PRAISE FOR *BRAIN STORM*

"A very powerful and unusual novel. I think you've got everything here that a reader loves—a hospital drama and thriller, a strong central character. Made much more interesting because the central character is a very unreliable narrator."

—Ann Cleeves, international bestselling author of the Vera Stanhope and Shetland series

"Elaine Viets has written the exciting first book in a multilayered crime novel series. Angela Richman is not only an investigator but a victim in this complex novel of crime, punishment, and medical malfeasance."

—Charlaine Harris, #1 *New York Times* bestselling author

"Elaine Viets's newest is both a timely medical drama and a compelling mystery. *Brain Storm* gives us a detailed look at the shattered life of a determined death investigator. Readers will want more of Angela Richman's adventures."

—Jeff Abbott, *New York Times* bestselling author of *The First Order*

"In *Brain Storm*, Elaine Viets takes a dangerous turn down a dark alley but manages it with panache and a touch of humor. Angela Marie Richman is a kick-ass protagonist who is victimized by the thing we all fear most—our own mortality. This is territory Viets knows well, and she does a fine job of showing the readers the terrain, all while entertaining them."

—Reed Farrel Coleman, *New York Times* bestselling author of Robert B. Parker's *The Devil Wins*

"Trapped in a nightmarish world after suffering six strokes, death investigator Angela Richman finds she can't trust anyone—including her own mind. A thrilling, suspenseful, twist-filled read that kept me up late into the night, *Brain Storm* marks a fascinating new direction for a wonderfully talented writer."

—Alison Gaylin, *USA TODAY* bestselling author of the
Brenna Spector series

"Haunting and creepy, with a fast-paced, twisty plot, and a protagonist you will not soon forget—this is Elaine Viets at her most deliciously dark."

—David Ellis, Edgar Award winner and author of
Breach of Trust and nine other novels

"I've been a fan of Elaine Viets's books since she debuted her leather-clad heroine Francesca Vierling. And now I am delighted to see her give us another strong female character we can root for—death investigator Angela Richman. I'm also stoked to see Elaine venture into darker territory with *Brain Storm*, a multilayered mystery that is rich in its sense of place and character and propelled with medical intrigue. *Brain Storm* has everything I love in crime fiction—complexity, intelligence, pretzel-plotting, and a touch of dark humor."

—P.J. Parrish, *New York Times* bestselling author of
Thomas and Mercer's *She's Not There* and the award-winning
Louis Kincaid series

"With *Brain Storm*, Elaine Viets offers readers a rare gem, a mystery that not only engages the head but also compels the heart. Following a near-fatal stroke, death investigator Angela Richman must struggle to regain her physical and mental health, while at the same time trying to solve the murder of the inept doctor she blames for her predicament.

Drawing on her own experience, Viets chronicles the harrowing journey back from the brink of death. And perhaps the most amazing aspect of the novel is that in the midst of such terrible darkness, Viets manages to deliver hilarious one-liners any comedian would envy."

—William Kent Krueger, Edgar Award–winning author of the
New York Times bestseller *Ordinary Grace*

"A huge welcome to Angela Marie Richman, an edgy death investigator with a rapier wit and even sharper powers of observation, who makes her debut in Elaine Viets's *Brain Storm*. I loved the deadpan humor from this character, a tough broad who's survived with a vengeance and has scores to settle."

—Hallie Ephron, *New York Times* bestselling author of
Night Night, Sleep Tight

BRAIN STORM

BRAIN STORM

ANGELA RICHMAN, DEATH INVESTIGATOR

ELAINE VIETS

THOMAS & MERCER

Published by Thomas & Mercer, Seattle

www.apub.com

Amazon, the Amazon logo, and Thomas & Mercer are trademarks of Amazon.com, Inc., or its affiliates.

ISBN-13: 9781503936317
ISBN-10: 1503936317

Cover design by Mark Ecob

Printed in the United States of America

To Don, who has kept his vows for better, for worse, for richer, for poorer, in sickness and in health . . . I love you.

CHAPTER 1

June 11, 2016

The doctor who nearly killed Angela Richman was buried today, and the Missouri medical establishment turned out to honor him. The eulogies were heartfelt: doctors, nurses, and patients praised Dr. Porter Gravois's compassion and skill as a neurologist. Their tears were genuine. His funeral cortege was nearly a mile long on the road named after his powerful St. Louis family. Everyone called him by his nickname, Chip, as if they were all part of his inner circle. Chip made them feel that way.

Angela didn't attend his funeral. She was still in the hospital, recovering from the damage he'd done to her. She'd been in there three months. Angela was glad Porter was dead, and so were the people who knew the real Dr. Gravois. They didn't call him Chip.

As she lay on the scratchy hospital sheets, she wondered how Dr. Gravois looked in his coffin. He had a long, pale face and a knife-blade nose, like a stone figure on a British tomb. Had the mortician managed to duplicate the fatherly smile that fooled so many? That smile didn't quite reach Gravois's hard, blue eyes, but those were closed forever.

Which suit was he buried in? Chip wore Savile Row suits from Kilgour in London. Chip pronounced it *Kilgar* and said only parvenus called the tailor *Kilgore*. His bespoke suits were lovely silk and light wool. It was a shame to put one in the ground. But Angela had no qualms about shoveling Gravois six feet under.

What about Dr. Gravois's bitter enemy, Dr. Jeb Travis Tritt?

He and his awful, off-the-rack suits were barred from the funeral. No matter how much he paid for his suits, he still looked more like a small-town insurance agent than a neurosurgeon.

His unwed mother had named him after her favorite country music star. Dr. Tritt was a country boy, from his badly cut hair to his thick-soled brown shoes.

Is he wearing a jail jumpsuit now? Angela wondered. Everyone heard Tritt threaten Gravois. He'd called him a crook and a killer and said the best thing Porter Gravois could do for his patients was die.

The next day Dr. Gravois was murdered.

CHAPTER 2

Fourteen weeks earlier

Angela Marie Richman lives in Chouteau Forest, a wealthy ghetto some thirty miles west of St. Louis. She investigates all the deaths in the county—murders, accidents, and overdoses—that don't happen under a doctor's care.

Chouteau County is about ten square miles. Its main town, Chouteau Forest—the Forest, to insiders—is mostly estates. And Chouteau, if you're local, is *SHOW-toe*.

She lives on the Du Pres estate in the house she inherited from her parents. She's one of the poor Richmans. Maybe not poor by your standards: her parents pulled down a fat five figures a year as servants for the Du Preses, one of the old Forest families. The Forest doesn't fritter away money on staff, but her parents did the work of at least six people: her mother, Elise, was the housekeeper, cook, dog walker, and errand runner, plus she cared for Madeline Du Pres, the family's demanding dowager, for more than a decade. Angela's father, Mel, took care of the vast grounds, as well as the upkeep on the hundred-year-old buildings.

Now Angela serves the Forest by dealing with their dead.

She was on call that Saturday night, the busiest time of the week for death investigators. That's when people partied, drank, shot up, and shot one another. Angela expected to be dragged out on this warm March night for a car accident, an overdose, or a domestic violence fatality. When her cell phone didn't ring by midnight, she went to bed.

She was out cold at 2:17 that morning when a tremendous bang woke her. She sat up, groggy and disoriented, then ran to the bedroom window and saw headlights reaching for the sky on the other side of the estate's stone wall. With the lights at that crazy angle, it had to be an accident.

She heard the sirens as she threw on her black pantsuit. By the time her cell phone rang, Angela was tying her shoes.

She clicked on her phone. The detective didn't bother with a greeting. "Richman," he said. "Ray Greiman." His voice frosted her phone.

Just my luck, she thought. *I've pulled Ray Foster Greiman, the laziest detective on the Forest force.* The man was impossible to work with.

"We got a situation here," he said.

"Can I see it from my upstairs window?" she asked.

"Yeah, that's it. Beemer ran into the Du Pres wall a hundred yards east of the main gate," he said. He said it right—Duh PRAY. Only insiders got to protect the Forest families.

"It's bad," he said. "The JJ twins, massive head injuries, one fatality."

"Oh no." Angela felt like he'd slammed her in the head with a shovel. The JJ twins were old Reggie Du Pres's granddaughters. Sixteen-year-old first cousins. Jillian Du Pres was a month older than Jordan Hobart. A little spoiled, but good kids. Both girls had long, dark hair, flawless, steam-cleaned skin, and curvy little figures. They looked so much alike, the whole Forest called them the JJ twins.

"Which one's dead?" she asked.

"Can't tell," he said. "Their faces are too messed up. I'm gonna guess it's—"

She stopped him. "We're on cell phones, Ray."

"Then get your ass over here," he said.

"I'll be there in five," she said.

Angela could have walked the quarter mile to the accident, but there was no time to waste. At forty-one, she had been investigating Forest deaths for almost twenty years. She knew the routine. She pulled her long, dark-brown hair into a practical ponytail. Her death investigator kit was packed in the trunk of her Dodge Charger. She grabbed her iPad, roared out of the garage, and was at the scene in two minutes.

When she saw the red Ferrari parked haphazardly next to the crushed Beemer convertible, Angela thought the kids had crashed while racing. But there wasn't a mark on the Ferrari or its driver, Sandiclere "Sandy" Warburton, the snotty teen son of a Forest defense contractor. Yes, the kid drove a Ferrari. Hey, Daddy Warbucks sells the military $600 toilet seats.

The police cars were parked to hide the accident from gawkers, and now two uniforms were setting up a privacy screen. She left her car on the grass. The powerful portable lights revealed the carnage.

A sporty blue Beemer two-seater convertible with the top down had bashed nose-first into the wall. The windshield was gone.

Four strapping paramedics wheeled a stretcher carrying a young girl in a blood-drenched pink party dress with a wristful of bangles. At first Angela thought the girl wore red gloves and a red scarf over her face. Then she realized that was the girl's face, now a raw mess of meat and blood-matted hair. Her arms were solid blood to her elbows, and one wrist dangled at an impossible angle.

Angela tried hard to hide her horror. *I'm supposed to be a professional,* she told herself. *I've seen worse, but I knew this girl, and she was still alive.* Angela watched as the girl was loaded into the ambulance, and it roared away.

The impact had thrown the other girl out of the car, onto the grass near the wall. *No seatbelt?* Angela wondered, hoping she'd died instantly.

She was lying on her back, the skirt of her black dress hiked to her waist, exposing a red thong. She wore a black leather jacket and a single see-through platform shoe. A glass slipper for a Cinderella whose prince would never come.

Near her hand was a red iPhone. No, a pink iPhone dyed red with blood. Her face had been put through a meat grinder.

When people learned about Angela's profession, they said, "You're a death investigator? How can you do that? The blood! The smell! And those dead bodies." Most of them shivered.

But they aren't dead bodies, she told herself. *Not to me. They're people who have died, like the JJ twin. An hour ago she was a gorgeous girl. She was loved—well, she still is—and will be mourned. Now she's trying to tell me what happened. It's my job to listen. This is the last service I can do for her.*

A teenage boy, white with shock and wide-eyed, was talking to Detective Greiman. Sandy, the defense contractor's son. The detective and the boy stood next to the Ferrari. For once, Sandy was missing his smug look of entitlement. He swayed like he was fighting a high wind and flung his arms in wide, sloppy gestures. He was drunk.

A teenage blonde in a blue party dress and silver shoes shivered next to him, teeth chattering and bracelets rattling. Lucy Chantilly, the senator's daughter. She was weeping, and her blue mascara blazed bizarre trails down her face.

Angela opened her car trunk and grabbed her death investigator kit and the blanket she kept to comfort shocked witnesses.

A Forest uniform nodded and let her through the yellow tape. As she passed the Ferrari, Angela saw a half-empty bottle of Captain Morgan's rum leaking onto the front seat, and she smelled pot. The death car reeked of weed and the coppery odor of blood. The kids had been drunk and high. Both cars.

Detective Greiman left Sandy and came over to see Angela. He was wearing black Hugo Boss. The Forest paid well, but not that well. Homicide detectives usually had two styles: rumpled, old-school Columbos and stylish metrosexuals. The only thing sharp about Greiman was his clothes.

Badge bunnies happily hopped into his bed, but she wasn't interested in stroking his ego—or anything else.

"What happened?" she asked. At six feet, Angela towered over the detective by four inches. He had to look up to her. Greiman hated that.

"Sandy and the girls were racing each other home from a party in Ladue." Another upscale burb, not quite in the Forest's league. "The girls lost control and hit the wall," he said.

"TWD?"

"Yeah," he said. "Texting while driving. They hit the stone wall head-on."

He pointed to the skid marks that left the road and turned into tire tracks plowing through the freshly mowed grass. "I checked the skid marks. The car was going about seventy when the driver lost control and hit the wall."

Angela winced.

"She was texting Sandy and the senator's daughter in the Ferrari. Her last words were USCK DNKY BLS. I think that's, 'You suck donkey balls.' At least that's how I translate it. That kid crap is hard to read."

"Whose phone?"

"Jillian's," he said. "Both girls were using it."

"Sandy was driving the Ferrari?"

Greiman nodded.

"There's an open bottle of rum in the car," Angela said. "They're underage. Have you Breathalyzed the driver and his passenger? Called for the drug dogs?"

"He's Daddy Warbucks's kid, for Chrissake," Greiman said. "And Lucy's the senator's daughter."

"So? Their parents have PR firms to paper over this mess and an army of lawyers. Do it, Ray. Everybody in this case is equally important, and all four families' investigators will crawl all over those cars. The paramedics don't live in the Forest. Someone will talk. Word will get out."

"Play it by the book," he said with a sneer. "You think you're hot shit because you're getting an award nobody's heard of." Resentment flared in his eyes.

Angela was getting the prestigious Harold Messler Forensic Specialist of the Year Award, and she owed it to Greiman's screwup. She didn't have to remind him. He knew it.

Two years ago, she and Greiman were called to what looked like a suicide. A Forest woman was found in her garage with her car engine running, vodka bottle on the floor, her face cherry-red from carbon monoxide poisoning.

"Suicide," Greiman said. His shift was almost over, and he wanted to go home.

But when she did the body actualization—the death investigator's examination—Angela noticed that the woman was wearing white socks, and the bottoms were clean. There was no way she could have walked to the garage behind her house and still have had clean socks. Someone had carried her to that car when she was drunk.

That someone stood to inherit $10 million. Word gets around in the Forest. Her family found out that Greiman had wanted to blow off the case, and they made sure he got a reprimand. Angela got a commendation and the prestigious Harry Award.

"I don't do this job for the awards," she said. "And there's no money in it." But there was recognition. Lots of it. She was leaving for the international forensics conference in Washington, DC, the first weekend in June.

Greiman had learned nothing from his mistake. "Look, the kids are pretty sure the dead girl is Jordan," he said.

"Don't guess, Ray. That's the road to lawsuit city."

"Jordan wore the black leather jacket to the party."

"Did Jordan leave wearing it?" Angela asked.

"They aren't sure."

"The JJ twins swapped clothes all the time," she said. "Even their grandfather says he can't tell them apart, and they'll switch clothes to confuse him. Jillian Du Pres could have worn the jacket home. We can't go by the witnesses' ID."

She hated his casual carelessness. She'd wanted to be a police officer when she was a kid. But as she got older, Angela didn't like some things about the Forest force, and Greiman was behind many of them. When Sisters of Sorrow Hospital wanted to hire a Chicago cardiologist, a board member invited the African American specialist to dinner at his Forest home. While driving back to his hotel, the specialist was stopped by Ray Greiman, then a young Forest patrolman. He asked, "Where'd you get a fancy Mercedes like this?"

The cardiologist did not sign on with SOS.

The Forest's hospital was run by French nursing sisters. In St. Louis, Barnes-Jewish and Saint Louis University hospitals were top-ranked nationally. SOS was in the top fifty. Exactly where, the Forest never said. A year later, Greiman was promoted to detective for reasons Angela never understood.

Death investigator combined Angela's love of forensics with a chance to protect and serve. She didn't have to wear a Forest PD uniform, but she did have to work with the police, including Greiman.

She managed to keep her temper when she told Greiman, "We'll need the girls' dental records. Most people in the Forest go to Dr. Stone. He can e-mail their digital X-rays to the ER and the medical examiner."

"You're going to call him at three in the morning?" Greiman asked. He looked at his watch. He wanted to go home—the same move that had gotten him into trouble before.

"Doc Stone won't mind," she said. "He's known those girls since they cut their baby teeth. The surviving girl's family needs to be at the hospital to make decisions about her treatment."

"I can't see why that will make much difference," he said. "The girl's in SOS. She'll get the same care anyway."

"Her parents may want to move her to another hospital or bring in an out-of-town specialist," she said. "That poor girl is going to need reconstructive surgery. If she survives. Her parents have to make those decisions."

"Then you'll have to inform the parents," he said. "A dentist can't e-mail X-rays without the parents' permission."

Angela knew that was coming. "Jordan Hobart's parents live down the road. I know them a little better. I'll tell the Hobarts and have them sign the permission forms. You test the kids."

Loud sigh.

Now she was shaking with anger. "Hey, I've got to tell two families that their beautiful daughter may or may not be dead. All I know is she's no longer beautiful. And I don't know which girl is luckier—the live one or the dead one.

"I'll get permission from the parents, and then I'll come back and actualize the body. Don't move the girl. Her body's mine. It's the law."

Before Angela left, she wrapped the weeping Lucy in the warm blanket, then gently pried the girl off her shoulder. She covered the dead girl with a clean white sheet she kept in her DI kit.

The headache started on the short trip to Jordan's home. It felt like a crown of thorns. No, a crown of barbed wire. Long, red spikes dug into Angela's brain, and pain shot down her neck.

She got migraines sometimes, especially after a bad death investigation scene. The last time was six months ago. A Forest housekeeper had returned from a weekend off to report a missing three-year-old and a "suspicious odor" coming from the locked bedroom of her employer, a divorced mother. The police broke down the door and found the shoe company heiress in bed, her blonde daughter, Mandy, curled up next to her. The commotion woke the little girl.

"Mommy seeping," Mandy said, rubbing her eyes.

Mommy was asleep all right—for good. She had a spike in her arm and $3 million in the bank. She'd decided to spend the weekend shooting up. Rather than get someone to watch Mandy, she'd drugged her little girl's milk to make her sleep until the housekeeper returned.

That headache had sent Angela to bed for three days. Sparkly glass halos invaded her vision. She was too nauseated to sit up. Tonight's headache felt even worse.

At this hour, the Forest looked enchanted. Its mansions were different styles, as if she'd stumbled into a book of fairytales. The English country house seemed perpetually shrouded in fog, and she swore she saw a stag in the woods near the Bavarian hunting lodge. The Romanesque castle seemed to echo with the rattle of knights' armor.

Jordan's French chateau always had a faint whiff of lavender. Her mother had married Holden Hobart III, known as Trip. Trip answered the door in striped pajamas, a dressing gown, and embroidered carpet slippers. He saw Angela's face, paled, and said, "What happened to Jordan?"

"Get Mrs. Hobart," she said. "I have bad news."

They went into the kitchen, the heart of the house, and Angela told the couple. Mrs. Hobart moaned like something had sucked out her soul. Trip turned to stone. He signed the permission form, his signature blurred by tears, and let her call Doc Stone from his office. She scanned the permission form and e-mailed it to the dentist.

Doc Stone cried, too. "I've known those girls all their lives," he said. "This is terrible. Terrible."

Dr. Stone could access his dental records from his home computer. He sent the digital X-rays to the hospital so the ER docs could figure out whether they had Jordan Hobart or Jillian Du Pres.

Jordan's parents wanted to go with Angela to the accident scene, but she said they couldn't. They insisted on going with her to break the news to Jillian's parents at the Du Pres home.

There was more. Much more—all hideously, horribly emotional. She hoped she'd never hear those anguished screams again. With each one, the barbed wire dug deeper into her head. The headache clawed into her brain. The families' sorrow weighed her down like a lead overcoat.

The JJ girls' parents were good and thoughtful people, even in their extreme distress. They knew Angela needed to return to the accident scene. They knew they were in no shape to drive to Sisters of Sorrow. Old Reggie Du Pres, the clan's patriarch, went with them. His driver took the family to the hospital in a beat-up Range Rover.

By the time Angela was back at the scene, the police had barricaded the road, and the JJ twins' families took another route out of the Forest. They were spared the sight of the bloody wreckage.

She parked on the other side of the barricade and hiked over. Greiman met her with, "The hospital got the dental records. The stiff is Jordan."

Angela had had enough. "The dead *girl* is Jordan Hobart," she said, in a whispering hiss, so the witnesses couldn't hear her. "Victims are dead people, not floaters or crispy critters."

"Okay, okay," he said. "Take the stick out of your ass. There's no point in trying to interview the witnesses. Jillian's in a coma, and the other two are lawyered up."

She could see Sandy, Otto Warburton's son, handcuffed and being shoved into a Forest police car. Lucy sobbed in the front seat of Greiman's unmarked car.

"After I Breathalyzed him, Sandy sobered up enough to realize he's in serious trouble," Greiman said. "He's eighteen. I saw a bag of green, leafy substance on the passenger-side floor in full view."

That's cop talk for a bag of pot. Whether or not he'd really seen it in full view, that's what he'd claim. Greiman didn't want the lawyers arguing about whether he needed a warrant to search the car.

"I Mirandized him and charged him with DWI, texting while driving, reckless driving, and anything else I could think of. His lawyer's meeting him at the station."

"Good work," she said.

"Waste of time. We both know he'll never be convicted," Greiman said.

"Maybe not, but it will cost Daddy Warbucks a pretty penny to get him out of this jam."

"Lucy, the girl in his car, is a minor," Greiman said. "The senator and the family lawyer are on their way."

"The senator is her father," Angela reminded him.

He gave her the case number, and she opened her death investigator kit, a black wheeled suitcase, and pulled on four pairs of latex gloves. As the examination proceeded, she'd strip them off to keep from contaminating the body with blood or evidence from another area. The forms she needed were loaded in her iPad. Angela used her own point-and-shoot camera to take photos for the medical examiner.

In the DI kit, she had a tape recorder, thermometers for body and ambient temperatures, a measuring tape, vials, bags, and containers of all sizes. Some of the plastic containers looked like they'd escaped from a Tupperware party, but no one ever wanted to open those bowls.

She photographed the body. Jordan Hobart was lying on her back, head facing north, neck at a sickening angle. Her left arm was thrown out. The wounds to her head were severe, but Angela tried to note and measure the ones she could see. She couldn't clean away the blood. That was the ME's job.

She noted every cut ("cutlike defect"), scrape ("contusion"), and bruise on the front of Jordan's body, from her head to her feet. She noted the dead girl's clothing and its condition, documenting every rip and tear, as well as the missing shoe.

Jordan's diamond-and-platinum jewelry looked expensive, but Angela couldn't say that. Officially, the girl was wearing "silver metal earrings with a large, clear stone, and six silver metal bracelets set with clear stones." She recorded it all, even the silver toe ring on Jordan's bare foot.

The harsh lights revealed that under Jordan's head and chest were "dark areas of significant blood, the largest measuring twenty by sixteen inches."

Angela recorded the ambient temperature—fifty-two degrees at 4:22 a.m. Then she used a scalpel to make a slit in a dress seam that ran under Jordan's rib cage and another slit in her skin in the same spot. She took the body core temperature with a refrigeration thermometer that cost fifty bucks at a food supply outlet. The forensic thermometer cost ten times that and didn't get the best temperature range.

She removed the thermometer, circled the slit on the body in indelible ink, and initialed the mark so it wouldn't confuse the medical examiner at the autopsy.

The glimpse of Jordan's perfect skin, now slightly greenish gray, made the barbed wire dig deeper into Angela's brain. She remembered Jordan and Jillian being wheeled through the Forest by their nannies in real British baby carriages. She'd watched them grow into mischievous little girls, riding their ponies on the Forest trails. Jillian still rode. Jordan played tennis and volunteered at the no-kill animal shelter. Both their charmed lives had ended today.

She was crying now. *Stop it!* she told herself. *Jordan needs your professional judgment, not your useless tears. Go back to work.*

The exacting work helped calm her. She noted and measured sixteen cuts on Jordan's right hand and ten on her left. Four nails were broken on her right hand. She covered both bloody hands in paper bags and taped them shut at the wrist. Then she brought out another clean white sheet from a ziplock bag and said to Greiman, "Help me turn her over, will you?"

He grumbled. She ignored him. Lifting dead weight was one of the harder parts of this job. Jordan weighed only a hundred pounds, but it took both of them to wrestle her small body onto the white sheet.

The back of her dress and her body were soaked with blood, and there was another wound at the crown of her head. Angela measured the wound and the blood stains, noted a small bruise on Jordan's left leg and two more cuts on the back of her right leg. Then the morgue attendants came forward with their body bag and paperwork.

Once the body was moved, Angela checked to see if anything was under it. She found nothing but blood stains on the grass. After she photographed and measured them, her work was done.

Angela could see the first gray light of dawn when she wearily climbed into her car and drove slowly, sadly, home. As she passed the Du Pres mansion, she saw that all the lights were on, even in the attic.

Back home, Angela's head was pounding, and she felt dizzy. She knew this was going to be a bad headache. The crystal halos blocked most of her vision. Lights shimmered around her, as if she were standing in a cut-glass candy dish.

She managed to read all the death investigator forms again and correct two spelling errors. Then she loaded the photos on to her home computer, sent everything to the medical examiner's office, and fell into bed, her head pounding with pain.

Angela was still on call Sunday, but the Forest didn't need a death investigator. She drifted in and out of pain in the darkened bedroom, lost in a fog of nausea and Imitrex migraine tablets.

She got one call from the Chouteau County Medical Examiner at five o'clock Sunday evening. Dr. Evarts Evans congratulated her for what he called her "sensitive handling of this sad case." He said he'd put a commendation in her file.

Angela faked it on the phone and managed to sound alert, but she was too dizzy and heartsick to enjoy her tiny triumph.

Three months later, she would be the most reviled person in the Forest. She'd be fighting for her life at SOS. Bald, crippled, and crazy, she'd commit the ultimate sin. She'd defend an outsider accused of murdering the beloved scion of a Forest family.

Angela would risk everything to rescue the man who'd saved her life.

CHAPTER 3

By Wednesday, Angela felt well enough to burn some toast and fix a cup of tea. The migraines wouldn't go away. She'd slept most of Monday and Tuesday, her days off. When she woke up this morning, Angela felt better, but her head still ached. She'd taken one Imitrex already. It didn't help that she'd found water all over the floor in the downstairs bathroom and had to call Rick DeMun, the Forest's handyman. Rick agreed to meet her at the house at five that evening.

When the ME's office called right after Rick and told Angela to report to Ben Weymuller's house, she'd hoped the exacting death investigation would distract her from the migraines and the plumbing problem. But the bright spring sun hurt her eyes, and her head throbbed.

Ben Weymuller, age ninety-two, had died at the bottom of his basement stairs, his mouth open in a silent scream. Ben's daughter, Lucille, found her father at eleven o'clock Wednesday morning, when she was supposed to take him to lunch.

By noon, Lucille was a murder suspect.

Angela knew Ben and his daughter. Ben's plain, pale-green house was nearly hidden in clouds of white dogwood. He lived in Toonerville, the sneery Forest nickname for the neat bungalows between Gravois, the main county road, and I-55. Toonerville was for Forest employees. Ben did custom woodwork for the local mansions. After he retired, he made exquisite carvings and custom furniture for chichi shops.

Angela parked her Charger on Ben's street and hauled her DI kit out of the trunk. She was shocked to see sixty-seven-year-old Lucille caged in a Forest patrol car. Worse, she was guarded by Ted Brixton Baker, the tactless new uniform. Angela heard Lucille weeping and started toward the police car to comfort her.

"Stop right there, Angela!" Ted said. "You can't talk to the suspect."

"Suspect?" she said.

"Detective Greiman's taking her in."

"Lucille's a retired schoolteacher," Angela said. "Please tell me you didn't cuff her."

"Not yet," Ted said. "But in my experience, you should never underestimate any suspect."

What experience? Angela wondered. Lucille had probably taught this twerp.

Lucille was a cushiony woman with pretty gray hair and a fondness for sherbet-colored pantsuits. Angela could barely see her through a haze of headache pain and hard, glittering halos.

"Detective Greiman is in the basement," Ted said. "The stiff went headfirst down the steps. When the daughter found him this morning, she called 911. EMS tried to resuscitate him, but he was deader than a doornail. The basement looks like a freaking slaughterhouse."

Lucille's wails grew louder. Angela blistered Ted with a glare, but the clueless rookie kept babbling. "Look at the blood on my new shoes," he said, exhibiting a huge, black lace-up with dark stains on its sole. "I stepped in it."

Lucille's anguished shrieks sliced into Angela's aching head. "Ted!" she said. "The victim's daughter can hear you. That's her father's blood. Show some respect."

He moved away from the patrol car, lowered his voice, and said, "She didn't show him any respect. Detective Greiman says she offed her father. You're supposed to go in by the basement door, around the side." He pointed to the entrance. "The geezer has his woodworking shop down there. He's at the foot of the stairs."

Angela popped another Imitrex. Then she put on four pairs of gloves, fired up her iPad, and opened the basement door. The stomach-twisting odors of death and coppery blood slapped her in the face, overpowering the sweet scent of fresh wood.

"There are booties by the door," Greiman said. Angela slipped them on and got the case number.

"Not that you could damage this scene," he said. "Goddamn basement's been trampled by a herd of buffalo. The daughter called EMS, and those assholes tried to revive him, even though he was DRT."

Dead Right There.

"That's why undertakers screw coffin lids shut," Greiman said. "Only way to keep EMS from resuscitating the stiffs."

Angela let him rant. EMS had to try to save Ben, no matter how slim the chance.

The dimly lit basement soothed her headache. As her eyes adjusted to the low light, Angela saw a frail, fine-boned old man lying on his back in a dark-red pool crisscrossed with footprints and dotted with medical debris. Ben's arms were stiff and bent at the elbow. Angela photographed the scene from the door.

As she got closer, she saw that Ben wore khaki pants and beige socks, and his chest and sternum were burned and contused by the EMS's efforts to restart his heart. IV lines trailed from his hands. She would document them and leave them in place. His red plaid shirt had been ripped off and tossed on the floor. Crushed gold spectacles crouched at the edge of the blood pool. Angela photographed them. She'd remind Greiman to check if they were the old man's prescription.

Ben's snowy hair was matted with black blood. The left side of his face and scrawny, pale chest were purple-red. *Livor mortis,* Angela thought. After Ben died, the blood pooled in his body and left those distinctive marks. He must have died lying on that side.

She sketched the basement for her report, diagramming the stairs splitting it down the center. On the east side was the furnace, hot water heater, and laundry area. Wooden shelves stacked with canned goods separated them from Ben's workshop on the west side.

Ben kept a neat basement. Angela saw dirty laundry piled in a basket. The concrete floor was swept. The smaller workshop tools were hung on pegboards. A short piece of smooth, unstained wood was clamped to the bench. More wood, ranging from slender, six-foot-tall wands to thick blocks, was arranged in bins and barrels. A tech was photographing it, working through a bin of one-by-ones.

"The daughter did him," Greiman said. "She said, 'It's all my fault.'"

Angela wasn't sure that was a confession. Family members often blamed themselves for a loved one's death.

"Why did Lucille say that?" Angela asked.

"She cried and carried on so much I had a hard time understanding her. I finally figured out she stopped by at eleven yesterday to bring her father mac and cheese for lunch. She was in a hurry to go to the church volunteers' lunch to get some two-bit award, and forgot to go downstairs to get him more canned soup. She says the old geezer probably went downstairs himself. He usually had dinner about six o'clock."

Greiman didn't dignify Toonerville residents with first names or sympathy. They couldn't advance his career.

"She thinks he fell down the stairs because he wore those slippery socks."

Up close, Angela saw that the stairs were made of some unusual reddish wood streaked with honey. "Why don't the steps have rubber safety treads?" she asked.

"He made the stairs himself," Greiman said, "and he thought rubber treads would ruin them. Must have been a stubborn old coot."

He was, Angela thought. *And a first-rate craftsman.*

"I figure the daughter got tired of waiting for the old man to kick the bucket and pushed him down the stairs."

No! Angela wanted to say. *Lucille's not like that.*

But she knew adult children did help demanding parents pass prematurely—with a shove downstairs, a pillow over the face, or an overdose of medication.

"Her father had a bad heart, and she checked on him every day," Greiman said. "Had to be a drag, with her being retired. My mom's retired, and she runs around with her friends. The daughter said she came by today to take the geezer to his regular Wednesday lunch at the Golden Corral. He insisted on going to the one all the way up in south St. Louis County. Another reason why she offed him—a sixty-mile round trip once a week because he liked that particular dessert bar.

"I figure she got tired of the old guy's demands and pushed him downstairs before she left for the lunch yesterday. End of demanding daddy. Those stairs are a death trap."

"They do look slippery," Angela said. She counted the steps—twenty-four—for her report, and noted their slick, polished surface and the single forty-watt bulb that lit them.

"Was the stair light on when you got here?" she asked.

"Yes, but I don't know who turned it on or when."

Angela measured the height of the handrail, then jiggled it to confirm it was sturdy. She photographed the blood streaked and spattered on the stairs, then measured the blood, including the dark clots painting the corner of the fourth step from the bottom.

Then she started the body actualization. Through the thick, crusted blood, she saw many bruises and scrapes on Ben's scalp and face. He had an ugly triangular indentation on his upper left temple. Angela carefully documented that "triangular-shaped indented defect" and counted, measured, and photographed everything.

"Did you see this blood on the fourth step, Ray?" she said, camera clicking. "It looks like it matches the triangular indentation in his head."

"Not sure it's a match," he said. "If the daughter didn't shove him, she clobbered him with a piece of wood. The tech is checking every stick. Also had her print the door, doorjamb, and the knob. No point looking for shoe prints on this floor."

Angela tried to head off another EMS rant. "No wonder falls are the leading cause of death for people over seventy-five," she said. As expected, Greiman ignored her hint, but they were getting along better than during the JJ twins' investigation.

"Will you arrest Lucille?" she asked.

"I'll question her and check her alibi," he said. "See how long she stayed at the church lunch and verify what she did after that. I'm taking her to headquarters. That will shake her up, especially after I Mirandize her. That always scares them."

A church lady like Lucille will be terrified, Angela thought. *She'll also be mortified, parading through the Forest in a cop car.*

"But unless the daughter actually says how she did him, I'll have to wait for the ME's report and TOD."

Time of death. Even the ME couldn't give Greiman an exact TOD. There were too many variables.

Angela was relieved that Greiman was being a little cautious. She photographed the bottoms of Ben's socks. They were slightly gray, as if he'd walked around his house without shoes.

"He's in full rigor," Angela said. "His arms and fingers are stiff." She described the plain yellow metal wedding ring on his liver-spotted left hand in her report.

Rigor was at its worst at eight to twelve hours. Then it left the body, starting with the smaller muscles. "I'm guessing he's been dead about sixteen to twenty hours," she said. They both knew that unless a witness had seen Ben die, there was no way anyone could definitely say when he'd died.

But Angela's guess supported Lucille's theory that her father had died around 6:00 p.m. She only hoped the ME's educated estimate would back up her guess.

Angela took the room's temperature, then made a slit in Ben's chest below his ribs and recorded his body core temperature. She circled and initialed the cut in his skin. His body temperature was ten degrees higher than the room's seventy-eight degrees.

She checked his lower right abdomen and found no greenish discoloration. That early sign of decomposition often showed up after twenty-four hours.

"How long was Lucille at the volunteers' luncheon?" Angela asked.

"She says she left the church about three o'clock," Greiman said. "After the lunch, she went with three old biddies to the Forest Tea Shoppe. Tea! That's how they celebrated. She was home by five to make hubby tuna casserole for dinner, and they stayed home all night. High living in Toonerville."

Angela ignored his sarcasm. "May I talk with Lucille?"

"Not till I cut her loose. *If* I cut her loose."

A grumpy Greiman helped her turn Ben's body. Angela found more contusions and blood on his back, as well as the expected dark, purple-red livor mortis on his left side, and photographed them.

"You about done?" Detective Greiman asked. "Can CSI finish their photos? I want to call the meat wagon."

Angela nodded. Her head felt like it might fall off and roll away. She stayed at the scene to oversee the removal of Ben's body. As the morgue attendants rolled Ben's body to the van, she heard fresh sobs from Lucille.

"I'm going upstairs to check his meds," Angela said. "Then I'm leaving."

"Living room hasn't been dusted for prints yet," Greiman said.

"I'll be careful." Angela peeled off another layer of gloves and rolled her DI kit out the door. Once again, she was temporarily blinded by the brilliant spring sun. She breathed in the fresh air. She could almost hear the plants pushing out of the moist ground.

She found more clues to the time of Ben's death on the front porch: the *St. Louis City Gazette* was still in its plastic wrapper, untouched this morning. The mail box was empty, and the living room curtains were pulled shut.

Inside, Ben's home was as neat as his basement, and it showcased his craft. She recognized Ben's custom-made designs. He'd made all the furniture, except the chunky brown recliner and matching couch.

The mellow oak kitchen cabinets and matching round table were carved with his delicate dogwood flower design. The table's centerpiece was a lazy Susan bristling with pill bottles. Angela checked for a doctor's name. Like most Forest dwellers, Ben went to Doc Bartlett. Judging by the medications, Ben had had a bad heart.

Angela stowed the medicine in a ziplock bag and labeled it. She would have to request Ben's medical records for the ME. Since Lucille was a suspect, Greiman would have to interview Doc Bartlett and any-one else who had information that might help his investigation.

She peeked in the dishwasher and saw a rinsed coffee cup, a cereal bowl, and a plate with a yellow residue. Mac and cheese? She photo-graphed them, along with the bag of foil-wrapped chocolates and the clean coffee maker on the countertop.

Angela opened the fridge with gloved hands. It was nearly empty: a quart of milk, a single chicken leg in clear plastic, a plastic bowl of leftover mac and cheese, half a loaf of bread, butter, and green grapes in a colander. She photographed the fridge's contents, then bagged the mac and cheese for testing, in case Ben had been drugged or poisoned.

Angela also wrote down what she didn't see in Ben's house. There were no liquor or beer bottles and no illicit drugs or paraphernalia.

She photographed the kitchen trash can. It held a candy wrapper and a rinsed soup can. Monday's newspaper was in the recycling bin.

Ben's bedroom was dark and soothing. Angela noted and photographed that the olive-green curtains were open, and the bed was made. *Ben should lie in state here instead of a funeral home,* she thought. His double bed was a burled oak masterpiece inlaid with fans of honey-colored wood. His nightstand, another work of art, held a lamp and an art deco clock. There were no books or TV in the room.

On the other nightstand was a silver-framed photo of Ben and a woman who looked like an older, white-haired Lucille. Her mother, Angela guessed. A vase of dogwood flowers was next to the photo.

HAPPY 60TH BEN AND HARRIET! a banner proclaimed over the couple's heads. Harriet's frilly white orchid dragged down the shoulder of her blue taffeta dress. In the photo she smiled sweetly at Ben, who looked uncomfortable in a dark suit with a carnation boutonniere.

Angela wondered if Ben would be buried in that suit.

The bathroom was spotless, and the toilet seat was up—another sign of a man who lived alone.

Almost finished, Angela told herself. The medicine cabinet contained only aspirin, corn plasters, and other over-the-counter medications. She photographed the inside, then packed all those medications into another ziplock. They would be delivered with the body.

She stowed her DI kit in the trunk. It was a relief to sit in her car. Angela rested her aching head on the steering wheel. Pound. Pound. Pound. The blood hammered in her head. She dry-swallowed another Imitrex.

Ben's long, useful life had come to a violent end. Angela was sure he was killed by his own creation, not his only daughter.

CHAPTER 4

After she left Ben Weymuller's house, Angela almost looked forward to seeing her friend Katie, the Forest's assistant medical examiner. The morgue was in the windowless basement of Sisters of Sorrow Hospital. There was no sunshine down there. Not in any sense.

On the short drive to SOS, the road danced and quivered. Angela parked her car in the back, then opened the unmarked beige door with her keypad code. The stink of spoiled meat and disinfectant hit her as she entered, and she tried not to gag. She never got used to the odor.

Carolyn, the receptionist, put down her romance novel to say, "Katie's in her office."

Katie's closet-size office was big enough for only a small desk and two skinny chairs. On the wall behind her desk she'd pasted a dramatic photo of the autumn woods with a plastic skull hidden in the foliage.

Katie was small, compact, brown-haired, and practical as a pair of walking shoes. Angela found her at her computer.

"I've been pallbearer for people who looked better than you," Katie said. "What's wrong?"

"It's that damned Greiman," Angela said. "Ben Weymuller died in his home. His daughter Lucille found his body when she went to take him to the Golden Corral for lunch."

"I'm sorry," Katie said. "Old Ben was a talented man, but his color was bad last time I saw him. Did he have a heart attack?"

"I think he fell down his slippery basement stairs. He was wearing socks."

"Dumb way to die," Katie said. "But not surprising. Seven percent of deaths are caused by falls."

"Greiman stuck Lucille in a patrol car and had his protégé, Ted Baker, guard her. That dipwad complained he got Ben's blood on his new shoes."

"Ted's a real AIT—Asshole in Training," Katie said. "He's learning from a master."

"Greiman's investigating Ben's death as a homicide," Angela said.

"I hate to say it, but Greiman's right," Katie said. "You know that. On unattended deaths, you always assume the worst. Always. Even if the suspect is a sweet, retired schoolteacher."

"But I saw where Ben's head hit the stairs," Angela said. "The wound matches the corner of the steps. I've photographed it."

"Good for you, but Greiman's still right. I agree he's a flaming asshole. If there was an asshole contest, I'd sponsor him, and he'd sweep the field in all divisions, even medical."

"I heard Lucille crying in the patrol car," Angela said.

"Very sad," Katie said. "Seriously, it is. But you couldn't hold her hand. Your main fault is you're not an asshole. You're too nice. And that's a major flaw, Angela. You're supposed to stick to the facts: Ben's death is suspicious. Elder abuse is common because families get fed up with cranky old people. Ben could have snapped at Lucille, and she could have pushed him down the stairs.

"Don't look at me like that. Happens all the time. It's the ME's job to determine how Ben died and when. It's your job to document the facts. This office will say if it was murder. Not you. Got that?"

"Okay," Angela said, "but I don't understand why they don't fire Greiman. He's sexist and racist."

"Hello?" Katie said. "We're in the Forest, wildlife preserve for white males. Greiman says what the Powers That Be think but can't say. They'll never get rid of him. Remember old man Du Pres's speech at the home-owners' meeting?"

"The one where he told the Forest families that if they were expecting a black guest or worker, they should tip off the police?" Angela said. "Reggie Du Pres told them, 'It's only polite to let the officers know it's one of our Negroes.'"

"And he's considered enlightened," Katie said. "At least he used the semiacceptable *N*-word."

"But the Forest hired my mentor, Emily, our first death investigator," Angela said.

"Emily *Du Pres*," Katie said. "The old man's niece. The Forest likes having its own DI. Gives them more control. They hire the medical examiner, and the ME hires the death investigator. Hey, we know what Greiman is. And like him or not, he made the right decision about Ben Weymuller. Even a stopped clock is right twice a day."

"The problem is knowing when it's right," Angela said. Her headache was so bad, she saw Katie through a shimmering glare.

"You're having migraines again," Katie said. "What triggered them this time? Ben's death?"

"They started before that. The JJ twins' investigation."

"That was Saturday night."

"I slept Monday and Tuesday," Angela said.

"You look like shit. You're popping Imitrex like candy, aren't you? And driving while you take it. You know better. Call Dr. Bartlett."

"If I don't feel better tomorrow, I'll call," Angela said.

"Look, Ms. Tough It Out, it's obvious you're in pain. Call Bartlett. Can't you ever react like an ordinary person?"

"I'm so ordinary I'm boring," Angela said. "I like margaritas, Nordstrom sales, and long walks in the woods."

"Sweet," Katie said. "Just like an online dating profile."

"Okay, I hate Disney princesses and pink power tools for women. I'm tired. Tell me some good news."

"Jillian Du Pres, the JJ twin, is still alive in the ICU."

"I guess that's good," Angela said.

"Damn right, it's good. They don't think she has any brain damage. She may not be as pretty as she used to be, but she's young, and she'll heal. Her parents can buy her the best care. That's good, and don't tell me otherwise."

"What's going on with the accident investigation?" Angela asked.

"It's a total clusterfuck," Katie said. "All four families are involved, and there are millions at stake. We're talking two branches of the super-rich Du Pres, plus Senator Chantilly, and Otto Warburton, the defense contractor. Legal eagles are swooping in from as far away as New York and California."

"Knowing the Forest, they'll choose local talent," Angela said.

"Depends on whether the outlanders can promise more money or better deals for the kids."

"Any charges filed yet?" Angela asked.

"Shitloads. The county prosecutor is covering his ass like a stripper in a police raid. From what I can figure out, the accident was a drag race. The JJ twins in the Beemer were trying to prove they could outrun Sandy's Ferrari. All four kids had been drinking and smoking weed.

"It was all in the kids' text messages. The cell phone time stamps show that the texting and drag racing began as soon as they left the party in Ladue. Sandy was driving while Lucy was texting in the Ferrari, but it's not clear whether Jillian or Jordan was texting when the Beemer smacked into the Du Pres's stone wall."

"So Jillian's looking at a TWD?" Angela said.

"For now. Remember, everyone involved is rich and powerful. Sandy was charged with DWI. He was Breathalyzed at the scene, which was smart."

"And my idea," Angela said.

"But Greiman went one step further and got a warrant for Sandy's blood," Katie said. "You may have jump-started the great detective, but he played it by the book. Jordan's autopsy found the steering wheel impression on her chest. That confirmed she was driving the Beemer. Sandy may be looking at vehicular manslaughter because Jordan died. To add to the fun, Lucy and Jillian may be liable for Jordan's death because they were in the drag race, too."

"Even if those two girls weren't driving?" Angela said.

"Yep. Jillian could be charged with killing her own cousin."

"That's awful," Angela said. "It's bad enough she'll have to live with the guilt over Jordan's death."

"Right now, the prosecutor is charging everyone with everything," Katie said. "Later, the charges can be bargained, reduced, or even dropped. And those are just the criminal charges. If there's a civil lawsuit—"

"And there will be," Angela said.

"All the survivors may be equally liable for Jordan's death and Jillian's injuries. Right now, the prosecutor is trying to figure out if he should confiscate Sandy's Ferrari, since it had drugs in it. The law says it can be sold and the money used to fund the state school system."

"A new red Ferrari could help a lot of schools," Angela said. "Except Sandy's father will just buy him another."

"It's still gotta sting," Katie said. "The senator's and Otto Warburton's spin doctors are in full wash and cover-up cycle. Stay tuned."

Angela's own head was spinning. "What are you working on?" she asked.

Katie peeked out into the hall and whispered, "Move your long legs, so I can shut my door."

Angela folded herself like origami. Once Katie's door was closed, she said, "A suspected Angel of Death at SOS. In the new telemetry unit."

"What's a telemetry unit?" Angela asked.

"Rooms where they hook patients up to computers to monitor them. Sounds impressive but allows the hospital to perform a full wallet-ectomy. The telemetry unit nurses say that in the past six months, eight patients with minor problems suddenly died while he was on duty."

"He? The killer is a male nurse?"

"Suspected killer. SOS paid him a big bonus—twenty-thousand bucks—to come here, and that pissed off the regular staff. Then the nurses noticed a sudden increase in their patient death rate. Patients who were expected to go home suddenly up and died. But only on his shift.

"The nurses watched him, but they couldn't catch him doing anything wrong. Then last night, a forty-two-year-old woman died suddenly, and her family raised holy hell. She was supposed to go home today. She was working on a big trial."

"Was she a lawyer?"

"She was a jury scout for ProWin Jury and Trial Consulting. She searched Facebook, blogs, and other social media to make sure the jury was following the judge's orders not to discuss the case. She had gallbladder surgery, and there was an a-fib, a slightly wonky heartbeat. The doc put her in the telemetry unit. She was fine, and then she died.

"The nursing staff threatened a walkout if the patient wasn't autopsied. I went over her body with a magnifying glass and found a bruise and a needle mark in a big vein on her foot."

"Not a standard injection site," Angela said.

"Tell me about it," Katie said. "The patient died of an arrhythmia, the kind that can be caused by high potassium levels."

"But that's a common hospital drug," Angela said. "And don't potassium levels rise after death?"

"They do, but not like this. And there's no reason for that weird injection site on her foot. Potassium is dangerous. The patient was in the telemetry unit and closely monitored. Her potassium was normal, and so was her ECG—that's her echocardiogram—until right before she died. Then everything went apeshit. Her T-waves suddenly peaked. Made no sense at all. Unless she'd been given a massive dose of potassium. When I found that weird injection site, I figured it had to be potassium poisoning."

"If she'd been monitored, couldn't they have saved her?" Angela said.

"Not after a huge dose. That's always fatal. Now the nurses are demanding that SOS investigate the seven other suspicious deaths, or they'll go public. They want the nurse arrested for murder. SOS is looking at a PR nightmare. They'll need exhumation orders for the other bodies, and I'm looking at seven more posts."

"I thought the head medical examiner would handle these autopsies, Katie."

"His Imperial Majesty Dr. Evarts Evans isn't going to offend the Forest families who run SOS," she said. "He dumped it in my lap."

"Oh boy," Angela said. "I'll keep you in drinks and dinners. You need wine and whine time."

"Good. Let's start tomorrow night," Katie said. "Our favorite Mexican place, Gringo Daze. Seven o'clock. Don't wimp out.

"I'll hunt you down if you don't show up."

CHAPTER 5

"Oh man, we got a situation here," Rick said, his thick work boots sloshing in the water in Angela's downstairs bathroom. He wore ancient jeans and a vintage Grateful Dead T-shirt, fragrant with pot smoke. Rick's rich, ambitious parents never understood how they had produced this lanky corporate dropout, but the rest of the Forest appreciated his skills.

Angela leaned against the doorjamb. Diamond-spangled halos danced and shimmered around the Forest's handyman. "How bad?" she asked.

"Seal's broken on the crapper. You'll need a new one. There's water damage to your walls and a blockage somewhere. I'll need to take out this here," he rapped on the wall behind the toilet. "We're looking at two or three weeks of work, but I can start tomorrow."

"Good," Angela said. Rick usually had a long list of jobs.

She could barely see him through the migraine's cut-glass shimmer. The tiny bathroom was a dark blur interrupted by those frightening gaps in her vision, like sparkling TV static.

After Angela had talked with Katie, she'd made it home just before Rick arrived, nearly blinded by her headache. She had known she was home only because she could see the vague outline of the white stone two-story house. She'd abandoned her car in the driveway and stumbled into the kitchen, where she'd dry-swallowed another Imitrex. The migraine gripped her brain with red claws.

"You don't look so good," Rick said. "Is something wrong?"

"I missed lunch. I'll fix an egg," Angela said.

"Good idea," Rick said. "I'll start measuring, so I can get to work early tomorrow."

Angela found an egg in the fridge, then reached for a fork in the silverware drawer. And didn't know what to do with it.

She looked at the stainless-steel object in her hand. Which end should she hold? Why did she need it? She knew it was a fork, but wasn't sure what a fork had to do with scrambling an egg.

"Rick?" she called.

"What's wrong?" he said.

"Can you scramble the egg for me? I can't figure it out." She handed him the fork.

"Angela, this isn't right. You need to go to the ER," he said.

"No!" she said. "I have a report to finish." She couldn't explain her panic, but she knew she had to act as if nothing were wrong. If she could fight this, she'd be all right.

"I'm having trouble standing up," she said, and stumbled into a kitchen chair.

"Do you go to Doc Bartlett?" he asked. "I'll call her."

"No!" she said.

"Yes, you're on some kinda bad trip, Angela."

While Rick waited for Dr. Bartlett's answering service to track down the internist, he nuked Angela's leftover morning coffee and scrambled an egg. Angela sipped the strong, sugared coffee and felt better.

Now the fork was no longer a mystery. She was eating the egg when Dr. Carmen Bartlett called back. "Angela, what's wrong?"

The death investigator could almost see the small, sturdy internist. "Rick DeMun is here," Angela said. "He called you. I have a really bad headache."

"How long?" Dr. Bartlett said.

"Since Saturday."

"What else?" Her voice was quick, urgent.

"I'm having trouble standing up. And I can't figure out how to scramble an egg."

"Throw your medications in a bag and have Rick drive you to the ER now."

"But—"

"Now!" Dr. Bartlett said. "Don't waste time."

"I have to find my medications," Angela said as she hung up.

"Tell me where they are," Rick said.

"Medicine cabinet. Upstairs bath."

Rick found a ziplock bag in the kitchen and ran upstairs. She could hear him tossing bottles into the bag: pink Zocor pills for high cholesterol, fat calcium tablets, and tiny white hormone replacement therapy pills. Her gynecologist had warned her those hormones carried a stroke risk, but Angela had started menopause at the relatively early age of forty.

Angela shared the fatalism that went with her profession: she'd seen too many seemingly healthy people keel over for no reason. "At least I'll make a good-looking corpse," she'd said, brushing away the objections.

Through the blinding pain, her sluggish brain pushed forward these words: *I take hormone replacement therapy. Must tell doctor.*

"Let's go," Rick said. He guided her outside to his battered blue van. The spring evening was cool, and the darkness was restful on the brilliantly beautiful breakup of her vision. Angela sat in the passenger seat, docile, clutching the bag of medicine, while Rick pushed his van way over the speed limit.

By the time they reached Sisters of Sorrow Hospital, she felt better. She could almost see clearly, except for the diamond bands of break-apart light. Rick rushed into the ER, came back with a wheelchair, and rolled Angela to the triage nurse for an evaluation while he parked.

"I feel better now," Angela said. She could see the nurse's face clearly. The headache was there but bearable. Maybe the Imitrex migraine tablets were finally kicking in.

But with those optimistic words, she condemned herself and Rick to a long wait with crying babies, sniffling children, and limping, after-work athletes. Fox News blared ceaselessly in the cold, uncomfortable waiting room, lit by the greenish glare of the fluorescent lights.

Finally, a nurse called Angela's name.

"Should I go in with you?" Rick asked.

"Uh, would you mind waiting out here?" Angela said. She didn't want to undress in front of the handyman.

Two hours later, Angela was in a hospital gown with her back-side hanging out, shivering in an exam cubicle. A freckle-faced Irish nurse with seen-it-all-eyes suddenly changed her tone from concerned to adoring. "Dr. Porter Gravois, the neurologist on call, will see you," she said, as if the Pope had granted Angela an audience. The nurse did everything but genuflect and throw rose petals at the specialist's shined shoes when the man strode into the room.

Angela knew Gravois by reputation: he was a respected neurologist from an old-money Forest family. His looks were impressively patrician. He'd given the hospital a pediatric oncology wing, named after his mother, Doris DeMun Gravois. Dr. Gravois was pale and lean, his thin nose as prominent as his pedigree. Angela was pretty sure he wore a Turnbull & Asser bespoke shirt and silk black rep tie under his starched white coat. Even his blond hair was graying impressively—just enough to make him seem mature, not old.

He nodded reassuringly at Angela, read the notes on her chart, then asked more questions about her family history.

Her sludgy brain reminded her, *Tell him about the hormone replacement therapy.*

He shined a light in her eyes, asked her to count backward from a hundred by fives, checked for numbness or weakness in her face, arms, and legs, then listened to her carotid arteries with a stethoscope.

Must mention the hormone replacement therapy floated into her aching head, but she lost that thought when Gravois commanded, "Balance on your right foot. Now your left."

She did both successfully.

"Now walk across the room, one foot in front of the other, like this," Gravois said, and demonstrated, putting the heel of his black wingtip against the tip of his polished toe.

Angela heel-and-toed her way across the small room, keeping her balance.

Don't forget the hormone replacement therapy, she reminded herself.

Gravois was trying to get her attention. "I said, do you have a family history of stroke or heart attacks?"

"No, both my parents died of cancer," she said. "And my grandparents. No strokes on either side of the family. Oh, one more thing. Dr. Bartlett told me to bring my medication."

Angela handed Gravois the ziplock bag. "I'm taking hormone replacement therapy."

Gravois didn't bother opening it. "I can't keep track of all that stuff," he said. "There's something new out every week. You're too young and fit to have a stroke. Keep taking the Imitrex and come back on Friday for a PET scan. You can get dressed now."

It was nearly midnight by the time Angela was dressed and checked out. Rick was working his iPhone. "I'm so sorry you had to wait," she said.

"No biggie," he said.

She climbed into Rick's van and told him what Gravois said.

"That's good," Rick said. "You're too young and fit to have a stroke."

Angela should have found Gravois's words comforting, but she knew something was wrong with that statement. She wished her head worked well enough to figure out what it was.

"I guess this is just a bad migraine," she said. "Katie's right. I'm too wrapped up in my work. I'm looking forward to margaritas with her tomorrow night."

"Good advice. We can all use more fun." The van rumbled and bumped into Angela's driveway.

"Thank you, Rick. I'm sorry I ruined your evening."

"Hey," he said. "If anything happened to you, that would ruin my evening. I'm glad you're okay."

She was better, but Angela knew something wasn't quite right. Maybe it was the Imitrex. She took another and fell asleep.

Angela woke up the next morning to Rick noisily pounding on her door. She quickly dressed and made her way downstairs.

"Ready for work," he said. "How are you this morning?"

"Better," she said, though another headache was gathering at the edges of her mind, like a storm on the horizon.

"Would you like coffee?" she asked.

"Brought my own," he said, holding up his thermos. Angela scrambled an egg, then swallowed another Imitrex.

She fought the headache all day as she struggled with her report on Ben Weymuller's death investigation. Angela turned it in about four o'clock. At four thirty, Rick poked his head in her study door.

"I'm leaving now," he said. "This is even more screwed up than I thought. It's gonna take at least a month."

"I'll give you the spare key, in case I'm at work tomorrow," she said. Like everyone in the Forest, she trusted Rick.

Angela could barely see him through the blinding migraine dazzle, as if he were spotlighted on a brightly lit stage. She was determined to push through this. She was too young and fit to have a stroke. The Forest's top neurologist had said so.

"Are you feeling better?"

"I'm fine," she said, forcing a smile. "I'll lie down until it's time to go out with Katie."

Angela crawled into bed for a nap that soft spring night, Thursday, March 10. And woke up nineteen days later.

CHAPTER 6

"What's your name?" the doctor in the white coat asked Angela. He looked like a fit forty and wore his stethoscope like an award.

"Angela Richman," she said.

"What day is it?" the doctor asked.

"Tuesday, March twenty-nine," Angela said. Her voice sounded funny, more a croak than her usual soft tones.

"Amazing," the doctor said. Then he left.

What's so amazing about that? Angela wondered. Over the doctor's shoulder, she could see the day and date on the giant calendar on the wall.

The beige wall. Her bedroom didn't have beige walls. And this wasn't her bed, either.

I'm in a hospital bed with a thin blue blanket and sheets like sandpaper, she thought. *The sun is shining. Is it morning or afternoon?*

Angela didn't know. She also didn't know the next doctor, who asked, "What's your name?" He was fiftysomething, his thin brown hair receding as if someone were erasing it off his scalp.

"Angela Richman," she said. *Why do I feel so groggy?* she wondered.

"What day is it?" he asked.

She checked the calendar over his shoulder. "Tuesday, March twenty-nine," she said. Her throat felt dry and scratchy.

"Astonishing," he said and left.

What am I doing in a hospital? she wondered. *Which hospital is it?*

Before Angela could ask, a third doctor barged into her room, a preppie as pale as a cave salamander. She didn't know him, either, but he asked the same question.

"What's your name?"

"Angela Richman," she said.

"What day is it?"

"Tuesday, March twenty-nine," she said.

"Amazing," he said, then left before she could find out more.

What's so amazing about March 29? she wondered. *Who are these doctors? Why do they keep asking my name instead of helping me? Why don't they ask how I feel? Or tell me what happened?*

Now a fourth doctor was at her bedside. He looked newly hatched, but he chirped out the same questions. She gave him the same answers, and he looked at her as if she were a prodigy spouting string theory.

Dr. Hatchling was followed by a fifth doctor, an older one with corrugated gray hair, who asked those same questions.

What day is it? she thought. *What the hell? Don't any of these birds have a calendar? Why are they bothering me? Can't they ask a nurse?*

Angela's left hand hurt. Now she saw an IV jammed into her badly bruised skin. These were old bruises, some turning yellow. Had she been in an accident? Her arm looked odd, too. Her usually tanned skin was a fierce, blotchy pink.

I look like a freak, she thought, and then slowly the pieces fell into place.

I'm in a hospital. A parade of doctors I've never met is coming through my room. They aren't helping me. They're putting me through my paces like a performing dog . . .

Oh no. Angela felt a stab of pure terror. She'd spent enough time around hospitals to know what that meant.

I am a freak. I'm the hospital freak show, and docs are gathering like vultures, fighting over my body, picking and pulling at what's left of me. They've come to see a show, and I'm supposed to perform. I'm a talking exhibit. Something bad has happened, but I don't know what.

I should charge admission.

"What's your name?" a sixth doctor demanded. Angela saw a pink porker with small, inquisitive eyes. *Show's over,* she thought and drifted away.

The next time Angela woke up, the room was dark and she was shivering uncontrollably. "Cold," she said. Her mouth was lined with cotton.

"Angela!" Her husband was holding her other hand, the one without the IV. "You're awake."

"Donegan," she said. "You're here." Angela smiled at her husband. His shirt was rumpled, and he needed a shave. "You look worried."

"You're cold," he said and rang for a nurse. "I've been here for days. This is the first time you've talked to me. When I'm not here, Katie is. She saved your life."

A nurse bustled in, saw Angela, and smiled. "You're awake," she said. "That's wonderful."

"I'm cold," Angela said.

"I'll get you a blanket from the warmer," the nurse said.

"What happened to me?" Angela asked Donegan.

"You had a stroke. Six strokes, the surgeon thinks."

"Surgeon? I had surgery for a stroke?"

"One was a hemorrhagic stroke. You had seizures, and there was bleeding in your brain. It was bad, Angela. Very bad. You're in Sisters of Sorrow, and thank God you had a good brain surgeon. But you're here now."

"Where was I?" Someone had stuffed her head with old rags.

"In a coma," he said. "A chemical coma. To give your brain a rest."

A rest. That sounded good. She felt like she'd been crawling through a long, dark tunnel. "Can I go home now?"

"Soon." Donegan said something else, but Angela was so tired she couldn't follow him. She remembered the feel of a warm blanket and Donegan's soft kiss on her forehead. Then the blackness swallowed her.

"Angela, sweetheart, how are you?" Her mother, a softly pretty woman with gentle brown eyes, was sitting by her bed, wearing her white polyester uniform.

"Momma," Angela said. "I'm so glad to see you." She reached for her mother's work-worn hand, and Angela's eyes filled with tears.

"How's your headache?" her mother asked.

"It's gone," Angela said, surprised. "It felt like iron spikes in my head, but it's gone. I'm woozy and tired, but the horrible headache is really gone. I'm just so tired."

"Then you sleep, my darling," her mother said and kissed her.

"Morning, sleeping beauty." Katie was sitting in a turquoise chair by Angela's bed. Her friend looked frazzled. Her short, neat hair stuck out in spikes. Katie never wore makeup, but her freckled farm-girl face was creased with worry.

"You scared the shit out of everybody," she said.

"I'm sorry."

"Not your fault. It's that flaming asshole, Dr. Porter Gravois. Chip to friends. Cow Chip is more like it. He should *never* have sent you home after you went to the emergency room. Dumb fuck."

Katie's more profane that usual, Angela thought in the part of her soggy brain that worked. Her friend's sentences registered ten and a half on the Katie Anger Index. The more upset Katie was, the more she swore.

"How'd you know about the ER visit?" Angela asked.

"Rick told me," Katie said.

"I heard you saved my life," Angela said.

"I didn't do a damn thing but get pissed off when you were a no-show at Gringo Daze."

A faint spot of clarity appeared in the gray fog of Angela's memory. Now she recalled days of blinding migraines. The pain had made her want to claw her head open and let her tortured brain escape. *I'd finished Ben Weymuller's death investigation,* she thought, *then stopped by the morgue to see Katie. She said I was overworked, and we were going to meet Thursday night.*

"We were supposed to have margaritas," Angela said.

"Right. At seven o'clock," Katie said. "When you weren't there by seven forty, I'd had enough. I called your cell phone and your home, and you didn't answer. I drove straight to your house to tell you what I thought of you.

"You were lying halfway out of bed. I tried to wake you, but you didn't respond. I was scared shitless. I called 911, and the paramedics hauled you to SOS. Dr. Tritt performed emergency brain surgery right before midnight."

"Dr. Tritt," Angela said. "Who's he?"

"Jeb Travis Tritt. You never met him?"

"I don't think so," Angela said.

"You'd know if you met Tritt," Katie said. "He was the neurosurgeon on call. He's the one who really saved your life."

Katie shifted in her tall-backed chair.

"You're uncomfortable," Angela said.

"I'm okay," Katie said.

"You're a lousy liar. Where do hospitals find those ugly chairs? Do they get a group rate from Torquemada's Warehouse of Unbearable Chairs?"

"Hey, you made a joke." Katie looked pleased. "You're going to be okay."

"That's nice," Angela said and fell back to sleep. Over the next few days, Angela drifted in and out of consciousness. Sometimes she talked with Donegan or her mother, other times with Katie. She'd find one of them at her bedside even in the middle of the night.

Nurses in scrubs drifted in and out in of her room. She was professionally poked, prodded, and stabbed by phlebotomists, then hauled through subterranean corridors for scans and X-rays.

Angela floated in a comfortable gray dream. Her mother had soft kisses and soothing words, but Donegan and Katie spoon-fed her bits of information, a little more each day. Donegan's words were shaded with worry and hesitation. Once Katie heard Angela joke, she was her usual blunt self. Except she was angrier than usual.

After two or three days, Angela had a time line of what had happened to her.

Donegan told her, "You had two seizures in the ambulance on your way to the ER. I saw your body try to rise up on the stretcher, but the paramedics strapped you down."

Now Angela had a horror movie vision of her zombiefied self in her mind.

"The paramedics thought you wouldn't make it," Donegan said. "One of them said to me, 'Sorry about your wife, man.'"

Angela teared up, then felt like a drama queen, crying over her own potential death. *I'm alive, dammit,* she thought.

Katie told her, "At SOS the fuckin' ER doctor said you had the worst blood stroke he'd ever seen."

Angela saw the fire in her friend's eyes. "What's a blood stroke?" she asked.

"A hemorrhagic stroke," Katie said. "Burst blood vessel. That twit said you'd be dead by morning, and if not, you'd be a vegetable. The asshole said 'vegetable.' I was devastated, and that dickwad doc left me standing there. Alone."

Angela felt ashamed, then sad, then angry for Katie. Her emotions were all over the place, like those of a hormonal teenager.

Katie said, "I asked him, 'What should I do?' 'There's coffee in the lounge,' Dr. Dickhead said and walked away. I finally got it together enough to e-mail the Forest ME. I told Evarts the ER said you'd be dead by morning."

"I was dead?"

"I had to prepare everyone at work," Katie said. "Dr. Evarts Evans was awake. He wrote your obituary. It's not everyone who gets to read their obituary."

"I have an obituary," Angela said and drifted off to sleep.

Donegan said, "Katie and I just sat there until nearly midnight, when Dr. Tritt came into the ER like a tornado. He said he could save you. I asked him, 'Will she be able to work? She won't be happy unless she can.' He said, 'Of course she will.' Dr. Tritt was the only one who believed you would live. He performed a craniotomy and removed a third of your frontal lobe. He's the only doctor here I trust."

Angela thought her husband looked ragged and tired. "Are you getting any sleep, sweetheart?" she said.

"Oh yeah. I'm fine."

No, he isn't, Angela thought. She could tell he'd lost weight. "What about food?" she asked.

"The bar across from the hospital has a terrific cheeseburger," he said.

"You can't live on cheeseburgers," Angela said.

"Don't worry," he said.

The next day, Angela told her mother, "Donegan's not eating right, Mom. He's living on bar burgers."

"Don't you worry," her mother said. "I'll take him lots of good home cooking." As soon as her mother left, Katie appeared.

"I'm glad to see you again, Katie, but how are you getting your work done?"

"I sneak away whenever I'm not working on my Angel of Death investigation. It's stalled while the lawyers try to get more exhumation orders on the possible victims. I've found another one with that distinctive needle site on the top of her foot. That makes two. We suspect there are eight or nine."

"At least the nurse is in jail," Angela said.

"No, he's still working at the hospital."

"You're joking," Angela said.

"I shit you not. Never underestimate the cowardice of hospital lawyers. They said he's had good evaluations, and we don't have any proof he's killed anyone. When his supervisor tried to cut his hours, the nurse called his lawyer, who threatened to sue the hospital. So they let the nurse stay on."

"Incredible."

"The hospital doesn't want trouble," Katie said.

"But the victims' families will sue," Angela said.

"You're damn right. The rumblings started in the nursing staff as soon as I got the exhumation order. The other nurses are watching him like hawks. If another patient dies unexpectedly, they'll go on strike."

"That won't be much comfort for the victim," Angela said.

"That's how chickenshit hospitals act," Katie said. "I wrote a memo to cover my ass. You're safe. You're nowhere near his ward."

"I don't feel safe knowing he's anywhere in SOS," Angela said.

Katie switched the subject. "Have you met Dr. Tritt yet? He stops by to see you when he gets off work at midnight."

"I remember a lot of doctors, but I don't think I've met him."

"You're his prize patient. He must let you sleep."

"What's he like?" Angela asked.

"Brilliant," Katie said. "Trained at the top neurosurgery hospitals—Mayo in Rochester and Cornell in New York. New to the medical staff here."

"Who's he know in the Forest?" Angela asked.

"Nobody," Katie said. "He married into a Forest family, but she's correcting that mistake. Meanwhile, he's pissing off everybody. His bedside manner sucks."

"Who cares, if he saves lives?" Angela said. "I have a vague memory of a big man with a bad haircut and a soft voice with a country accent."

"That's him," Katie said. "Dresses like he fell off a hay wagon. Doesn't know a fish fork from a fish finger. That asshat Gravois looks like a *GQ* model and is slick as goose shit, but we'd be picking out your tombstone if it hadn't been for Dr. Tritt. That Gravois . . ."

They heard the rattle of a rolling computerized work station, and Katie stopped. "I'm in your john," she said and slipped away before a no-nonsense blonde nurse rolled into Angela's room.

"Welcome back to the land of the living," the nurse said. She examined Angela with businesslike precision, then trundled her computer work station to the next room.

When Katie returned, Angela asked, "Why did you suddenly shut up when the nurse appeared?"

"She adores Dr. Gravois," Katie said, her voice hushed to a whisper. "Everyone does. Except me."

"And me," Angela said. "I'm here because of his screwup. If he's as bad as you say, why does everyone love him?"

"He's a wizard at avoiding trouble. He knows how to shut down complaints and investigations. In your case, he made himself invisible. He's never come to see you, never asked how you were. He's been the golden boy since he donated fifty million dollars for that pediatric oncology wing five years ago—and twisted arms for the rest of the money," Katie said. "He donated enough to name it after his mother. She lost her first boy to brain cancer when he was two years old."

"I knew about the wing," Angela said, "but not the story behind it."

"It's heartbreaking for any woman to lose a child," Katie said. "He wanted some good to come out of his family tragedy. It also doesn't hurt that Gravois is a major money maker for the hospital. The insurance companies adore him—he'll always testify on their behalf. And he has the right connections, the right clothes, and all the social graces. That's important here. The Forest isn't a meritocracy. They'd rather die at the hands of a man who dresses properly, than be rescued by a talented hick in a bad suit. Tritt is a gifted surgeon, but he'll never know or understand the Forest. The staff is taking bets on how long Tritt will last. We're in a fight for the soul of the hospital."

CHAPTER 7

Angela woke up shivering in the dark hospital room. She knew it was late. No TVs blared, no carts rattled down the hall. The herds of chattering visitors were gone. She heard the soft beep of the monitors and saw the greenish fish-tank light of the night nursing desk.

Angela's skin itched, and her arms were purple, blue, and green with more needle stick bruises.

"You're awake," the man at her bedside said. Large and lumpy, he was twice as wide as Donegan. The man's dark hair was badly cut and plastered with oil. His noble nose made his round, fleshy face oddly attractive. Even sitting in the ugly turquoise chair, he radiated energy.

Angela saw his green scrubs and cap, and her slow, sleep-clogged brain put the information together.

"You're Dr. Tritt," she guessed. "Katie said you saved my life."

"I am, and I did," he said. No false modesty for Tritt. "You have a terrific friend, you know that? You don't have any next of kin, and she handled everything."

Angela was confused. Why hadn't Katie called her mother? Or Donegan? She started to say something, but Tritt didn't give her a chance.

"You were an FTD delivery," he said. "That's fixing to die. The idiot in the ER said you'd be dead by morning. He told your friend Katie, without consulting me. Lucky I was on call. I saw you and knew you'd make it. Katie was really worried about you."

Of course she was, Angela wanted to say, but Dr. Tritt steamrolled ahead. "Most people—even husbands and wives—say they're worried, but they're really worried about themselves: How will I live with this drooling cripple? You two aren't partners, are you?"

"No, she's—"

Angela wanted to say that Katie was the sister she'd never had, but Dr. Tritt barged through her feeble words. "Katie said she'd take care of you if you were disabled. I said you'd be fine. I opened your head about six minutes to midnight."

Opened? An image flashed through Angela's mind. She saw Katie in an autopsy suite, peeling back a dead woman's face like a rubber mask and cutting off the top of her skull with a Stryker power saw.

Where was my head cut open? Angela wondered. She wanted to reach up and touch it, but she was too afraid to know.

Tritt's nonstop talk drained her energy. She lay back on the rough pillow and listened to him. His voice pushed on, warm and friendly. His pleasant country accent made scary facts seem less frightening.

"You had a venous stroke," Tritt said. "The sagittal sinus, that big vein at the top of your head, ruptured. That kind of stroke is usually seen in pregnant women during labor or new mothers. It's rare. Few women survive, much less in your shape."

Angela wanted to tell him about all the doctors in her room, but she didn't get a chance.

"Doctors are coming from as far away as Illinois to see you," he said. "Seventy miles!"

She heard his pride. Dr. Tritt hadn't saved her life. He'd raised her from the dead.

"Everyone wants to see you," he said. "They don't usually get a chance to talk to a venous stroke survivor. This is a real coup."

For you, she thought. *I'm a living, breathing trophy.* Angela felt angry but wasn't sure why.

"Let me check you out," Tritt said.

He shined a light in her eyes and ran his fingers over her scalp. She couldn't feel his fingers, but she saw them. He had the hands of a concert pianist—long and strong with short, square nails and clean, pink skin. No calluses or scars on those fleshy instruments.

"Healing nicely," he said. "The drain is open."

Drain? I have a drain? Before Angela could ask about the drain, she drifted off to sleep as Tritt droned on about his achievements. The next morning, Angela checked the giant wall calendar. It was April 2.

"Welcome to the step-down ICU," a big, cheerful nurse with fried blonde hair said to her. "I'm Chris. You're making progress."

Angela didn't remember being moved out of the critical care unit, but this room looked about the same. Her hospital breakfast arrived on a tray, with a tin pot of coffee and a bottle of vitamin-enriched chocolate Ensure. She gobbled her cold, lumpy eggs and greasy sausage, her first solid food since the stroke.

Angela stayed awake after breakfast, listening to the code calls and blaring TVs.

"May I come in?"

A gray-haired woman in a powder-blue suit and flowered blouse rolled a computer workstation into Angela's room. She looked like a sweet old grandma, until Angela saw Grandma's ice-chip eyes. This was a woman who weighed wallets and found them wanting.

"I'm Gina Lorraine Swinny. From the hospital billing office," she said, confirming Angela's suspicions. Gina had a soft, fluttery voice, but Angela detected steel underneath.

"There's been a little problem with your insurance," she said. "When you were admitted on March tenth, your friend Katie told us that you had double insurance—from your job and also your husband's—but she failed to say which one was primary."

"What's primary insurance?" Angela asked.

"Your main policy," Gina said. "You have to designate one of them as primary."

"I'm not sure what you mean," Angela said. "When I go to the doctor, I give the office both cards, and they work it out."

"Oh no, no, no," Gina said. "That's not right. You have to choose one."

"Well, I didn't," Angela said, "and it's never been a problem."

"I'm afraid you've caused this hospital a great deal of difficulty. Since our records were confused, you were without insurance when you were admitted. There are penalties. You owe SOS one hundred thousand dollars."

"What?" Angela said. She was glad she was lying down. "That's outrageous."

"It's the law," Gina said. "We waited until you were well enough to help us straighten this out. I realize that's a large sum. I'll give you time to work it out. I'll be back in a little bit."

Angela could hear Gina's workstation rattling down the hall. *I should be upset,* she thought, *but this is so ridiculous, and I'm so tired.*

She woke to find her lunch tray in front of her: warm milk, a cold, skinless chicken breast, flabby white bread, green beans, and a stingy square of yellow cake. By the time she drank the milk and ate the cake, Angela decided Gina Swinny was a bad dream.

Katie stopped by after lunch with *Thin Air*, a new Ann Cleeves mystery.

"Thank you," Angela said, clasping the treasure to her ugly hospital gown.

"Good to see you awake," Katie said. She seemed more relaxed today. She was wearing a clean lab coat, and her brown hair was neatly combed.

"How's the Angel of Death investigation?" Angela asked.

Once again, Katie checked the hall, then pulled the privacy curtain around the bed and lowered her voice to a near whisper. "I autopsied a second victim yesterday. Thirty-six-year-old mother of three. She'd come to the ER with a concussion. No sign of bleeding in the brain, but they kept her in the telemetry unit overnight. Sure enough, she died, but not from a hematoma. She went into sudden, unexplained cardiac arrest. I checked her records. Normal potassium levels until just before she died, and there were those damned high T-waves again on her cardiogram. It looks like another massive dose of potassium."

"Did you find the telltale needle stick?" Angela asked.

"Yep. This time I didn't have to go over her body with a magnifying glass. I found it right away on her foot."

"What did she do for a living?"

"She was a health insurance company executive."

"Which one?" Angela asked.

"Does it make any difference?" Katie said.

"Do the Angel of Death victims have anything in common?" Angela asked.

"The suspected victims—the nurses say there are eight—are all women, ages twenty-five to fifty, all good-looking."

"Single?" Angela asked.

"Fifty-fifty. Some married, some single. Victim two was married."

"So the Angel of Death is a woman hater?"

"Maybe," Katie said. "Maybe he feels threatened by attractive women. Maybe they made him feel inferior. Maybe he hit on them, and they turned him down. Maybe he got off watching them die. We don't know what twisted excuse he's using. Remember that Angel of

Death case in Italy? A nurse killed thirty-eight patients because they or their relatives were rude to her."

"Guess I'd better be polite until you catch the creep," Angela said. "He has to know the nurses are on to him."

"Of course he does. But he's clever. And the longer he can't kill, the more desperate he'll become. The staff can't watch him every minute. Next major crisis in that ward, he'll lose his bodyguard, and someone else will die."

"What about the other six autopsies?"

"The lawyers are still futzing around," Katie said and made a face. *A much milder F-word,* Angela thought. *She's feeling better.*

"The hospital lawyers can't—or won't—come out and say SOS wants the bodies exhumed because the women were probably poisoned. And the families haven't caught on that their deaths weren't natural.

"SOS doesn't want the victims' families lawyered up, and they sure as hell don't want this story leaked to the press. The lawyers' requests are so delicately phrased, you'd think the hospital was inviting the dead women to a party. Naturally, the families won't consent."

"So SOS will let the matter drop?" Angela asked.

"Can't," Katie said. "The nurses are raising holy hell. One knows an investigative TV reporter. Not some local yokel. A big-deal national reporter with brains and serious connections."

"Then the Forest can't buy her off or threaten her," Angela said.

"Exactly. The nurses are really tightening the screws. They promised a mass walkout unless the hospital investigates the deaths—even the Forest couldn't cover that up. Then they brought out the ultimate weapon. They want to report those deaths to the Joint Commission."

"What's that?" Angela asked.

"The commission does hospital accreditations, and if SOS loses that, it's in big trouble. That sucking sound you'll hear will be the big bucks going down the drain, along with the hospital's reputation. The nurses are smart. They got their own lawyer. They know that gang of weasels in white coats will pull the usual doctor trick and blame the nurses. I gotta run. Enjoy your book."

Angela's head was spinning from this new information. She read Cleeves's latest Shetland adventure, until Gina Swinny rolled in with her rattling workstation. The only thing grandmotherly about her now was her short gray hair. Gina had the hard, flat eyes of a seasoned enforcer.

"Well?" she said. "Did you take time to consider my request?"

Angela heard the threat. "Yes. I don't owe you anything. All you have to do is rebill the insurance companies."

"You owe the hospital a considerable amount. I was prepared to offer you a deal of ten thousand dollars."

"I don't want your deal," Angela said. "Get out!"

"You'll be hearing from me again!" Gina said and pushed her workstation into the hall like a battering ram.

Angela was shaking with anger. She needed to call Tom Wymen, her lawyer. She fumbled for her bedside phone, charged the information number to her account, and was eventually connected to Tom.

"Angela," he said. "You must be feeling better if you're calling me."

"Yes and no," she said and told him about Gina Swinny's threat. Tom's laugh warmed Angela's heart. "That's ridiculous," he said. "Tell her to pound sand. What's she gonna do, repossess your brain? Better yet, I'll call this Gina now and end this today."

"Thanks, Tom," Angela said.

Angela's dinner had arrived, and she attacked this meal. It was still hot, and she was hungry. Donegan stopped by as she was finishing her roast chicken. "I brought you these," he said, handing her a dozen velvety red roses.

Angela inhaled their perfume. "My favorite. They smell so sweet."

Donegan smiled and kissed her, then sat by the bed and asked about her day.

"Katie came to see me," she said. "Mostly I slept." She didn't want to worry him by mentioning Gina Swinny. She'd fixed that problem.

He was wearing her favorite rust suede jacket with the leather patches on the elbows, the one that made his eyes look deep-brown. The one that set the coeds' hearts fluttering.

Hers, too. Donegan had been her English professor, and Angela fell in love with him the first day of class. He was the smartest, funniest man she'd ever known.

A recorded voice announced that visiting hours were over. Donegan kissed her cheek. She wished she were back in his arms, feeling his strength and warmth. They'd make love—hot, sweaty love instead of staid kisses.

Angela dozed after Donegan left and woke up at midnight to find Dr. Tritt at her bedside, studying her chart. "I hear you're eating," he said. "That's good. Tomorrow, we'll get you up on a walker. Then I'm moving you to the stroke unit to start physical therapy."

"I had a stroke, right?"

"Six strokes," he said. "Including a hemorrhagic stroke. That's why I had to do brain surgery."

"The day before I had the strokes, I went to the SOS ER," she said. "Dr. Porter Gravois was the neurologist on duty. He said I was 'too young and fit to have a stroke' and sent me home."

Tritt's words started low, slow, and measured. Then they exploded. "That incompetent fool. It's bad enough that he testifies for insurance companies. Now he's killing ER patients. You're never too young for a stroke. Never! Babies have them."

Tritt's face was so red, Angela was afraid he'd stroke out. "What do you mean, he testifies for the insurance companies?" she asked.

"He helps insurance companies screw people out of money they have coming. Exhibit A is right here in this hospital. Gravois testified against Patrick Fargo, a twelve-year-old boy injured in a car accident. He told the jury that the boy's neurological injuries were mostly imaginary."

Is Tritt supposed to mention the boy's name? Angela wondered. *What about patient confidentiality?*

"Now Mariah, the boy's mother, can't pay his medical bills, thanks to Gravois," Tritt said. "The kid is dying of kidney failure—imaginary kidney failure, I guess. Except that poor boy will be dead soon. Really dead."

His brown eyes glowed with fanatic fire. "I'm sick of Gravois. You sue him, and I'll testify on your behalf. He's done enough damage. I want to get him."

CHAPTER 8

"I'm Tink Warren, your physical therapist." The tiny blonde barely came to Angela's shoulder.

"Short for Tinker Bell?" Angela asked.

"Congratulations, you win a free walk down the hall," Tink said, and grinned. Relentlessly cheerful, the hospital PT had dandelion spiked hair, an infectious smile, and pale skin showcasing dragon-and-flower tattoos.

"Nice tats," Angela said. "How do you get by with visible ink at a hospital?"

"Are you kidding? If SOS didn't hire people because their ink showed, they wouldn't have any employees. Besides, my mom works in radiology."

Ah, Angela thought. *The Forest connection.*

"Let's get to work. Grip your walker, Angela, and stand up. Slowly. Slowly."

Slowly was the only way Angela could stand. She sat up on the edge of her hospital bed, grabbed the aluminum walker's gray plastic handholds, and pushed up.

Angela was on her feet for the first time in almost a month. The room tilted, and her knees shook. She wasn't used to standing.

"I feel a draft at my back," she told Tink.

"No wonder," Tink said. "Your tush is flapping in the breeze. Put this gown on to cover your back end."

"Hospitals turn you into a flasher," Angela said as Tink helped her slide into a second greenish-blue hospital gown like a robe. The physical therapist closed the gown's shoulder snaps, then fitted a heavy canvas belt with a big ring for her to grab if Angela fell.

"The belt doesn't go with my socks," Angela said, wiggling her toes in the hideous yellow hospital-issue socks with the nonslip soles.

"Too bad. For what SOS charges, those should be Jimmy Choos," Tink said. "Up you go again. I'll follow with your stand." IV lines tethered Angela to a rolling metal stand hung with three clear bags. A urine collection bag was taped to her thigh.

"Stand up straight," Tink said.

"You sound like my mother," Angela said.

"Standing up straight reduces the stress on your shoulders," Tink said, grabbing the ring on Angela's belt. "Come on. I've got you, if you start to fall."

Angela thought Tink was too tiny to keep her from falling, but she did see the muscles under those tats. Angela took one step and then another, pushing the walker forward.

"Good," Tink said. "Keep going."

They rounded the foot of the bed, passing a chest of drawers covered with flowers, metallic balloons, and a pink orchid plant. Cards swarmed between the gifts.

"Somebody has friends," Tink said. "Who sent the gorgeous red roses by your bed?"

"My husband," Angela said.

"Lucky girl," Tink said. "Doubly lucky. You almost didn't make it."

Angela trundled into a hall that was fifty shades of bland. She blinked at the morning bustle, a hick gawking at the big-city traffic. People stared at her. A little boy blurted out, "Mommy, that lady's head looks funny." His mother dragged him toward the elevator.

Before Angela could ask why her head looked funny, Tink said, "Turn left. There's less traffic at this end of the hall. You're doing good. Keep your weight on the walker and your back straight."

As they made slow, rattling progress down the wide hall, Angela took voyeuristic peeks into the rooms. She saw a pale old man on his back, snoring. In another room, a bored young woman flipped through TV channels, her dark room drained of life and color.

Through the arrow-slit window at the end of the hall, Angela glimpsed the tender, green Missouri hills. It was late spring. Hospitals had no seasons.

"You made it," Tink said, as if Angela had finished a marathon. "Now turn slowly, and let's start back. Dr. Tritt will be pleased you took a walk."

"He's a wonderful surgeon," Angela said.

"He certainly thinks so," Tink said, her voice flat.

The physical therapist was clearly no fan of Tritt. Neither were the nurses. Last night, after Tritt's monologue ended at about 2:00 a.m., a nurse had checked Angela's vitals. "If he's bothering you, honey, press your call button, and I'll get rid of him," the nurse had said.

Why doesn't the staff like Dr. Tritt? Angela wondered as she pushed the walker toward her room.

"Excellent," Tink said. "You're making real progress."

"When can I go home?" Angela asked.

"In a little bit," Tink said vaguely. "You've got some recovering to do. You're so lucky."

Lucky? That word again. Angela didn't feel lucky. Not with an unpleasantly warm urine bag taped to her leg. She wasn't ready to return to her room yet. "What's around that corner?" she asked.

"The pediatric unit," Tink said.

"Can we go there?" Angela asked.

"I don't want you overdoing it," Tink said.

Angela couldn't stand going back to her room after her brief taste of freedom. "Please?"

Tink gave in, and Angela turned the corner. Now she was sorry she'd insisted on going down this hall. The unit's bright crayon colors and happy cartoon characters seemed to mock the pale, sickly children.

Through a thicket of balloons, plants, and flowers in the second room, Angela could make out a boy's unmoving figure in the bed, so small he barely made a mound under the covers. He was connected to a spaghetti-tangle of tubes, IV lines, and wires. A worried-looking woman, her brown hair streaked with gray, was talking to a man in a dark suit. Angela could see only the back of the man's head and his dark-suited shoulders.

"That's Monty Bryant," Tink whispered. "The famous personal injury lawyer. That man is sex on a stick."

"Have you dated him?"

Tink snorted. "As if. Montgomery Anderson Bryant is way outta my league. Monty is rich, divorced, and has a horse farm in the Forest. He and his ex-wife share custody of their son, who's the same age as that little boy in there."

Angela waited until a laundry cart rumbled past, then whispered, "Is that Patrick Fargo? I hear he isn't going to make it."

"Who told you his name?" Tink asked.

"Dr. Tritt," Angela said.

"Figures," Tink said. "I shouldn't be saying this, but Monty is taking Patrick's illness hard. He's one lawyer who actually cares about his clients. The hospital is crawling with ambulance chasers, but Monty's not like that. If they could clone Monty, there wouldn't be any lawyer jokes."

Angela stumbled, and Tink grabbed her belt. "Tired?" she asked.

Angela nodded. She was so exhausted, she could hardly push the walker back to her room.

"Let's get you back into bed," Tink said. "It's almost lunchtime." Tink folded the walker and propped it against the wall, then settled Angela into the hospital bed and adjusted its height.

By that time, an orderly arrived with a tray of spaghetti, a limp salad with a transparent slice of cucumber, khaki green beans, more chocolate Ensure, and vanilla ice cream. Angela ate it all.

Donegan arrived as she was finishing her ice cream, and the room suddenly seemed brighter. She kissed her big-shouldered, brown-haired husband, inhaling his scent of coffee and citrus, and wished they were home.

"I brought you these," he said, handing her a stack of novels. She spotted her favorite authors: Jeff Abbott, Naomi Hirahara, Charlaine Harris, Brendan DuBois, and David Ellis.

"Hours of good reading," she said, stacking them on the nightstand next to her roses.

"Thought I'd have lunch with you," Donegan said, pulling a supermarket sandwich on a puffy white bun out of his briefcase, along with a Diet Coke. "I see a walker against the wall. Were you up and about?"

Angela told him about her epic walk and said, "Your whole department chipped in and sent that orchid plant. I love the delicate color. About half of those cards are from your colleagues."

"I work with good people." Donegan checked the black-and-white schoolhouse clock on the wall, tossed his lunch wrapper in the trash, then kissed her good-bye. "I have to go back to work, sweetheart. I'm glad you're making progress. I'll see you tonight."

Angela stroked his soft hair and kissed his velvety ear. His brown eyes looked tired. "Stay home and rest tonight, will you? I'll read my books"—she patted the pile of novels—"and get some sleep after my hike down the hall. Promise?"

"Promise," he said and kissed her again. The light and warmth left the room with him.

Angela sank back into her Ann Cleeves novel like a warm bath, forgetting the hospital world until Katie barged into the room two hours later. "Hey, is that a walker I see?"

"It is," Angela said. "Tink, the PT, walked me all the way down the hall and over to the pediatric unit."

"That's progress."

"She doesn't like Tritt," Angela said. "None of the nurses do. Why not?"

"He's a bumpkin," Katie said. "He may be a skilled surgeon, but the women here like the smooth moves of Dr. Gravois. Good ol' Chip can fool them all."

"Except you, me, and Donegan," Angela said.

Katie frowned when Angela mentioned Donegan's name, then said, "We're immune to the Forest's magic spell. Tritt's divorcing Donatella Dubois. She refused to go by Donatella Tritt."

"So that's his debutante wife," Angela said. "Let me guess: she was a Daughter of Versailles."

"Only a maid of honor," Katie said. "Her title should be ice princess. Her mother was a queen."

"Considering what happened to Marie Antoinette," Angela said, "wouldn't it bother you to be named Queen of Versailles?"

"Not a problem for either of us," Katie said. "We weren't rich enough to be presented to society at a debutante ball. Mark my words: before the ink is dry on Dr. Tritt's divorce decree, the hospital will find a way to get rid of him. Gotta go. My patients won't wait forever."

"At least they won't sue," Angela said. It felt good resuming their familiar banter. *Another step toward normal,* she thought.

After Katie left, Angela felt energized. And curious. *Why did that little boy say, "Mommy, that lady's head looks funny"? Why did his embarrassed mother whisk him away?*

What does my head look like? Angela wondered. She couldn't bring herself to touch it, but she had to see it. She didn't see a mirror in her room, but there would be one in the bathroom, a room she hadn't used yet, thanks to the catheter. She scooched to the edge of the bed, opened the walker, then stood up, back straight, and pushed toward her bathroom.

She felt less woozy this time. She flipped on the light and looked in the mirror.

A misshapen creature stared back at her. This woman looked much older than Angela. Her face was swollen, and her skin was bright-red. Dark panda circles surrounded her eyes. On the right side, her long, dark hair was shaved off, exposing her ear. The scalp was covered with ugly stubble. A swollen, blood-rimmed oval about five inches long was cut into her head. Staples held it closed. A tiny pipe stuck out of the top of the woman's half-shaved head. The left side of the woman's head was covered with dark, stringy brown hair.

Oh my God, Angela thought. *That's me. I'm grotesque. My hair is gone. Half-gone. This is what I look like now.*

Angela screamed.

CHAPTER 9

"What the hell were you doing?" Katie yelled as she burst into Angela's room.

"Wha'?" Angela dragged herself out of a drugged sleep to find a furious Katie glaring at her. Angela had been out cold for hours, ever since two nurses had hauled her back to bed, then called Tritt. The sedative he'd prescribed had plunged her into a merciful sleep.

Now she had to deal with an irate Katie.

"Why did you get out of bed without calling a nurse?" Katie asked.

Angela wasn't brave enough to look into her friend's angry eyes. "I wanted to see what I looked like," she said.

"You could have asked for a mirror. You're not supposed to get up without assistance. You can barely walk with a walker. If you fall, you could have another stroke. You could die!"

Katie was shouting now, frantic to make her point.

"I don't want to live," Angela said. "Not like this. I used to be pretty." Tears rolled down her red, swollen face.

"Well, pardon me if I don't join your pity party," Katie said. Her sarcasm stung like a splash of disinfectant. "I admit punk patient isn't your best look. Your face is swollen from the drugs and surgery, and God knows what crap they pumped into you to keep you in a chemical coma. You're going to look worse until you get better, and that will take a while. Tritt removed a third of your frontal lobe. You've had six strokes. But you're alive, dammit. You're alert. You can walk and talk, and you're eating like a Clydesdale. You can see. You can taste your food. Do you know how many stroke survivors wish they could do those things? You're damn lucky."

"Lucky?" Angela said. That word again. Something snapped. She held up her needle-bruised hand, covered in tape and draped in IV lines, and said, "This is lucky? Lucky is winning the lottery, not looking like the star of a horror movie."

"You're too stupid to know how lucky you are," Katie said, and Angela flinched at the anger flashing in her friend's brown eyes.

Katie was so furious, she shifted in the turquoise chair. Angela noticed that she looked tired, pale, and rumpled, and she felt even worse. She'd pushed her friend to the limit.

"If you want to see courage," Katie said, "haul your sorry ass down the hall to the ICU, where Jillian Du Pres is recovering. She's awake now and knows she's looking at years—*years*—of plastic surgery, but nobody hears her whining. She's fighting and fighting hard. You don't even have to go that far. In the pediatric unit, a twelve-year-old boy is struggling to stay alive. Patrick is going to die of kidney failure, but he won't give up. He wants to live, but that's not gonna happen. Dr. Gravois testified against him, so when Patrick does die—any day now—his mother will spend the rest of her life paying off her son's medical bills. Because Dr. Gravois's so-called expert testimony protected the insurance company. But I don't hear Patrick complaining—or his mother."

Now Angela was awash in shame and guilt. "I'm sorry," she said. "You're right. I've been selfish. But I wasn't prepared for the shock. I didn't think I'd look this bad."

"What the hell," Katie said, and her voice softened. "Did you think you'd look like those brain surgery patients on TV, all pretty and pale, with a nice white bandage wrapped around their heads like they're at a spa? Doesn't work that way, girl. Your head's been opened with a power saw. The surgery was bloody and brutal, and you're going to look like shit for a while. But you will get better. And you will look better. Do you understand?"

Angela nodded. "I'm sorry," she repeated. "I'm doubly sorry you had to come here. I know you're busy."

"Good. Now get your ass in gear and start fighting. I brought you something to keep your strength up."

Katie opened a foam container that she'd set on Angela's bedside table. "This is broiled lobster, a baked potato with sour cream, and asparagus in hollandaise sauce." She produced a small box. "And here's double-chocolate cake. You slept through dinner, and I can't stand to watch you shovel in more of that hospital dog food. You'll forget what real food tastes like."

"Really? Lobster?" Angela's voice trembled, and her eyes teared up.

"You cry, and I'll take it home," Katie said. "Start eating before the cholesterol police catch me."

Angela ate. Katie was right. This was better than the hospital meals. As the delicious food warmed her, she began to feel hopeful.

Nobody looked good after surgery. Angela knew that, just like she knew crime scenes didn't look like the ones on TV. When was the last time she'd seen a young, beautiful blonde murder victim artfully spattered with blood in a mansion?

Most death scenes were dirty, smelly, and ugly. The old and poor died far more often than the young and beautiful. Even in the Forest,

Angela had investigated far more deaths in roach-ridden rooms than ritzy mansions.

When she finished her rich chocolate cake, Angela said, "That was wonderful. Can I start my beauty sleep? I have a lot of work to do." She failed to hide a yawn.

"Get well," Katie said, and smiled at her. "Good night." Her anger had vanished like a summer rainstorm. Angela was asleep before Katie caught the elevator.

CHAPTER 10

"Squiz your butt chicks!" Svetlana, the Russian physical therapist, screamed to the four stroke patients. Angela thought the PT
sounded like Natasha, the cartoon Russian spy in *The Rocky and
Bullwinkle Show.*

The four patients were exercising in the hospital's stroke rehab center, on two platform mats the size of king beds. The exercisers worked
out on their backs, hospital pillows under their heads.

Two older men exercised together on the giant mat. One was bald,
red-faced, and meaty, his dark, surly eyes buried in pads of angry fat.
No surprise he had a stroke, Angela thought.

His exercise partner was gray and thin. His hair, skin, and sweat suit
were worn and colorless. His left arm trembled constantly. Svetlana's
forceful commands made the shaking worse.

Next to Angela on her double mat was Trixie, a tiny, wrinkled doll
in a red velvet duster. She kept a towel between her stick legs for modesty, or what passed for it in a hospital. Trixie wore a red velvet bow in
her long, curly gray hair, and red lipstick crept into the cracks around

her lips. Angela could see the urine bag taped to Trixie's thigh. It, too, had a jaunty velvet bow. That brave act touched her heart.

Angela, the youngest person in the exercise class, was reveling in her new freedom. Her catheter was out, and she was untethered from her IV pole for the class. Chris, the blonde, frizzy-haired nurse, had lent her a pair of soft, much-washed jeans and an old shirt. Chris was as tall as Angela but bigger-boned, and the clothes hung on her. Angela still felt better in real clothes.

With her powerful legs, sturdy shoulders, and beefy arms, Svetlana looked strong enough to lift a Russian troika with all three horses. Even her blonde hair seemed muscular.

"Angela!" Svetlana shouted. "Squiz your butt chicks! Are you squizink them?"

Angela started giggling. She couldn't help it. The cartoon accent, the absurd exercise patients, Trixie's urine bag with the velvet bow, were too much. Angela's giggles burst into hearty, full-fledged laughter.

Now the other exercisers stared at her. So did the rest of the patients in the stroke rehab center. In the exercise area, a cotton-haired old man in a plaid bathrobe walking with the help of the parallel bars, halted his progress.

The patients in the section of the rehab center that was set up like a home stopped and glared at Angela. The solemn older woman in a long pink robe practicing in the pretend kitchen halted, a saucepan in one hand. The shaky fiftysomething woman in the open training bathroom stopped, too. She'd been learning to sit on a toilet seat—while wearing double hospital gowns.

Toilet training, Angela thought. *Now that's how to squiz your butt chicks.* She was laughing so hard, tears streamed down her face.

An angry Svetlana loomed over her. "You must take training serious if you want to get well," she said.

Angela wiped the tears from her eyes and said, "I'm sorry. It's my first day up. I'm a little punchy."

"I forgive your joke," Svetlana said with great dignity. "It's the drugs."

Ever since she came out of the coma, Angela's emotions were raw and close to the surface. She was confused by their intensity. She'd always prided herself on her cool, professional demeanor. Had Tritt removed that, too? Had he cut away an essential part of her personality? Would she be able to function as a death investigator when she went back to work? She couldn't be laughing uncontrollably at crime scenes.

When would she be able to work? Death investigations were hard. She had to climb stairs, scramble down hillsides, wedge herself into cars, and pick her way through burned buildings. Right now she could barely make it down the hall with a walker.

Svetlana's class lasted only twenty minutes. Then Tink Warren, the perpetually cheerful physical therapist, was at the platform mat to collect Angela. "Sit up straight," Tink said, opening the walker and positioning it in front of Angela. She snapped the canvas belt around Angela's waist.

"Swing your legs around and stand up. Slowly. Are you dizzy?"

"A little," Angela said, gripping the walker. "I'm fine now."

"Back straight? Perfect," Tink said. "You've been moved to the stroke ward. We're going to your new room. They're working on something in the hall, so we'll take the back way though the pediatric unit."

Tink's two sleeves of tattoos added much-needed color to the bland hospital scene. Angela scooted the walker over the shining beige tile floor, Tink hovering nearby, ready to grab the ring if Angela started to fall. The tiny blonde PT reminded Angela of a small, friendly Chihuahua as she danced at her side, peppering her slow, lumbering charge with questions and comments.

"How was your first class?" Tink asked as they turned into the pediatric hallway.

"It didn't last long, but I'm tired," Angela said. She tried not to look into those sad rooms.

"Give it time. You're just starting PT," Tink said. "I heard you got the giggles."

Angela nodded. Now she was ashamed that she'd laughed at the Russian physical therapist.

"Svetlana has a funny accent, but she's smart. She's a good PT," Tink said.

"I know she is," Angela said. "My emotions are all over the map these days."

"Brain injuries do that," Tink said. "You'll be more in control as you start to heal. What did you used to do?"

Used to do? Angela thought, feeling the panic grip her. Her identity was slipping away. She was reduced to a helpless creature in a hospital.

"I am a death investigator," she said, as if those words could conjure up the woman she used to be. "I work for the Forest medical examiner."

"Cool. So you, like, work with dead bodies?"

"Exactly. At a crime scene, the dead people are my responsibility. I photograph, measure, note their wounds, clothing, jewelry, body temp, and more."

"Intense," Tink said.

"How soon before I can go back to work?" Angela asked.

Tink's silence stretched for a long moment. "Dr. Tritt will tell you that," Tink said. "I'm here to beat you up." She grinned, but Angela didn't like her evasive answer. Why wouldn't anyone give her a straight answer?

Angela's trek back was blocked by a commotion in Patrick's room. She couldn't see the frail twelve-year-old, but a medical team surrounded the boy's bed. Monty Bryant, the family attorney, was in the hall, holding Patrick's weeping mother. Mariah's gray-streaked head was buried in Monty's chest, and he held her close.

Angela saw the crash cart inside the room, the floor littered with used vials and other medical debris, and heard the commands and responses pronounced in unnaturally calm voices. This was serious. She and Tink averted their eyes to give the boy privacy during his struggle.

Then she heard someone say, "Sorry, people, it's over." Someone else said, "Pronounce at eleven forty-three."

Mariah started wailing before the defeated doctor told her that Patrick was dead.

CHAPTER 11

"Your new room is on the right," Tink said. "Nearly there. Only five doors away."

Angela's walker felt awkward and heavy. Those five doors seemed like five miles. As she trudged down the wide hall, she concentrated on her goal and tried not to think about the futile fight to save Patrick.

Finally, she was inside her new room, which looked just like her old one. "Dr. Tritt arranged for you to have a private room," Tink said. "You're lucky. Hospital roommates can be real doozies."

The hospital bed's clean sheets looked fresh and inviting. Tom Wymen's balloons were floating a little lower today on a similar chest of drawers. Donegan's roses were fully open, a dazzling display of velvety red next to her bed.

Those roses are a fragrant reminder there's still romance in my life, Angela thought.

"So, you gotta pee?" Tink asked.

Romance, maybe, but no privacy.

"Might as well, since I'm up," Angela said, pushing toward the bathroom. The toilet had a raised seat and safety-grip metal bars.

"Leave the door partly open. I'll wait out here," Tink said. "I can hear if there's a problem."

Well, that beats a nurse watching me, Angela thought. She was regaining her freedom in tiny increments.

She washed her hands and avoided looking in the mirror. After her screaming session, she didn't have the courage to examine her ruined face. She hoped it would be healing by the time she looked again.

Tink settled her into bed and folded the walker away. A cheerful aide brought in a tray with chopped and formed chicken slices in pus-yellow gravy, a scoop of gluey, white mashed potatoes, and limp string beans. Angela pushed away the remains of her sad meal when she heard a knock on the door.

"Ms. Richman, may I come in?"

The man in the doorway was ridiculously handsome: chiseled chin, white teeth, large, delicately shaped nose, wavy blond hair, and shrewd blue eyes. The Romans would have wrapped him in a toga and made him a minor god. Today, he wore the signs of modern success: a hand-tailored navy suit, designer tie, and handmade shoes.

"Hello," said this vision of masculinity. "I'm Monty Bryant." His handshake was firm. "May I talk with you a moment?"

He sat in Angela's turquoise chair before she could answer. She suspected few women ever said no to Monty Bryant.

"You're Patrick's lawyer," she said. "I'm so sorry he died."

Monty shook his head and sighed. "That poor boy. He fought so hard." He wiped his eyes, and Angela wondered if he was tearing up. "I tried to help him and failed."

"How's his mother?" Angela said.

"About like you'd expect," he said. "Her sister came to take Mariah to stay with her, so she won't be alone. Patrick's death spurred me to come see you. Dr. Tritt told me that you were misdiagnosed by Dr. Porter Gravois."

"I showed up in the ER with the classic symptoms of a stroke," Angela said. "I was taking hormone replacement therapy, which should have been a warning sign to any doctor, but Gravois said he couldn't keep track of all that stuff. Then he said I was too young and fit to have a stroke and sent me home. You see what happened."

"Awful," he said. "Just awful."

Angela wasn't sure if he was talking about her appearance, the stroke damage, or Dr. Gravois's incompetence.

"That's why I came to see you," Monty said. "Patrick is my worst failure. A great injustice was done to that boy—first by the damage from the car accident and then by Porter Gravois's testimony at Patrick's trial."

"Dr. Tritt said Gravois testified that Patrick's injuries were mostly imaginary," she said.

"I thought the jury would have to have hearts of stone to deny that boy justice—and the money he needed. But Porter Gravois got up on the stand, did his *Father Knows Best* routine, and said, 'The boy will be fine. What he needs is an incentive to recover.'"

"How could anyone believe that?"

"The insurance company poured a lot of money into fighting that suit," Monty said. "They hired a jury consulting service. The jury consultants held mock trials to see which arguments a jury would buy. They even had someone watching the jury's Facebook and Twitter accounts. I lost a woman juror I know was sympathetic. She was disqualified by a Facebook post. It was a blow. Patrick got nothing, and he isn't Gravois's only victim. That man has done so much damage to innocent people. I wish I could have helped poor Patrick. I have a son his age. Young Patrick's brave fight is over. But yours is just beginning. Angela, would you be interested in suing Dr. Gravois?"

"Do you think I have a case?"

"I can't make any promises, but it looks like that to me."

"I'd like to kill him," Angela said.

"He's not worth twenty years of your life."

"Then let's sue him to death," Angela said.

CHAPTER 12

"When you were in the coma, do you remember anyone talking to you?" Dr. Tritt asked.

It was one o'clock in the morning. Each night after his shift ended, Tritt would stop by to talk to Angela. Talk at her, actually. His hatred of Chip Gravois boiled out like streams of molten lava. Angela couldn't stop him any more than she could stop an erupting volcano. She was the human sacrifice to his white-hot fury.

Angela had endured the neurosurgeon's nightly nonstop rant against Gravois for nearly an hour. This question caught her by surprise.

"Gravois nearly killed you, and nobody did anything about it," Tritt said.

How often had she heard that line? That's why she nearly missed his question. "When you were in the coma, do remember anyone talking to you?"

"Did I what?" she asked. Angela was startled that he'd actually spoken to her. Even in the dim light of her hospital room she could see that Tritt looked uneasy, maybe guilty.

He was an ungainly figure sitting in her turquoise chair. A big man with a strong face, a bizarre bedside manner, and beautiful hands. She tried not to think that he'd had his fingers in her brain. She shivered. The hospital was so cold at night, and the blue blankets were thin.

"Well? Could you hear people talking to you?"

"No," Angela said.

"Good," he said.

She heard Tritt's obvious relief. "Why?" she asked.

"I used to come by every night and say, 'Angela, this is God. Wake up!' but the nurses made me stop."

Angela laughed. Tritt had made a lot of shocking, outrageous statements, but this one was funny.

"Did anyone else talk to me?" she asked.

"Your friend Katie came by every day, held your hand, and talked to you for hours. A nice guy spent some time with you, too."

Katie and Donegan, Angela thought. She wondered why Tritt hadn't talked to her husband. *Too wrapped up in himself,* she decided. Angela felt touched and sad. All those hours they'd spent in the ICU, and she never knew they were there.

"I don't remember anything," she said. "On March tenth, I had a bad headache and went to bed. The next thing I knew, it was March twenty-ninth, and a bunch of doctors were asking me what day it was. My coma wasn't anything like the ones I've read about."

Did I just say "my coma"? Angela wondered. *Could my life get any more surreal?*

"I have a nineteen-day hole in my life," she said. "I have no memory of that time, and I had no idea I was dying. I didn't hear anyone. There was no tunnel to the hereafter or bright lights, and my relatives weren't waiting on the other side. In fact, for me, there was no other side. I fell asleep at home and woke up here."

In another dimension, with a new face and an obsessed neurosurgeon.

"I know I . . . ," Tritt said.

But Angela never heard the rest of the sentence. She was asleep. She had no idea when Tritt left or if he realized how long he'd been talking to himself.

CHAPTER 13

The sun was shining as a nurse threw open the curtains. "Good morning, Sunshine," the nurse said. She had beautiful, milk-chocolate skin and a gospel singer's contralto. "My name is Victoria, and I'll be your nurse today."

A nurse with a sense of humor, Angela thought. *She's comparing herself to a server.* Angela blinked at the tall, pillowy African American woman as she wrote her name on the whiteboard in the room.

"I understand that you are Dr. Tritt's prize patient." Her smile was warm. "I also understand that you are stubborn as a mule and think you're well enough to go wandering around on your own. You wanna get up, you call me, understand?"

Angela nodded. Victoria was not quite as friendly now.

"You get up without me, and you will regret it. I'm not having you passing on my shift, is that clear?" Her voice was an angry rumble.

"But sometimes I can't wait. I need to use the bathroom," Angela said.

"And sometimes I'm being run ragged and can't get there in time. Stay put! I'd rather change the bed than have you wearing a tag on your toe. Understood?"

Angela nodded again.

"Breakfast is on the way," Victoria said, giving Angela a dazzling smile. "Eat up. Then I'll give you a sponge bath, and by that time Tink will be here to take you for your workout."

After Angela obediently ate her food, Victoria washed her with brisk, no-nonsense movements like she was cleaning a car, then helped her dress in the exercise clothes Katie had dropped off. Angela's sweat pants drooped so badly, she had to tighten the drawstring to keep them from falling off.

"I've lost weight," she said.

"Fifteen pounds," Victoria said, "the last time you were weighed. It'll come back soon enough."

Tink delivered Angela to a busy morning in physical therapy. She prided herself on doing all her exercises, and they seemed easier today. She didn't find Svetlana's accent funny at all.

Angela smiled at the two old men on the other exercise platform, then complimented Trixie on her appearance. Today Angela's dainty, shriveled exercise partner wore a powder-blue duster and matching ribbons in her curly gray hair and on her urine bag.

"You look nice," Angela said.

"Thank you," Trixie said in her soft, quavering voice. "I find it improves my mood if I make the effort to look better."

After a full half hour of exercise, Angela practiced walking using the parallel bars. "You're doing good," Tink told her. The tattooed PT had dyed her hair raspberry pink. It went well with her unnaturally cheerful disposition.

Angela didn't bother hiding her yawn.

"Tired?" Tink asked.

I'm bored, Angela thought, but she said, "It's been a long morning."

"Let's go back," Tink said. "I hear the lunch carts."

Their rattle was like a dinner bell. All around the rehab room, patients heard the carts, looked up hopefully, and then their physical therapists helped them shuffle back to their rooms.

As they passed the double-doored entrance to the ICU, Angela said, "One of my neighbors is in there. Jillian Du Pres. May I see her?"

Tink shook her head. "That poor girl. She's taking her cousin's death hard. They've been friends since they were born. She couldn't go to Jordan's funeral. It really tore her up."

Funeral? Jordan must have been buried while I was in a coma, Angela thought.

"Jillian's quite the fighter. A real warrior woman. But she's still not allowed any visitors except her immediate family."

Now Angela felt like an intruder. "I understand," she said. She realized she didn't have the energy—emotional or physical—to visit the surviving JJ twin. *I have to get stronger, so I can get out of here,* she thought.

"Tink, can I do more workouts?" she asked.

The PT looked surprised. "More?"

"Today was an off day, but I have to get stronger."

"You worked out before your strokes, right?"

"Four times a week," Angela said.

"Good. The old muscle memory will kick in, and you'll be back up to speed soon. I'll give Dr. Tritt a good report and see if he'll let you have an afternoon class, too."

"Thanks. I like working out," Angela said. "I'm a real gym rat." That wasn't quite true, but if exercise was the ticket out of SOS, she'd work out more.

As she and Tink turned the corner, they heard shouting near the nurses' station. Men's voices. One was Dr. Tritt's soft Kentucky accent, now with a slicing, angry edge. "Thanks to you, Patrick's mother will have something to remember her son by until the day she dies," Tritt said. "A bill from SOS. And you know this hospital will hound that woman for every last nickel till she's in her grave."

Angela could see Tritt now, red with fury, his cheap brown shirt and polyester tie shifting under his wrinkled white coat, cowlicked hair tense and oily.

"And what will the insurance company do with the millions you've saved them?" he asked. "Split the money with you? Huh? Huh?"

Silence. Porter Gravois didn't bother answering. His Savile Row suit had an expensive, silvery sheen, like polished armor, and Tritt's clumsy jabs bounced off it.

The two doctors were near the thick books of patients' charts. Two nurses hovered close to the desk, openly eavesdropping. A third was on the phone. She kept glancing first at Gravois, then at Tritt, and whispering into the receiver in a low, urgent voice. Angela wondered if she was calling hospital security. Patients and visitors were gathering around the edges, watching the warring doctors. Dr. Tritt turned and saw Tink and Angela. He pointed at Angela.

"What about my patient?" he shouted. "Look at her: lost her hair, skin peeling, using a walker. But she's alive, no thanks to you."

Oh no, Dr. Tritt, Angela thought. *Please don't do this.* She could feel the spectators' eyes on her, taking in her semishaved head, swollen face, and drug-damaged skin. Angela could see the pity on their faces and wished her too-big clothes would swallow her. There was no place to hide.

Tritt pointed at Angela. "She didn't look like that when she saw you in the ER, did she? Then she was so gorgeous, it hurt to look at her."

Angela felt herself turn red with shame, but she doubted the blush would show on her unnaturally pink, peeling skin. Tink hissed between her teeth at his tactless comments and grabbed the ring on Angela's safety belt to steady her.

"She'd be dead if it wasn't for me," Tritt said. "Why? Because you sent her home when she showed up in the ER with classic stroke symptoms. And you didn't recognize them."

"Really, Tritt," Gravois said. He sounded relaxed, calm, and in control, an executive dealing with a rude underling. Angela noticed that Porter Gravois didn't use Dr. Tritt's title. "It's illegal to reveal a patient's confidential details."

"Confidential? Confidential?" Tritt said, his voice a snarl. "It's not going to be confidential for long. That information will be in the court records when she sues your ass sideways. You're the one who said she was too young and fit to have a stroke. I can't believe you said that. Babies can have strokes, asshole! Why did you send her home?"

More silence. Dr. Gravois seemed to enjoy watching his rival unravel.

"You're a crook and a liar," Dr. Tritt said. "The best thing you can do for your patients is die. That will save lives."

The nurses gasped. Dr. Gravois could have been stone.

Tritt tried to goad the neurologist into answering. "I didn't have everything handed to me on a silver platter," he said. He was shouting now. Angela no longer saw the lifesaving healer. Now he was a big, awkward man in an ill-fitting shirt and a wrinkled white coat, wearing brown clodhoppers.

Porter Gravois's silence infuriated Dr. Tritt. "I worked my way through college, something you never did. Hell, I worked my way through high school. I baled hay. I shoveled shit on a farm."

More silence. One beat. Two. Angela no longer heard the hospital's constantly ringing phones and beeping monitors. The spectators held their collective breath, waiting for a reply.

Porter Gravois's eyes traveled from Tritt's badly chopped hair to his thick-soled shoes.

"It shows," Porter Gravois said.

One nurse giggled, then another. Then the other spectators burst into mocking laughter. The elevator dinged as if a round had ended, and out strode a tall, white-haired, pink-skinned man in a navy suit and a red power tie. His low voice caught every ear.

"Gentlemen! Gentlemen! Stop this at once!" he said. He didn't shout. He commanded silence.

"Who's the suit?" Angela asked Tink.

"Dr. Stanleigh Elkmore, SOS director. Head of the hospital," Tink said. "The nurse must have called him."

"This is unseemly," Dr. Elkmore said. "You will both meet in my office. Immediately."

Gravois started to follow. Tritt didn't move, and the director glared at him. "Unless you want to lose your privileges."

He marched both men to the elevator.

"Wow," Tink said as the doors closed on the drama. "That was better than a WWF grudge match."

"Except Tritt was the one with the grudge," Angela said. "I thought he was going to punch Gravois."

"Not a chance," Tink said. "A surgeon would never risk his precious hands. Chip Gravois handled himself well."

Her approval annoyed Angela. "But Tritt was right," she said. "Porter Gravois did say I was too young and fit to have a stroke and sent me home. He ordered a PET scan for later. My friend found me in a coma, half-dead. Why would Gravois do that? I don't understand how he could send me home."

"He thought you had a tumor," she said. "That's standard procedure."

"Except I really did have a stroke," Angela said. "Six of them. And I needed brain surgery. So Tritt was right."

This hospital-wide hatred of Dr. Tritt was beyond Angela's comprehension. She had to know what was going on. "Tink," she said. "I don't understand. Why does everyone at the hospital hate Dr. Tritt?"

"Because he's arrogant," she said.

"Of course he is," Angela said. "He's a surgeon. He saws open skulls. You have to be arrogant to do that. But he's good."

"And he never stops telling us how good he is," Tink said. "And he's a hound. He thinks the nurses and staff—including PTs like me— exist for the pleasure of the great man, and we should be honored to be summoned for a quickie. Contrary to what you see on TV, hospital staff aren't always having sex. This isn't the Playboy mansion. We're run ragged taking care of sick and dying patients. Vomit, blood, and pee aren't big turn-ons. Tritt's marriage has been falling apart for ages, and he made it clear he wasn't getting any at home. He expected the staff to take up the slack. He had an affair with a nurse here, Linda. A good nurse, funny and popular. Her own marriage was rocky. At first Linda figured no harm, no foul, and had a little fling with Tritt. Then she changed her mind and decided to try to mend her marriage. She broke off the relationship with Tritt. He managed to sweet-talk her into resuming their affair. They had make-up sex in the janitor's closet."

"Ick," Angela said.

"Right," Tink said. "The janitor caught them *en flagrante*. I don't have to draw you a picture. But the nurse is gone."

"She was fired?" Angela asked.

"Not quite. SOS arranged to get her a job at another hospital—for less money. But nothing happened to Tritt. The hospital didn't punish him because the relationship was 'established and consensual.'" She made air quotes around those last three words.

Now Angela understood the staff's animosity to Tritt. She also understood that the hospital was similar to City University—or her husband's view of it. Donegan told her that teaching students was beside the point at a university and wouldn't advance his career. City University was run for the convenience of the professors and instructors, and their career advancement was the real purpose. The hospital was the same way: patients were beside the point. They were the backdrop for the staff politics.

"Dr. Gravois is a married man," Tink said. "He's no skirt chaser. I don't have to worry about him getting handsy in the halls or asking if I wanna fuck in the bathroom."

"Ew," Angela said. Now she not only knew, but knew too much.

They were at Patrick's former room, now an empty accusation. Angela knew there was no point in bringing up Porter Gravois's testimony against the boy. They rounded the corner, and she could finally see her own room. Angela was so tired she could hardly make the short trek. She carefully steered her walker around the fridge-size dinner cart that nearly blocked the hallway.

"Ready for lunch?" Tink asked as she settled Angela into her bed and folded away the walker.

"And a nap," Angela said. "Might as well catch up on my sleep."

She knew Dr. Tritt would be in her room at midnight, raving far into the night.

CHAPTER 14

"Do you know what I have to do with that son of a bitch?" Tritt shrieked. He was pacing in Angela's room, his anger too great to be contained in the turquoise chair. His voice shook with emotion.

Angela didn't bother to answer his question. She'd lost count of how many times she'd heard the answer.

"I have to meet with the SOB!"

He didn't have to say who that was. Porter Gravois. Tritt had lost the battle in the hallway. Gravois had kept his cool while Tritt ranted, then stabbed him with a stiletto. Those two words, "It shows," had neatly, cruelly skewered Tritt's heroic career struggle. Worse, the head of the hospital had stepped off the elevator and ended the confrontation. Personally, Angela thought that timely intervention had probably saved Tritt from saying something worse.

But his punishment was swift and humiliating.

"I have to meet with him," Tritt said. "At his convenience! In the hospital cafeteria tomorrow afternoon. We're supposed to drink coffee together. Coffee! I'd rather drink rat poison!"

Angela was afraid he'd stroke out in her room. Tritt's face was contorted with rage: his eyes bugged out, his face was a scary shade of fuchsia, and he was frothing at the mouth. She brushed his spit off her arm and wondered how she could calm him down. It was one thirty in the morning, and his tirade showed no sign of slowing.

Angela's fingers twitched over the call button. If she summoned a nurse, Tritt would be shooed out of her room, and she could go back to sleep.

"And I have to apologize!" he said. "Apologize! Gravois nearly kills you, and I have to apologize. That smug son of a bitch, Stan Elkmore, said my behavior was 'unseemly.'"

Dr. Tritt minced his words and said those last three syllables with one pinkie extended.

Stan Elkmore? Angela's drugged, sleep-deprived brain tried to remember who that was. Oh, right. The head of the hospital. White guy, white hair, dark suit, power tie.

"It's bad enough he made me shake that asshole's hand in his office." Tritt held up his right hand as if it had been wounded.

"But that's not enough. Oh no. Stan says because our disagreement— that's what he calls it—was public we have to have a public reconciliation in the hospital cafeteria, or I lose my privileges. I'll lose my privileges after I saved a patient Gravois nearly killed. Does the great neurologist get threatened with that? Oh no, he's the fair-haired boy here.

"I called Monty Bryant and asked if I had to drink coffee with that asshat in the cafeteria. The lawyer said he was there and saw the whole thing."

He was? Angela thought. *I didn't see him. But I was too busy avoiding everyone's eyes when Tritt turned me into Exhibit A for Gravois's screwups.*

"Monty said I had to do it," Tritt said. "He says employment law is not his specialty, but I broke about nine thousand rules and regulations when I pointed out what Gravois did to you. Now SOS has me by the short hairs, and Monty says I should cooperate. But Monty's going to be there tomorrow as a witness. For moral support."

Angela's mind was drifting when she heard Tritt say, "That's why I want you there, too."

"Huh?" This was new. "You want me where?" Angela asked. Now she was fully awake.

"This will be a test for you. Tink can walk with you, but you won't wear a safety belt or anything. If you make it to the cafeteria and back on your own, you'll be well enough to start walking with your walker. You'll still need physical therapy and cognitive training, but this will be a big step forward."

"I'm glad you think I'm ready to walk by myself," Angela said. "No, I'm thrilled. But why do you really want me in the cafeteria tomorrow?"

"I need witnesses. Friendly witnesses. Everybody's mad at me because I attacked dear, sweet Dr. Gravois. You and Monty know what he's really like. He doesn't fool you. Also, I want Gravois to see what he's done. He misdiagnosed you and screwed you up big-time. You used to be a major babe."

Major babe? The nurses were right. Tritt was a hound.

"Gravois should confront his mistake," he said.

Mistake? Tritt's calling me a mistake? Angela had endured too much. The anger boiled out of her. "What the hell is wrong with you?" she said. "I know I look terrible, but do you have to keep mentioning it? How do you think I felt in the hall today when you told everyone what Gravois had done to me? Do you have any idea how embarrassing that was? I was humiliated to have strangers staring at my half-bald head and peeling skin. Worse, they felt sorry for me. Stop it! Just stop!"

Tritt was smiling now. He quit his restless pacing. "I like it when you're feisty," he said. He dropped into the chair by her bed.

His smile irritated Angela. "Feisty? Old ladies are feisty," she said. "I'm angry, dammit."

"I know," he said. "And I'm thrilled. That's good. Okay, you're not feisty. You're a force of nature."

"That's better," Angela said.

"And that force is why you're still alive. You're willing to fight to live. That's what I like about you. It's why you're getting better. You're looking better, too. If Monty is going to sue Gravois, he'd better get a photographer in here fast. In another week or so, you won't look bad enough to convince a jury how much damage that man did. The best time to photograph you is after your PT tomorrow. Monty should have someone here about eleven, eleven thirty. You'll look tired after your workout, and you won't have had lunch or a nap yet. We want you to look really bad so you can sue that asshat sideways."

"Uh, thanks," Angela said. "I think. Should I call Monty tomorrow?"

"No, I'll talk to him," Tritt said. "He's helping me deal with the administration. I can't do anything about Gravois testifying against Patrick, but I've filed a raft of complaints about you. I've made formal complaints to the CEO, the chief of staff, the peer review officer, and the risk manager."

Fat lot of good that will do, Angela thought. *This is SOS's game, and you're playing with their deck of cards. It's stacked against you.*

"I know SOS isn't going to listen to me," Tritt said. "I'm not one of the old boys. But there is a way to nail them."

"How?" Angela asked.

Tritt leaned forward as if he was telling her a bedtime story. "What happened to you is called a 'sentinel event.'"

"What's that?" Angela asked.

"The day before this so-called event, you showed up at the ER with the symptoms of a stroke. If Gravois didn't have his head up his ass, he would have paid attention to your symptoms, and you wouldn't have had six strokes and brain surgery. Gravois may have suspected you had a tumor—that's probably why he ordered a PET scan—but your hormone replacement therapy put you at risk for strokes. He should have known that. He shouldn't have sent you home with no follow-up until you had that PET scan. He should have kept you here in the hospital, where you would be monitored. But that would have cost money.

"Instead he was worried about protecting the goddamn insurance companies, so he sent you home, and you nearly died. Your case is a sentinel event, and it needs to be investigated, but SOS will sweep it under the rug, no matter how many reviews I request. So I sent a complaint to the only thing that SOS fears."

Tritt stopped and smiled. His eyes gleamed, and his thin smile was a seething mad-dog slit.

"I've sicced the Joint Commission on them," he said. "They do hospital accreditations. SOS could lose its accreditation."

Angela remembered Katie telling her that the nurses were threatening to report the Angel of Death killings to the Joint Commission.

"The Joint Commission doesn't care whose mother was a Daughter of Versailles and whose grandfather was a big-deal surgeon," Tritt said. "They'll run their own investigation."

Angela wanted to wipe that self-satisfied smile off his face. "Did you tell the hospital you filed a complaint with the Joint Commission?" she asked.

"Of course," he said. "I'm not like one of the old boys in the Forest. I don't make sneaky backroom deals. I was perfectly up-front about it. I told them what I did and what they could expect."

He sat up straighter. She could feel his pride—his overwhelming, overweening, destructive pride. "What can they do to me?"

He'd seen an example when Gravois had eviscerated him in the hall, and the hospital had threatened to revoke his privileges if he didn't go through the handshaking farce. Now he'd declared war on SOS and told the hospital when and how he was going to attack. Worse, he'd rushed in and never checked to see if the Joint Commission protected whistle-blowers.

Oh, Dr. Tritt, she thought. *How can anyone so smart be so stupid? Your brilliant technique saved my life, but you don't know how to save yourself.*

CHAPTER 15

The hospital's version of *High Noon* took place at three o'clock the next day.

Doctors, nurses, and support staff were waiting for the cafeteria showdown between doctors Tritt and Gravois. Angela had felt the ripples of excitement since early morning and heard excited, whispered conversations.

When Tink collected Angela at two thirty, she was still dressed in her workout clothes—her own jeans and a blue T-shirt. Angela's clothes hung on her, she'd lost so much weight. The physical therapist's spiked hair was lime-green today. Angela liked the way it mirrored the color of the dragon scales in Tink's tattoos.

"I'll stand over here and watch you," Tink said, holding the safety belt. "If you're wobbly, I'll put this on you."

But Angela's performance was flawless. She snapped open the walker and stood up, back straight, hands on the grips, like a demonstration video, then rolled down the hall with Tink. She felt good being out of her room.

They arrived at the cafeteria twenty minutes before three and found an empty table near a small section in a back corner with a RESERVED sign. The scene of the sham reconciliation had four tables partly screened by a planter with fake flowers.

Angela showed off her new skills by buying coffee and brownies for herself and Tink and delivering them to the table.

"You didn't spill a drop," Tink said as she accepted her cup.

The cafeteria was filling up fast. Two nurses in scrubs sat near Angela, and she tuned in to their conversation. The gray-haired fire-plug in the teddy bear scrubs said, "I saw Tritt attack Chip Gravois in the hall yesterday. Really, I don't know why the administration puts up with Tritt."

"Because he married well," the blue-eyed brunette in butterfly scrubs said, shrugging. "At least his wife finally realized he was screwing anything that moves."

"Not until her father showed her the private detective's report—and the photos," the older nurse said. "That woman needed wising up." She smiled, a hanging judge condemning a guilty man.

The Forest really wants Tritt gone, Angela thought. *And he's helping them.* She couldn't say anything to Tink. The PT would cheer if Tritt lost his privileges.

The two nurses hailed another nurse standing in the cafeteria doorway. "Linda!" Nurse Butterfly called. "Grab a drink. We saved you a seat."

Linda? Is that the nurse who had the affair with Tritt? Angela wondered. Linda was pretty in a countrified way, with curly, big hair and soft, brown eyes. The new arrival bought a soda and joined the nurses at the table.

"Thanks for calling me," Linda said. "Today's my day off. I wouldn't miss this for the world."

The nurses suddenly went silent. Angela watched Tritt, the underdog, enter the cafeteria at exactly three o'clock like a boxer before a title match. Angela winced when she saw him, dressed like a shady sales-man in a beige suit, chocolate shirt, and light-brown tie. His hideous suit shifted like sand. *He must not have had surgery today,* she thought. *He didn't wear his white coat, the medical mark of authority.* Sweat and resentment rolled off him.

Tritt was greeted with thunderous silence. The standing-room-only crowd parted as he barged through the cafeteria to the clearing in the center. Monty Bryant was with him, as promised. The popular lawyer's smiles slid off the granite-faced crowd.

"I hope Monty knows what he's doing," Tink said.

Angela said nothing. She admired Monty for his unpopular stand.

The silence grew tense as everyone waited for Porter Gravois to appear. The dull beige cafeteria was overwhelmed by raw anger, antici-pation, and curiosity. Neutered music oozing from the speakers calmed no one. Doctors who usually dined in their staff lounge or the execu-tive dining room stopped in for a late cafeteria lunch. Most skipped the woody fish sticks and chose spaghetti with a meatball as big—and hard—as a racquetball. Angela enjoyed watching the white-coated docs wrestle with the sloppy sauce. She wondered how many would wind up wearing it.

This afternoon, hospital administrators had a sudden urge for the watery cafeteria coffee, and a stout, harried woman with a hair-net kept refilling the urn. The first SOS big gun was a rotund, self-important doctor with patent-leather hair. His white coat crackled with starch.

"Who's he?" Angela asked Tink.

"Carlton DeVree, the chief of staff," Tink said. "The scrawny doc with the big ears next to him is Hampton Mann, the peer review officer. The older woman with the black cat's eyeglasses and prison matron suit is Drake Bynes, the SOS risk manager. Those glasses are not an ironic fashion statement. I think she was born with them."

Chief of staff, peer review officer, risk manager, Angela thought. *Tritt filed complaints with all of them. They turned their backs when he entered and refused to acknowledge Monty's greeting.*

3:02. No sign of Porter Gravois. The bigwigs stood with their coffee cups like awkward guests at a cocktail party. Angela noticed Dr. Stanleigh Elkmore, the head honcho who'd orchestrated this farce, talking to the Forest ME, Evarts Evans.

Tritt paced in the center of the room, sweaty and unhappy, his hair slick with oil. Monty looked cool and relaxed, despite the brutal shunning by Gravois's supporters.

Angela ate her brownie but abandoned the coffee after two sips. Even cream and sugar couldn't make lukewarm dishwater drinkable.

"You're doing good," Tink said. "Are you tired? Do you need to go back to your room?"

"I feel terrific," Angela said. She glanced at the cafeteria clock. 3:05. The head of the hospital, Dr. Stan Elkmore, checked his Cartier tank watch, frowned, and headed toward the dirty dish tub. Was he leaving?

As Elkmore dropped off his empty cup, Porter Gravois hurried in. "Sorry I'm late," he said to Elkmore. "Last-minute emergency. ER."

Gravois didn't sound sorry, and he didn't look like he'd been fighting for a patient's life: his white coat was crisp. Tritt snorted but said nothing.

Chip Gravois basked in the crowd's approving smiles. Elkmore escorted him to the center of the room, making it clear who he supported.

Elkmore stood before the two doctors and announced, "Colleagues have their differences, but we have one goal at Sisters of Sorrow Hospital—to serve our patients. I'm glad you two have ended your disagreement and agreed to shake hands in friendship."

That smug bastard, Angela thought. She shifted slightly, hoping Porter Gravois would see her, but his eyes were on Elkmore.

For a brief moment, Tritt looked like he might punch Elkmore and Gravois in the face and then run for it. He finally presented his right hand. Gravois left it hanging in the air a fraction too long, as if he thought Tritt's hand wasn't quite clean. Then he shook it.

Angela could barely hear Tritt ask Porter Gravois, "Can I buy you a cuppa coffee?" His question was a line from a badly rehearsed play. His soft Kentucky accent was thicker than usual, and sweat streamed down his forehead.

"You may." Gravois's clipped, two-word answer underlined Dr. Tritt's poor grammar and mush-mouthed diction.

"I'd like another cup, too," Monty said, his voice hearty. "Dr. Elkmore, may I buy you a cup?"

"No," Elkmore said. The cafeteria, which was already chilly, felt positively frosty. "I'll buy my own." The head of the hospital wasn't accepting anything from Monty, now that he'd sided with the enemy.

Monty patted Tritt on the back, and the two walked toward the coffee urn, where Tritt filled two mugs, and Monty filled one. Angela couldn't tell what the two men said to each other. All three mugs were on the same tray, and Monty carried it to the checkout line.

Dr. Elkmore stalked toward the urn. His comment that he'd buy his own coffee started a stampede. The hospital brass, nurses, and support staff suddenly wanted coffee, and the harried woman with the hairnet raced around, trying to keep the urn filled. Every doughnut, cookie, and pastry disappeared off the racks.

Angela watched a stoop-shouldered woman with gray-streaked hair and beige scrubs enter the cafeteria. "She looks familiar," she said.

"That's Patrick's poor mother," Tink said. "Mariah works here in the laundry to help pay his bills." She shook her head. "She has three jobs now." Tink didn't see the connection between her beloved Chip Gravois's testimony and the bereaved woman's financial ruin.

Monty hurried to embrace Patrick's mother. He must have invited her to join him. Mariah shook her head no and stood against the wall by the meeting spot.

Tritt handed the cashier a twenty for the three coffees and told her to keep the change. She was the only other person there who smiled at the neurosurgeon.

"Hello, Monty," a grandmotherly woman said as she walked next to him. *Gina Swinny,* Angela thought. *From the billing office.*

"Hi." Monty didn't bother to make conversation with Gina. She tried to talk to him, but he ignored her and told Dr. Tritt, "I'll take that." Monty carried the tray with the three coffees to the meeting spot.

Gravois was already seated on the long, upholstered banquet seat against the wall, the *St. Louis City Gazette* in front of him. Monty talked to him briefly, pointed to something in the paper, then left Tritt's cup. Monty sat down one table over on the same beige seat with his coffee and a free paper. Dr. Elkmore and three more big shots took the table across from him. When Dr. Tritt sat down, the reserved section was filled.

It was hard for Angela to see everything, but she heard Tritt and Porter Gravois make awkward small talk for about three minutes. Then Gravois yawned. He didn't bother covering his mouth. "I'm tired," he said. "I want to read."

Angela saw Gravois rudely stick his nose in the newspaper, but his supporters were lined up to see him. They shook his hand, patted him on the shoulder, or simply smiled at him and shunned Tritt.

"So good to see you, Dr. Gravois," Gina said. She gave him a warm smile and kept patting his hand while she talked to him. Angela was grateful when Elkmore, the hospital head, cut short the receiving line. "Please respect Dr. Gravois's privacy, Gina," he said. "His time is limited."

Tritt stopped to talk to Monty, then left. Monty read his paper and stayed until he finished his coffee. By the time he left, the cafeteria was nearly empty. The drama was over.

Tink was talking about the search for a new SOS physical therapist, but Angela wasn't listening. She was too angry. Tritt's public shaming wasn't fair. The man who'd saved her left the cafeteria in disgrace. The doctor who'd nearly killed her was heralded as a saint.

Porter Gravois had taken Angela's job, her looks, and her life. He was going to see what he'd done. Angela couldn't contain her fury. She snapped open her walker and stood up.

"Are you going back?" Tink asked, surprised by Angela's sudden movement.

"Yes," Angela said, "but first I have to do something."

She pushed her walker over to the neurologist's table. "Dr. Gravois," she said.

He ignored her.

"Dr. Gravois! Look at me!" she said sharply.

"Angela," Tink said, "what are you doing?"

"I want him to see what he's done," she said, and grabbed Porter Gravois by his white-coated shoulder. *He looks pale,* Angela thought.

That's when Porter Gravois toppled forward into his newspaper.

Tink screamed. "He's dead! Dr. Gravois is dead!"

CHAPTER 16

Was Porter Gravois dead?

Tink kept shrieking, "He's dead! He's dead!" but Angela wasn't sure. The neurologist was definitely unconscious.

She shook his shoulder and said, "Dr. Gravois? Are you okay?"

He didn't move. She lifted his head. His eyes were shut.

Tink's screams had summoned the three nurses who'd been sitting near their table—the women had moved from the cafeteria to the hallway to say their good-byes. One nurse called a Code Blue while the other two tried to revive Gravois. They dragged the nearby tables, including the one with Gravois's newspaper, out of the way, then stretched Gravois on the long bench seat and tore off his clothes.

Angela moved to the farthest corner of the area, where she was out of the rescuers' way but could watch. Tink sat next to her, weeping and wringing her hands.

Soon a hospital medical team rushed in. The cafeteria corner became a battlefield as they fought to save the neurologist. Gravois's white coat and beautiful shirt and tie were in a pile on the floor. His pale, lean, runner's body was exposed.

But Gravois was beyond help. The staff's violent chest compressions were pointless. Finally, the team realized that the frantic resuscitation attempt had failed. Porter Gravois died in navy silk boxers and black executive-length socks, a porno movie reject. Angela had wanted the man dead. She'd made up vengeful scenarios where he suffered her pain and humiliation. Now she watched her wish come true.

Sorrowful wails rose from two first responders. But one nurse's voice was different—angry and insistent.

"Dr. Gravois was murdered," said Nurse Butterfly, whose name was Becca Parlo.

"What? That can't be," Tink said.

But this time, no one noticed the PT. She turned to Angela, her eyes wide and frantic. "You don't believe that, do you?"

"No," Angela said. "We don't know what happened to him. Maybe he choked or had a heart attack or a stroke. There are any number of ways healthy people die every day."

"No one would kill Dr. Gravois," Tink said. "We all loved him."

That wasn't true, but Angela didn't mention Gravois's enemies. She couldn't understand why, but Tink didn't want to believe the man she admired had been murdered. Becca Parlo continued to insist he had been.

The rescuing doctor looked surprised. "Ms. Parlo, it's too soon to say anything."

"It's important to say this now," Becca Parlo said. "Dr. Gravois was murdered. The police should be called before the evidence is thrown away. There was nothing wrong with Dr. Gravois."

"And how do you know this?" Dr. Condescending asked. "Are you a family member? A confidante? A doctor? Or just hysterical?"

Now Becca was furious. Her voice shook with rage. "I'm not hysterical," she said. "Dr. Gravois had his blood done at this hospital two days ago. I drew it. He asked for me because I have steady hands. I saw the results when I went to the lab to pick up blood for another patient. His blood work was perfect. Perfect! He passed his physical with incredible results. That man was in amazing shape for forty-two. For twenty-two! Look at him!"

Gravois was perfect, Angela thought. *His body could have been sculpted out of marble.*

The doctor patted Becca on the back, but his tone patted her on the head. "Now, now," he said. "Even seemingly healthy people die of heart attacks and aneurysms. We see examples every day."

"Maybe," Becca said. "But that's not why Dr. Gravois died. I saw Tritt put something in his coffee cup. Test that cup right there." She pointed to Dr. Gravois's table. "See if I'm not right. This is a crime scene, and Tritt killed Dr. Gravois. He hated him."

"That's a very grave charge," said Dr. Condescending.

And an amazing leap in logic, Angela thought. *Just because Tritt hated Porter Gravois doesn't mean he'd murder him. Does it?*

Angela wasn't sure. Night after night she'd endured Tritt's white-hot hatred. Today, he'd been publicly humiliated and forced to shake hands with the man he detested. Yes, he was angry. But mad enough to kill? To risk his career?

Lynette Riskin had no doubt. The compact nurse in the teddy bear scrubs said, "Becca is right. I saw Dr. Tritt fiddling with Dr. Gravois's coffee."

"So did I," said Linda, the nurse who'd had the affair with Tritt. "Don't you dare try to tell us we didn't see him. We're all witnesses and trained observers. I'm calling 911 right now."

All three nurses dialed the emergency number. They wielded their cell phones like magic wands, changing Dr. Gravois's death scene into a crime scene and Tritt into a murder suspect.

Angela scrambled through her memory. *I was sitting near him,* she thought. *The planter blocked some of my view. I saw Tritt hand Gravois a coffee cup. Gravois added his own cream and sugar, made a face, but sipped it. Nothing unusual about that. The coffee here is terrible. I wonder if he even tasted it after the first sip, or if he drank it out of nervousness.*

"Did you see Dr. Tritt do anything to Dr. Gravois's cup?" Angela asked Tink.

"I wasn't paying attention," Tink said. "But I wouldn't be surprised. Tritt hated Dr. Gravois. He was jealous."

Angela felt her heart freeze. Everyone in the cafeteria—except her and Monty—would have that reaction.

Now the police burst through the cafeteria doors. Forest patrol officers secured the scene and strung yellow tape around the far corner. The evening meal would be delayed. The chunky woman in the hairnet and the cashier on duty wouldn't be leaving when their shift was over at five. They were witnesses now, along with the three nurses, Tink, and Angela.

I wonder which detective is catching this case, Angela thought. *Please don't let it be . . .*

Detective Ray Greiman rushed in, slick with self-importance.

Terrific, Angela thought. *Dr. Tritt's life is in the hands of the most careless detective in the Forest.*

Greiman should have separated Tink and Angela, since they were both witnesses, but he let them sit together. Angela didn't object to this mistake. She was glad to have Tink's company. The detective also let the nurses stay in their angry cluster and the cafeteria staff huddle together.

Angela watched Greiman talking to the nurses. Naturally, he spent the most time with cute, black-haired Becca. She eyed his two-button navy suit and subdued gray plaid tie and smiled brightly for a woman who'd just witnessed the death of a beloved doctor.

Angela wanted to warn the nurse in the butterfly scrubs: don't be fooled by the pretty packaging. But she knew Becca would find out what he was really like. Probably the hard way.

The CSI team had arrived. They collected Gravois's remaining coffee and bagged the cup, the sugar packets, and the empty creamer containers. Greiman complained about the zillion fingerprints but insisted that CSI print everything—the tables, chairs, banquette, dishes of little creamer containers, and the sugar dispensers, as well as the coffee tray that had not been set in the dirty-dish pile.

Good.

Angela wished she were the death investigator on this case. For the first time since her stroke, she wondered who was doing her job now. When Dr. Evans had visited her at SOS, the medical examiner had assured Angela that her job would be waiting when she recovered. "Get well and don't worry about it," he'd said. "That's an order."

An order she'd followed too well. *The Forest didn't go into suspended animation while I've been in the hospital,* Angela thought. *Did they promote the other death investigator, Gwen Steer, Greiman's distant cousin? That woman's as slippery as Ray. Or did the Forest hire someone new?* Angela had taken a vacation from office politics, but maybe it was time to return to the world of workaday worries.

Then a white-haired sprite in a black suit hurried into the room, hauling a black rolling suitcase. Angela smiled with relief and called, "Emily!"

Emily Du Pres, the seventysomething niece of the Forest patriarch Reggie Du Pres, was the death investigator for this case. "Be with you in a moment, sweetie," she called. "Hugs!" She waved, parked her suitcase outside the yellow tape, and unzipped it.

"Who's that?" Tink said.

"Emily Du Pres," Angela said. "She was the Forest's first death investigator. She trained me before she retired. She must have come back to fill in for me."

"You look relieved," Tink said.

"You have no idea," Angela said.

She watched Emily take out her iPad and confer with Detective Greiman. Angela guessed the death investigator was typing in the case number and wondered what form she'd use. Maybe Injured Person

Died After Arrival at Hospital? No, Gravois wasn't brought to the hospital because he'd been injured. He worked there.

Emily would probably use a standard Death Scene Investigation form. Angela could almost see the familiar form in front of her. She wished she were the one filling it out on her own iPad. Emily spent a long time photographing Gravois from every angle.

"Why is she taking more photos?" Tink asked. "Didn't the cops take them?"

"Death investigators take their own," Angela said. "She has charge of the body. The detective handles the crime scene."

Emily was tapping on her iPad. "Now she's noting the location of Dr. Gravois at the scene," Angela said. "She'll say he was in the northwest corner of the cafeteria, lying faceup on the beige vinyl banquette adjacent to the west wall, with his head facing north."

Tink nodded, and they watched Emily glove up, putting on four pairs, and take out a thermometer. "She's taking the ambient—air—temperature," Angela said. "I'm guessing the cafeteria's in the chilly upper sixties. She'll note that the AC is turned on."

"Definitely on," Tink said. "I'm freezing. Wish I had a blanket from the warmer. How are you?"

"A little tired," Angela said. "But not bad."

Tink gasped when Emily pulled a big meat thermometer out of her DI kit and cut a slit under Gravois's rib cage. The physical therapist's face turned green as her hair. Angela felt dizzy, too.

"What's she doing?" Tink asked, swallowing hard.

"Taking his body core temperature," Angela said. "It's important for time of death, even if that's already been documented."

Emily shoved the thermometer into the slit. "I think I'm gonna hurl," Tink said.

"I feel kinda queasy, too," Angela said. "If you're really gonna let loose, duck under the tape and run for the trash can over there. Don't contaminate the scene."

Tink took several deep breaths, gulped, and then said, "I'm fine. I'm fine. I thought I had a strong stomach after working here."

"It's different when you know the person," Angela said.

Emily peeled off one set of gloves and stashed them in a ziplock bag in her suit pocket. "She's taking them off so she doesn't contaminate the body as she examines it," Angela said. "The crime scene has been compromised by the rescue effort. Emily will have to note all the damage on the body. If Gravois was dead when the medical team tried to resuscitate him—"

"He was," Tink said. "I'm glad they tried to save him, but he was definitely dead."

"In that case," Angela said, "there won't be any bruises from the intravenous lines, the chest compressions, or the blood pressure cuffs, but there will be needle punctures, elliptical burns on his chest, and maybe fractured ribs or liver lacerations."

Tink started to cry again, and Angela realized she'd been too clinical.

"Hey," she said. "Saving someone is a rough business. You know that. And if he was really dead, then he didn't feel anything." Tink was sniffling now and nodding her green head.

"At least Emily is experienced enough to know what medical trauma injuries look like," Angela said. "When I was a newbie, I missed a gunshot wound when I did the body actualization on a man who'd been shot during a holdup. He survived but died after arriving at the hospital. His body was a mess after the paramedics worked on him, and then he had emergency surgery. The surgeon screwed up and put a catheter into a gunshot wound. Nice, ready-made hole, and I didn't see it."

"Angela! I don't want to hear this," Tink said. "Not unless you want me to gorp in your lap."

Angela shut up, until Tink asked, "What's the death investigator doing now? She's over by his watch, typing on her tablet."

"Describing the jewelry on Dr. Gravois's body," Angela said. It felt odd to say his "body," but it helped distance her from his death. Her own stomach calmed as she watched Emily go through the death investigator's familiar ritual.

"He's wearing a gold wedding band, but a death investigator can't say that. We're not trained to appraise jewelry," Angela said. "She'll put down 'yellow metal ring.' His watch, which looks like a Cartier tank, will be described as a yellow metal Cartier watch with a rectangular face and brown leather band."

"Didn't the head of the hospital have a Cartier tank, too?" Tink asked.

"It's the Forest's official old-money watch," Angela said.

"What will happen to it?" Tink asked.

"The jewelry will be left on his body and transported to the medical examiner's office. He'll keep wearing his navy shorts and black socks. The police will bag his other clothes."

Now Emily and Detective Greiman turned over Gravois's body. As usual, the detective complained about this chore. Tink hissed when she saw Gravois's stained shorts.

"He stinks. That death investigator should clean him up," Tink said.

"She can't," Angela said. "No one can change or remove anything on the body. It belongs to the ME."

"It's disrespectful." Tink was growing more upset.

"No, it's important," Angela said. "It's what happens when people die. You know that."

"I do," Tink said, "but it's so unfair."

Death is unfair and undignified, Angela wanted to say. That was true but no comfort for Tink. The strong little PT was deeply troubled.

"When the police catch the killer, that person will pay," Tink said. "Tritt deserves to go to jail."

Tink had switched from "I wasn't paying attention, but I wouldn't be surprised" to condemning Tritt for murder. Worse, she was observant.

She'd noticed what type of watch the head of the hospital wore. That would add to her credibility.

That damned Greiman should have interviewed Tink right after the nurses, Angela thought.

He was swaggering toward them now. Greiman stood over Angela, noting her folded walker, baggy clothes, and scabbed, half-bald head.

"Nice haircut," he said.

CHAPTER 17

"Nice haircut."

Ray Greiman really said that. Angela saw Tink staring at the Forest detective, her mouth open. In an afternoon of unpleasant shocks, Detective Greiman had delivered another. She could almost read Tink's thoughts: *How can he be so cruel?*

Welcome to my world, Angela thought.

She felt tired and muzzy, but she'd tear out her tongue before she'd let Greiman know his barbs hurt. He'd like that. She wanted to spoil his fun.

Angela forced herself to smile. "I like the West Coast vibe," she said. "You should think about changing up your look. Is that a trick of the light, or is your hair getting a little thin on top?"

Greiman's hand went automatically to his hair. *Gotcha!* she thought.

"You found the stiff?" he asked, reverting to his favorite way of annoying her. She must have scored if Greiman spoke so disrespectfully about a prominent Forest doctor.

"Yes," Angela said.

"He's not a stiff," Tink said, eyes flashing with anger. "Dr. Gravois is—was—a wonderful doctor. Everybody loves him."

"Okay, okay," Detective Greiman said, backing away. He flashed the smile that charmed so many badge bunnies. "You're Tink Warren, right? The problem with being a homicide detective is it desensitizes you. I'm sorry if I offended you."

His smile had no effect on Tink. "What's your excuse for being rude to Angela?" she said.

"I was just kidding," he said. "Angela and I go way back."

"Are you going to interview me, or can I go?" Tink said. "Angela's been up longer than usual. She needs to go back to bed."

"I'll get to you in a minute, Miss Warren," he said. "Now, if you'll move, I'll interview Angela."

"It's Ms. Warren," Tink said, but she moved to the other side of the partition. "I'm right here, Angela, if you need me."

Greiman leaned forward on the cafeteria table, talking as if he and Angela really were old friends. "I gotta problem here," Greiman said. "Someone found dead at a hospital cafeteria table doesn't scream 'crime scene.'" He nodded toward the far corner, where Emily was still examining Gravois's body, and techs were crawling around taking prints. "This crime scene—if there is one—is well and truly fucked," he said. "We bagged the coffee and cup, empty sugar packets and creamer containers, but I didn't see or smell anything but bad coffee with a lot of cream and sugar. I never drink that shit when I'm here. Even the coffee in the machine is better. But it has to be tested, or the nurses will scream."

How do nurses put up with men talking down to them all the time? Angela wondered. *It's a miracle more men aren't murdered.*

"Did you know the vic?" he asked.

"He was the neurologist on call when I went to the ER before I had the strokes." Angela wasn't convinced Porter Gravois had been murdered. A berry aneurysm could have killed him—a land mine planted in his brain before his birth. Happens all the time to otherwise healthy people. Only an autopsy could determine the cause of his death.

For now, she'd stick with the facts. If Greiman asked the right questions, he'd get the right answers. But she wasn't leading him to Dr. Tritt, the obvious choice for Gravois's killer—if there was a murder. Greiman never saw past the obvious. He'd arrest Tritt and close the case.

"Did you see the victim again after that ER visit?" the detective asked.

"No," Angela said, relieved he didn't ask her anything about Gravois's misdiagnosis or when or how she was admitted to the hospital. *It wasn't a lie,* she thought. *Not really. I saw him arguing with Tritt in the hall, but Gravois never saw me as a patient again.*

"The nurses say he was killed by a"—he checked his notes—"Dr. Jeb Travis Tritt, a brain surgeon. I can't believe that name. What kind of brain surgeon is named after a country singer?"

A good one, Angela thought, but she said nothing.

"Did you know this Dr. Tritt?"

"Yes," Angela said. "He operated on me." She didn't mention that Tritt had saved her life. If Greiman knew that, he'd discount her opinions as biased.

"When was the last time you saw Tritt?"

"In the cafeteria today."

"When did you get to the cafeteria?" he asked.

"About twenty minutes before three," she said. "My trip here was a test. It's the longest walk I've taken by myself. Tink came with me, but only to help in case I couldn't finish the walk. I got us coffee and brownies, and we sat at that table there."

Angela pointed to the spot and hoped the detective wouldn't ask why she was in the cafeteria. She didn't want him to know that Tritt had asked her to be there as one of his supporters.

"Who else was present when you arrived?" Greiman asked.

"Mostly staffers stopping by for coffee or a snack," she said. *Buying refreshments before the show started,* she thought.

"Who else was present who may have seen or overheard a conversation?" Greiman asked.

"Dr. Elkmore sat closer to them. He can tell you who else was at his table. Monty Bryant was nearer, too. They'll know if anyone else was closer."

Patrick's mother was standing behind Gravois, leaning against the wall, she thought. *Mariah definitely had a reason to kill Gravois. But that poor woman has suffered enough. I'm not siccing Ray Greiman on her.*

"The nurse"—he checked his notes—"Becca Parlo, said she saw Dr. Tritt put something in the victim's coffee. Did you?"

Becca Parlo, she thought. *Miss Blue Eyes in the butterfly scrubs.*

"And Lynette Riskin, another nurse, corroborates her story."

Lynette, the stocky woman in the teddy bear scrubs. "They were in the group of three nurses sitting near Tink and me?" Angela said.

"Right. Where was Tritt when the nurses saw him put something in the vic's coffee?"

"I don't know what you mean," Angela said.

Greiman sounded impatient. "I mean, was Tritt at the coffee urn, where it would be normal to add things to coffee? Or did he step into a darkened corner, and that's why the nurses' attention was drawn to his actions?"

"Whatever the nurses say they saw, I didn't," Angela said. "There is no cream and sugar at the urns. It's at the service bar, with the napkins and the plastic utensils, or on the tables. Dr. Tritt didn't go to the service bar. I saw Dr. Gravois add his own cream and sugar from the table. The sugar packets are in white china holders. The little creamer containers are in dishes. Both are next to the salt and pepper. Didn't you bag his sugar packets and creamer from the table?"

"If they were Dr. Gravois's," he said. "What about Tritt? Did he use cream and sugar?"

"I don't know," she said. "All I can say is I didn't see Dr. Tritt do anything but hand a cup of black coffee to Dr. Gravois. Dr. Tritt never added anything to Dr. Gravois's coffee."

"How did you discover the body?" he asked.

"I wanted to ask Dr. Gravois a question. He didn't answer. I asked it again, and he fell forward onto the table." Her voice trembled at the memory.

"With all the stiffs you've seen, you didn't realize he was dead?" Greiman said.

"No. He was fine. I thought he was reading his paper—until he fell over dead."

"And you'd be willing to put that in a statement?" he said.

"Sure, I'll write one now," she said.

Greiman gave her a Witness Statement Form and a pen. "Fill that out and sign it, and I'll talk to Mizzz Warner." He gave Tink's preferred title a mocking buzz, but Angela ignored him.

She was familiar with the form, but she was exhausted. She'd been up for more than three hours now, the longest time since she came out of the coma. Her head hurt. Angela filled in her name, address, title, and contact information, grateful that she could remember her phone number.

Then she stared at the command: "Please write a concise description of the actions you personally witnessed. Do not include information provided to you by others. Please be as specific as possible when stating the names of those involved, locations, and times of the witnessed actions. (Use the back of this page if needed.)"

I have to get this right the first time, Angela thought. *I'm using ink, and if I cross out too many words, Greiman will get suspicious.* She chewed on the plastic pen cap, trying to organize her thoughts, then wrote her statement. It was as spare as possible. She wasn't giving Greiman any details to use against Dr. Tritt.

At last she was done. She printed her name, then signed it. Greiman could add the date.

"Finished, dear?" Emily Du Pres was at her table now. "Me, too."

The death investigator's face had delicate, beautiful bones. Her pale skin was wrinkled tissue paper, but she seemed as strong and smart as ever. "So when are you coming back to work?" she asked.

"As soon as Dr. Tritt gives the okay," Angela said.

"Hurry," she said. "I want to go back to retirement. I've taken up bridge, and I miss my lunches with my friends. What did Dr. Evans say about you returning? Has he been to visit you?"

"Twice," Angela said. "He brought a gorgeous bouquet and said my job would be waiting when I was ready to work again."

"I'm only doing this because I like you," Emily said. "I don't want to worry you, but hurry and get well."

Don't want to worry me? Angela thought. *I hope Emily doesn't know the effect of what she is saying.* But now Angela was really worried. She was out of touch with the office politics.

"Evarts called me out of retirement to work as a DI until you're back on your feet. He's managed to avoid hiring someone new so far."

Which means someone is lobbying to oust me? Angela thought. *Who would do that?*

"Finish your statement yet?" Greiman said.

There's my answer, she thought. *He'd love to get rid of me.*

"Here it is," Angela said. She heard the metallic clack of a stretcher unfolding. "The body snatchers are here," Ray Greiman said.

The medical examiner's attendants zipped Porter Gravois into a body bag.

Katie will have to autopsy him, Angela thought. *Evarts Evans, the chief medical examiner, was here this afternoon, so he's a potential witness.*

The attendants rolled the stretcher toward the door. Angela watched the body of the man who'd nearly killed her disappear down the hall and felt nothing.

CHAPTER 18

Angela was walking down the dimly lit hospital hall late that night. Her hospital gown barely covered her, and she shivered with cold. But she could see her goal, the double doors at the end of the hall. There was no light behind them, but she had to get to them.

Almost there. Almost there. Now Angela was close enough that she could nearly touch them. She was almost free.

Angela reached out and heard a nurse's soft voice say, "Go back to bed, honey."

The doors vanished, and she was back in her hospital bed, fully awake now, but still cold. She felt the same crushing disappointment she always did after that recurring dream.

Angela wanted to cry. She'd almost made it to the doors when the nurse's voice stopped her. Ever since she came out of the coma, Angela had the same dream each night. In the dream, she never argued with the nurse. It always ended the same way: she woke up in her hospital bed, freezing. Sometimes her teeth were chattering. It was like sleeping in a morgue drawer.

What time was it? She checked the wall clock. Twelve thirty. No visit from Tritt tonight. She was grateful she didn't have to listen to a vitriolic monologue, but she felt uneasy. Was he celebrating Porter Gravois's death? Tritt was tactless enough to do that. Or worse, had he been arrested? If Gravois really was murdered, then Tritt was the prime suspect, and at least three credible witnesses claimed to have seen him tampering with Gravois's coffee. Would Greiman believe Angela over the nurses?

She knew the answer to that: she was drugged and had a head injury. But Gravois could have died of natural causes. It was too soon to determine the cause of his death today. No, yesterday. The new day was only half an hour old.

The contents of the neurologist's coffee cup would have to be tested, and Katie would have to do his autopsy. That would take time. Gravois's death would slow down Katie's investigation into the Angel of Death murders, unless Evarts Evans took over those autopsies. But she doubted he'd want to get involved in something so politically risky.

Angela was so sleepy. But she couldn't stop worrying about Katie. Her friend had a lot on her shoulders. And there was Katie's daughter, Sarah.

What's she doing in my hospital room? Angela wondered. The room seemed out of focus, though she could see Sarah just fine.

Katie's daughter was twenty-five, with brown hair. She was prettier than her mother. Sarah and another nurse Angela didn't know, a young African American woman, were pushing Angela's bed out of the room and into the elevator. Now her bed was in the depths of the hospital, rolling through a maze of corridors. Angela watched, amazed, as Sarah expertly steered her bed. She had no idea that buried deep in the basement was a series of hidden hospital wards that were copies of the rooms upstairs.

"I never knew these were down here," Angela said to Sarah. "They even have the same signs."

"It's our hospital, and we want to run it right," Sarah said. "We'll take care of you." The African American nurse was hauling away big bags of dirty linen.

"But what happens when you get off work?" Angela asked.

"Don't worry, we'll take you with us," Sarah said. She had a dark smear on her blue scrubs. *Dirt?*

"That's what we're going to do now." Sarah pushed Angela's bed out into an alley—a narrow city alley, surrounded by tall buildings. The alley was crisscrossed with electrical and telephone wires.

What's this alley doing behind SOS? Angela wondered. *I don't remember it.*

Angela's bed was bumping down the rough surface, and she was starting to panic. "You can't do this," she said. "You'll get in trouble. It's illegal."

"No one will find us," Sarah said.

And then Angela was awake. In her hospital room. She was frightened—sweating in panic. It was daylight. Almost eight o'clock, according to the clock on the wall. Somehow Sarah had brought Angela back to her hospital room. But Katie's daughter was in danger. The hospital would find out about this alternate hospital, and Sarah's scheme would be discovered. Angela had to stop her, but she didn't know how to reach her.

Katie! she thought. *I have to tell Katie.* Angela didn't have her cell phone with her in the hospital, but she used her room phone to call the medical examiner's office. She was grateful that she still remembered that number. It rang five times before Carolyn, the romance-reading receptionist, picked up the phone.

"Hi, Carolyn. It's me, Angela," she said.

"Yes?" Carolyn said, sounding bored. No "How are you?" No "Glad you survived." Nothing.

"I need to talk to Katie," Angela said.

"She's busy and can't be disturbed."

"But it's important," Angela said. "It's an emergency. Her daughter is in danger."

"Sorry," Carolyn said. She sounded so bored that the single word was an effort. "She left strict instructions. No interruptions. I'll transfer you to her voice mail, and you can leave a message."

"But—"

Too late. She heard Katie's voice say, "Please leave a message at the beep."

"Katie, it's Angela. I'm worried about Sarah. Your daughter is running an illegal operation at SOS. There's a whole duplicate hospital ward in the basement, and she and a friend started it. She took me down there last night, Katie. She's going to get caught. You have to do something. She's only twenty-four, and I don't want her to ruin her career."

She heard the rattle of the food cart and said, "Oops. They're bringing my breakfast, and then I have PT, but I'll be back about eleven thirty if you want to talk to me about it. Please, Katie, do something. I don't want anything to happen to you or Sarah."

Angela was still frightened. She called Donegan and got his voice mail. Of course. His class started at eight fifteen. She started to tell him about Katie's daughter Sarah, but an aide was coming in with her breakfast tray. *Better not say anything,* Angela decided. *Too risky. Hospitals are hotbeds of gossip.*

"Please call me, Donegan," she said. "It's important. I love you."

The aide smiled at her and said, "Good morning. It's pancake day, your favorite."

That was the last smile Angela saw that day. All the stroke wards, even stroke rehab, were in mourning for Porter Gravois. She heard nurses weeping in the hallway and whispered conversations among the staff. "That poor man . . . such a loss . . . his wife fainted dead away when they told her . . ."

Emily Du Pres, the death investigator pitching in for Angela, would have had to deliver that news. *Fainters are the worst,* Angela thought.

I'd rather deal with weepers, screamers, or cursers. Even the wall punchers were better. She'd had two of those, both men. They were so upset when she told them, they rammed their fists into the walls. Angela never went alone if she could avoid it. *The least likely people will faint when they hear the awful news. Some just drop like their strings have been cut. I have to try to grab the poor fainters before they fall and hurt themselves.*

The other odd reaction—though Angela had seen it often enough— was denial that the deaths happened. She still remembered breaking the news to a tall blonde in her twenties whose handsome husband had shot himself in the head.

"No!" the new widow had screamed, as if Angela had torn out her heart. Then she began beating her head against the wall and shrieking, "No, no, no! You're lying! Liar! Liar!"

A homicide detective—one more sensitive than Greiman—was with Angela that afternoon, and the two of them had to hold the woman to keep her from hurting herself. It was a relief when she started crying, but Angela would hear her hard, harsh sobs for a long time.

Angela had called the woman's mother, and she stayed with her daughter. "The poor boy was bipolar," Mom had said. "So charming. So talented. But I knew there would be trouble. He'd gone off his meds again."

Angela shook her head as if she could erase that memory and tried to eat her rapidly cooling breakfast. She took two bites of a pancake but couldn't finish it. Her stomach was twisted into a knot. She was too worried about Katie and her daughter.

Fortunately, the nurse thought Angela's poor appetite was caused by Porter Gravois's death. "It's okay, honey," she said as she removed the nearly untouched tray. "We're all upset today. The Sisters of Sorrow are holding a special memorial mass this afternoon in the hospital chapel at four o'clock, if you'd like to attend. Now, you'd better get dressed for your physical therapy. Do you need help?"

"No thanks," Angela said. She'd made real progress. She could wash her face and brush her teeth without looking in the mirror. By the time she changed into her workout clothes, Tink was at her bedside.

"You don't look so good today," Tink said. "That asshat kept you sitting in the cafeteria too long."

Tink didn't look like her usual perky self, either. Her lime-green hair was oily, and she wore a plain white blouse and black pants. Maybe the outfit was a hip-to-be-square fashion statement, but ordinary clothes were not becoming to the exotic physical therapist.

"I can't believe you want to go back to work with that detective," Tink said.

"I want to go back to work," Angela said, "in spite of Greiman. He's the downside of a good job. You have to put up with a jerk or two even in the best jobs. He's mine."

"He asked me out after he interviewed me," Tink said. "Can you believe it? I wouldn't go out with him if I'd spent six months in a freaking lighthouse. I'd rather be with my battery-operated boyfriend."

"TMI," Angela said, and grinned. Tink shrugged and grinned back.

They were in the hall now, passing the physician photos on the wall. Angela saw that Dr. Gravois's photo was draped in black. Underneath his photo was a shrine: heaps of hothouse flowers, supermarket bouquets wrapped in paper, and cut flowers from gardens, along with prayer cards, sympathy cards, and a doctor teddy bear wearing a white coat and a stethoscope.

"Look at that," Tink said. "People loved Dr. Gravois."

A flyer taped to the bottom of his photo frame announced the memorial mass and said that donations in his name could be made to Sisters of Sorrow Hospital.

"Sad," Angela said. It seemed the safest response.

"It looks like work here at SOS will improve for a lot of us once Tritt's arrested for Dr. Gravois's murder."

"Whoa, whoa," Angela said. "Who says Dr. Gravois was murdered?"

"Everyone," Tink said.

"Have the autopsy results been released yet?"

"No, but those are just a formality. We saw Tritt put something in Dr. Gravois's coffee."

"We?" Angela asked.

"Sure, the three nurses who sat near us in the cafeteria—Becca Parlo in the butterfly scrubs, Linda with the country singer hair, and Lynette Riskin—she wore the teddy bear scrubs. All three saw him tampering with Dr. Gravois's coffee. I did, too."

"You did? I thought you said you weren't paying attention."

"I thought that at first," Tink said, "but when I had time to think about what really happened . . ."

And listen to the three nurses talk to Detective Greiman, Angela thought.

"I distinctly remember him dropping something into Dr. Gravois's cup before he set it down," Tink said. "It's like they say on TV, you know. Tritt has motive, means, and opportunity."

She counted them off on her fingers: "One, he hated Dr. Gravois. He was jealous. Two, they had that huge fight in the hall by the nurses' station, and Tritt started it. Everybody saw that. He told Dr. Gravois the best thing he could do for his patients was die. Three, a brain surgeon can get his hands on all sorts of drugs. Tritt did it, and we're finally gonna be rid of him. It's a shame we had to lose Dr. Gravois, but at least he didn't die in vain."

They were at the door to the rehab center. "Workout time," Tink said. She helped settle Angela on the exercise mat, next to Trixie, the old woman with the bows. Today she wore green velvet, with matching bows in her hair and on her urine bag.

Svetlana, the Russian PT, started counting off leg raises. "One. Two. Lift leg higher. Three . . ."

Now Angela was doubly distracted: she was worried about Katie's wayward daughter and about Tritt. *The hospital will cheer when Greiman arrests him,* she thought. *Hell, he'll probably get a promotion for his work.*

"Angela!" Svetlana shouted. "You are not paying attention. You are staring at the ceiling."

"Sorry," Angela said. But she couldn't concentrate. She bungled her exercises. Tink put her through her paces on the parallel bars, but Angela stumbled and nearly fell. Good thing Tink was paying attention and caught her before Angela hurt herself.

"That was close," Tink said. "You could have hit your head. Let's call it a day and get you back to your room. It's eleven o'clock."

Angela was grateful. The return trip took a little longer than usual. Angela steered her walker around a trio of weeping nurses trying to comfort one another over the loss of Dr. Gravois. The impromptu shrine under Dr. Gravois's black-draped photo in the hall was gone. Instead there was another note taped to the wall: Please leave flowers and tributes for Dr. Porter Gravois in the Chapel on the Second Floor, next to the Cafeteria. A mass will be said for the repose of his soul at 4:00 p.m. today.

Angela sank gratefully into bed, while Tink put her walker away. The PT patted her hand. "It's hard when we lose one of the good guys," she said. "You rest up. Yesterday was a terrible shock. Tomorrow, you'll do better. Get some rest before lunch."

Angela's eyes were closed, but she wasn't sleeping. She was upset, but not about Dr. Gravois. Katie's daughter worried her. The hospital would find Sarah, and they'd punish that young nurse for sure. But Katie was a strong person. She'd make Sarah stop. She'd save her daughter.

"What the fuck's wrong with you?"

"Huh?" Angela opened her eyes and saw a furious Katie.

"Why did you tell Carolyn there was an emergency with my daughter?"

"Because—" Angela said.

"Because I don't have a fucking daughter."

"You don't?"

"No. Especially not a twenty-four-year-old daughter who's a nurse. Since I'm your age, that would mean I got pregnant at sixteen. I did a lot of stupid things at that age, but getting pregnant wasn't one of them. Would you care to explain yourself?"

Katie's glare burned her skin. "But it was so real," Angela said. "I saw her. She had brown hair and wore blue scrubs. I talked to her. She rolled my bed down to the basement and . . ." She told Katie the whole story.

"An alley?" Katie said. "Outside this hospital? We're in the fucking burbs. We're in a fourteen-acre parking lot. There is no alley. I don't have a daughter. I've never had a daughter. Let me guess what happened. You woke up in this room."

"Right," Angela said. "My bed was right back here."

"And how did this nurse disconnect your monitors without setting off an alarm? You're still hooked up at night."

"Oh," Angela said.

"It didn't happen," Katie said. "I don't know what shit they gave you when you were in that coma, but I told you, you aren't thinking straight yet. You're going to have crazy dreams for a while. And you're going to have panic attacks till your head is on straight. But I thought you were far enough along that you'd know the difference between a dream and reality."

Angela was truly frightened now. Maybe she was crazy. Maybe she'd never be able to know the difference between what was real and what was imaginary. How could she go back to work if her brain was this messed up?

"I'm sorry," she said, and now she couldn't hold back the tears.

"Hey," Katie said. "It's okay. You're going to be all right. You probably overdid it yesterday when you were in the cafeteria. I heard you found Gravois's body."

"Yes," Angela said. "It was scary. I stayed up for nearly four hours. My longest time yet."

"Too much, too soon," Katie said. "You never did know when to quit."

"Did I make trouble for you when I called your office?" Angela said.

"Nothing serious," Katie said. "Except that Carolyn, the receptionist who loves romance novels, thinks I have a secret love child."

CHAPTER 19

Katie stayed by Angela's bedside in the ugly turquoise chair after her tirade. Angela's wonky memory made her cringe. How could she have invented a daughter for her best friend?

Angela's lunch tray arrived during the uncomfortable silence, and Katie said, "Hell, I have to eat sometime. Might as well have lunch with you."

Angela took that as grudging forgiveness.

Katie pulled the privacy curtain and said, "I got another body."

"An Angel of Death victim?"

Katie nodded and opened her brown bag. Angela eyed Katie's lunch with envy: peanut butter on whole wheat and a crisp, green Granny Smith apple. She was facing a gray scouring pad oozing brown glue, limp white bread, and the ever-present green beans. Angela ate her chocolate ice cream first, before her only edible food melted away.

"Courtney, a thirty-five-year-old lawyer who had unexplained headaches. She was supposed to go home for her wedding," Katie said, noisily chomping her apple. "Died of sudden cardiac arrest. Her heart-broken fiancé was sure she'd been murdered and wanted the medical examiner to investigate. Her mother said her daughter's death was God's will and fought the exhumation. But the fiancé had a good lawyer and power of attorney. He was able to approve the exhumation. I posted Courtney this morning."

"Same spiked T-waves and the telltale needle mark?" Angela said. She took a tiny bite of the meat. It was like chewing rubber bands.

"I knew exactly where to look," Katie said. "God didn't call her home. That woman died of a massive dose of potassium." Katie bit completely through her apple and tossed it into the trash basket, while Angela hid the unmanageable meat in her paper napkin.

"What kind of lawyer?" Angela asked. She'd abandoned the alleged meat and turned to the soft, gummy white bread.

"The fiancé? Real estate, I think."

"No, the victim," Angela said. She gave up on the bread and tried the green beans. They were dull but predictable: at least she knew what she was eating.

"Oh, this is rich," Katie said. "Courtney was an insurance company lawyer. In fact, I think she was one of the cast of thousands that fucked up Patrick's case. And she winds up dead in the same hospital. SOS better batten down the hatches—it's in for a real shitstorm. The fiancé is not going to keep quiet about his bride-to-be's death. I expect to get the rest of those exhumation orders by the end of the week. I can't wait."

"Only you would look forward to five more autopsies," Angela said.

"I'm looking forward confirming my theory. And I'll enjoy watching the SOS shysters squirm. I'm praying nobody else gets killed because those pin-striped cowards have been pussyfooting around."

Katie shoved her sandwich wrapper in the paper bag, balled it up, and tossed it toward the wastebasket.

"You missed," Angela said.

Katie picked it up and tried again. "Rim shot," she said. "LeBron James taught me that. I'll tell you about it someday."

"Are you doing the autopsy on Porter Gravois?" Angela asked.

"Yep, but I couldn't get to him this morning. I had orders to autopsy the latest Angel of Death vic."

"I thought the Forest came first," Angela said.

"The hospital is getting nervous that the national press may start sniffing around. So far, the hospital's managed to keep the murders out of the news, but the story's going to break soon. Either that, or the killer will attack someone else."

"The killer nurse is still working here?" Angela said.

"Oh yeah," Katie said. "In finest SOS fashion, they're ignoring the problem and hoping it will go away. But it won't. Mark my words. Another innocent patient will die before he's arrested."

Katie pushed the privacy curtain back and resumed her regular voice. "Oh, I ran into Mario at the grocery store."

"My hairdresser?"

"He wants to visit," Katie said.

"Good, he's always fun."

"I wish he wouldn't look at me like he wants to kidnap me and do a makeover," Katie said.

"He looks at every woman like that," Angela said. "I've asked Tritt for more PT classes so I can get out of here."

"Ask him if you can have your laptop, and I'll bring it. What are you doing this afternoon?"

"Reading Charlaine Harris's *Midnight Crossing*. Then I'll have dinner and fall asleep until Tritt comes by and wakes me up. Maybe Mom and Donegan will stop by and see me."

Katie looked at her oddly and said, "Angela, you know—" Then she stopped. "Gotta run."

And Katie was gone. Neither Donegan nor her mother visited. Angela, who'd once wished she'd have enough time to sit around and read, now realized she'd gotten her wish—and didn't want it.

Angela fell asleep before the end of visiting hours and woke up to an outraged Tritt sitting by her bed. Tritt's words gushed out in torrents, and she was powerless to stop them.

"I don't get it," he said. "He's dead. He's dead, and they're carrying on like he was the world's greatest doctor."

Porter Gravois was chilling in a morgue drawer, but his archenemy was alive with hate. Tritt's dark hair stuck up in oily spikes, and he couldn't stop running his fingers through it.

He paced around Angela's bed, waving his arms, his rage cycling through three stages: simmering, boiling, then exploding: "It's poor Dr. Gravois this, and poor Dr. Gravois that, and saintly Dr. Gravois, and talented Dr. Gravois, and . . ."

Angela saw the green-eyed monster staring from Tritt's crazed eyes. He was possessed by jealousy. Now that his enemy was dead, he was more alive than ever.

"How can they love the man who ruined Patrick?" he asked. "That little kid suffered because of the great Porter Gravois. Patrick's mother is a slave at this hospital. And you—look at what he did to you! A good-looking . . ."

Angela rose up on the scratchy hospital sheets and pointed her bruised hand at him, IV lines trailing like a tattered shroud.

"Stop!" she said. "Just stop."

He did. They both looked surprised.

In the heavy silence, Angela felt angry adrenaline charge through her, burning away the drowsy comfort of apathy and self-pity.

"I'm sick of being your pathetic poster child," she said. "Yes, Porter Gravois screwed up his diagnosis of my strokes. Big-time. And I'll have to live with the consequences. But I am not the woman Porter Gravois ruined. I'm Angela Richman, death investigator. I'm getting well, and I'm going back to work. Don't you ever, ever, mention my looks again. Are we clear?"

Tritt gave a strangled *Irk!* and Angela rushed on. "I'm grateful you saved my life, but I have more reasons to hate Porter Gravois than you do. Better reasons than you'll ever know. So don't wrap yourself in my pain. You aren't sitting here with a drain and staples in your head and needles in your arm."

"I like your spirit." Tritt looked pleased as he settled his bulk into the turquoise chair.

He isn't going to leave, Angela thought. *Sleep is my only escape, but I'm awake, and he keeps talking.*

"Tink says you want more exercise," Tritt said.

"I want out of here," she said. "If exercise will do it, then bring it on."

"As of tomorrow, you'll get your wish," he said. "And you'll start some cognitive skills training."

"What for?" Angela asked.

"What's your phone number?"

"That's easy," she said. "It's—" It's what? She couldn't remember. "It's gone," she said. She was shaken. Why couldn't she remember a number she'd rattled off daily?

"What about your Social Security number?" he asked.

"Sure," she said. But it was gone, too. She couldn't even remember the first number.

"They're gone," she said. "What about my passwords? How will I get into my computer? How can I work if I can't remember routine numbers?"

"You're upset," he said. "That's good."

"It is?"

"Strong emotion will help imprint those numbers. You'll find them. When you do, write them down. Keep a list. It will help jog your memory. Your brain will construct new pathways as it heals, but that information will come back. I'll write the orders."

I'm on a roll, Angela thought. "Can I have my laptop?" she said. "Katie said she'd bring it."

"Definitely," he said. "I'll write another order to allow it."

But he still didn't leave. *The brilliant Dr. Tritt seems lonely,* Angela thought. *He should be going home when he gets off work instead of talking to me. I wonder why he doesn't go home.*

His next sentence answered her question. "My wife's divorcing me," he said.

Angela knew that, but it seemed odd to hear it from her doctor.

"Her family's a big deal in the Forest. She was a Daughter of Versailles, whatever that is."

"A DV," Angela said. "She was a debutante from an important Forest family."

"Right. She told me her father paid one hundred thousand dollars so she could make her debut and another twenty-five thousand dollars for the dress. She took off a whole semester of college to practice for her presentation. She knows how to use finger bowls, fruit knives, and things I've never heard of."

Angela was touched. The great surgeon mentioned those achievements as if they were equal to his.

"My wife loves to shop," he said. "She thought a brain surgeon would make millions, and she could queen it in a mansion like her mother. I don't. I have my own practice and make decent money, but not the millions she expected. I can't charge whatever I want. The insurance companies control everything. My fees are based on what Medicare will pay. I only got three thousand dollars for your surgery, and I did Japanese twist drill holes."

He never bothered explaining what those were.

"I bought her a big house with twenty rooms, but she says it's too close to Toonerville. She's ashamed to have her friends there. I'll be happy to sell that fucking white elephant. It's a money pit with pillars."

On the wrong side of the tracks, Angela thought.

"When my wife found out I don't make the big bucks, she wanted a divorce. Never was any good in bed. Just lay there, like you did, except you were in a coma."

Did I just hear that? Angela wondered. *He can't be implying he had sex with me.* But as he kept talking, Angela realized this had nothing to do with her. Tritt was telling her way too much about his failed marriage.

"We weren't getting along for a long time," he said. "She hated sex. She took Ambien to avoid screwing me. She'd be asleep when I got home."

Yep, Angela thought. *He really said that.*

CHAPTER 20

"If Farmer Bob sells twenty-three pounds of tomatoes at six cents a pound, and Farmer Tom sells twenty-one pounds of tomatoes at eight cents a pound, which one makes the biggest profit?"

Angela reread the math problem in the workbook, then stared at Kayleigh, the earnest cognitive therapist. Somewhere in her late twenties, Kayleigh's pale gray eyes were hidden behind horn-rimmed glasses, the kind screen queens wore until the hero whipped off the specs and revealed the glamorous beauty behind them.

Angela was sure that Kayleigh was plain, with or without the glasses. But her drab brown hair was long enough for a ponytail, and Angela envied her that hair. She still hadn't gotten the nerve to look at herself again, but she knew that half of her head was covered with stubble.

They were in a classroom near the stroke rehab center, sitting at a round blond wood table. Angela had finished her morning physical therapy. These word problems were supposed to sharpen her brain.

"Angela? Do you understand the question?" Kayleigh asked, her voice irritating, insistent, and unpleasantly nasal. "If Farmer Bob sells twenty-three pounds of tomatoes at six cents a pound, and Farmer Tom sells twenty-one pounds of tomatoes at—"

"Who the hell cares?" Angela said.

Kayleigh looked startled, but Angela felt good for the first time since this session began. Angela had hated word problems even in school. She'd always wanted to say "Who cares?" when the nuns asked her to unravel mathematical riddles about the yards of ribbons sold and trains leaving New York traveling sixty miles an hour.

Angela really didn't care, but she'd wanted a good grade, so she'd kept her mouth shut. Now, thirty years later, she'd finally said the truth. She savored her satisfaction. For almost an hour, she'd been wrestling with word problems, while Kayleigh treated her like a slow learner.

"Well, you must be feeling tired," Kayleigh said, dismissing Angela and her bad behavior. "I'll ask Tink to take you back to your room."

The green-haired physical therapist appeared as if Kayleigh had clapped her hands to summon her. The two therapists had a brief conversation in the hall, then Tink helped Angela stand up and start walking back toward her room.

"You're doing well," Tink said. "Keep it up, and Dr. Tritt might let you take unescorted trips to the john and down the hall."

"More freedom," Angela said.

They were out of earshot of Kayleigh's classroom, but Tink lowered her voice anyway. "I heard you were a little snappish in class today," she said.

"Kayleigh talks to me like I'm mentally challenged," Angela said.

"She can be condescending, but you do say off-the-wall things sometimes," Tink said.

"I do? What things?" Angela said, suddenly alert. So far, everyone had told her how well she was doing.

"Sometimes, you don't make sense," Tink said. "When the step-down ICU nurse asked, 'Where's your friend Katie?' you said, 'She's with my father.'"

Angela stopped in the hall, and Tink reached for the canvas safety belt ring to hold her steady. "But my father's been dead for years," Angela said. "I don't remember saying that."

"I know, I know. Don't get upset," Tink said. "As the drugs leave your system, you're getting better. But your brain needs time to heal. And be careful what you say to Kayleigh. You don't want her giving Dr. Tritt a bad report. Recovering patients should show a little spirit, but you don't want to be too snarly. Not if you want out of here."

This is like prison, Angela thought, but she kept that observation to herself and resumed the walk back to her room.

No sooner had Tink settled Angela into bed and left than Katie burst into the room. She pulled the privacy curtain, plunked herself down, and whispered gleefully, "The dam has broken. I'm getting the rest of those exhumation orders by the end of the week. I can't wait."

"Merry Christmas," Angela said.

"More news! The tests on Gravois's leftover coffee are back."

"Already? Holy cow, that was fast. Ridiculously fast."

"They're in a ridiculous rush. They found zolpidem."

"What's that?" Angela said.

"A sedative. Most likely Ambien."

"Maybe he took a sleeping pill," Angela said.

"In the middle of the day? When he was supposed to be working? I don't think so. Ambien is tricky. The FDA lowered the recommended dose in 2013. It can really mess with your brain and cause memory loss. Some people take it and then forget they were eating, walking, making phone calls—even screwing. Been some major lawsuits over that memory loss. No doctor, not even a dud like Gravois, would take that hypnotic while on duty.

"But I double-checked with his wife, Cora. Gravois never had insomnia. Slept like a log. She said he was extra tired because he was on call the night before he died. He didn't need Ambien."

Angela froze. Ambien. Someone had mentioned Ambien to her recently. Someone at SOS. Who was it?

"Cora said Gravois just had his annual physical. His blood work came back perfect. Even his cholesterol was good.

"Somebody put Ambien in Gravois's coffee, Angela. That shit they serve in the cafeteria is so bad, he probably never knew it. He loaded his coffee with cream and sugar and couldn't taste anything."

Three witnesses—all nurses—had insisted they saw Tritt put something in Chip Gravois's coffee, Angela thought. *They told Detective Greiman. That's when Tink decided she'd seen Tritt fiddling with the neurologist's coffee, too. Was it Ambien? And why do I keep thinking I've heard about Ambien in the last couple of days? It's important, but I can't remember why.*

"Was the dose big enough to kill him?" she asked Katie, fighting to keep her voice steady while searching her damaged brain. *Ambien. Ambien. I've heard it. I know I have. I'm not making this up. Ambien is real. And someone really mentioned it.*

"Don't think so. We'll know for sure when we get his tox screen back. But right now it looks like he drank enough to zonk a healthy adult. The Ambien would make him groggy, but it wouldn't kill him."

Ambien, Ambien. If I can remember, I'm not crazy, Angela thought. She could picture Gravois sitting in the cafeteria, saying he wanted to read his paper, then rudely yawning in Tritt's face.

"Then why give him Ambien at all?" Angela asked.

"I found that answer when I posted him," Katie said.

That's when Angela remembered who'd mentioned Ambien. It was Tritt, complaining about his estranged wife.

He'd said, "We weren't getting along for a long time. She hated sex. She took Ambien to avoid screwing me. She'd be asleep when I got home."

Oh, Dr. Tritt, she thought. *What have you done?*

CHAPTER 21

"Look what else I brought," Katie said.

"My laptop! Thank you, thank you." Angela hugged the silver laptop to her chest.

"I also brought us lunch," Katie said. "Grilled chicken salad for you and a French dip for me, with chocolate-covered strawberries for dessert."

"Yum," Angela said, opening the square foam salad container and staring at the fresh greens with slices of chicken. "Beautiful. The lettuce isn't old enough to get Social Security. Tell me the gossip. What's going on with the Gravois investigation? What did you find when you autopsied him?"

"It's gonna be a fuckup orgy," Katie said. She took a big bite of beef and French bread. Angela tried to wait patiently while her friend chewed.

"First time through, I didn't find any obvious cause of death," Katie said. "Porter Gravois was in perfect condition, except he was dead. So I Sherlocked him."

"What?"

"Examined his body with a magnifying glass. That's how I discovered the needle bruise on the back of his hand."

"He was stabbed in the hand with a needle and just went on having coffee and talking?" Angela said. "I don't get that."

"He wasn't talking. He couldn't. Like I said, we got the report back on the coffee. He was sedated first."

"With Ambien?" Angela asked.

"That's right—or something damn close to it."

"I think I saw it take effect," Angela said. "Gravois yawned in Tritt's face and said he wanted to read his paper. I thought he was being rude, but maybe the drug was starting to work."

"Sounds like it. Believe me, once he was injected with potassium, it was lights out."

"But it was the potassium chloride that killed him?"

"Yep," Katie said. "Gravois's death is now officially murder."

"Did the Angel of Death murder him?"

"I don't think so," Katie said. "He wasn't stuck in the foot. This needle stick was on the back of his hand."

"Couldn't the mark be from an old blood test done earlier?"

"No, he'd had routine blood tests a few days before he died. I found that site on his arm, with an old bruise. Where else could they stab him with his clothes on?" Katie asked. "They couldn't jab him through his lab coat. He wore shoes and socks, so his feet were out. His hands were about the only targets, and they weren't easy. That's why Gravois was sedated first. He wouldn't calmly sit there while his killer stuck his hand with a needle. That's not a quick, easy stick. The killer had to find a big vein in the doc's hand. And potassium burns like hell."

"Does Detective Greiman know Gravois was murdered?"

"The Forest's lapdog was at the autopsy," Katie said. "I did my best to make the dude turn green. Showed him the stomach contents and pulled out the intestines. He's got a weak stomach for a homicide detective."

"I know," Angela said.

"Stupid bastard wore a face mask," Katie said. "You'd think he'd know a mask only traps the smell in his nose hairs."

"I just take a few deep breaths and move on," Angela said. "But I want to hear more about Gravois's murder investigation."

"Greiman should get an Olympic medal for jumping to conclusions," Katie said. "Because the killer used potassium, the great detective says the killer has to be on the hospital staff."

"Maybe. Not necessarily," Angela said.

"Look," Katie said. "I know you hate Greiman, and his trolley's on the 'has to be the hospital' track, but he could be right. Don't look at me like that. He's your blind spot, Angela. The killer has to have some kind of medical background to know how to do the injection. It takes practice to hit even a big vein in a hand. But that doesn't mean Dr. Tritt murdered him. The killer could be a nurse, an X-ray tech, a paramedic, a military medic."

"Even a junkie," Angela said.

"That, too," Katie said. "The whole hospital was in the cafeteria, and Lord knows we have our share of substance abusers."

"Are you sure Gravois's killer isn't an Angel of Death copycat?" Angela asked.

"Could be," Katie said. "The police held back the injection site information on the Angel victims, but the nurses know, and they talk. The Forest wants Dr. Tritt out of here, and Greiman is itching to slap the cuffs on Tritt. He knows that's an instant promotion."

Angela was losing her appetite. "Tritt tells everybody how much he hates Gravois. He's so jealous he can't see straight."

"Tritt still stopping by your room for his midnight rants?" Katie asked.

"How do you think I got permission for this computer last night?" Angela said. "Tritt rattled on until two thirty in the morning. It was an epic hate fest: he paced, ran his fingers through his hair, and flung his arms in the air."

"Sounds like an opera," Katie said.

"More like Shakespeare, without the good dialogue. I'm sure the night nurses heard him carrying on."

"They'll go running straight to Greiman," Katie said.

"Three nurses have already said they saw Tritt drop something in Gravois's coffee," Angela said. "I was there when Greiman interviewed them in the cafeteria right after they tried to save Gravois. Tink, my PT, told me she wasn't sure what she saw during the so-called reconciliation, but she changed her mind after she heard the nurses talking to Greiman."

"He didn't separate the witnesses?" Katie asked.

"Hell, no. He's too lazy. And too busy flirting with the cutest nurse. I hope she goes out with him—she deserves it. I'd hoped Tritt would stop raving about Gravois after he died," Angela said. "Instead, he's gotten worse. He's jealous that Gravois is so popular and that so many people mourn him."

"Death would improve Tritt's popularity."

"Katie!" Angela said.

"Look, I love the guy. But he's hopeless. Nobody here's ever going to like Tritt, even if he wins the Nobel Prize in Medicine. He'll always be a bragging, bumptious outsider. Once his divorce is final, SOS will get rid of him. You've listened to him more than I have," Katie said. "Do you think Tritt killed Gravois?"

"No," Angela said. "For a brilliant surgeon, he's awfully stupid about people."

"All surgeons are," Katie said. "They only deal with patients under anesthesia."

"Tritt has this naive idea that he can somehow convince people he's a better doctor than Gravois," Angela said. "He hated him, but he'd never kill his rival. You don't think he did it, do you?"

Angela had finished her salad and bit into a chocolate-covered strawberry. "These are fabulous," she said.

"Thanks," Katie said. "They're double health food—fruit and chocolate. I'm not saying Tritt did it, but if I was going to kill another doc, I'd use potassium. I only found out how Gravois died because I was on the lookout for it, after working the Angel of Death case. I just hope he isn't railroaded for Gravois's murder. Greiman is sloppy. I know you love your mentor, Emily, and I don't think she'd lie, but if she can tweak the facts to make Uncle Reggie happy, she will. The Forest wants beloved Porter Gravois's killer. Convicting Tritt would kill two birds—settling the case and getting rid of the inconvenient Dr. Tritt."

"But the cafeteria was full of suspects," Angela said.

"Who hated Tritt and loved Gravois," Katie said. "You mark my words: Tritt will be trading his butt-ugly suits for orange jumpsuits before the month is out."

"I hope not," Angela said.

"Hey, considering what he wears, the prison suit's better tailored."

Angela balled up her napkin and threw it at her friend. Katie laughed and ducked.

"You've finished your strawberries. Fire up your computer," Katie said. "I want to see your face when you read your obituary on the Chouteau County website."

"It's still online?" Angela said.

"With comments. They're priceless. Hurry up," Katie said.

She plugged in the computer while Angela tried to get on the SOS Wi-Fi. After four tries, Angela said, "There's something wrong with me. I still can't get on the net."

"Nothing's wrong with you," Katie said. "The hospital Wi-Fi works about half the time, like most things here."

Angela found the page and winced. "Where did they get that photo of me? It's horrible."

"It's your employee ID picture," Katie said. "Evarts had a hard time finding something worse than your driver's license photo, but he managed. And quit bitching. At least you have hair in the photo. Do you like the black border and the gothic type around your obit, like a bad holy card? He's very proud of that stylistic touch."

"It's definitely funereal," Angela said and started reading out loud:

> My Dear Colleagues,
> We regret to inform you . . .

"What's with this 'we'?" Angela asked.

"This is a royal proclamation by His Imperial Majesty," Katie said. "Keep reading. It gets better."

> . . . that Chouteau County Death Investigator Angela Marie Richman passed away yesterday following a series of strokes. Ms. Richman, forty-one, is the wife of the late City University professor Donegan Archibold Marshall.

"No! Evarts used Donegan's middle name," Angela said. "My husband hates that name. He never uses it."

"Too bad. Might have helped him in the Forest. The Archibolds are hot shit in England. They have a crest and everything."

"Donegan's family is Irish. They came over during the potato famine," Angela said.

"Keep that secret," Katie said. "And keep reading."

> The couple was married twenty years and lived on the Du Pres estate. Ms. Richman is the daughter of the late Melrose B. and Elise Frances Richman, lifelong employees of the distinguished Mr. Reginald Du Pres.

"Distinguished!" Angela said. "The only thing Reggie Du Pres does is live off his family's money and stay out of jail."

"Hey, he's not a drunk, and he didn't squander the family fortune. In the Forest, that's distinguished. Go on, you haven't gotten to the good part yet."

> Angela Richman was mentored by Chouteau County's first death investigator, Mrs. Emily Hanley Du Pres, niece of Reginald Du Pres. Mrs. Du Pres became a widow at a young age. After rearing three sons—now partners in the premier Forest law firm Du Pres, Hanley & Hampton—Mrs. Du Pres went back to City University to be trained as a death investigator. She served Chouteau County until her retirement twelve years ago.

"What the hell?" Angela said. "Is this my obituary or the history of the Du Pres family?"

"Go on," Katie said. "You still haven't reached the good part."

> The late Angela Richman worked many difficult cases. She was supposed to receive the prestigious Harold Messler Forensic Specialist of the Year Award for her distinguished service this June. No funeral plans have been announced.

"Because I'm not dead," Angela said. "Did Evarts run a correction for this travesty?"

"He put a line on the Chouteau County site two weeks later that said you were on the road to recovery," Katie said. "He sounded disappointed you'd ruined his masterpiece."

"Masterpiece! My own obituary isn't about me!" Angela said.

"You've lived in the Forest long enough to expect that," she said. "And you still haven't gotten to the best part. That's the first one in the comments section."

Katie got up, checked the hall, then nodded. "Okay, you can read it."

"What were you doing?" Angela asked.

"Making sure there's a nurse nearby when you see this. My patients don't have blood pressure, and I don't want to see you on my slab after all you've gone through. Okay, you've been warned. I think you're strong enough to take it. Go!"

"The first comment is by Detective Ray Foster Greiman," Angela said. "I can't believe it. The time stamp says he wrote it at two in the morning on March eleventh."

"You were in surgery then," Katie said. "The Forest ER doc said you weren't going to make it. Tritt said you would, but no one listened to him. I called Evarts, and he checked with the ER doctor, who said you'd be dead by morning. Then Evarts put up your obituary," Katie said. "He posted it at one fifty-seven."

"And Greiman posted his comment three minutes later," Angela said.

"He's a lousy cop but a good politician," Katie said. "Greiman knows Evarts is very proud of his blog, so that ass licker Greiman is a regular commentator."

Angela put her hands over her eyes. "No! I can't unsee that image."

"Okay, ass kisser. Read. I have to get back to work."

Angela's voice trembled with rage as she read Greiman's comment:

Angela and I worked many cases together. I was thrilled when she won the Harry—that's what we in LE call the Harold Messler Award.

"LE?" Angela said.

"Law enforcement," Katie said.

"And he was thrilled? At the JJ twins' accident, that bastard Greiman told me, 'You think you're hot shit because you're getting an award nobody's heard of.'"

"Control yourself and read the rest of the comment," Katie said.

Angela took a deep breath and read:

My friend and colleague, Angela, was kind enough to credit me—along with Mrs. Du Pres, of course—with teaching her the investigative techniques that helped her win that important award. Angela may have been a newbie, but she was eager to learn the right stuff from an experienced pro. I am truly, sincerely sorry she died. I only hope the next Forest death investigator will be her equal.

"That liar!" Angela shouted. "That unmitigated, bald-faced, cock-sucking, mammer-jamming liar."

"Wow, your speech faculties are definitely not damaged," Katie said. "I'm not sure even I could muster that string of swear words."

Angela lay back on the pillow, trying to take deep, calming breaths.

"How do you feel?"

"Mad as hell," Angela said.

Katie took her pulse. "Slightly elevated, but not dangerously so. How are you going to get revenge on this son of a bitch?"

"By trashing his case against Tritt for killing Porter Gravois."

"Good," Katie said. "But he hasn't arrested Tritt yet."

"He will," Angela said. "And when he does, he deals with me. I'm out for blood. Ray Greiman's blood. He's going to be sorry that I'm not dead. Truly, sincerely sorry."

CHAPTER 22

Angela had two goals: save Tritt and get Greiman. The Forest's fuckup-in-chief had all but crawled over her dead body to steal her victory.

She started searching copycat killings on the Internet, typing "Angel of Death" in her laptop's search bar. Angel of Death was a poisonous mushroom, a pro wrestler, a song by Hank Williams Sr.

Those three words had a long, vicious history. Angela read about the evil ones who earned that name: Nazis like Josef Mengele and Irma Grese. Medical serial killers, including nurses, male and female, who'd killed anywhere up to ninety patients, and an English doctor who'd hustled 250 older people to the churchyard before their time.

Angela read about copycat killers inspired by movies, from *The Dark Knight* to *Natural Born Killers*. The Tylenol murderer, who killed seven innocent people, inspired others, including a woman who wanted rid of her husband.

Was Gravois's death a copycat killing? Katie thought there were seven or eight SOS Angel of Death killings. But what if someone else used the hospital's Angel of Death murders as a cover for his own killings? Someone who wanted rid of Gravois? But who? The hospital stroke units were awash in teary-eyed staffers distraught over the neurologist's sudden death, and there would be more weeping when Gravois was laid to rest.

But not me, Angela thought. *I won't be crying for him. Neither will Katie. Certainly not Monty. Monty. The lawyer who mourned Patrick's death and had a son the same age. Monty sat in my room and said, "Patrick is my worst failure. A great injustice was done to that boy—first by the damage from the car accident and then by Porter Gravois's testimony at Patrick's trial. I thought the jury would have had hearts of stone to deny that boy justice—and the money he needed. But Porter Gravois got up on the stand, did his* Father Knows Best *routine, and said, 'The boy will be fine. What he needs is an incentive to recover.'"*

What else had Monty said? Something else about Gravois. No, not Gravois. Patrick's lawsuit. "The insurance company poured a lot of money into fighting that suit. They hired a jury consulting service. The jury consultants held mock trials to see which arguments a jury would buy. They even had someone watching the jury's Facebook and Twitter accounts. I lost a woman juror I know was sympathetic. She was disqualified by a Facebook post. It was a blow."

Didn't another Angel of Death victim have something to do with a jury consulting service? What had Katie said?

Angela searched her brain until she remembered Katie talking about the forty-two-year-old woman—an Angel of Death victim—who'd been working on a big trial. Katie had said, "She was jury scout for ProWin Jury and Trial Consulting. She searched Facebook, blogs, and other social media to make sure the jury was following the judge's orders not to discuss the case." Like all the others, she'd died of a potassium overdose.

But the Angel of Death took a lawyer, too. Courtney. That's right. Katie had said, "Courtney was an insurance company lawyer. In fact, I think she was one of the cast of thousands that fucked up Patrick's case."

Three Angel of Death victims connected to Monty. Granted, the Forest was small and inbred but . . .

"Angela!"

Angela was so lost in thought she nearly dropped her laptop when the voice intruded. She slammed the computer shut and saw a dramatically handsome man standing by her bed.

"Mario!" she said. "Katie said you'd stop by." She smiled at him.

Mario had leading-man looks: long black hair, longer eyelashes, and soft brown eyes that made hearts—and other body parts—throb.

"Don't you work at the salon today?"

"I sneaked out. I don't have to be back until four. I've been so worried about you," Mario said in his soft Cuban accent. He was fashionably dressed in black, but he brought life and color to the drab hospital room. "I cried when I got the news that you were sick." He folded her in a hug, and she caught his expensive, woodsy cologne. Then he lifted up a huge peach orchid plant. "For you," he said.

"So extravagant," she said. "Put it on my nightstand where I can enjoy it."

"And this!" He opened a silver thermos, and Angela breathed in the rich smell.

"Cuban coffee!" she said. "Rocket fuel."

He unpacked a bone china espresso cup and poured her a shot of the thick, black coffee laced with sugar.

"This is so wonderful," she said, taking a sip. "The coffee here is dishwater. How are things at Killer Cuts?"

He shrugged. "The usual. I want to hear about you. Katie said you were in a coma."

Angela nodded.

"What was it like?"

"I went to sleep with a terrible headache on March tenth and woke up on the twenty-ninth. Those nineteen days were incredibly restful. Being in a coma is peaceful. Coming out of it, not so much."

He lowered his voice. "Tell me. Was there a tunnel of light with relatives waiting for you?"

"No," she said. "Definitely not."

"Thank God," he said. "I was afraid that's what would be waiting for me. I can't take the Cuban drama of all my family on the other side." Angela laughed.

"Not that I'm going to heaven," Mario said. "My mother is praying for me to find a nice Cuban wife."

"She doesn't know you're gay?" Angela said.

"My mother believes prayer can work miracles. And it will be a miracle if I marry a nice wife. I talked with your friend Katie. I'd love to do a makeover on her."

"Good luck," Angela said. "Katie cuts her own hair."

"I noticed. She says you're working hard to exercise and get well."

"Six days a week," she said.

"Good, good," he said. "And how are your spirits?"

"I'm okay." She tried to believe that, but her hair stylist knew her too well. He looked at her shrewdly.

"Mario," she cried. "Look what happened to my hair." The tears she'd been holding back leaked out.

"Honey," he said. "Hair grows back, but you don't come back from the dead."

"You're right," she said.

"I have to get back to the salon for my four o'clock," he said.

"Thank you for your gifts," she said.

"A flower and a cup of coffee?" he said. "It's nothing."

"And words to live by," she said. "Hair grows back, but you don't come back from the dead. That's my mantra until I recover."

Angela felt energized after Mario's visit. At dinner time, she eyed another desiccated cheeseburger with the inevitable green beans. She thought green beans should be the official vegetable of SOS.

She was too exhausted to continue her research. Angela woke up to see Tritt's hulking frame in the turquoise chair by her bed. He looked tired tonight, and a little sad. But he never tired of criticizing his dead rival. "Who cares if his father was some bigwig surgeon?" he said.

Everyone in the Forest, she wanted to say. *The Forest believes in ancestor worship. They know his great-grandmother and his grandmother were Daughters of Versailles queens, and his mother was a maid of honor. They know that his grandfather, a famous surgeon, helped found SOS. And they'd rather die than go to a better doctor.*

And why do you care anyway? He's dead.

But she didn't say it. Tritt wouldn't get it.

Angela had nearly fallen asleep, lulled by Tritt's predictable, impassioned denunciation of Gravois. She wondered how much of it was envy.

Chip Gravois had had everything Jeb Travis Tritt wanted: good tailoring, social acceptance, admiration, a name that wasn't a joke. Gravois had had everything but talent. And in the small, insular world of SOS, Tritt's talent couldn't compete with Gravois's pedigree. It didn't make any difference that Gravois was dead, and Tritt was alive. Somehow that made the situation worse.

He stopped for a moment, and Angela hoped he would leave. Instead he said, "Sorry about your hair." Now his voice was soft, his country accent soothing.

"It must have been a shock, the first time you saw yourself like that. You had pretty brown hair. But you'll look better, I promise. Healing takes time."

"Why is my skin so red and itchy?" Angela asked.

She'd managed to get in a whole sentence.

"You had an allergic reaction to the first seizure meds I gave you. Isn't that gone by now?"

"No," Angela said.

"Then I'll order some cream to stop the itching. I had to shave your head for the surgery, but I burned your hair, because I knew you were going to make it," he said. "If you're gonna die, I save your hair, so your undertaker can put it back on your head. People like to look good in their coffins."

Huh? Angela was stunned speechless.

"Anyway, I'm sorry about your hair."

Tritt sounded so sincere, she said, "Well, in the grand scheme of things, it's not a big deal." Mario's visit had altered her perspective.

But now she wondered about Tritt's presentation of the hair ceremony. If she were going to die, would he have walked into her room and said, "Well, you're screwed, Angela, but here's your hair. The undertaker can stick it back on your head. You'll look terrific in your coffin"?

I don't care how I'll look in my coffin, Angela thought.

Then she remembered Mario's words—"Hair grows back, but you don't come back from the dead"—and started laughing.

CHAPTER 23

"They don't want me at the funeral," Tritt said. It was 12:10. Another night, another rant. Angela could tell the neurosurgeon was gearing up. At least he was sitting down, instead of restlessly roaming her room.

"What funeral?" she asked.

"Porter Gravois's," he said.

Oh, right. Porter Gravois's burial would be a state occasion in the Forest. Missouri had been a border state during the Civil War, Southern enough to revel in the theatrics of death. Gravois would have a three-day wake at the Forest Mortuary, followed by a funeral mass at Our Lady of the Forest Catholic Church. The Forest not only believed in a personal God, it claimed his mother, too.

Then Gravois would take his place next to his ancestors under the grim granite obelisks and weeping angels in Chouteau Forest Cemetery. On a hilltop, looking down on everyone.

Tritt said, "Stan Elkmore, the hospital's head honcho, called me in for what he called 'a little talk.' Blew smoke up my ass for ten minutes before he got to the point."

Angela was sure stuffy Stan would have been deeply offended that he "blew smoke" and maybe by the makeshift title. She could see the old boy in his office, making genteel small talk before he slipped his stiletto into Tritt's thick hide. Angela hid her smile. She wasn't going to add fuel to the surgeon's fiery hatred.

"Stan said I'm barred from the wake, and 'it would be better for all concerned' if I had surgeries scheduled the day of the funeral."

Angela didn't have to ask why—she knew, and it gave her chills: the Forest had decided Tritt had killed Porter Gravois. The beloved neurologist's killer would not be welcome at his funeral.

"I don't get this place," Tritt said. "First, Stan wanted me to make nice with Gravois, and now I'm supposed to keep away."

Would you want to go to his funeral? Angela wondered, but she didn't get a chance to interrupt his monologue.

"I would have gone, too," he said, and for a moment the crazy rage flashed in his eyes. "Just to see that bastard in his coffin. The undertaker will have a hard time getting that smug look off his face."

I saw Gravois's body, Angela thought. *Some dead people look surprised or in pain or even asleep. But Gravois didn't look smug. He was a blank slate. He looked like nobody was home.*

"They usually don't have open coffins at Catholic funerals," Angela said.

"Then I'll look at his closed coffin and know the bastard is rotting inside," Tritt said. His teeth were bared, and his eyes were a raging fire.

Angela's eyebrows shot up.

"What?" he said. "You think I'll get all weepy because Gravois is dead? Who knows how many lives he saved by keeling over in the cafeteria."

Angela saw Nancy, the night nurse, frozen in the doorway. From the shocked look on her face, Angela could tell she'd heard Tritt's harsh words. Nancy rattled into the room with her portable workstation and said, "Good, you're up, Angela. I'll take your vitals." She rolled past Tritt as if he didn't exist.

Nancy, a honey blonde with high cheekbones and jutting breasts, checked Angela's blood pressure and temperature with swift, practiced movements. Angela caught Tritt studying his hands instead of scoping out the nurse. Angela thought he was trying to shrink into the shadows. A hound like him ignoring a well-built blonde? She wondered if the pair had a history.

"Okay, you're good," Nancy said. "Call me if you need anything."

Angela waited until the nurse rolled out of the room. *Tritt has never asked how Gravois died,* she thought. *He's too wrapped up in his vengeful little world.*

Before Tritt could restart his diatribe, Angela said, "Dr. Tritt, you may not know this, but Gravois didn't die of a heart attack. He was murdered."

"Good," he said. "Who offed the bastard?"

"Not good," Angela said. "The Forest thinks you killed him."

"Me? I wouldn't soil my hands." He held up his precious instruments.

"You didn't have to," Angela said. "He was injected with potassium chloride."

"Not nearly painful enough, but at least we're rid of the asshole."

"That's why you were told to stay away from his funeral," Angela said. "The Forest thinks you're his murderer."

"How are they going to prove I killed him?"

"Four witnesses say they saw you dump something in Gravois's coffee during the Great Reconciliation in the cafeteria."

"I thought you said he was injected," Tritt said.

"He was, but first he was drugged with Ambien."

"How?"

"Not sure," Angela said. "Supposedly someone dropped Ambien in Gravois's coffee to make him sleepy. Then the killer injected him with the potassium, and he died."

"Surrounded by witnesses?" Tritt said. "Sounds overcomplicated. Why give Gravois the sleeping pills first?"

"Maybe the killer wanted Gravois to sit still when he was stuck with a needle. Maybe he needed time before Gravois's body was found."

"Who are these witnesses?" he asked.

"Three nurses."

"Nurses!" Tritt said and snorted. "Buncha gossips."

"And a physical therapist."

He shrugged. "So nobody serious."

"The detective investigating the case is taking them very seriously," Angela said.

He still didn't look impressed. *Time for a big reality check,* she thought. "Now that you're getting divorced, you don't have any protection in the Forest."

"They aren't going to fire me," he said, laughing at her. "SOS doesn't have another neurosurgeon. Nobody's as good as I am." Overbearing, arrogant, and clueless, Tritt continued praising himself—and missing the point.

I tried, Angela thought. She looked up at the wall clock: 1:15 a.m.

Her room was dark and cold. Tritt's midnight monologue had lasted more than an hour. His angry words poured over her in waterfalls, and she was powerless to stop them. She had trouble tracking them. Finally, she figured out he was still fulminating about his late enemy, Porter Gravois.

"It's bad enough that the incompetent asshole protected the insurance companies," Tritt said. "But he was a crook, too. He was involved in some kind of scam."

"What kind of scam?" she asked, wedging in four words.

"I don't know, but he had something going."

"Do you have proof?" she asked.

"Not yet, but I know he was crooked as a dog's hind leg. Once the Forest knows, that will shut off the tears."

And then, mercifully, he marched out of Angela's room without even a good-bye. She heard the elevator ding, and the nurse, Nancy, was back in the room. "Look, if you want rid of Tritt when he's in here on a late-night rampage, ring your bell and I'll come rescue you."

"Thanks, Nancy." But Angela knew she couldn't do it. She couldn't abandon the man who'd saved her, no matter how obnoxious he was.

The nurse sensed her hesitation but misread Angela's reason. "He'll never know," Nancy said. "I won't tell. I'll be so glad when Tritt is arrested. We'll all feel safer. I hate having a killer walk these halls, especially late at night."

"Do you think Dr. Tritt did it?" Angela asked.

"Of course he did. Three nurses and a PT saw him drug Chip's coffee. All he had to do was stick him in the hand, and then Chip was dead. He didn't have a chance of rescue."

"And what did Tritt do with the syringe?"

"Hid it in his pocket until he dropped it in a sharps container. They're all over the hospital. We all know how much he hates poor Dr. Gravois. We've heard him carrying on. It's worse now that Dr. Gravois is dead. I heard what Tritt said about wanting to see him rotting in his coffin. I'm reporting that to Detective Greiman as soon as I get off work. He's been talking to the nurses. We think he'll arrest Tritt any day now, and we'll be rid of him for good."

She patted Angela's arm. "You get some sleep now. You look tired."

Nancy turned off the reading light, leaving Angela brooding in the dark.

CHAPTER 24

When Victoria, the imposing brown-skinned nurse, took Angela's vitals later that morning, she was subdued and teary-eyed.

"Is something wrong?" Angela asked.

"Tonight's the last night for Dr. G's wake," she said, "and I can't make it. Between the children and my work schedule, there's no way I can fit in a visitation."

"I'm sorry," Angela said. "But I'm sure he would understand."

"He would. He was a good man," Victoria said, wiping her eyes.

"May I ask you a question about Dr. Gravois?" Angela said.

Victoria nodded.

"I'm not a nurse, but I have spent some time hanging around hospitals. I've never seen nurses cry like this over a doctor. From what I can tell, most doctors are sneery and abusive to the nurses. They order them around and ignore their opinions."

"*Many* doctors are sneery," Victoria said. "*Some* are abusive. But there are a bunch who can be gentlemen and ladies, and Dr. G was the best of that bunch. He took care of my friend Caril's mother. She was broke, and he never charged her. He was caring, always polite. He was never impatient and he never pulled rank. Which is more than I can say for the man who killed him."

"But Dr. Gravois threw Patrick under the bus in the lawsuit," Angela said.

"Great men make great mistakes," Victoria said. "He was sincere in his testimony against Patrick, but the good he did far outweighed the harm. Everyone in the stroke units is grieving. Dr. G had a fine reputation."

A fine reputation? Angela thought. *Victoria is a good nurse. Why can't she see what Gravois was really like?*

"He misdiagnosed me," Angela said. "When I showed up at the ER with classic symptoms, Gravois said I was too young and fit to have a stroke, and sent me home. I was supposed to come back for a PET scan. Instead, I had six strokes the next day and nearly died."

"I was nowhere near the ER when you came in the first time," Victoria said. "Maybe Dr. G shouldn't have sent you home between the time you presented to the ER and your PET, but he did not do anything wrong. I know Monty talked to you about suing Dr. G, but that lawyer would have had a hard time proving his case. Especially since you're making such a good recovery."

Because of Tritt, Angela wanted to say, but she knew it was useless to argue. This was the Forest, where appearances mattered more than facts. Porter Gravois had appeared to be the perfect doctor. Those who worked with him regularly had admired and respected him. Nothing Angela could say would change that.

The aide who brought in Angela's greasy breakfast was subdued, and Tink was teary-eyed. She was wearing all black, but Angela knew it wasn't a fashion statement. She was genuinely mourning the late doctor.

I'd better get a nap in this afternoon, Angela thought. *Three days of the stroke units mourning his enemy will drive Tritt wild.*

After her exercise class, Tink insisted that Angela practice domestic duties. She folded laundry at a table for ten minutes until she wanted to throw it across the room.

"Now we're going to practice in the kitchen," Tink said. "Today, we'll boil water."

"I wasn't very good at that before the strokes," Angela said. But she went through the motions in the model kitchen, learning the safe way to bend and reach for a pot on the bottom shelf in the cupboard, how to turn on a faucet, then pretending to turn on the stove—all the while using her walker.

"This is like playing house with broken dolls," Angela said. "I know how to do this."

"Do it anyway," Tink said. "You'll be using that walker when you go home."

Angela realized she wasn't the worst off in the rehab room. Other patients clearly envied the way she was mastering her walker. *I'm improving,* she thought. *I will get out of here. But how long will I have to go through this farce until I'm free?*

Angela was glad to be back in her room, where she didn't have to pretend to be sad about Porter Gravois. She was delighted when Katie stopped by at lunchtime with grilled chicken sandwiches, artichoke salads, and chocolate cupcakes.

"A feast!" Angela said. "What's the occasion?"

Katie put a finger to her lips, closed the privacy curtain, and said, "We caught the Angel of Death."

"At last," Angela said. "Congratulations."

Katie seemed more angry than relieved. She unwrapped her chicken sandwich, then stabbed an artichoke with a plastic fork.

"Why aren't you celebrating?" Angela asked. She wanted to revel in the sight, smell, and taste of real food, but her friend was upset.

"Nothing to celebrate," Katie said. "Nurse Daniel Cullen Anniston is behind bars. But not before that bastard killed again. That scurrying sound you hear is the SOS brass heading for the hills before the shit-storm hits."

"At least you get to say 'I told you so,'" Angela said. She took a generous bite of her chicken sandwich.

"So fucking what? Another good woman is dead," Katie said. "I covered my ass with a memo when I posted the first Angel of Death victim, recommending that Anniston be relieved of his duties. But the hospital lawyers overruled me. Their memo said it would be 'prudent' and 'reasonable' to keep the goddamned killer working. Now a high school math teacher—who's far more useful than a flock of lawyers—is dead. So you won't hear me cheering."

"Jeez," Angela said. "That poor woman."

"And her husband. And her teenage daughter. And her mother," Katie said.

"I hope they're suing," Angela said. "Their lawyers will have a field day when they find those two memos. Unless SOS has destroyed them." She tried to savor the salad and concentrate on her friend's anger.

"I'm sure the hospital will scream privilege," Katie said, "cite HIPAA privacy, and use every damn dodge they can to hide them. But e-mails have a way of turning up from the most unlikely sources."

Angela saw a sly smile on her friend's furious face. Katie would make sure the plaintiffs' lawyers saw those explosive memos.

"Damn, this makes me mad," Katie said. "Anniston should have been jailed after the last victim. At the very least, they could have given him a paid leave. But the 'prudent' lawyers"—she made finger quotes—"didn't want to spend the money. Well, they're gonna spend it now. And I don't think the hospital's insurance covers negligence. I hope the victims' families hire sharks who strip the hide off the hospital's country-club cowards," Katie said. "Those assholes think doing deals at the nineteenth hole makes them hotshots."

"How did you catch the killer?" Angela asked.

"Just the way I predicted," Katie said. "The nurses watching Anniston dropped their guard during a crisis."

"Which crisis?" Angela asked. She bit into the cupcake. It had at least an inch of chocolate icing.

"Gravois's death distracted them," Katie said. "The nurses suspected Anniston might go after Judy, a forty-seven-year-old math teacher. She fit the profile: a good-looking woman who was scheduled to go home the next day. The nurses really watched her. Judy might have made out it of here, except her mother caught Anniston slacking off the night before Judy's release. When he didn't answer Judy's call for twenty minutes, Mom went to the nurses' desk and raised holy hell."

"That's when he decided Judy was too much trouble," Angela said.

"He hates criticism," Katie said. "All he needed was an unguarded moment."

"Judy's mother condemned her daughter to death," Angela said. "I hope she doesn't blame herself."

"She shouldn't, but she will," Katie said. "The day Judy died, the nurses had doubled their guard. One nurse bought a 'nanny cam'—a teddy bear with a camera in it—as a present for Judy. She was that worried. Then Gravois died, and the nurses were weeping and wailing over that useless shitbird. Finally, one remembered they'd left Judy unguarded. By then it was too late. Anniston had already injected her with a massive dose of potassium."

"So her death was painless?" Angela asked.

"That's what I'm telling her mother," Katie said, "but I sure as shit wouldn't want to go that way. Potassium burns like a son of a bitch. The only good thing is the fucking Angel of Death is toast. The nurse's nanny cam caught him. When they couldn't save Judy, one nurse ran down to the chapel. That's what made the staff suspicious in the first place: they noticed that Anniston lit candles in the chapel after each death in their unit. Sure enough, the nurse found him lighting nine candles."

"One for each victim," Angela said.

"Exactly. Last time he lit eight, and before that, seven. The nurses were alert enough to snap the candles with their cell phones. This nurse got Anniston lighting the ninth candle, then called her superior."

"And since the police were already here for Gravois's death," Angela said, "they arrested Anniston."

"No. The asshole got away," Katie said. "He was off duty when he lit the candle, and he slid out the side door and disappeared. Arresting him wasn't a priority, not with Gravois dead, so the hospital waited till he came into work this morning."

"Don't tell me Detective Greiman caught this case?"

"No, Greiman's assigned to clear Gravois's death as soon as possible," Katie said. "That's a Forest priority. Butch Chetkin got this one."

"He's good," Angela said. "I like working with him."

"I hope Chetkin can survive the SOS politics," Katie said. "He's got the evidence: the nanny cam, the candle shots, and nine autopsies. The hospital is very careful about potassium—there have been accidental deaths from that stuff. That's why nurses check three times before they administer it. At SOS, you have to get it directly from the pharmacy. Anniston liked to bullshit with the night pharmacist, and when the dude was distracted, he'd help himself to a vial. Anniston is on camera going into the SOS pharmacy each night before the last four Angel of Death killings. The cops found his prints in the cabinet where the vials were kept. The Sisters of Sorrow better say their prayers."

"Are there even any sisters at this hospital?" Angela asked. "I've never seen one."

"I've seen two," Katie said. "One is Sister Bridget, the token nun on the SOS board. The other is Sister Rita. Both wear business suits and silver crosses. But those crosses don't make them religious any more than flags on politicians' lapels make them patriots. Both sisters worship the almighty dollar."

"Who's Sister Rita?" Angela asked.

"Head of patient services," Katie said. "Sister Rita has taken a vow of poverty—for the patients. She's out to get every last nickel." She paused. "You know Mariah Fargo."

"Patrick's mother, the boy who died of kidney failure," Angela said. "She's working in the hospital laundry now."

"Sister Rita got her that job," Katie said. "Called her into the business office before Patrick was buried. Mariah's insurance was maxed out. She owes more than two hundred thousand dollars for Patrick. Sister Rita said Mariah could take a third job at the hospital in the laundry."

"What?" Angela said. "Mariah will be working for the hospital until she drops."

Angela finished the last bite of her cupcake and said, "Katie, I know you don't like nuns, but I'm not sure even Sister Rita could be that bad. The mean nun is an old stereotype. I went to a Catholic school. Sisters aren't like that anymore. They don't torture children with rulers."

"You went to a rich kids' school because both your parents worked in the Forest," Katie said. "Those nuns weren't going to touch your lily-white asses."

"Okay, but where did you hear that about Sister Rita?"

"From Mariah," Katie said. She smiled, a gambler playing her trump card. "The people who do the work hang out behind the morgue."

"That little patch of grass next to where the funeral homes park their body vans?" Angela said. She shuddered. "It's hot, airless, and has one skinny tree. I wouldn't want to take my break where I could see the bodies being wheeled to those spooky black vans."

"The staff hideout behind the morgue is no flower garden, but it's boss-free," she said. "I sit back there sometimes. The mucketys—doctors, nurses, and administrators—never go there, but I meet a lot of janitors, cleaners, laundry workers, and aides. The poor dumb fucks who do the work and see everything. That's where Mariah told me about her third job. And screw the stereotypes. Sister Rita carries a concealed ruler."

Angela laughed, but she wanted more information, not more nun-bashing.

"Can you answer one more question?" she said. "What's a Japanese twist drill hole? Dr. Tritt said he used them when he operated on me."

"It's a technique perfected by Japanese neurosurgeons," Katie said. "They drill holes into the skull at an angle, instead of going straight in. Cuts the death rate by ten percent. Another sign of Tritt's skill. I gotta run. Eat that cupcake. It'll sweeten Tritt's rant tonight."

CHAPTER 25

At midnight, Mount Tritt erupted, spewing white-hot hatred over his dead rival. He paced Angela's room, wearing out the same path on the tiles.

"I can't believe the tears wasted on that fraud," Tritt said. "If the staff knew what he was really like, they'd stop their pointless crying."

But Angela, fortified by the caffeine in that extra cupcake, interrupted him.

"If you want to rant about Gravois, tell me something I don't know."

Tritt was so surprised, he stopped in midsentence.

"Hey, you stopped me," he said and smiled at her.

Angela wanted to slap his smug face. "So fucking what?"

"That's good. You're getting stronger." Tritt looked pleased as he settled his bulk into the turquoise chair.

"Don't pat me on the head," Angela said. "If you want me to hate Gravois, give me a new, improved reason. I've worn out the old ones. I'm sick of hearing that he's incompetent."

"Gravois was crooked."

"Prove it."

"He has a thirty-room mansion in the Forest on Du Barry Circle."

"Had," Angela said. "He's dead."

But she could see the Gravois mansion in her mind, a gray stone country-French castle with pillars, skinny turrets, lacy wrought iron, and gargoyles roosting on the waterspouts, surrounded by a topiary garden and acres of woods. The Gravois family kept a stable and a pack of hunting hounds.

"He also had a summer home in Michigan."

Angela had seen the photos. The Gravois summer "cottage" looked like a resort hotel, down to the green-striped awnings.

"This is the Forest," she said. Angela yawned. It was 12:40. He still wasn't telling her anything she didn't know.

"And an indoor and an outdoor pool."

"So? He's Forest old money," Angela said.

"He had art on loan to Momma."

"Who?"

"Momma. The fancy art museum in New York."

"Oh, you mean MoMA—the Museum of Modern Art."

"Yeah, that one."

"It's pronounced Moe-Ma."

"I don't care how it's pronounced. It's a big deal, and he had the kind of stuff hanging on his walls that museums want."

"Look, all this goes with living in the Forest," Angela said. "My parents worked for the Du Pres family, and I know how the Forest rich live: They summer in Michigan because their ancestors used to escape the heat there before air-conditioning. They live in massive castles and shiver all winter because they're too cheap to heat them. Du Barry Circle is the top of the tree in the Forest, but Dr. Gravois had old money."

"The hell he did," Tritt said. "His father was a lush and lost most of the family fortune in bad investments."

"How do you know?" Angela said.

He shifted uncomfortably and looked down at his powerful, beautiful hands, the source of his success. "Uh, I did some research. A girl I know. Knew."

Between the sheets, she thought. Resentful Forest employees sometimes spilled secrets, even though the penalty was banishment without a reference.

"He couldn't be short of money," Angela said. "He donated the pediatric oncology wing."

"His mother donated the fifty million dollars for that wing," Tritt said. "Her money came from railroads. My source said she donated that wing anonymously and wanted her son to get the credit. Gravois named the wing after his mother."

But nothing was really anonymous in the Forest. "Didn't his mother leave any money?"

"Dad blew that, too, trying to prove he was a Wall Street whiz," Tritt said. "My source said Gravois was short of cash. He sold his private plane and joined some kind of rich people's club where they pool their money to buy and maintain a plane. There's a hefty discount if you pay your Chouteau County taxes early. Gravois didn't take it. In fact, he hasn't paid them yet."

"So?"

"His wife stiffed the Forest Party Shoppe in Toonerville nine hundred bucks for her annual holiday party. I know the owner."

How? Angela wondered.

"The owner said Cora looked her right in the eye and said, 'What are you going do about it? I live in the Forest.' She knew the attorney's fees for that amount would make it silly to pursue unless she was willing to go to small claims court. But that's not all. My ex saw Cora take her diamond necklace and tiara, the one she wore as a Daughter of Versailles queen, to the Ladue Elite Jewelers up near St. Louis."

"Maybe she needed them cleaned."

"She could have that done in the Forest. My ex said Elite makes exquisite fakes, and all 'the best' people use them. Supposedly you lock up your real stuff and wear the fakes for safety purposes. However, everyone knows that Elite will discreetly sell the real pieces in New York or LA, and you can wear the fakes and not say anything. My ex says both were pieces by nobodies, but they had good stones."

"What was your ex doing there?" she asked.

"Selling her engagement ring. I paid a pretty penny for that ring, and she didn't want the Forest to know how much she got. She told me when we signed the papers at the lawyer's. She also told me how much she got for her ring. She got cheated. I told her what that ring was really worth, just to see her face."

Tritt smiled triumphantly, enjoying his double victory over his ex and Angela. This time, he knew more about the Forest than Angela. "Gravois's lifestyle ate up tons of money," he said. "Money he didn't have in the first place."

"But his wife is a Stillman Rockefeller," Angela said.

"My ex says those are the poor Rockefellers," he said. *Score two for Tritt,* Angela thought. *But the divorce must be final. That means Tritt will be fired any day now.*

"So where did he get all that money?" Tritt asked. "He needed an endless flow, and someone was turning off the tap."

"Investments?" Angela guessed.

"Everyone here took a bath in the last stock market crash," he said. "He needed ready cash. All the time."

"That's still not proof he's a crook," Angela said.

"Hey, you're the investigator," Tritt said. "Investigate."

"My specialty is dead bodies," she said.

"Try cold cash. I already gave you your laptop. Now I'll give you a place to start your investigation," he said. "The hospital billing office. I used to see Gravois hanging around there all the time, talking to Gina Swinny."

Gina Swinny. The billing office woman who'd tried to dun Angela for extra money—when she had two insurance policies.

Tritt stopped his anti-Gravois tirade to take a breath, and Angela slid in a whole sentence. "Maybe they were having an affair," she said. "Dr. Gravois and Gina."

As soon as she blurted out that suggestion, she knew it was wrong. Gray-haired Gina was at least twenty years older than Gravois.

"The faithful Chip Gravois? Mr. Family Values? I doubt it," Tritt said. "I never heard he's a player, and I can't make that claim about most of the docs at this hospital."

Including you? Angela wondered.

"Besides, Gina has three grandkids. No gossip about her love life, either, and hospitals are hotbeds of gossip."

Angela had wondered why the SOS billing office would threaten her with fraud. Angela had two insurance policies: hers and Donegan's. Why would SOS demand cash from her? It didn't make sense. She'd never had that problem before at any doctor's office. Unless Tritt was right, and something crooked was going on at Sisters of Sorrow Hospital.

"I'll look into it," Angela said.

"Hurry," he said. "His funeral is next week. I've circled it on my calendar. Saturday, June eleventh."

"Oh my God!" Angela said.

Tritt stopped. At last. "What's wrong?"

"Today is June fourth. The Harry Award dinner at the international forensics conference in Washington, DC. I have to pack my things."

"I had Katie cancel your trip. You're not going."

"What? You never said anything about it."

"I didn't want to upset you."

"Too late," Angela said. "I'm upset. Why can't I go?"

"You're not strong enough to travel yet. You still have a drain in your head. You can't walk without a walker."

"I want my award," she said. "The nurse took the staples out of my head today. I'll look like hell, but I want to be there."

"Let me repeat. You've got a drain in your head. If the plane's cabin pressure decompresses, it will kill you."

"And how often does that happen?" Angela said. "It's rare."

"Not that rare. It happened on Southwest Airlines, Japan Airlines, Aloha Airlines, Helios Airlines in Greece, and more."

"Nobody died on that Southwest Airlines flight," Angela said. "I remember the story."

"You would have died if you were in that cabin," he said. "That plane had a five-foot hole in the ceiling. How are you going to get to the St. Louis airport? Board the plane? Get to the hotel in Washington?"

"Cabs," Angela said. "And I'll tip!"

"Using what for money? You're not leaving this hospital. Got that? You're not undoing my good work!"

"Your good work? This is my life."

"Exactly," he said. "Good night."

CHAPTER 26

Angela's red, roiling thoughts were no match for her hospital room's bland beige decor. *I'm going to Washington,* she told herself. *I don't care what Tritt says. The Harry Award is the highest honor in my profession, and I'll be on that stage to accept it if I have to crawl there.*

I'll take it easy, Angela decided. *I'll fly to DC at three this afternoon. That way, I'll miss the Saturday lectures and panels. I'll get into DC in time to make it to the Saturday evening ceremony. I already have my new dress. It will be too big—I've lost fifteen pounds since the strokes—but I could cinch the waist with a silver belt and wrap my head with my silver scarf. The outfit will look chic. I'll have to wear ballet flats instead of heels, but that's not a big deal. I'll talk it over with Donegan when he visits. He'll understand how important this is. I'll make him see what it means to me.*

Angela fell asleep planning her acceptance speech. Someone told her, "You're looking better," and she thought it was a colleague at the award ceremony. Then she opened her eyes. Donegan was standing over her in the pale morning light.

"It's you," she said. "My favorite way to start the day." She threw her arms around Donegan and kissed him. She liked how he felt—strong and muscular, but not muscle-bound. He was wearing his blue-checked Brooks Brothers shirt and navy jacket.

"I love that outfit on you," she said, running her fingers through his soft brown hair. She kissed him again.

"I'm sorry I woke you," he said.

"I'm not," she said. She smiled at him. "You don't look so tired today. Is Mom still feeding you?"

"Too well," he said, patting his flat stomach. "Last night was chicken and dumplings with carrot cake for dessert. I wanted to bring you a piece, but I ate it all."

Angela laughed. "Mom's carrot cake is irresistible. You're forgiven."

"You're looking so much better," he said.

"I'm stronger every day," Angela said. "That's what I wanted to talk to you about. Tritt said my trip to the award ceremony in Washington was cancelled."

"We had to, Angela. You're not well enough to go."

"I am now," she said.

"No, you're not," Donegan said. "Do you think I don't keep track of your progress? You exercise in the morning, eat lunch, then sleep all afternoon. Tritt keeps you awake late at night, jawboning. I bet he did last night, too, didn't he?"

Angela didn't answer him.

"You asked if you could go and he told you no, didn't he?"

Angela said nothing.

"I'll take that silence as your answer."

Donegan took her hand. "I love you, Angela. Your friends love you. We're proud you're fighting so hard. But you're still not thinking straight. You can't travel yet, especially not alone. You've come too far for us to lose you. Stay home. They'll send you your award." He looked at the clock. "Oops. I have to run. Department meeting at seven thirty."

He kissed her forehead and was out the door. Angela chased the cold, uncooperative lumps of scrambled eggs and greasy hash browns around her plate and considered her options. She'd seen the Harry Award, a gleaming crystal obelisk. Her mentor, Emily, had one, and Angela had admired the glorious way it caught the sun.

That award symbolized Angela's achievements and her losses. The Harry was her professional standing, her hard work, her triumphant solution of a baffling death. When she got the news that she'd won the Harry, Angela had been admired and attractive. Now she was a pitiful, crippled, half-bald creature. But if she could get her hands on that award, if she could touch its smooth, sparkling surface, she'd be whole again.

Angela knew Katie would understand. She'd rejoiced with Angela when she got the news. The two friends had drunk so many margaritas at Gringo Daze, they'd had to call a cab. Angela checked the wall clock: 8:10. Katie had promised to stop in before she went to work.

By the time the aide took Angela's breakfast tray, Katie was there. She looked harried. "I'm swamped, but I wanted to tell you to mark tonight on your calendar. I'm bringing you dinner."

"You're a true friend," Angela said. "But I'm not going to be in SOS tonight."

"What?" Katie sounded wary.

"I need you to drive me to the airport today. I'm going to the Harry Award dinner."

"Are you fucking nuts?" Katie roared. "Hell no, I'm not taking you to the airport. I was afraid you'd try to pull some kind of stunt, but I didn't think you were that crazy. But I was wrong. You haven't the faintest grasp of reality. Listen and listen good: a trip to DC will kill you. Got that? If you die, I'll make sure Evarts autopsies you, and Greiman is there, upchucking at the sight of your innards. I'm not lying to you. You will not survive this trip! Hell, you can barely make a trip to the john, much less seven hundred miles to DC."

"But—" Angela wanted to tell her friend what the award meant.

Katie cut her off. "Don't fuck with me, Angela, and don't concoct some clever scheme to escape to the airport. I know most of the people doing the shit work at SOS—the ones mopping the halls, cleaning the johns, and hauling away the dirty linen. I'll tell them to be on the lookout for you."

"But—"

"Keep your butt in that hospital," Katie said.

Angela was desperate to make Katie understand. "I don't sleep all afternoon. I take extra classes. I'm almost well, don't you see?"

"You're still batshit crazy."

"I realize you don't have a daughter," Angela said.

"What about Donegan?" Katie asked. Now her face was sad and serious.

"He's fine," Angela said. "He stopped by before class this morning to check on me. He's looking better. Mom promised to make him good meals, and her home cooking seems to be working. He's even put on a pound or two."

Katie sat in the turquoise chair, took Angela's hand, and looked her in the eye. Angela was gripped with fear. "What's wrong?" Her words came out in a frightened squeak.

"I'd hoped you'd realize this before I had to tell you, but you need to know the truth. Donegan is dead, Angela."

"Noooooooooo! That can't be true." Angela felt like Katie had torn out her insides. But some part of her, the healing part, had kept that fact hidden because it was too terrible to face.

"I'm sorry, Angela," Katie said. "He died three weeks before you got sick."

Now Angela remembered that horrible time: the uniformed cop at the door at eleven o'clock in the morning, when Donegan was supposed to be at City University. The fast and frantic drive to SOS. The sight of her dead husband on a gurney in the ER, his chest burned and covered with ECG tabs left over from the futile effort to save him. The ER docs had broken three ribs in the struggle.

Her Donegan had looked so beautiful—a dead Viking ready for Valhalla. Angela had wept and screamed her denials while Katie held her and kept her from banging her head against the wall. Then Doc Bartlett came and gave Angela something, and she drifted through the funeral and burial in a numb haze. She remembered tossing a red rose onto the lid of Donegan's polished wood casket and the awful finality of that nearly soundless gesture.

But now Angela felt a thin tendril of hope. She grabbed it, desperate. "The red roses!" she said. "Who sent me the red roses?"

"Monty," Katie said. "He asked the florist for your favorite flower."

"Red roses are my favorite," Angela said. *But only from Donegan,* she thought. *My wedding bouquet was red roses. He sent me roses for my birthday and on our anniversary.*

"And the books?" she asked.

"From me," Katie said. "I know who you like to read."

"Who was the man Tritt said sat by my bed when I was in a coma?"

"Monty visited you. So did Rick."

"Oh," Angela said.

The terrible silence stretched on. "My mother is dead, too, isn't she?"

"For almost twenty years," Katie said. "You took care of her during her long illness. She left the house to you and Donegan. You'd been married about a year when you moved in."

Now the sorrow was crushing Angela. She could hardly breathe. She remembered the gray numbness after Donegan died, the pill-fogged days and sleepless nights. She'd begged Evarts Evans to let her go back to work so she wouldn't be rattling around in her empty home with its constant reminders of Donegan. Outspoken as ever, Katie had told Angela that she was going back too soon, before she'd had time to grieve.

Now she realized Katie was talking to her. "I'm sorry, Angela," her friend said. "Tritt decided to let you believe Donegan and your mom were alive until you were stronger. It was nearly time to tell you. But when you started with this crazy shit, I had to tell you. A trip to Washington would kill you."

"I want to die," Angela said.

"Don't be an asshole," Katie said. "You can't do that to your mother. She was so proud that you were a death investigator. And what about Donegan? Do you think he wants you dead? You've got a job to do, lady. Stay alive and make them both proud."

Katie wanted to call Tritt and get Angela a sedative, but Angela refused. "I need to think about Donegan," she said. "I buried myself in work before I got sick, trying to forget my loss. Now I have to face it. But I think I'll skip PT today."

Angela spent the afternoon thinking of the good times she'd had with Donegan. She cried. She slept. She woke up and remembered the night, nearly a week after Donegan's funeral, when she'd thought about taking sleeping pills to end her pain and be with him. But she knew that would be rejecting her mother, who'd brought Angela into the world and believed everyone is here for a reason. Angela had decided her reason to live was to be a death investigator and went back to work.

It was still her reason. Angela knew that Donegan was the love of her life. She would always miss him. He would always be with her, but not as a hallucination. Their love was real, and she'd had that rare gift. Angela cried again and knew there would be more tears.

CHAPTER 27

Guacamole with thick chunks of ripe avocado. Crunchy tortilla chips and hot salsa. Platters of steak fajitas, chicken burritos, and steaming bowls of black beans and rice. All Angela's Mexican favorites were spread out on a pink, orange, and green Aztec tablecloth Saturday night.

"You brought a feast from Gringo Daze!" Angela said.

"Katie and I decided you should have your Harry Award dinner in your room tonight," Monty said. "We got permission to set up a table, and we can stay past eight, when visiting hours end. I brought you these."

With a flourish, he handed Angela a huge vase of red, yellow, pink, and orange Gerbera daisies.

"This is the perfect centerpiece," Angela said. She set the flowers on the table, then hugged her friends.

"What a treat. Food with color and taste," Angela said. "How did you score the restaurant's brown dishes?"

"Compliments of Lourdes and Eduardo," Katie said, "along with flan for dessert. They're waiting for their favorite customer to make a personal appearance. Now sit down and eat."

"Since it's a formal occasion, I'll wear my robe," Angela said. Her new pale-blue robe hid the needle bruises on her arms, though she could hardly stand the soft fabric on her peeling skin. But tonight was special. She'd endure the discomfort.

Monty pulled out a chair for Angela, and she inhaled the scent of the rich, spicy food. "Why is your cell phone out, Katie?" she asked.

"Evarts is out of town, and I'm on call. Now eat before your dinner gets cold."

Angela didn't need a second invitation. She helped herself to a scoop of guacamole, then fixed herself a steak fajita, piling on the sour cream, *salsa fresca*, and guacamole, until her flour tortilla was dripping.

"Mmm," she said, after the first bite.

Katie produced margarita glasses rimmed with salt and a thermos of their favorite drink. "Virgin margaritas," she said as she filled their glasses.

After all three filled their plates, Katie and Monty toasted Angela. "To our award winner," they said. "You did us proud."

Angela enjoyed the food and the conversation. She forgot about her pain, her shaved head, and her lost looks. She didn't feel her bruises or her itching skin.

"I have good news," she said. "I get a scan tomorrow morning, and if all goes well, Tritt will remove the drain in my head."

Angela knew the drain stuck out of the crown of her head like a tiny exhaust pipe. The rest of it was buried deep in her brain to regulate the pressure of her cerebrospinal fluid.

"Once that's gone, it won't be long before I'm outta here."

"That's real progress," Katie said. "The nurses won't have to monitor you so much, and you won't have to sleep with the head of your bed raised. Plus, there's much less chance of infection once that drain is out. You'll be home before you know it. You're not ready to go home alone, though. You'll need a caregiver."

"I'll start looking for one tomorrow," Angela said. "And that's the last serious thing we're saying tonight."

Katie and Monty applauded Angela's news and toasted her with another round of drinks. Then the three talked about nothing and everything, until Katie's cell phone rang at 8:20, and she leaped on it.

"Yes, she's here," Katie said and handed her phone to a surprised Angela.

A man with an educated voice and precise diction said, "Angela, this is Ian Broward, president of the International Forensics and Death Investigators Association. How are you?"

"Me? I'm fine." Angela could barely muster those three words.

"We've heard you put up quite a fight after your strokes and brain surgery," he said, "and we're sorry you couldn't attend tonight." Ian's words were oddly echoey.

"Me, too," Angela said. She was grateful Ian didn't know the details of that fight.

"Let me set the scene for you," Ian said. "We're at the IFDIA dinner in the hotel's grand ballroom in Washington, DC. We have an excellent photo of you projected on our screen on the stage. Dr. Evarts Evans is onstage, ready to accept your award for you. But we wanted you here, too, so we have you on a speaker phone, so the audience can hear you."

That explains the echoey sound, Angela thought. She was suddenly stricken with a powerful case of long-distance stage fright. She looked up and saw Monty grinning. Katie gave her a thumbs-up.

"Angela," Ian said, "you're receiving the Harold Messler Forensic Specialist of the Year Award tonight because you represent the best of the profession. Though it is not a death investigator's job to solve crimes, meticulous attention to detail can significantly aid the police. Because you noticed and documented that a victim's socks were clean, and therefore she couldn't have walked to her car and killed herself by carbon monoxide poisoning, her case was changed from an apparent suicide to murder. Better yet, her killer has been brought to justice and is now serving twenty-five years in prison. For this reason we are proud to present you with the Harold Messler Forensic Specialist of the Year Award."

The crowd's cheers and applause washed over Angela. She reveled in the energy. After nearly five minutes, the cheering quieted enough that Ian Broward said, "We're waiting for your acceptance speech."

"Uh, thank you," Angela said, her voice shaking with emotion. "I'm deeply honored. I really am. I would not have this honor without the love and support of my"—she paused and gathered her courage—"my late husband, Donegan Marshall. I want to thank my friend and colleague Katherine Kelly Stern, Chouteau County's assistant medical examiner."

"Don't forget Evarts," Katie stage-whispered.

"Not to mention Dr. Evarts Evans, Chouteau County Medical Examiner," Angela said.

"You almost didn't," Katie said, but she looked relieved.

"I wouldn't have this award without your help and guidance. Thanks to you all, I'm on the road to recovery and planning to return to work any day now."

"Any words of advice, Angela?" Ian Broward asked.

"Never let a brain surgeon cut your hair," she said. "They do a half-assed job."

Angela enjoyed the crowd's laughter and applause. Monty and Katie applauded along with them, but Katie rolled her eyes and said, "Will you forget about your fucking hair for once?"

Monty shushed both of them.

Angela heard Evarts say, "I'm pleased and proud to accept this award on behalf of Angela Richman, Chouteau County's rising star. We knew from the day we hired her that she was special and . . ."

The three listened dutifully while Evarts droned on. They could hear the audience's restless coughs and whispered conversations, until even Evarts figured out he was boring everyone and hurried to finish his speech.

"I've been told that Angela Richman will make a full recovery, and we couldn't be happier," he said. "We in Chouteau County eagerly await her return."

More applause.

"His applause sounded almost louder than yours," Monty said.

"The audience was clapping with relief when he finally shut up," Katie said.

"Angela, are you there?" Ian Broward asked. "Congratulations."

Angela thanked him and Katie clicked off her phone.

"You two set that up, didn't you?" Angela said. "Chouteau County didn't need an on-call medical examiner."

"Guilty as charged," Katie said. "I e-mailed Ian Broward a decent photo of you, where your hair looks good."

Angela felt like she was floating. She finished the last of the flan, then tried to help Katie and Monty pack up. "No, this is your night," Katie said. "Go sit on the bed, so we can fold up the table and put the chairs away."

"Thank you so much for a wonderful evening," Angela said. "I'm glad I didn't go to Washington. My award dinner was more fun here with you."

"Our food was better than the hotel's rubber chicken, too," Katie said.

Angela was surprised by how tired she suddenly felt. She realized that Katie and Dr. Tritt were right: she wasn't well enough to make the trip to Washington, DC. She could barely make the trip to the table in her own room.

When the dishes were packed into the empty coolers, Katie helped Angela out of her robe and into her hospital bed.

"We're so proud of you," Monty said and kissed Angela good night on her cheek.

By the time they left the room, Angela was almost asleep. She prayed that Tritt, the man who had kept her alive so she could receive her award, did not visit her that night.

CHAPTER 28

At 6:00 a.m. a slender, coffee-skinned man in maroon transport scrubs slid a sleep-drugged Angela onto a gurney. He adjusted the gurney's front end so Angela's head was propped up, then wrapped her in a thin blanket that was cold comfort. A fat medical records file, thicker than an unabridged dictionary, rested at her feet.

Angela was half-asleep as the man expertly rolled her into an elevator, then steered her through a dizzying maze of corridors and double doors until she was in a chilly white room deep in the hospital.

There, she was swallowed by an ice-white machine that looked like one of Katie's autopsy tables in white plastic with surreal growths on its sides. Faceless techs adjusted her position and made soothing sounds while the machine beeped and blurped. Then she shivered under the useless blanket in the hallway while the techs evaluated their findings.

The process was as cold and impersonal as death. But in the lifeless sci-fi setting, Angela nursed a small ray of hope. She was getting better. She knew it. Soon she'd have that drain out, and she'd be back in her book-lined home. She'd recuperate there, feel the summer sun on her skin and the green grass tickling her bare feet. She'd breathe in the scent of rambler roses and honeysuckle instead of disinfectant and frigid, stale air.

She wondered if her mother's pink peonies were blooming yet. Reggie Du Pres hated them—the plants were full of ants—but Angela invoked her mother's memory and the ancestor-worshipping Reggie let her keep them in the backyard.

"You're good to go," a tech told Angela, and she dreamed of a soft summer afternoon while she waited for a maroon-scrubbed transport tech to take her away. Then she woke up in another cold room, with nurses, computer monitors, and hard, white machines with wild tangles of wire, cords, and accordion tubes.

Tritt was there in green scrubs, wearing a surgeon's cap and a face mask.

"This won't hurt," a nurse said, but it did. Angela slid from the cold, white world into a deep black one until she saw a shadowy face and heard someone call her name. Someone familiar.

"Katie?" Angela struggled to open her eyes, but the bright light hurt.

"Afternoon," Katie said. "You're awake." Angela saw that her friend was wearing a fresh lab coat, something she donned in case she needed to pull rank in the hospital.

"You're going to be okay. I'll ring for the nurse."

"It's over?" Angela asked. She was still groggy from whatever they'd given her for the pain.

"It's over. The drain's out. You no longer have a stovepipe sticking out of your head. Oh, and since you're obsessed with your fucking hair, the rest of it's been buzzed off. It was falling out, anyway. With all the shit they poured in you, you were bound to lose it all."

Maybe she was still numb from the procedure, but Angela didn't care about the hair. "At least both sides are even," she said.

"Good. I think that was a joke. A feeble one, but it beats your drama queen routine. Now that you're awake, how do you feel?"

"My head aches."

"It will, for a little while, but you came through with flying colors—and a flapping mouth."

"Oh no. Did I swear? I do that when I'm drugged. I called the surgeon who took out my gall bladder a son of a bitch."

Katie laughed. "Most of them are. Your language was fine, but you saw Tritt wearing a face mask and told him, 'If you wore that over your big mouth more often, you'd be in less trouble.'"

Angela groaned.

"Tritt thought it was funny. So did the nurses. Your smart remark is the talk of the hospital."

"Oh God, the one person I want to help, and I did that to him," Angela said.

"You may have helped Tritt, in spite of yourself," Katie said. "It gave the hospital gossips something new to chew on besides how he killed Porter Gravois."

"Tritt is still the chief suspect?" Angela asked.

"He's the only suspect," Katie said. "Nobody can figure out why he hasn't been arrested yet. Since you'll be going home soon, I have two caregivers you can interview. When do you want to see them?"

"Now! Today! As soon as possible," Angela said.

"I thought so. The first woman is stopping by at three thirty. The second will be here at four o'clock."

Madison Muson, Katie's first caregiver candidate, was a pale twentysomething with long, dark-red hair. She was brisk, efficient, and utterly humorless.

"How are we this afternoon?" Madison asked, handing Angela her résumé.

She sat in the turquoise chair, hands folded in her lap, while Angela read her achievements. "So you're a licensed practical nurse?" Angela asked.

"Five years," Madison said, and Angela saw her pride. She also heard a high-pitched, two-note bird whistle.

"What was that?"

"My cell phone," Madison said. "That's my boyfriend. I have a different alert for all my regular callers. Now, as an LPN, I'll monitor you and report any adverse reactions to medications or treatments. I assume your doctor is Carmen Bartlett?"

Ding!

"Excuse me?" Angela said.

"Oops. Text message," Madison said, but she made no move to pick up her phone.

Ooogah! The blare of an old-time horn.

"That's my mom." She gave Angela a wobbly smile. "As I was saying, the health information I record can be used to complete insurance forms, preauthorizations, and referrals."

Ding!

Madison looked flustered. "Sorry. I never answer my cell phone when I'm"—*Ooogah!*—"on duty. My time is completely dedicated to you."

Whistle!

Angela skimmed the rest of Madison's impressive résumé and said, "Thank you for coming here. I have another interview at four. I'll call and let you know."

Ding! Ooogah!

Angela suspected that Madison already knew her decision. A final whistle followed her out the door.

Ten minutes later, Mrs. Leota Raines bustled in. She was a comfortable, motherly woman in her late sixties with tightly curled white hair and faded blue eyes.

"My, you've been through a lot," Mrs. Raines said. "You must be a strong person. You're healing fast, and I'll be happy to work with you until you're completely independent."

Angela studied her extensive résumé.

"My current client has advancing Alzheimer's and needs to go into long-term care at the Willingham in the Forest," Mrs. Raines said. "I'm staying with her until her room in the memory unit is ready. For the life of me, I don't know why that place calls its Alzheimer's wing the memory unit. It's like they're making fun of their patients. I can't tell you exactly when I'll be free. It could be two days. It could be two weeks. I just don't know."

But Angela knew she wanted Mrs. Raines. After the woman left, Angela called Katie and told her the situation.

"I like Mrs. Raines, but she may not be able to work for me until her current client's room is ready at the Willingham. It could be two days or two weeks."

"I'll stay at your place for a couple of days until she can start," Katie said.

Angela was doubly grateful. She could go home soon, and she wouldn't have to face her empty home alone.

CHAPTER 29

"Angela! You're up and walking at six in the morning?" said Chris, the funny nurse with the fried blonde hair. "Before breakfast?"

"Before breakfast, after lunch, after visiting hours, and in the middle of the night," Angela said. "I'm walking to build myself up so I can walk out of this hospital. I'm committed."

"You probably should be," Chris said, giving Angela a good-natured grin. "Just don't overdo it, honey."

Angela pushed her walker past the nurses' station. She saw a white-coated doctor dictating his notes in a cubicle. James, an SOS janitor, stopped sweeping as she passed him. "Morning, Angela," he said, pushing a fluffy gray pile out of her way. "You're looking good."

She wasn't. Angela knew she was an odd sight. Her baggy jeans and worn cotton T-shirt flapped on her scrawny body. At least her socks and gym shoes still fit.

She didn't have the nerve to look in the mirror yet, but last night she'd gingerly felt her head. Her buzzed hair was a bristly half-inch long on one side and even shorter on the other. She figured it was growing in gray. Angela had started dyeing her hair dark brown about five years ago.

On the right side of her head, where she'd had the surgery, Angela felt a cobblestone-like bulge where Tritt had sawed a five-inch-wide porthole in her skull. The skin around it felt puffy and scabbed.

She couldn't imagine what she looked like—and that was a blessing. *Katie's right,* she decided. *I am obsessed with my hair. Any more shallow and I'll have my own reality TV show.*

At eleven o'clock, Tink collected Angela for her exercises. This morning, the physical therapist had pink hair, ripped jeans, and a black leather jacket crisscrossed with zippers.

"Like the jacket," Angela said as they headed down the hall.

"Vintage nineties," Tink said. "Goes with the tats."

Svetlana still led the exercises, but Angela had a new workout group. Trixie, the older woman with the beribboned urine bags, had been sent home. So had the quiet, pale old man. The red-faced grump had had another stroke. *No surprise there,* Angela thought.

Now she worked out with Rosie, a retired schoolteacher who'd been planning a cruise to Alaska when she'd been felled by a mild stroke. "Thank God I bought trip insurance," the zaftig teacher said.

A ghostlike man who used a wheelchair worked out next to a heavyset construction worker in dingy sweats. Based on his behavior, Angela thought his name—Dick—was a perfect fit. Dick stroked his belly bulge as if it were a beloved pet. When Svetlana adjusted his mat, Dick boldly patted her bottom. The athletic blonde slapped his hand.

"Aw, come on," Dick said. "I'm feeling frisky. That's a sign I'm getting better, right?"

"I am not dating a patient," Svetlana said, in her charming, wonky English.

"I'm pretty sure this bird isn't looking for a date," Angela whispered to Rosie.

"Try another four-letter word," the schoolteacher said, "but I doubt he can get it up right now."

"A date!" Dick said. "I was thinking more like a little fun later." He winked. "I have a private room."

Rosie rolled her eyes.

"You are married man," Svetlana said. "I am telling your wife when she visits this afternoon."

That shut him up for the rest of the class.

Afterward Tink said, "Now I have a treat, Angela. Today we start practicing the proper way to get in and out of a car. We only begin that exercise when you're about to go home."

"At last!" Angela felt a surge of pure joy. She missed her sleek black Charger. "Do you know when I can leave?"

"Your surgeon will tell you. You'll have to do some other things, too, so don't expect to walk out tomorrow."

The training car was enshrined in its own corner. It was a yellow metal frame made to look like the front of a car, but with no dash, a scaled-down door, and a thinly padded passenger seat.

Angela started to sit down in it, but Tink stopped her. "No, we're doing this the right way. You're here to learn." Angela moved away. This was too important.

"Using your walker, back up to the passenger seat," Tink said. "No, don't reach for the door frame to steady yourself. Keep one hand on the walker and use the other hand to reach for the seat.

"There. Got it. Good. Now lower yourself carefully into the seat. I said carefully! Go slow. No! Too fast! Don't brace yourself on the door—use your walker. Better. Better. Be careful not to hit your head. Swing your body forward. There. You did it." Tink applauded. "Again."

"When I can drive?" Angela asked, backing her walker up to the car for a second try.

"When your surgeon clears you," Tink said. "You're bracing your hand on the door again. Forget about driving for now. You have to know the right way to get in and out of the passenger seat."

After three tries, Tink pronounced Angela's technique perfect, then took her back to her room for a gluey pasta and warm Jell-O lunch. Angela didn't care. Soon she'd be home.

Angela was so excited by the prospect of leaving that she couldn't take an afternoon nap. She snapped her walker open and was up again, scooting through the stroke rehab ward, then the oncology ward. In each room there was a small tableau, illustrating a theme. Angela could almost read the titles over the doorways.

Boredom. She saw a washed-out woman sitting at the bedside of a wasted, white-haired man. The couple sat in silence, neither talking nor touching.

Greed. A middle-aged woman whined at the bedside of a hefty patient, "You promised me your diamond cocktail ring, Mama, but Sissy wore it to church on Sunday. That's not right. If you die, you know she'll keep it."

Sorrow. Angela watched a thirtysomething man hugging his chemo-bald wife. Both were weeping. Angela turned away, ashamed of her voyeurism.

Now that the Angel of Death was safely stashed in jail, Angela roamed all the hospital's halls. She was fascinated by the dreaded isolation section at the end of the third-floor hall. She read the frightening warnings posted on the doors to each cell-like room and watched nurses enter the air locks.

Down on the second floor, Angela savored the chapel's peace. The horrors of the hospital never penetrated its serene beige walls. She sat on a plush upholstered bench and watched the dust motes dance in the stained-glass light.

Angela explored the first-floor lobby, a mausoleum of gray marble with a stainless-steel cross. She watched tired women with squirming children and slump-shouldered men sign in and get their ID photos. The white-haired security guard, looking like a beardless Santa in a blue uniform, remained cheerful in that dispirited crowd. When the check-in line disappeared, the security guard said, "Hi, sweetheart, haven't seen you down here before."

"This is my first trip down here alone. I'm Angela Richmond. My next stop is the cafeteria."

"I'm Terry." The guard held up a Kit Kat candy bar. "You want my advice, get yourself one of these out of the machine. Only edible food in the place." A twentysomething woman with a clipboard cleared her throat, and Terry went back to work.

Angela wished she'd followed the guard's advice. Instead, she'd treated herself to a cafeteria cookie. Katie had given Angela twenty dollars cash but refused to bring her purse to SOS. "The hospital says your credit cards and ID could be stolen," she'd said. Angela didn't quite believe her. She thought Katie didn't trust her after her escape attempt before the Harry Award dinner.

Angela took her chocolate chip cookie to an alcove far away from Gravois's death scene and read a free paper.

That's where Katie tracked her down. "Hey, you're racking up some miles," Katie said. "I had to ask three people before I found you down here."

"May I treat you to a cookie?" Angela said. "It's not too stale."

"Despite that rave review, I'll stick with my water," Katie said, hoisting a bottle. "It's the one thing the cafeteria cooks can't ruin. I hear you're walking morning, noon, and late at night."

"I'm trying to," Angela said. "But it's still not as much as I want. Some afternoons, I'm so tired I fall asleep until dinner. Or I'll sleep after dinner until Tritt comes by."

"You're supposed to," Katie said. "You're in the freaking hospital. Sleep is how you heal."

"I want to be strong," Angela said. "I wake up feeling good, and then I get tired."

"That's how healing works," Katie said. "Are you working on your computer?"

"I'm so slow," Angela said. "I have more than four hundred e-mails, mostly get-well wishes. I can only do one or two a day. I'm frustrated."

"Don't be," Katie said. "Build slowly. Do one or two e-mails, then three, then four, and before you know it, you'll be back up to speed."

Mildly annoyed by Katie's upbeat advice, Angela changed the subject. "What's going on with the Angel of Death?"

"They nailed nurse Daniel Cullen Anniston for nine counts of murder one—which means he's set to fry if he's convicted. The hospital is covering its ass with stainless-steel pants. They know they're in for it when the Angel victims' families start suing. So far, nobody's filed. Yet. It's like those old Westerns—it's quiet. Too quiet. The attack begins soon.

"Meanwhile, the national press is like an overturned ant hill—crawling all over SOS, getting in any way they can. Security's trying to stop the reporters, but the press has big expense accounts, and our underpaid staffers have their hands out. A janitor got a Benjamin to prop open a side door."

"A hundred bucks?" Angela said.

"Not bad for two minutes' work," Katie said. "There's a brisk business in used visitor passes in Lot A—twenty bucks is the going rate. And a New York tabloid offered me a thousand bucks if I'd photograph the last victim on a slab."

"You didn't," Angela said.

Katie glared at her. "Do you know me at all? I told the asshole to get lost. Her family doesn't deserve that. With so many reporters scuttling around, I'm surprised one didn't try to interview you in the hall."

"But I don't know anything," Angela said.

"That didn't stop a patient from giving an interview to the *National Star* called 'My Night of Fear.' She claimed she could tell nurse Daniel Anniston was a killer because of his glowing eyes, and she sat up all night so he wouldn't attack her."

"I bet SOS is thrilled," Angela said.

"Here's the best part," Katie said. "She wasn't even in his ward. She was in here for a gallbladder operation. SOS is afraid to say that because they don't want to draw more attention to the controversy."

"Too late now," Angela said.

"I hope the tell-all patient got paid," Katie said. "The billing office is really rackin' up some monster bills. Even *I'm* hearing complaints, and my patients don't talk."

"You know SOS demanded that I pay cash upfront when I came out of the coma," Angela said.

"You were smart to get a lawyer," Katie said. "That made the billing office back off."

"I don't understand why I had two insurance companies," Angela said.

"The university had changed its health insurance plan. You and Donegan were deciding if his new plan was any good. You talked to me about dropping his insurance, but then he, uh—"

Katie stopped.

"Died," Angela said. That word stabbed her heart, but she said it. "And the university told me I had thirty days to cancel, but I never did. I was in SOS before the month was up. I guess they cancelled it for me."

"No, Donegan's department head left you a message—and also told me—that the university would keep you on Donegan's insurance until you were able to make your own decision. So you still have double insurance."

"That's so kind," Angela said.

"They really liked Donegan," Katie said. "But I'd go over your bills carefully as soon as you feel well enough."

"I'm dreading them already," Angela said. She finished her cookie, which tasted like chocolate-flavored cardboard, while Katie sipped her water.

After her burst of energy, Angela was suddenly tired. "What do you hear about Tritt?"

"He hasn't been arrested yet, which surprises the hell out of me. The whole Forest wants him behind bars."

"Why the delay?" Angela asked.

"Not sure," Katie said. "They're having trouble finding another neurosurgeon. Those are in short supply—especially ones with connections to the Forest. The hospital may also hope the Angel of Death case dies down, but that ain't gonna happen. Could be Greiman's waiting for something. Knowing him, he'll make it a real TV news spectacle. He's gunning for Tritt."

"I thought the hospital would at least put him on administrative leave."

"Monty convinced them that would be a very bad idea. Angela, when you're on your rambles, if you hear anything—and I mean *anything*—that can help Tritt, you let me know. Because as sure as I'm sitting here, his ass is gonna be in jail. Tritt killed one of their own, and the Forest is out for his blood."

CHAPTER 30

"So, you want to leave our fine accommodations and go home," Tritt said.

The neurosurgeon woke Angela out of a sound sleep just after midnight, but she didn't care. Not when she heard her favorite four-letter word—*home*.

"When can I go?" she said, sitting up in bed.

He held up a sheaf of papers. He seemed alert and energized. "Your latest blood tests are good, and so are your PT reports. You're working with your cognitive therapist, even if she is a major pain in the ass. And I hear you're walking all over the hospital."

"When can I leave?" Angela asked. She had to pin him down before he started his midnight monologue.

"As soon you have two safety features in your shower: a grab bar and a shower chair."

"I'll call Rick, the handyman, first thing tomorrow," Angela said.

"Katie already did," Tritt said. "You can go in two days."

"Yes!" Angela did a fist pump. "Freedom!"

"Free of the hospital, but lots of sitting in doctors' waiting rooms."

"I don't care," Angela said. "I'm still out of here."

"Just hope you like two-year-old copies of *People* magazine," he said.

"What doctors do I need to see?"

"You're still on warfarin," he said. "That blood thinner takes careful monitoring. Very dangerous drug. It's the same ingredient that's in rat poison. The rats aren't poisoned. They bleed to death."

"Good to know," Angela said. "So how does this rat avoid drowning in her own blood?"

"You'll need blood tests two or three times a week."

"A *week*!"

"Just till your blood levels settle down," he said. "Doc Bartlett can handle them. You'll have to watch what you eat. Spinach and broccoli are natural blood thinners and will screw up your levels."

"They won't cross my lips," Angela said. "Am I on warfarin forever?"

"Depends on if the carotid arteries open up in your neck."

"I hate needles," Angela said. "I'm bruised all over."

"If you want out of here, suck it up," he said. "You'll have to see me at least once a month until I release you, and a dermatologist should check your skin."

Angela looked at her red, itchy arms. Even in the dim light, she could see that her skin was peeling off in strips.

"Here's the name of a good derm doc. Make an appointment ASAP."

"When can I drive?"

"You want to go back to work?" he asked.

"I want my life back, and my death investigator job is a big part of it."

"You have to be seizure-free for six months in Missouri to drive again," he said. "Your last seizure was March tenth. I noted it in your chart. You can start driving in mid-September."

"September! That's forever."

"*If* you don't have any more seizures," Tritt said. "Today is June sixth. You're already halfway through the wait. Be careful not to overdo those late-night walks up and down the halls. You need a full night's sleep."

And your midnight rants don't count, she thought.

"You didn't stop by last night," she said.

"I was in the ER. Double accident. A bad one. Young lawyer—twenty-eight—was clobbered by a truck driver. She was in a Honda. The truck driver was on speed. He wasn't wearing a seatbelt and went through the windshield. He was circling the drain when I got there, but the lawyer survived surgery. She'll make it, but she wasn't as lucky as you."

That word again, Angela thought.

"Why not?" she asked.

"She could be permanently crippled, and she's a trial lawyer. Well, that didn't hurt Ironside."

"Ironside?" Angela asked.

"The TV lawyer, Raymond Burr. Fat cripple stuck in a wheelchair. Remember?"

"Vaguely," Angela said. "That's an old show. It ran in the early seventies."

"Right. The wheelchair didn't hurt Ironside's career."

"His fictional career," Angela said.

"This lawyer's a hell of a lot better-looking than Burr," Tritt said. "Hell, this could be an advantage. The jury will give her a sympathy vote."

"Is the truck that plowed into her owned by a rich company?" Angela asked.

"One of the richest—Cheap and Easy, the big-box company right up there with Walmart and Target."

"Then she'll get a fat settlement," Angela said.

"Not so sure," Tritt said. "Remember Tracy Morgan, the comedian crunched by the Walmart truck? They fought him tooth and nail to avoid a payout. At least this one's a lawyer. Her family's already hired Monty Bryant. Plus, I'll testify for her."

He said this as if the jury were already handing the lawyer a massive check.

"She's got another advantage: that asshole Chip Gravois is dead. He can't screw up her chances for a decent settlement." Angela could see the change in his eyes. They glowed with hatred. Tritt was off, in full doc-dissing mode.

He's obsessed, she thought. *If Tritt is arrested—no,* when *Tritt is arrested—he'll sign his death warrant when he opens his mouth.*

Katie's right, Angela thought as the neurosurgeon ranted. *I'll have to save Tritt from himself. I'll spend tonight roaming the halls, hoping to hear something that will help him.*

Tritt stopped midinsult and looked up at the clock. "Is it really two fifteen?" he asked. "I better get home. I need some sleep."

"You and me both," Angela said, but the clueless doc was already out the door.

CHAPTER 31

Angela was wide awake, dread and excitement coursing through her. Home. She was going home. She snapped open her walker and started scooting down the halls.

"Hey!" Nancy, the blonde night nurse with the magnificent endowment, called from the nurses' station. "Going for a late-night stroll?"

"I need the exercise," Angela said.

"As skinny as you are?" Nancy laughed, and Angela kept walking. After three trips around the floor, Angela became invisible, another accepted part of hospital routine, like the ringing phones and the code calls over the speaker system. Just what she needed for serious snooping.

When Angela passed the nurses' station again, half an hour later, she heard Nancy gossiping with Deb, a hard-faced older nurse with dyed black hair.

"Monty Bryant was in the ICU today," Nancy said. "I offered him a home-cooked meal, but he said he was busy. I don't think he's over his divorce."

"Keep trying," Deb said. "Rich, good-looking, good personality, and his own horse farm. Monty's a nice guy, too. Gave me some of those fancy heirloom tomatoes he raises. They were amazing. Way better than the heirloom tomatoes I got from old man Du Pres. It was nice of the old boy to share them, and his heirlooms looked beautiful. But when I cut his tomatoes open, they were hard and white on the inside."

"My father raises heirlooms," Nancy said. "Old man Du Pres's tomatoes probably had 'white core.' Big problem with tomatoes. They need potassium and nitrogen. That old cheapskate Du Pres probably gave away his heirlooms because he couldn't sell them to the local restaurants."

"Sh," Deb said, looking around. "Be careful what you say about Reggie Du Pres. He's a big deal here."

"Well, Monty's tomatoes were perfect."

"A hottie like that shouldn't go to waste," Deb said. "If I wasn't an old married lady, I'd screw him myself."

Nancy looked up and saw Angela. She waved and scooted down the hall, where she saw an untended computer running, and filed away its location in her mind.

Next Angela headed to the stepdown ICU. Through the double glass doors, she saw Jillian Du Pres, asleep in the solemn darkness. The surviving JJ twin was shrouded in bandages.

Angela gulped back her tears and pushed on to the ICU. She was sorry she did. Angela couldn't enter the unit, but through the glass doors she glimpsed an even sadder sight: a young woman, her head buried under white bandages, breathing to the robotic hiss of a ventilator. Was this the lawyer Tritt had saved? A worried man and woman sat on either side of her bed, each holding one of her hands.

"She's lucky," Tritt had said.

Angela had seen enough luck tonight. She was so tired she could barely trudge back to her room. She crawled into bed and slept until the rattling breakfast cart woke her.

"Rise and shine," said Deb, the black-haired nurse. "I hear you're going home tomorrow."

"Can't wait," Angela said.

"I'm supervising your shower," Deb said. "The hospital wants to know how well you manage on your own."

"I'm ready and rock steady," Angela said.

But when she reached for the walker, she was wobbly. She tried to distract Deb by asking, "You're still on duty?"

"For another hour," Deb said. "You don't look too steady this morning."

"I'm fine," Angela said, but she wasn't. She'd overdone it yesterday. Deb helped her unbutton her gown. Angela forced herself to walk with good form, remembered her training about stepping into the shower. When she was done, she carefully toweled off and dressed for her exercise class.

"Good job," Deb said.

Angela called Mrs. Raines, and her caregiver said, "I'm sorry, but I won't be able to take care of you yet. My current client won't be able to move to her new home for four days."

"I understand," Angela said, wondering if she'd be stuck in the hospital until Saturday.

With that, Tink was in the doorway. "Hey, hey," the PT said. "This is our last day." She was wearing outrageous silver overalls and Day-Glo orange sneaks.

"And you dressed for the occasion," Angela said. "I'll miss you and your fashion sense."

Class went off without a hitch. A harried Katie stopped by after lunch to reassure Angela. "Rick the handyman has installed the grab bar and put together your shower chair."

"That was quick," Angela said. "I'll call and thank him."

"You can do that in person," she said. "A pipe burst in the downstairs bathroom. I told him to go ahead and fix it. Rick is tearing out the damaged drywall and putting in new. He'll be around the house for a while."

"I've got a problem," Angela said. "Mrs. Raines can't stay with me for another four days."

"Then I will," Katie said. "I can stand you until Saturday."

"Thanks," Angela said. She felt the tears gathering.

"Turn off the fucking waterworks, or I'll leave you here," Katie said.

The rest of the day passed in a blur. Angela ate the greasy gray muck passing as beef stew, then fell asleep.

An outraged Tritt woke her at 1:10 that night. "I don't believe it," he said. "That son of a bitch detective questioned me for four hours today. Four hours. Greiman thinks I killed Chip Gravois. I said I wouldn't waste my time killing that asshole."

"You talked to a homicide detective?" Angela said. "Without calling a lawyer?"

"Why should I? I didn't kill the asswipe."

"But Greiman thinks you did," Angela said.

"That's his problem."

"No, it's *your* problem," Angela said. "And it's a big one. The whole Forest thinks you killed Gravois. They want you arrested for murder."

"Then they're all stupid. I can't wait to have my day in court. When I tell the jury what Gravois was like, they'll give his killer a medal."

She closed her eyes. *It's almost over,* she thought. *This is the last time I have to hear about Gravois.* But she wished the neurosurgeon would shut up.

Her wish was granted at 1:20.

"Well," he said. "Guess this is it." He stuck out his hand and allowed her to shake it. It felt strong, smooth, and dry.

"Good luck," she said.

"You, too," he said and was gone.

Now Angela was wide awake. *This is my last night to snoop,* she thought, opening her walker. At the nurses' station, buxom, blonde Nancy stopped her conversation with the hard-faced Deb. "I was gonna rescue you, Angela, but you didn't ring the bell," Nancy said.

"Tritt was just blowing off steam," Angela said.

"I don't like you alone in the room with a killer," Nancy said.

"Tritt's no killer," Angela said.

"Like hell," Nancy said.

"That man's a stone killer," Deb said. "Look, honey, it's nice of you to defend him, but we know you've been a little loopy since your surgery. You can't trust your instincts."

"Tritt's insane," Nancy said. "After I heard him say that he wanted to see poor Chip Gravois in his coffin, I called that nice Detective Greiman. The detective gave me his card—with his personal cell phone number—and said I should call him if I feel I'm in danger."

"He's one sizzling detective," Deb said, fanning herself. "If I were you, I'd need a lot of protection."

Nancy glared at her coworker and said, "He was strictly business. He had me sign a statement and said I'd be called as a witness when Tritt went to trial. Meanwhile, Detective Greiman said I should never be alone with Tritt."

"Too late now," Deb said and snorted.

Is Deb referring to Nancy's rumored affair with the brain surgeon? Angela wondered.

"Detective Greiman says he has four witnesses who saw Tritt drug Dr. Gravois's coffee," Nancy said. "His case is falling into place, and I'm a big part of it. Tritt's getting the death penalty, and I want to be there when he dies."

"If SOS sells tickets, they'll make a fortune," Deb said.

CHAPTER 32

The tree-shaded yard at Angela's white stone house greeted her with a full summer display: red and white impatiens lined the walkway. Red geraniums, purple iris, phlox, and red rambler roses rioted in beds along the freshly mowed lawn.

The air smelled green and alive. Birdsong had replaced the heartless hum of hospital machinery.

Angela was a different person from the woman who'd left here half-dead in an ambulance three months ago. Now she was battered but determined to resume her life. Tears slid down her face as Katie helped her out of her pickup truck.

"What's wrong?" she asked, handing Angela her walker.

"Nothing," she said. "I'm happy to be home." *And I miss my husband.*

Angela felt the warm sun on her skin, thawing the permanent hospital chill. As she scooted along the walkway, Rick met them on the lawn in his handyman uniform of ancient jeans and vintage Grateful Dead T-shirt, with a rather pleasant whiff of sweat and pot smoke. "Hey, there, Angela," he said. "Welcome home. Good to see you."

Rick's dopey smile was genuine. He acted as if Angela always had a shaved head and a walker.

"How are you feeling?"

"I'm home, and everything's fine," she said. It was. Summer had arrived in the Forest. Angela breathed in the green, velvet scent of the grass and felt the soft wind on her skin.

"Mrs. Adams, old Reggie's cook, sent over dinner," he said. "Roast beef, mashed potatoes, asparagus, and a whole apple pie."

"That's so nice," Angela said.

"There's enough to feed an army," Rick said.

Angela got the hint. "Make yourself a plate for dinner, Rick. And thanks for setting up my shower chair and grab bar."

"No biggie," Rick said.

"Angela, how are you getting up the stairs?" Katie asked when they reached the front porch.

"The way Tink taught me in physical therapy," Angela said. "I won't break." Her friend stayed too close, watching while she mastered the two porch steps to the front door.

"See?" she said. "Easy."

Angela's home smelled of lemon polish, old books, cinnamon, and something new—freshly cut wood and an odd, chalky odor. Fresh-cut Sheetrock? She saw dusty footprints leading to the downstairs bathroom.

Ponytailed Rick emerged from the room, wearing clear safety glasses and carefully carrying a monster yellow nail gun.

"New gun?" Angela asked. "Looks like a major machine."

"Just got it. Is this cool or what? This sucker can shoot a three-inch nail more than a hundred miles an hour. It's powerful."

"I know," Angela said. "I was the death investigator on a case where a construction worker got a nail through his skull."

"Accident?" Rick asked.

"That's what his buddy told the police," she said. "But the detective discovered the dead guy was having an affair with his buddy's live-in lover. His buddy nailed his former friend for nailing his lover."

"Wowza," Rick said. "What a way to go. Did you see that story on the Internet about the dude who got a three-inch nail in his head and lived? Awesome X-ray."

"My DI case wasn't so lucky," Angela said. "I still don't like to think about it." She sat in the closest chair for a quick rest.

"I've seen some amazing nail-gun scenes in movies," Katie said. "There's a classic in *Straw Dogs*—the updated version by Rod Lurie."

"I loved that scene, even if I did piss off Mother," Rick said.

"How did that happen?" Angela asked.

"You know my parents sent me to business school. Mother's not happy I'm a handyman, even though I run a successful business. It's too blue collar for her. I'd go nuts if I had to sit at a desk all day. I like my freedom. But Mother is still trying to hook me up with what she calls 'suitable young ladies,' so every once in a while I go out with one to get her off my case. Andrea was the latest. She was a senior at Smith, and she'd broken up with the dude she'd dated since her freshman year. Mother asked me to take Andrea out and escort her to the Daughters of Versailles Ball.

"Andrea had tickets to *Julius Caesar*, and I like Shakespeare. I liked her, too. She wasn't bad for someone Mother picked out. Andrea and I got to talking about how much we liked the classics. So next time, I took her to see *Straw Dogs*."

"For a date?" Angela asked. She couldn't hide her disbelief. "It has a rape scene."

"Hey, it's no more violent than Shakespeare. Ever see *Titus Andronicus*? That has rape and cannibalism. In *Othello*, Desdemona is slaughtered on stage. Shakespeare's chock full of revenge, murder, suicide, and sword fights."

Angela was laughing so hard she had to hang on to her walker, but Rick was serious.

"The fucking *New York Times* said this *Straw Dogs* held up a funhouse mirror to a polarized America. I thought a Smith girl would like to see a movie about the culture wars. Mother was well and truly pissed about *Straw Dogs*. I guess Andrea was, too. She refused to go out with me again."

"Her loss," Katie said. "I'm sorry."

"I'm not," Rick said. He shrugged. "I didn't have to put on the soup and fish and go to the DV ball."

"Too bad you didn't get to show Andrea the nail-gun scene in *Lethal Weapon 2*," Katie said.

"Another classic nail-gun shoot-out," Rick said. "But it bites my butt when the cheap actioners get it wrong."

"How so?" Katie asked.

"They shoot a nail gun like a firearm. You can't do that. *Mythbusters*, the TV show, proved it. They shot a nine-millimeter pistol at fourteen feet—the usual distance for a shoot-out. The gun was accurate. So was the nail gun, but it didn't have enough force. The nails bounced off the target. Nail guns are not lethal weapons unless the gun is actually on the target."

"Didn't know that," Katie said.

"My gun has a sliding safety tip," Rick said, patting his big yellow gun. "The safety tip has to be pushed down first. You can't just pull the trigger and shoot. The new guns force you to push the safety tip against the wood, then pull the trigger, to shoot one nail. You can't have a Wild West shoot-out with a nail gun like this baby. Wanna shoot it, Angela?"

"Sure," she said. She was curious about the machine.

"The gun looks heavy," Katie said.

"It's only about seven or eight pounds," Rick said.

"I can lift that," Angela said.

She was determined to try Rick's nail gun. She scooted her walker into the gutted first-floor bathroom. Only the toilet and sink, gray with dust, remained. The Sheetrock walls were gone, and Rick was working on the wood framing.

"You can shoot a nail right here," he said, pointing to a waist-high two-by-four in the side wall. "First, put on my safety glasses." He slipped his slightly sweaty glasses over Angela's eyes and handed her the nail gun.

Angela thought the power tool felt awkward, but not as heavy as it looked.

"This is a good place to start," Rick said. "No knotholes—I checked. Knots are harder than the rest of the wood, and if your nail hits a knot, it can change direction and hurt you.

"I've marked the spot with a carpenter's pencil. Press the gun tip down. There. Good. See how it grips the wood? Now, keep your free hand away from the nailing point and fire!"

Ka-chunk!

"Hey, I like that," Angela said. "Can I shoot another one?"

"The next mark is six inches away," Rick said. "Put the tip down. Right. Fire when ready."

Ka-chunk!

"Bravo! Want another?"

Suddenly the gun felt like it weighed seventy pounds instead of seven.

Katie looked at her and said, "You're gonna fucking pass out from fatigue. Drop that gun and go to bed."

Angela didn't fight her.

The stairs to the second floor rose before Angela like a mountain. She had no idea fourteen stairs could be so high. She'd climbed only six stairs in physical therapy.

"Can you climb those?" Katie asked.

"Watch me."

Katie stayed two steps behind her as Angela climbed the stair mountain, taking short rests between each step. One. Two. Three. She rested a little longer at the sixth step, then made the other eight at a measured pace. Katie applauded when she reached the hall at the top.

At last Angela was in her bedroom, a light-filled room with pale-green walls and sheer lace curtains. Through the double windows, she could see her mother's deep-pink peonies blooming in the sunny backyard. Katie had a big crystal vase of them on her bedside table.

"Mmm," Angela said. "Peonies smell wonderful."

"The petals fall off too soon when you bring them inside," Katie said.

"Even that's pretty," Angela said. "Your bouquet looks like an Impressionist painting."

The double bed with burled insets had belonged to her great-grandparents. An elaborate sunrise was carved out of mellow wood. Donegan's side of the bed was empty and always would be. She steeled herself to get used to the sight.

Katie must have made the bed. Donegan's soft, plush black robe was neatly folded at the foot of the bed. Angela had slept with the robe in the weeks after he died, lonesome for his familiar smell. She sat down on the pale duvet. The room spun slightly.

"What's wrong?" Katie asked.

"Just tired," she said and yawned. "It's only four o'clock, but I'm ready for dinner and bed."

Katie brought up two plates of Mrs. Adams's hearty food. Angela ate dinner in bed while Katie sat in the easy chair nearby, wolfing down her dinner. By six that night, Angela was asleep, knowing there would be no midnight rant by Tritt.

CHAPTER 33

Angela woke up the next morning feeling weak, tired, and depressed. *Why do I feel so low?* she wondered. *I'm home. I'm getting better. Slowly. I need work to distract me, but right now I can barely climb the stairs. Still, there is one case I can work on: Porter Gravois's murder. Now that I'm out of the hospital, I'll have a clearer perspective.*

She could smell coffee. Katie must have started breakfast. She heard her friend rattling around in the kitchen. Angela had two doctors' appointments today. She showered, then brushed her teeth. Unfortunately, she caught a glimpse of herself in the bathroom mirror: Her face was still swollen, and her skull had an ugly scabbed patch at the surgery site. Gray stubble shot up like weeds on a lawn.

Deal with it, she told herself. But she couldn't help flinching.

She sat on the bed, resting a moment before she dressed, then began the slow trek downstairs to the kitchen.

Katie met her halfway and walked her to the kitchen. "Morning," she said. "I was going to bring you breakfast in bed."

"Thanks, but it's a treat to sit at a table instead of eating off a tray," Angela said. "Yum, oatmeal with honey and strawberries."

While Katie dished out their breakfast, Angela set the kitchen table herself, loading napkins, place mats, and silverware into the basket on her walker, and then sat down.

"Real food," she said. "Hot coffee. Such luxuries." A white mound on the dining room table caught her eye. Three-foot-high stacks of white envelopes were heaped on the dusty surface.

"Are those piles of mail on the dining room table?"

"Bills," Katie said. "Hospital bills. Lots of them. I picked out all the get-well cards and brought them to you."

"How can I deal with all that?" Angela asked. She heard the whine in her voice.

"Later. When you're stronger. Now eat up," Katie said. "You're due at Doc Bartlett's at nine for a blood test, then you see Dr. Hector Mignon, the dermatologist, at ten."

Angela reported to Gerri, Doc Bartlett's phlebotomist. The generously proportioned black woman presided over a closet-size room plastered with funny cat photos and hung with rubber chickens.

"Take this, honey," Gerri said. Angela gripped a worn, brown teddy bear and closed her eyes while the nurse searched for a usable vein. "You've gotta drink more water, Angela," she said. "Here's one. Here's one. Gotcha, sucka!" Gerri stuck her, and Angela yelped.

"Finished, Countess Dracula?" Angela said.

"Till next time," Gerri said. Angela rolled out to the waiting room. Thirty minutes later, she was in Doc Bartlett's exam room. Katie stayed with her.

"You're making progress," Carmen Bartlett said. The internist was a small, smart compact woman. "But promise me you'll start eating healthier. Any questions?"

"When will I stop feeling tired?" Angela said.

"In another month or so. Keep at it, start eating healthy, and rest up."

They barely made the eleven o'clock appointment with Dr. Hector Mignon. The dermatologist's office looked like an upscale spa, complete with bamboo plants, smooth, decorative stones, and semi-Asian music. A slide show on a screen extolled the advantages of Botox, laser vein surgery, and acne treatment while Angela filled out the patient history form.

Angela and Katie were shown into an exam room. Angela sat upright in what looked like a space-age barber chair, and shed dead gray skin on the protective paper. Katie paced.

Dr. Hector was a boyish forty with the red cheeks and pale skin of an English schoolboy. He was shadowed by a twentysomething woman in a white coat and high heels, model thin and creamy skinned, with dark, wavy hair and perfect makeup.

"Olivia Arcola, a dermatology resident," he said. Olivia gave Angela such a contemptuous look, she wanted to shout, "I used to be pretty, too!" Instead Angela felt a deep, wounding shame.

It helped when Dr. Mignon said, "You've been through a lot," as if he admired her, then prescribed a cream.

Angela and Katie were walking back to the shiny red pickup when Angela cried out in pain. Katie turned paper-white. "What is it?" she asked.

"I don't know. I feel like hot wires are stabbing my scalp."

"I'm calling Dr. Tritt's office," Katie said.

"No, it's okay," Angela said, but Katie was already dialing the number on her cell. She explained the problem and said into the phone, "We'll be over in twenty minutes."

Katie told Angela, "That was Gracie, Dr. Tritt's office manager. He has office hours today. He'll wait for us. He doesn't think it's serious, but he wants to check you."

Dr. Tritt's office was empty when they arrived. The long, narrow room reminded her of a railroad car, with better chairs. She smiled when she saw a two-year-old copy of *People* magazine. Angela was looking at photos of Miley Cyrus twerking with Robin Thicke when a nurse said, "Dr. Tritt will see you now."

Angela sat on the exam table, while Katie paced until Tritt bounced in. *The man looks like a bargain-in-a-bag bedding set,* Angela thought. *Where did he get that puffy, pale-blue suit, navy shirt, and color-coordinated striped tie?*

He was carrying a grinning skull with a porthole cut in the right side. Angela had seen enough real skeletons to recognize a high-grade plastic teaching model.

"Thought you'd like to see what you look like now," he said, putting the medically mutilated skull on the exam table. Angela's stomach flip-flopped like a freshly caught fish.

"So what's going on with you?" he asked.

"I feel like someone's shoving hot wires into my scalp."

"That's good," he said.

"It is?"

"It means the nerves are coming back to life." He examined her scalp carefully and said, "You're okay. You have to watch for infection. If you suddenly develop a red lump with fluid running out, then you'll have a real emergency. That's when you call me."

He settled his powder-blue bulk on the counter when his harried-looking office manager stuck her head in the door and said, "You have a meeting in five minutes, Dr. Tritt."

"Thanks, Gracie," he said and gave Angela this cryptic advice: "You need to eat healthier if you're going to get well." Then he hurried out.

"He's the second doctor today to say that," Angela said.

"We were lucky he was called away," Katie said. "He was settling in for a long chat. We would have grown old together in Tritt's office. Let's go home and eat the rest of Mrs. Adams's roast beef. Then I'll get some healthy food."

An hour later, Angela was back in bed with two roast beef sandwiches on whole wheat. She finished her lunch and stared out her open window. A light breeze stirred the lace curtains.

She could see the green rolling hills of the Du Pres estate horse farm, surrounded by pristine white fences. Angela watched the groom, a sun-blasted strip of rawhide named Bud, unloading sacks of feed for the horses and bags of potassium nitrate.

Potassium. Tomatoes. Old man Du Pres raised gourmet tomatoes.

That's when she knew who killed Porter Gravois.

CHAPTER 34

Monty Bryant killed Porter Gravois.

Angela knew it. The answer was right across the way, in the Du Pres horse farm. Like the Du Pres family, the personal injury lawyer kept horses and raised heirloom tomatoes. She felt alert, alive, and electrified. Yes! She was right. Her brain was working.

Wasn't it? For a moment, Angela felt uneasy. *Did I make a massive leap to a dangerous conclusion?* she wondered. *But I didn't imagine Bud or the potassium. Monty is a real person. My skills are back on track.*

She stared at the rolling green hills out her bedroom window and watched old Bud, the groom, feed the majestic beasts after he'd unloaded the sacks of feed and bags of potassium.

Detective Greiman said Porter Gravois's killer would have to be someone connected with the hospital, because the doctor was poisoned with potassium.

But gentlemen farmers used it by the bag for their gourmet tomatoes. Angela's father said it was used in welding and metal casting, and during the winter garages were filled with potassium chloride to keep people from slipping on the ice.

Am I jumping to conclusions? she asked herself again. *Sure, Monty had access to the stuff, but that doesn't mean he killed Porter Gravois.* But she remembered the Angel of Death victims: one was a lawyer for an insurance company. Another worked for a jury consulting business that ruined Monty's chances of getting a big settlement for Patrick.

What if Monty was revenge-killing? She thought about the third victim, a schoolteacher. Was there a connection to the case? Angela checked her laptop. She found the woman's full name: Judy Brown. Her search was complicated because there were a zillion Judy Browns, but Angela finally figured out which one was the Angel of Death victim. Judy had a Facebook page, but Angela didn't see anything useful. Until she read this: "I'm a star! Check out my interview on *Home Court!*"

The Home Court was a local TV program that discussed major cases, from Michael Brown's death in Ferguson to Patrick's court case. Judy Brown was one of the jury members interviewed after Patrick and his mother lost the case. She had a rather plain face, but Judy carried herself as if she were a real beauty. Long hair and expert makeup reinforced the illusion.

"I voted no," Judy said. "Patrick was a nice little boy, but Dr. Porter Gravois said he would be fine, and all he needed was an incentive to recover. I thought it was in Patrick's best interest to vote no, and I don't regret my decision."

Did you regret it when Patrick died? Angela wondered. *Did you even know the incentive plan didn't work, and you condemned Mariah Fargo to a lifetime of hard labor?*

Angela knew Monty Bryant had killed Porter Gravois, but she hoped he'd killed the neurologist to save other lives. He had good reasons.

Gravois was a shill for the insurance companies. He'd cost the lawyer and his clients the money and justice they deserved. Patrick's sad case was the last straw. The lawyer had been at the hospital the day Patrick died, and he'd comforted Patrick's grieving mother.

Tink had told Angela, "Monty is taking Patrick's illness hard. He's one lawyer who actually cares about his clients. The hospital is crawling with ambulance chasers, but Monty's not like that. If they could clone Monty, there wouldn't be any lawyer jokes."

Angela knew Tink wasn't exaggerating. The lawyer had visited Angela in her hospital room and said, "Patrick is my worst failure. A great injustice has been done to that boy—first by the damage from the car accident and then by Porter Gravois's testimony at Patrick's trial."

And Monty had said, "I thought the jury would have had hearts of stone to deny that boy justice—and the money he needed. But Porter Gravois got up on the stand, did his *Father Knows Best* routine . . . That man has done so much damage to innocent people. I wish I could have helped poor Patrick. I have a son his age."

Monty saw himself as a white knight. If he couldn't help Patrick, then he could save other innocent people by killing Porter Gravois. Hell, if he'd offed the neurologist in March, I wouldn't have had to go through the strokes, brain surgery, and a coma.

Porter Gravois was killed by a potassium injection in his hand. Monty could have brought the potassium chloride from his home or stolen it off the crash cart in Patrick's room when he stayed to comfort Patrick's mother after her son died. Either way, he had an easy way to get the potassium.

Monty had been Dr. Tritt's major supporter during the fake reconciliation in the hospital cafeteria. *I admired the way Monty stood up to the hospital administration. The lawyer insisted on going to the cafeteria with the disgraced Dr. Tritt. Monty even got the coffee and carried it to the cashier. Once again, he looked like a white knight.*

But what if he wasn't that noble? What if Monty slipped Ambien into Gravois's coffee then? No one would have noticed.

Monty had sat at a table not far away from Gravois and Tritt in the cafeteria, on the same bench as Gravois. Once Tritt left, Monty could have easily injected the doctor with potassium and walked away.

Monty killed Gravois in front of hundreds of witnesses and left a free man.

It was perfectly clear. But a dolt like Detective Greiman would never see the subtlety. He'd go for the obvious choice—as well as the one that would help his career. He was going to arrest Dr. Tritt, and there was no way the neurosurgeon would get a fair trial in the Forest.

If Angela accused Monty of murder, no one would believe her. But she could trick the lawyer into admitting he killed Dr. Gravois.

Except what excuse could she use to see him? The waning afternoon sun was sliding behind the Du Pres stables, turning the paddocks golden green. Angela loved the view.

My own case! she thought. *I'll call Monty and ask if he'll talk to me about my options now that Porter Gravois is dead. See if there is some way I can sue SOS.*

Yes! She felt elated. Finally, she was getting . . . nowhere. She still couldn't drive. How would she get to Monty Bryant's office?

She heard the garden gate open, and there was Katie lugging an armload of groceries into the backyard.

"I don't know why I'm an expert on healthy food," she said. "My patients don't even eat."

"You at least know what they should have eaten," Angela said. "All I'm getting are sheets of paper with the food pyramid on it. What am I supposed to do with that?"

"Make nifty paper airplanes," Katie said. "Aren't you cold with that window open? The sun's going down. Get your walker, and we'll do Good Food 101 in the kitchen."

The evening breeze was chilly, but it still felt good after months of refrigerated hospital air. "Why are you asking me for cooking advice?" Katie said. "Since when did you get so helpless? Didn't your mother teach you how to cook?"

"Mom was old-school Southern," Angela said. "Everything was either fried, covered with sugar, or both. I got out of the habit of cooking like that. I quit cooking, period."

"Time to get started again. Sit down at the kitchen table. You look exhausted."

"I'm not," Angela said, but she and Katie both knew she was lying.

She watched her friend unpack the bags. "I'm giving you a cooking lesson for noncooks," Katie said. "This is a supermarket roast chicken." She put a domed plastic container in the center of the table.

"Smells good," Angela said.

"It's not the healthiest type of chicken, but I've had your grilled chicken breast. Tasted like a broiled tree stump."

"It wasn't that bad," Angela said.

"The hell it wasn't. I was chewing a rubber glove." Another bag. "These are potatoes, sweet and Idaho whites. Bake 'em both at four hundred fifty. Which do you want for dinner?"

"Sweet," Angela said.

Katie washed and forked a sweet potato.

"Aren't you eating with me?" Angela said.

"Not tonight," Katie said. "I have a date."

"Who with?" Angela asked.

"Never you mind," Katie said. "It's a first date, and I don't want to jinx it. If it works out, I'll tell you more. Now, back to your dinner."

She brought out a bag of carrots and a package of corn on the cob. "These colorful yellow and orange things are called vegetables. You can't have spinach and broccoli, since you're on Coumadin, but there's nothing wrong with carrots and corn. Just dump these in boiling water." She filled two pans with water and dropped in the veggies.

Another bag, this one heaped with dark-red Delicious apples.

"These are apples, and this is a hunk of cheddar. An easy lunch, especially if you use this whole grain bread. Even you can handle that." The cheddar went into the fridge, along with the bread.

"These are bags of salad mix, cut up and ready to go: Italian, seven lettuces, veggie lovers. Pour them in a bowl and add this liquid. It's called salad dressing."

Katie put the bags and a wooden bowl in front of Angela, along with a set of salad tongs, and Angela fixed a salad.

"And this is uncured turkey bacon. No nitrates or nitrites. It's healthy but doesn't taste like it." She flipped the package onto the table.

"Add a tomato"—she put a fat one on the table—"and you have a TLT sandwich. Also healthy. And this is butter. Real butter."

"Isn't that fattening?" Angela asked.

"Have you looked at yourself in the mirror lately?"

"Not if I can help it," Angela said.

"Take my word for it, you can use some fat. Most women can. One thing I'm learning from my patients—the ones I cut up—is they aren't eating enough milk and butter. You need the calcium from dairy products. I'm seeing too many dowager's humps on women who've been dieting for thirty, forty, fifty years. Eat your fat. It's good for you."

"Now that I can do," Angela said.

"And here's your secret ingredient: soy milk."

Angela turned up her nose at the blue half-gallon of soy milk. "Yuck."

"Not as yucky as getting stuck with needles every two days. This will set you free, I promise. I'll make you a soy milk smoothie, my special recipe."

Katie dumped vanilla soy milk, cinnamon, strawberries, and blueberries into the blender on Angela's sink top, whirled it, and poured the mixture into two glasses, then sat down.

Angela took a tentative sip and then a long drink. "That's actually good."

"You don't have to sound so surprised," Katie said. "Even I can grind up fruit in a blender."

"I have to ask one more favor," Angela said. "I need to see Monty Bryant. His office is on your way to work. If I can get an early appointment with him, will you take me tomorrow morning?"

"Of course," Katie said. "He works late—until seven or eight. Why don't you call him now?" She handed Angela her cell phone.

Monty answered his phone. "Angela!" he said. "Why are you calling on Katie's phone?"

"She's at my house, fixing our dinner," Angela said. "May I see you tomorrow morning—early?"

"Eight o'clock okay?" he said.

Angela looked at Katie, who nodded.

"Perfect," Angela said.

"Then I'll see you in the morning. And tell Katie our dinner reservation is for eight thirty tonight. I'll pick her up at eight."

Angela hung up and said, "Monty Bryant, huh? Not bad."

"It's just dinner," Katie said. "Nothing serious."

I sure hope not, Angela thought. *Because I want Mr. White Knight in jail for killing Porter Gravois.*

CHAPTER 35

The next morning Angela woke up and saw Donegan's black robe still folded at the foot of the bed. She hadn't slept with it last night. She gathered the soft robe into her arms and inhaled her husband's scent one last time.

I'll always love you, Donegan, she thought, *but it's time to face reality, no matter how terrible it is.*

She draped the heavy robe over her walker and scooted to Donegan's closet, where his clothes were still neatly on hangers. She hung up his robe and gave it a final pat.

Angela sat back down on the bed to slip on her pants, then stood up again, both hands planted on her walker for balance. She zipped her pants, and they nearly slid off her hips. She cinched her belt to the last notch, then buttoned her blouse. It hung on her like a shroud. Angela stuffed it into her pants. Now she looked like she was wearing another woman's clothes.

She heard Katie in the kitchen. Good. She could put the rest of her plan in place. She pulled her death investigator's kit out of the bedroom closet, fished out the digital recorder, slipped it into her shirt pocket, and buttoned it.

One-party conversations can be legally recorded in Missouri, she thought. *I'll start by getting Monty to discuss Porter Gravois. Then I'll gently lead him into admitting he killed the doctor.*

I'm good at that. I got old Mr. Moulton to break down and say he killed his wife of sixty years. It took more than hour, but he finally admitted that he put a pillow over her face while she napped because she was "cranky" and refused to fix him breakfast.

Even the police had thought Mrs. Moulton's death was natural. But Angela saw—and documented—the saliva on the pillow, and DNA proved she was right. The poor old guy was in the early stages of dementia, and his family quietly got him into care.

Monty was far more formidable, but Angela knew she could handle the lawyer. *I feel sharper today, after a night's rest in my own bed. I'm ready to match wits with Monty.*

Angela felt a little dizzy after getting dressed, but she was thrilled to be on her own for the first time since the strokes. She ignored the hot wires sparking in her scalp, now that she knew that meant she was recovering. She felt an odd, insistent itch at the surgery site. She steeled herself and checked her head in the mirror. It looked okay.

I'm turning into a hypochondriac, she decided. Another reason she needed to go out. She stumped down the stairs with her walker, where Katie had breakfast waiting in the kitchen. After a quick meal, Katie asked, "What's with the carryall? Are you running away from home?"

"No, but since I have another day of doctors' visits, I want to start on that stack of bills. I'm going to be sitting in a lot of waiting rooms."

Angela rolled her walker into the dining room and began stuffing the bag with the bills to the screech of Rick's power saw. Then she carefully made her way to the front porch. Katie's shiny red truck was waiting in the driveway.

"You'll need help up into the truck, but you can do it, Angela," Katie said, throwing Angela's walker in the back. Then she helped Angela climb into the big truck and handed her the carryall.

"Today's a good day for an outing," Katie said. "Sunny and warm." She put the truck in gear and rolled down the drive. "You've got your head stuck out the window. Do you want the air-conditioning on?"

"It's too nice," Angela said. "I'm enjoying the fresh air. I haven't had it in three months." She took a deep breath of the warm June air.

"How are you feeling?" Katie asked.

"Better," Angela said. "Especially after real food—thank you again for dinner—and a night in my own bed."

"Sweet. Now cut the shit and tell me how you really feel. You look pale, Angela. Something's bugging you. What hurts?"

"The nerves are reconnecting in my scalp, and it's torture," she said. "It feels like someone's poking hot wires in my head."

"Ouch. That's natural, but Mother Nature can be a bitch," Katie said.

Angela didn't mention the itch, which was getting worse. That was probably natural, too. "How was your date with Monty?" she asked.

"Nice," Katie said.

"Nice? You went out with the hottest bachelor in the Forest, and that's all you can say?"

"That's all I'm gonna say," Katie said. "You'll get more out of the folks in my steel drawer hotel, so don't try it."

"Can you at least tell me if you have another date with Monty?" Angela said.

"Yes."

"Yes, you can, or yes, you have another date?" Angela asked.

"You figure it out," Katie said.

Katie keeps quiet about her love life only if she's seriously interested, Angela thought. *She'll talk when she's ready.*

Angela was glad she was seeing Monty first. His law office was a low-slung brick building with massive, polished, brass double doors. *Brass is the right material,* Angela thought. Monty had plenty of it. Jealous rivals joked that the lawyer's office was a short ambulance chase from SOS.

"We're here," Katie said. She parked the red pickup in the driveway and helped her friend climb down. "Easy," she said. "Watch your step. You're sure you're okay?"

"Never better," Angela lied. The itch on her scalp had turned into a throb. "Are you coming in, Katie?"

"Nope. I have to stop by the office if I'm going to be running you to doctors all day. I'll be back in an hour."

"Deal," Angela said, "and thanks."

Katie held open a massive brass door for Angela, then ran to her truck. Angela scooted into a waiting room with hunter-green walls and brown leather wing chairs, presided over by a freckle-faced brunette. The receptionist's girl-next-door looks surprised Angela. She thought the dashing lawyer would surround himself with cool Bond beauties.

"Please have a seat," the receptionist said.

Angela didn't sit. Instead, she studied the art on Monty's walls—oil paintings of horses, including what looked like a good copy of George Stubbs's prancing *Whistlejacket.* She switched on the digital recorder in her shirt pocket and was startled when the receptionist said, "Mr. Bryant will see you now."

Monty was on the phone when Angela entered his office, a perfect showcase for a successful lawyer. The massive mahogany desk promised stability. The walls lined with legal books said he was smart and prepared, and a stunning view of the green Missouri hills shouted his past triumphs.

The lawyer was equally scenic. Angela wondered how his exquisite features added up to such a manly face. His wavy hair glowed in the morning sun.

Then she saw those alert blue eyes and knew she shouldn't underestimate this man.

He hung up and said, "Good to see you walking again, Angela. You've made amazing progress."

"Thank you," Angela said.

The freckled receptionist returned with coffee. "Coffee okay, Angela?" Monty asked. "Or would you rather have tea?"

"Coffee," Angela said. "I take mine black."

He handed her a bone china cup and said, "How can I help you?"

"What's happened to my lawsuit now that Porter Gravois is dead?"

"Your suit died with him, Angela," he said.

"But he did so much damage."

"He did," Monty said. "But your damage will heal. You can talk, eat, and walk. You need a walker now, but eventually you won't. Your hair will grow back. In a year, no one will be able to tell you've even had strokes."

"What about his estate? Can we sue that?"

Monty shook his head. "No luck there, either. And there may not be much estate to sue."

"What do you mean?" she asked.

"There are rumors," he said, "that Dr. Gravois was having trouble meeting his financial obligations."

"But he donated fifty million dollars for a pediatric oncology wing," Angela said.

"Yes. But his mother did that, and he got the credit. His father's bad investments and Gravois's high living took care of the rest of the money."

Hadn't Tritt said the same thing, that Porter Gravois was hard up for money? The Forest fed on rumors.

"I hired a gardener he'd let go, and his pool man," Monty said. "Both told me they hadn't been paid in weeks. His widow has quietly put their estate up for sale. I agree that he was a terrible doctor, and

I won't weep at his funeral, but he's gone, Angela. You're alive and recovering."

"But what about my bills? My dining room table is piled with them."

"I'm sorry, Angela, but you're stuck paying them."

"So I can't sue the hospital, either?"

"No. I'm sincerely sorry."

He looked it, too. *Time to try a different tactic,* Angela thought as she sipped her coffee. "I've always admired you," she said. "And if ever a man needed killing, it was Porter Gravois."

He laughed. "Don't quote me, but I agree."

"His death was a public service," she said.

"That's a bit extreme, Angela."

"Is it? After what he did to Patrick? And that boy's mother, who's in debt to SOS forever? Gravois nearly killed me—and God knows how many other people."

"I don't know all his victims, Angela," he said. "I only represented a few. I'm sorry I can't help you."

"You knew about potassium because you grow those fancy tomatoes," Angela said. "Did you take it off the crash cart in Patrick's room or bring your own from your farm?"

"Did I *what?*" Monty set down his coffee cup. "What do you mean, I knew about potassium?"

Here goes, Angela thought. "You killed Dr. Gravois." She kept her voice soft, a simple fact, not an accusation. She got her best results when she sympathized.

"You went to the cafeteria with Dr. Tritt the day of Gravois's death," she said. "You could easily slip Ambien into his coffee, then inject Gravois with potassium and walk away."

"No! Angela, that's crazy." He looked alarmed.

"I'm glad you killed him, Monty," she said. "Who knows how many innocent lives you've saved?"

"Angela?" Monty said. "Are you feeling okay?"

"Sure, why wouldn't I be?"

"Katie said you were making terrific progress, but you still had off-the-wall ideas. This is one of them, Angela. I didn't kill Porter Gravois."

Stay firm, and he'll confess, Angela told herself. "You did," she said. "You're such a white knight, you sacrificed yourself to save others."

"I didn't like Gravois," Monty said. "I'm glad he's dead. But I do my fighting in a court of law."

He needs a little more softening up, Angela thought. "You're a good lawyer, Monty. You could get off with manslaughter. Maybe even community service."

"Angela," he said, "I would never, ever kill Gravois. Think this through," he said. "We both know Detective Greiman wants to arrest Tritt for Gravois's murder, right?"

"Right," she said.

"And it's a matter of time before Greiman cuffs Dr. Tritt and waltzes him through the hospital halls. We also know that arrest would please a lot of important people in the Forest. Yes?"

"Yes," Angela said.

"But I need Dr. Tritt. His testimony is crucial in the personal injury suit for Carter Williams White."

"Who's he?" Angela asked.

"She," Monty said. "She's a trial lawyer who was in a head-on crash with a truck driver. He died, but she survived, just barely."

She remembered the pale figure buried in bandages in the ICU, her parents holding her hands. "I saw her," Angela said.

"I'm going up against the lawyers for a multinational company," he said. "Tritt is my chief weapon. Why would I frame him for murder? I need him to fight the biggest case of my career."

"But—" she said.

"Angela! Look at me." Now Monty's eyes were blue steel. "I would never, ever kill Porter Gravois."

Angela felt her heart freeze. *He's right,* she thought. *How could I be so stupid? I can't trust myself. This is as bad as Katie's nonexistent daughter. And my imaginary hospital visits from Donegan and Mom. No, it's worse. How can I crawl out of here?* She looked around wildly, as if there were a convenient trap door in the floor.

"I'm sorry, Monty," she said. How long should she apologize before she could make her escape? Was there any way out of this?

Then Angela saw salvation standing in the door of Monty's office, covered with freckles.

"Mr. Bryant," Monty's receptionist said. "I'm sorry to interrupt, but Judge Waters is on the phone."

"I have to take this call," Monty said.

"Bye," Angela said. She put down her cup, snapped open her walker, and slid out of the room.

CHAPTER 36

"What the fuck happened?" Katie asked when her red pickup roared to a stop in front of Monty's law office.

Katie, wearing a white lab coat over her gray pantsuit, jumped out to help. Angela was so tired, she could hardly scoot her walker to the truck. Angela collapsed into the seat and closed her eyes, hoping the endless video of her humiliation in Monty's office would quit playing in her aching head.

"An hour ago, when I dropped you off, you looked okay," Katie said. "Now you're shot to shit. What did you do?"

"I made a mistake," Angela said. She could feel the hot wires burning into her brain. Her head was electric with pain and her scalp uncomfortably tight. She was hot and sweaty on this cool June day.

"What kind of mistake?" Katie sounded cautious.

"A big one," Angela said. She took a deep breath before she confessed. She'd have to tell Katie before her friend heard Monty's version. Except there was no way Angela could explain this debacle.

"Uh, I came to a wrong conclusion."

Silence. Ominous silence. Angela pushed on, hoping to get this over with. "I thought Monty killed Porter Gravois."

"You *what*! You accused Monty of murder?"

Angela's scalp felt like it would split like a rotten tomato. She touched the surgery site and felt a hard lump the size of a grape. Something was wrong. Why was she so feverish? She was frightened.

"Angela!" Katie said sharply, to get her full attention. "Let me get this straight. You marched into Monty's office and called him a killer."

"Yes," Angela said. She wasn't sure which was worse—the physical pain in her head or her intense shame, burning her psyche like acid.

"That makes no sense," Katie said.

"It did, kind of," Angela said. "At the time."

Katie glared at her. *At least I didn't accuse Monty of killing the Angel of Death victims, too,* Angela thought.

"No, really," she said. "I used logic: Monty is a personal injury lawyer. Porter Gravois testified against Monty's clients and ruined their lives. Gravois cost Monty's clients the justice they deserved. Patrick Fargo's case was the last straw."

"So Monty fuckin' killed Gravois?" Katie gripped the steering wheel as if she wanted to strangle it—or Angela.

Angela pressed on, her voice shaking with fear. "Hear me out. My idea wasn't that crazy."

"I doubt it, but go on." Katie was seething. For the first time, Angela wondered if their friendship would survive her latest disaster.

"Monty is a good guy," Angela said. "He's practically a saint in a three-piece suit."

"Cut the crap. What's your alleged reasoning?"

"Monty was at the hospital the day Patrick died of kidney failure," Angela said. "The boy was the same age as Monty's son."

"So are thousands of other kids," Katie said.

"But Monty doesn't know them," Angela said. "He didn't watch them suffer. He didn't hear their mothers cry. Patrick's death was personal. Patrick wanted to live but couldn't. Patrick's mother, Mariah, wept on Monty's shoulder. He was in Patrick's room when the boy died. And Patrick didn't die peacefully—his final moments were a brutal rescue attempt. He died while the medical team pounded, shocked, and stuck him with needles. After Patrick died, Monty stayed to comfort Mariah. She'd lost more than her only son. Monty knew that woman was getting a life sentence at her son's death. She was condemned to hard labor to pay Patrick's bills. Monty had failed to get her any money."

Now Angela's voice rose so that it was almost, but not quite, a question. The pain in her scalp was intense. The new nerves danced and capered like demons, poking red-hot pitchforks into her brain. Her scalp felt like it might split. The swollen knot at the surgery site throbbed with her pulse. Fever sweat ran down her neck.

Something was wrong, but Angela tried to ignore it. She had to make Katie understand her misguided trip to see Monty—a trip that now seemed insane. She couldn't lose her best friend.

"Porter Gravois was injected with potassium. I saw Bud, the Du Pres groom, unloading potassium at their horse farm," Angela said. "I realized both Reggie Du Pres and Monty raise those fancy tomatoes. Monty was around potassium all the time. He could have taken it off Patrick's crash cart. Or he could have brought the potassium from his own farm, where he keeps it by the bag. See?"

Seething silence was the only answer.

"Dr. Tritt's fight with Porter Gravois gave Monty the opportunity he needed," Angela said. "The next day, he went to the cafeteria with Dr. Tritt. Monty carried the coffee tray to Gravois's table. That's when he slipped in the Ambien tablets. Then he sat nearby, and when Gravois fell asleep, Monty injected him and left."

"And that's why you accused Monty of being a fucking killer?" Katie said. Her voice was dangerously low. "That's your so-called logic? Monty, a stand-up guy, would betray Dr. Tritt, his friend and ally, and frame him for murder?"

When Katie said it, Angela's reasoning seemed ridiculous. Shame shot through her. Her head was alive with hot needles, and her scalp was about to crack open like an egg.

"You do realize that Monty couldn't kill Gravois by injecting him with the potassium from the bags on the crash cart?"

Angela stayed silent, but Katie's voice was dangerously low. "A little knowledge is a dangerous thing, Angela, and you know just enough to be criminally stupid. You kill someone with *undiluted* potassium. That's why the stuff is kept in vials in the fucking pharmacy. Potassium in the bags in the hospital has been diluted."

"Oh."

"He could have used the potassium in the fertilizer if he'd mixed it with water, but he'd have had to guess the lethal amount."

"Uh."

"And while we're talking stupid, where the hell did Monty get the Ambien?" Katie asked. "Did you even check to see if he takes sleeping pills? Or do you think he keeps them by the bag?"

Angela said nothing.

"So you decided that Monty, an all-around good guy, was so cold-blooded, he injected Porter Gravois in front of dozens of witnesses and then walked away?"

"Uh," Angela said.

"Uh, my ass. Answer me, dammit!"

"Uh, yes," Angela said. "But when you put it that way, it doesn't make a lot of sense."

"Brilliant deduction! Too bad you didn't come to it sooner. So you actually accused Monty of killing Porter Gravois?"

"I tried to get him to admit it," Angela said. Her scalp throbbed so bad, she could hardly talk. The pain was blinding, almost as bad as the migraines she'd had before the strokes.

Through the fog of pain and fear, she heard Katie fuming. "Angela, that is the most assoholic thing you have ever done. It's beyond stupid. It's worse than accusing me of having an imaginary daughter who's running a scam at the hospital. Or those hospital visits from Donegan and your mother! You should be locked up."

"I know," Angela said. She tried to hang her head, but it hurt too much to move. The grape-size lump on her head felt bigger now. It throbbed and ached until she felt it would tear through her skin.

She could hardly hear Katie's next question. "How did Monty react when you accused him of murdering Porter Gravois?"

"Like I was crazy," Angela said. Her jaw seemed to pop from the pain. She wanted to claw her scalp off her head.

"Finally," Katie said. "Somebody reacted normally. Then what did you do?"

What did I do? Angela wondered. She couldn't think. Her head was about to burst. Through lightning flashes of pain, she saw that Katie's truck had stopped at a red light.

"I—" Angela's thought slipped away. Throb. Throb. *Concentrate,* she told herself. Katie was staring at her, her face dark with fury.

"I—" she tried again. Then Angela felt a tremendous pop, and warm liquid ran down the side of her head as if she had a gusher in her skull.

Katie stared at her. "My God, what's the yellow crud running down your head?" she said. Her anger dissolved into concern. "No, don't touch it, Angela. Your head's infected. Fuck, fuck, fuck! What if it's in your brain? No, no, no! This can't be happening."

Angela wasn't worried. Now that the warm liquid ran down her head, the pain was gone. The gunk smelled bad, though. She started to wipe it off with her hand when Katie shouted, "I said, don't touch your head!"

Her voice softer, as if Angela were a spooked animal, Katie said, "Just hold still. Don't move. Easy now." She dug around in her purse for a packet of tissues, pulled out a handful, and gently pressed them to Angela's head to blot the liquid.

"Hold those there while I get off this road." Katie parked the truck in a supermarket lot. "How do you feel?"

"Better," Angela said. She did, too.

"Why are you shivering?"

"I'm cold."

"It's eighty degrees." Katie felt Angela's forehead. "You've got a fever."

Now she was on her cell phone, talking in a serious tone. "Jeb? It's Katie Stern. Angela's got a nasty abscess at the surgery site, and it just burst. Yeah, yellow pus is running down her face. I'll bring her in. On our way. We'll meet you at the ER."

"The ER?" Angela said. "You're taking me back to SOS?"

"Sorry, sweetie, but this is serious." Katie's fury was gone. She gently removed the tissues from Angela's head, now sticky with an evil yellow goo, and dropped them in a plastic grocery bag on the floor.

"Don't touch that bag," she said, giving Angela more tissues. "These aren't sterile, but they'll have to do until I get you to the ER. Watch it! Don't get that yellow gunk in your eyes, or they'll get infected, too. Hang on!" Tires squealing, engine roaring, Katie's truck bounced across the potholed lot toward SOS. Angela clung to the chicken bar with one hand and held the tissues to her head with the other. She dreaded the sight of the sprawling hospital, the source of her loss and pain.

Katie screeched to a stop in front of the ER, grabbed a wheelchair, half carried Angela to it, and rolled her inside.

"Angela Richman," Katie told the ER nurse. "She has a burst abscess on a healing brain surgery site. Her neurosurgeon, Dr. Jeb Travis Tritt, is meeting us here."

The intake nurse bristled at Tritt's name. "This is an emergency room, not Dr. Tritt's personal clinic," the nurse said. "She'll have to be evaluated by the ER physician." She didn't seem to realize that Katie was an assistant medical examiner who worked in the morgue at SOS.

"You're playing politics," Katie said. "If Angela has sepsis, you're looking at major brain damage and an even bigger lawsuit. I'm Dr."—she emphasized her title—"Katherine Kelly Stern, and I'll testify on her behalf."

By the time Katie returned with the walker, Angela had been whisked into an ER room, where a newly hatched doctor met her. He had the fine blond hair and preppie sneer that Angela recognized as the hallmarks of Forest aristocracy. His name tag revealed a powerful Forest surname: B. HOBART.

"What's the *B* stand for?" she asked as a nurse took her temperature.

"Bunny," he said.

Yep, definitely Forest old money. "Related to Jordan Hobart?" she asked.

"Distantly," he said as he probed her head with gloved hands. "That's definitely an abscess. We need to get the rest of that infection out."

He was pressing a handful of gauze on her head when the cubicle door opened, and an enraged Dr. Tritt shouted, "What are you doing, you dumb fuck?"

"Are you speaking to me?" Dr. Bunny Hobart asked.

"You're the only dumb one in here. Angela's the patient. *My* patient. Get your incompetent hands off her and explain yourself."

"This is a spontaneously ruptured abscess," Dr. Hobart said. "I'm draining it by pressing on it."

He pressed a square of gauze on Angela's head, and Tritt screamed, "Get away from her, you stupid shit. That's exactly how *not* to treat an abscess. If you press on the infection, it will spread under the skin and go into the deeper tissues. You'll kill her. You'll ruin her face if that pus gets under the skin there. You'll disfigure my patient. Last thing she needs is another overprivileged asswipe who got a job trading on his name. Get out. Now!"

The young doctor slunk out.

"I don't know how that one even got through med school," Tritt said. "This place is a magnet for dud docs."

"We've got some beauties," Katie said. "But I don't think SOS has cornered the market on incompetents. We keep them as pets. What do you call a med student who graduates at the bottom of his class?"

"I'll bite," Tritt said.

"Doctor," Katie said. "How can I help you with Angela's abscess?"

"I need room," Tritt said. "You're cramping my style and telling jokes because you're nervous. Go wait outside. And don't look so worried. I'll take good care of Angela."

Tritt checked a computer. "At least he had a nurse take your vitals," he said. "You have a fever of one hundred and two. You'll need antibiotics."

"But I'm allergic to all the major antibiotics," Angela said.

"That's why I'm calling in an infectious-disease doc to see if he can find something that will work. You're going to be fine, Angela, just fine. But I'm going to have to get this infection out."

He snapped on latex gloves, then stacked packets of cotton swabs and gauze on a tray. Slowly, gently, he blotted the goo oozing from the abscess. As Tritt carefully patted the wound, the infectious-disease doc came by and prescribed a rare and expensive antibiotic—intravenous Cubicin.

"You'll have to stay in SOS for about a week until we get this under control, Angela," Tritt said. "The hard part will be finding you a bed.

We're short of rooms with the remodeling in the main building. I've got a nurse checking."

Tritt had been working for two hours when a nurse came by. "We found a bed," she said.

"Good!" he said.

"The only one we have is in the new hospice section," the nurse said.

"Even better," he said. "She'll be one of the lucky ones who gets to go home from there."

Angela didn't feel lucky at all.

CHAPTER 37

Angela's hospice room looked like an upscale funeral home. The touches of luxury—velvet curtains, gloomy gold walls, and dark wood—made it feel cold and lifeless. She missed the beige blandness of her old hospital room.

It was five o'clock before she was wheeled into this plush prison. Tritt had worked on the ruptured abscess, making sure the infection hadn't penetrated her brain, and then she was hooked up to intravenous Cubicin.

Katie kept popping in to check on her. Angela was tired and discouraged. After a brief, cruel taste of freedom, she was shut up with the living dead.

She must have slept through dinner. She woke up in the cold, dark room about eleven o'clock that night, lying in state in a hospital bed.

Too restless to fall back to sleep, Angela saw that her hand was once more needle-bruised and shrouded in IV lines. At least her fever had broken. She reached for her walker, scooted over to the closet, and found an extra gown. She slid into it so her backside was covered. She was adept at using a walker and pushing an IV pole—skills she wished she didn't need.

This hospice unit was different from the hospices Angela had visited as a death investigator. Those were more like resorts, with plants, flowers, and pictures of families and pets. They tried to fulfill their patients' wishes, even if the wish was not to die alone and in pain.

This was a money-making mockery of hospice treatment, a warehouse for the dying. On the SOS bulletin boards, Angela saw no programs for hospice patients or their families. No music therapy, pet visits, grief counseling. The pictures were etchings of urns—urns! As if people here needed more reminders of impending death.

Angela heard a man crying for his mother—and fled to the lighted nurses' station.

"You're up, Angela," said a nurse named Suzi. "Would you like a sandwich?"

Angela didn't want to go back to her grim room. She dined on a dry chicken sandwich, graham crackers, and orange juice in a family waiting room with sad, gray furniture.

Then she haunted the dreary hospice halls, restless, lonely, and frightened. She could hear Katie yelling at her: "Angela, that is the most assoholic thing you have ever done. It's beyond stupid. It's worse than accusing me of having an imaginary daughter who's running a scam at the hospital. Or those hospital visits from Donegan and your mother! You should be locked up."

That last sentence scared her. This snafu with Monty was another major miscalculation.

What if Tritt had saved her life, but her mind was permanently damaged? Before the strokes and surgery, Angela would have spotted the flaws in the flimsy case she had built against Monty. She would have never barged in and accused him of murder.

Angela desperately wanted her useful, fulfilling job back. But no matter how healthy she became, Angela couldn't go back to being a death investigator. Not until she regained her reason.

By Angela's fifth circuit of the hospice unit, the nurses didn't look up when she passed. She heard two of them gossiping about Tritt at the nurses' station.

"That detective was here this afternoon. What's his name— Greimer?" That was Suzi, the blonde pixie who'd brought her a sandwich.

"Greiman," said the other nurse, a stately African American beauty named Bethany. "Looks like an actor in a cop show."

"That's the one," Suzi said. "He interviewed me before I clocked in. Spent quite a bit of time with me."

"Oh yeah?" Bethany said.

"Strictly business."

"If you say so."

"I do." Suzi sounded huffy. "I told him I heard Tritt say: 'Someone should do the world a favor and get rid of Gravois.'"

Bethany nodded. "I heard him say that, too. Man wasn't shy about dissing Chip Gravois. Tritt told me, 'Death is the only way to get rid of Gravois for good. The good old boys here will never fire him.' Maybe I should talk to that detective."

"I kept his card," Suzi said. "When is poor Dr. Gravois's funeral?"

"Tomorrow afternoon," Bethany said. "The chaplain is holding a special service in the chapel for staff who can't attend. I'll be there. It's a sign of respect. I used to work in the stroke unit. I heard Tritt is barred from showing his face at the funeral."

"I wonder if Bobbi Heagy will show up at his funeral," Suzi said, lowering her voice. Angela slipped behind a pillar to eavesdrop better.

"She wouldn't dare," Bethany said. "What if Dr. Gravois's wife saw her?"

"Does Cora even know he was banging Bobbi?" Suzi asked.

"The wife is always the last to know," Bethany said. "Chip Gravois was a good man, but even the best ones are human. I blame Bobbi for taking advantage of him. Gravois said he regretted he didn't have a son to carry on his great talent."

"I heard him say that," Suzi said. "But I thought he and his wife were trying to adopt."

"Maybe, but it never happened. Bobbi got herself knocked up on purpose. She thought he'd divorce Cora and marry her."

"That woman was a fool," Suzi said. "A man like Dr. Gravois would never marry a Toonerville nurse. He needed a refined, educated wife who could run his estate and help his career. Bobbi wouldn't have fit in his world."

"But she closed her eyes and opened her legs and thought she caught herself a big-deal doctor," Bethany said.

Angela was shocked by the women's casual condemnation of their colleague.

"The minute she said she was pregnant, Dr. Gravois wanted rid of her," Suzi said. "He gave her money for an abortion."

"I thought he was pro-life," Bethany said.

"They all are—until it's their life," Suzi said. "He didn't want to see Bobbi anymore, but she followed him around like a hurt dog. So he complained that her performance was slipping at the hospital. Pulled some strings and got her another job at Mother of Mercy Hospital. Then he gave her a good reference and got rid of her."

"She got a raise when she moved, didn't she?" Bethany said.

"A nice one—or so she told me," Suzi said. "She drops by here a couple of times a week, but now she makes sure Dr. Gravois's not on duty."

"Guess that won't be a problem anymore," Bethany said. "She can come back any time she wants. Call light's on in 232. I'd better check."

Angela slipped away quietly, trying to understand what she'd just heard. She took the elevator down to the cafeteria. It was twelve thirty, and the workers on the late shift were starting their lunch hour. Angela couldn't drink the sludge that passed for coffee, but Katie said the cafeteria couldn't ruin water.

I'll have a nice, hot cup of tea, Angela thought. *How could they ruin a tea bag and hot water?* She bought a chamomile tea and took her cup to a quiet corner to sort through what she'd heard:

Saintly Dr. Gravois had had an affair with Nurse Bobbi. She'd become pregnant, and he'd forced her to have an abortion.

Angela took a wary sip of tea and quickly set it back down. The tea wasn't hot or nice. It tasted like stewed sweat socks.

Could you force a woman to have an abortion? she wondered. Gravois said he would not support the baby. If Bobbi took him to court, Gravois could get more and better lawyers.

Rather than raise the child alone—or give the baby away—Bobbi had had the abortion. Gravois had then neatly maneuvered her into working at another hospital, for more money. Bobbi was bought off and bundled out of sight.

The nurse had gambled big-time in the marriage market and lost. Bobbi had a good reason to kill Gravois. And access to the fatal drugs. But was she at the hospital the day he died? Who would know?

Angela idly stirred her undrinkable tea and tried to think. There were so many people in the cafeteria the afternoon of the staged reconciliation between Tritt and Porter Gravois, and some were outsiders. Visitors, even ex-employees, had to sign in.

She stared at the machines lining the cafeteria entrance. *Maybe I should have bought machine coffee,* she thought. *Nope, the machine served coffee, hot chocolate, and chicken soup, but it all tasted like soup.*

She saw a tired, gray-haired man buying a candy bar and thought of Terry, the lobby guard who loved Kit Kat bars. All the hospital visitors had to sign in with him. Was he on duty? She'd take Terry a Kit Kat bar and see if he'd talk.

At that hour, the SOS lobby was a vast, high-ceilinged room with a giant steel crucifix on one of the gray marble walls. A janitor was buffing the black marble floor near the door. Terry sat alone on the other side, behind a swoop of stainless steel, with a camera for the visitors' photo IDs, a log book, and a radio on his belt. He was a big-bellied, white-haired Santa, with pink skin and a thick mustache.

"Angela!" he said and smiled. "I'm sorry to see you back."

"You and me both," she said.

"What's with the IV?"

"Scalp infection," she said.

"You be careful," he said. "Hospitals breed superbugs that are hard to kill."

"I know," Angela said. "If the docs don't kill you, the infections will. I brought you a present." She handed him the Kit Kat.

"My favorite!" he said. "I don't get a break until two, and I'm coffeed out. I was wondering how I'd stay awake until then."

He unwrapped the candy bar. "Thanks, sweetheart, I appreciate this."

"Are you bored working nights?" she asked.

"Not really. The days were *too* exciting. First, there was that folderol when Dr. Gravois and Dr. Tritt had the fight and had to kiss and make up in public. I never did like Tritt. The nurses hated that arrogant SOB, and they called all their friends to come watch the show. Tritt slept with most of them. I missed my break, signing in all those angry women. I hope you won't take this wrong, but they were like a coven of witches."

"Was Bobbi Heagy there?" Angela asked.

"The little redhead who transferred to Mother of Mercy? No, she didn't show. She has too much class to sleep with Tritt. Nice girl, Bobbi, but she definitely wasn't here that afternoon."

"Oh," Angela said. Her theory was dead.

"But that same afternoon, Dr. Gravois up and died. Now I'm spending every break and lunch hour talking to the cops. That Detective Greiman, mostly. He took up hours of my time, and I didn't get paid. When it wasn't cops asking me questions, it was reporters trying to get in here. I got my ass chewed out because a TV reporter sneaked up to the telemetry unit. He said he was visiting his Aunt Martha, and there was a Martha by that name in the unit. How was I supposed to know he'd bribed someone in Admitting for a patient's name?"

Terry finished his Kit Kat bar with a resentful crunch.

"I asked them to move me to the graveyard shift. I took this job to supplement my Social Security. I don't need the hassle."

"Why were the cops talking to you?" Angela asked.

"First, it was the Angel of Death business."

"Did you know the nurse, Daniel Cullen Anniston?"

"Sure. I knew the women resented him because he got that big signing bonus, but it didn't bother me. The nurses caught on to him long before the hospital did. There's going to be a hell of a lawsuit over that. A hell of a lawsuit."

"He was arrested the same day Gravois was killed," Angela said.

"If you ask me, that nurse, Anniston, killed Dr. Gravois," Terry said. "I saw him."

"You did? You saw him kill Porter Gravois?" Angela felt a flare of excitement. If the Angel of Death had killed Gravois, then Tritt would be safe.

"Well, I didn't see him stick Dr. Gravois with a needle," Terry said, "but I was making my rounds on the second floor, and I saw Anniston in the chapel, right after Dr. Gravois was found dead, lighting those damn candles. He lit one for every person he killed."

"That's what I heard," Angela said. "Did you tell the police?" For the first time, Angela felt hope.

"I did. I put it in my report, too. The unit nurses were suspicious of him by then and asked me to keep an eye on Anniston. I showed that Detective Greiman my report, but he wasn't interested. He was more interested in flirting with the cute nurse who photographed the candles in the chapel. He took her out for a fancy dinner. Me? I lost my lunch hour, and my report got ignored."

Figures, Angela thought.

CHAPTER 38

"What the fuck is this place?" Katie said.

Angela's breakfast tray had just been hauled away when her friend bounced into her room the next morning, smiling like the first day of spring. One look at Angela's room, and the sunny smile slid off Katie's face.

"This was the only room the hospital could find for me. It's in the hospice unit," Angela said. "You were in here yesterday."

"I was too worried about you to notice your room was decorated as a haunted hospital scene."

Katie pulled over a spindly, black plastic chair and sat by Angela's bed. "Sweet suffering Meryl Streep, this is grim. It's like a fucking Stephen King movie."

"Please, stop," Angela said. "It's scary enough at night."

"Your room makes my morgue look cheerful as a kindergarten," Katie said.

"At least the morgue residents are dead," Angela said. "I can't imagine ending my days here. SOS turned this floor into a hospice unit for fast cash, but they don't offer the victims anything but a bed. They stick people in here until they die, with no comfort or counseling."

"Let me open the curtains." Katie yanked on the dark velvet curtains, and sunlight flooded the somber room.

"The sun makes it worse," Angela said. "It's a tantalizing view of something I'll never see."

"How do you sleep in here?" Katie asked.

"Not very well. I fell asleep right after I was wheeled in here and woke up about eleven. Then I felt like someone had sucked all the air out of this room. I spent the rest of the night roaming the hospital halls."

Angela lowered her voice. "I learned things, too. I overheard the night nurses say Dr. Gravois had an affair with a nurse named Bobbi."

"You're shittin' me." Katie looked genuinely surprised. "I've never heard a whisper that Saint Chip was doing the wild thing. You say it was Bobbi. Bobbi Heagy, that curvy little number with the long red hair?"

"I think so," Angela said. "I've never seen her."

"Gravois had good taste," Katie said. "Bobbi has looks, brains, and personality."

"The story gets better," Angela said. "Gravois liked to talk about how sad it was that he didn't have a son to carry on his great talent."

"For screwing up lives?" Katie said. "I thought he and his wife were looking to adopt."

"So did the night nurses. But they said nurse Bobbi took him seriously when he said he wanted a son and got herself knocked up on purpose."

"Don't tell me," Katie said. "She thought he'd leave his wife and marry her?"

"Yep," Angela said.

"Some women never learn," Katie said. "And it's the smart ones who fall for the old wheezes."

"I don't know how smart Bobbi is, but she fell for it," Angela said. "She got pregnant, and Gravois forced her to have an abortion."

"Forced her how?" Katie said. "Kidnapped her and held her down?"

"Refused to give Bobbi any money, except to terminate the pregnancy."

Katie looked shocked. "This is definitely news to me."

"It gets better. Gravois wrote a bunch of reports criticizing Bobbi's performance."

"In bed or on the job?" Katie asked.

"At SOS. Until she had to leave here. Then he found her a better job with higher pay at another nearby hospital, Mother of Mercy."

"Well, I'll be damned," Katie said.

"Probably," Angela said with a grin. "But I hope you won't be in the same circle of hell as Porter Gravois."

"That miserable hypocrite," Katie said.

"The night nurses wondered if Bobbi would show up at Gravois's funeral," Angela said.

"The funeral service is by invitation only," Katie said, "and I didn't get an invite. Since I autopsied him, it would have been polite. After all, I had my hands in the man."

"I don't think Miss Manners covers that etiquette problem," Angela said. "But I'm betting Bobbi didn't get an invite, either."

"She can't go to the funeral," Katie said. "But there's nothing to keep a rejected lover from making a hell of a scene at the cemetery."

"That would send the Forest gossip mills into overdrive," Angela said. "Lord knows nurse Bobbi had a good motive to kill Porter Gravois—and the means."

Katie tensed. "Oh no, Angela. Don't tell me you've got some half-assed theory."

"No! I tested it first. You'll be so proud of me. I didn't know if Bobbi was at the hospital the afternoon Gravois died. Instead of jumping to conclusions, I checked with Terry, the desk guard."

"He's working nights now?" Katie said.

"He requested a transfer," Angela said. "Between Gravois dying, the Angel of Death, and the hordes of reporters trying to sneak into the hospital, it was too much. He was on duty last night. I got him a Kit Kat bar."

"The only edible thing in the cafeteria," Katie said.

"You got that. They can't even boil water. Terry told me Bobbi was nowhere near the hospital the day Gravois was killed."

"You checked with him?" Katie said.

"You bet," Angela said.

Katie smiled. "That was the sensible, logical thing to do. You're getting your mojo back."

"I hope so," Angela said. "I still have to apologize to Monty."

"Forget about it," she said. "I talked with him last night. The best thing you can do is never mention the incident again."

"You went on a date last night?" Angela asked.

"Did I say that?" Katie asked.

"Still playing your cards close to the chest," Angela said.

"Leave my boobs out of this discussion."

"Speaking of boobs, Terry told me something about Ray Greiman," Angela said. "Terry says he ran into the Angel of Death—Daniel Anniston—right after Gravois's body was found. Terry was already watching for Anniston. The nurses had tipped Terry off that Anniston was a suspect. Terry noted what he saw in his report, but Greiman ignored it. He was too busy flirting with the nurse who took the photos of the candles. Typical Greiman, careless as usual."

Katie sighed. "I hate to bust your balloon, Angela, but Greiman was right."

"What?"

Katie held up her hands. "Hey, I know you don't like him. I'll personally nominate him for Jerkoff of the Year. He's careless and dumber than a box of hammers. But this time, Greiman was right. Nurse Anniston, the Angel of Death, always lit one candle for each victim. That's how the nurses in his unit caught him. They noticed his habit of lighting candles in the chapel, first one, then two, all the way up till there were nine. The candles corresponded to the number of Angel of Death victims. And the last victim was Judy, the math teacher."

"But Gravois died the same day," Angela said.

"Yes, and the Angel of Death went to the chapel and lit nine candles," Katie said. "Only nine. A suspicious nurse followed him and photographed the lit candles with her cell phone. The Angel of Death didn't confess to murdering Gravois. He never lit ten candles. They were part of his ritual. If he'd killed Gravois, he would have lit another candle.

"Also, the Angel's victims were injected in the foot, not in the hand, where Gravois was injected. Much as I'd like to pin Porter Gravois's death on Anniston and make this go away for Tritt, the Angel of Death isn't guilty of killing Gravois."

"Oh." Angela felt like she'd been punched in the stomach.

"But, hey, you deserve a pat on the back for checking before you started pointing fingers. Good move. Good thinking. Did you learn anything else from Terry?"

"He gave me some medical advice," she said. "He said I should get out of here ASAP because there are superbug infections."

"Terry's right on target, but you're stuck here for a while. Tritt thinks he let you go home too soon. I brought your books and that carryall full of bills. There's enough in there to keep you busy."

"And more bills on the way," Angela said.

Angela looked around the funereal room. She heard someone moaning across the hall and shuddered. "I have to get out of here," she said. "I can't stand a week in this place."

"Come on," Katie said. "I know it's scary, but you can do it. See what you can find out about Tritt. He needs you."

"Why?"

"Because I heard he's going to be arrested right before Porter Gravois's funeral: sacrificed to the gods of the Forest."

CHAPTER 39

"Hey, Angela, you look a helluva lot better this afternoon," Tritt said. The neurosurgeon's big voice and bigger personality filled Angela's dreary room, chasing away the gloom.

Dr. Tritt wore the only clothes that suited him—green hospital scrubs and a surgeon's cap. He checked her chart, then said, "Temp is normal and has been since last night. Good." With gloved hands, he removed the gauze covering the ruptured abscess on her head and said, "Nice. Pink and healthy. The Cubicin is kicking in."

"What happens if I get allergic to the Cubicin?" Angela asked.

"Then you'd better pick out a comfy casket, because that's the last resort."

"The longer I'm in the hospital, the riskier it is. Get me out of here," she said.

"Can't. You need at least six more days of IV antibiotics."

"Hospitals are growing bigger and badder bugs."

"That's why I put you in another private room. It cuts the risk of infection. Your lunch is here. Eat. Food will make you feel better."

The hospital lunch lived up—or down—to Angela's expectations. She picked at her mushy green beans and poked her limp salad. The gristly gray hamburger, grandly christened a Salisbury steak, was a perfect example of dead meat. She wolfed down her chocolate cake and fell asleep, dreaming of her brief time at home.

"Angela, darling, did I wake you?"

Emily Du Pres, the Forest's first death investigator, swept into the room carrying a huge bouquet. She looked like a small, elegant bird of prey in a slim black suit and an honest-to-God black hat with a veil.

"I did wake you up, didn't I? I'm so sorry." Emily oozed insincerity.

"Darling, we're all devastated you're back in the hospital. Reggie sent me with these flowers from his own garden—iris, phlox, and roses. Aren't they lovely? So much nicer than hothouse flowers, don't you think?"

So much cheaper, too, Angela thought. *Old Reggie Du Pres didn't get to be the richest man in the Forest by throwing money at florists.*

"Lovely," Angela said.

"Reggie hopes you'll see his daylilies when you're out of the hospital. They're especially fine this year, but they don't make good bouquets. You need a vase, don't you?" Emily said *vahz*.

"How is Mr. Du Pres after the JJ twins' terrible accident?" Angela asked.

"He's doing as well as can be expected," Emily said. "But those beautiful girls were the apple of his eye. Jordan's death caused him great distress. And poor Jillian will never be the same. What a shame she was so disfigured before her coming out. She'll still be a Daughter of Versailles, but she would have made a much prettier queen before the accident."

A nurse appeared in the doorway and asked, "How can I help?"

Emily handed her the bouquet and said, "Find a vahz for these flowers. Make sure you cut the stems before you put them in water."

If the nurse objected to being ordered around like a servant, she didn't say anything. In the Forest, a Du Pres wish was a command.

"Reggie wanted to thank you, Angela dear, for the sensitive way you handled the JJ twins' tragedy. We're glad you insisted the driver of the other car be Breathalyzed. He'll be held accountable. I'm on my way to poor Porter Gravois's funeral," Emily said. "Such a loss."

"Sad," Angela said, a comment she hoped could be taken many ways.

"Reggie is hoping you'll show the same good judgment and sensitivity with dear Porter's death."

"I'm not sure what you mean," Angela said.

"We've heard you've been asking questions about Porter's death, wanting to know who was in the hospital the afternoon he was murdered."

Terry, Angela thought. *The sweet old security guard sold me out. He went running to the Du Pres family when I asked him about Bobbi Heagy.*

"I mentored you, Angela," Emily said. "And I did the death investigation for Porter. A very thorough one. There is no reason for you to investigate his killer. It's not your place. Detective Greiman is in charge of the murder investigation. He has a suspect who will be arrested soon."

Emily didn't mention Tritt's name.

"What if the suspect didn't kill Dr. Gravois?" Angela asked.

"Of course he did, dear. There's no question. I know you believe he saved your life. Loyalty is a commendable quality, but your first loyalty is to your community."

Angela didn't say anything.

Emily, delicate, fine-boned, daintily wrinkled, rushed on. "You may own your house, but you don't own the land it's on," she said.

Angela heard the steel behind that gently quavering voice. "Reggie has the right to buy it back if he decides he wants the land it's on—and the terms of the deed say he has to pay the purchase price, not the market value of your home. Your parents paid twenty-five thousand dollars for that house. You couldn't buy much for that, could you, dear? Especially if you don't have a job to go back to." Emily checked her watch. "I must run. Porter's service is starting soon." She patted Angela's hand.

"Your job is waiting when you get well. Rest up, dear. Don't do anything foolish. I want to go back to Palm Beach as soon as possible."

CHAPTER 40

Angela watched Detective Ray Greiman slide out of the shadows in the sunless marble lobby at SOS, like the predator he was.

Tritt, striding across the lobby, stopped when Greiman ambushed him. Angela saw the spectacle from the far corner of the vast, dark space. Angela had been too upset and restless to go back to sleep after Emily's visit. She roamed the halls until she wound up in the lobby on a hard marble bench.

It was three o'clock, and everyone who was anyone was at Our Lady of the Forest Catholic Church for Porter Gravois's funeral.

In the hospital lobby, Tritt was surrounded by Greiman and four uniformed officers, unable to move in any direction. Behind the police, a TV camera lit the scene with a harsh glare. The photographer looked like he had slept on a park bench.

Greiman was dressed for TV success in a tailored blue suit, blinding white shirt, and power tie. Tritt's brown polyester suit looked like a mudslide. Even his clothes looked guilty.

"I know you killed Dr. Porter Gravois," Greiman said. "I have a warrant for your arrest for murder one."

Angela was glad she was sitting down. First-degree murder was a death penalty offense in Missouri, a state that eagerly executed the guilty. The Forest would use all its political muscle to kill Tritt.

As the church bells tolled for Porter Gravois's funeral, Angela heard Detective Greiman give the familiar chant, "You have the right to remain silent . . ."

But Tritt didn't. He screamed, "What the fuck? I'm a doctor. I never killed that asshole, but he deserved to die. Do you know how many people he killed? Legally? And got away with it?"

Shut up, Tritt, Angela wanted to say. *Please shut up and get yourself a good lawyer.*

But he didn't. The neurosurgeon's face was red with rage, and his eyes were wild. His sweat-damp hair was plastered to his big head. Tritt looked like a crazed killer. Everyone who saw this scene on TV would assume he was guilty.

Now the vast, empty lobby was filled with people—and all of them hated Tritt. They were silent, but they reminded Angela of the mob outside Dr. Frankenstein's castle, armed with torches and pitchforks.

Angela saw Nancy, the honey-blonde nurse with the high breasts, glaring at her ex-lover. Tink had dyed her hair powder-blue and stood out in the crowd. Deb, the hard-faced older nurse, was smiling. Pretty Linda Marie Partod, the countrified nurse, looked frightened. Lynette Riskin, the short, robust nurse in the teddy bear scrubs, crossed her arms and watched, stone-faced.

Dr. Bunny Hobart, the "overprivileged asswipe who got a job trading on his name," as Tritt said, sported a satisfied sneer.

Now a flying wedge of hospital hierarchy pushed through the crowd. Angela recognized them from the cafeteria reconciliation: starchy, rotund Carlton DeVree, the chief of staff, and skeletal Hampton Mann, the peer review officer, his giant ears flapping like open car doors.

They were led by the hospital director, Dr. Stanleigh Elkmore, his pink skin a dangerous red. "Who let in this TV person?" he demanded.

He clapped his hand over the camera lens and asked, "Is your microphone on?"

The TV photographer nodded. "Then get this," Dr. Elkmore said. "You do not have permission to tape anything on hospital property, do you understand? If this appears on the news, you'll be hearing from our lawyers. Now get out."

Dr. Elkmore waited until the TV photographer scuttled away, not realizing that his outburst would ensure the tape of Tritt's arrest would run endlessly for the next forty-eight hours.

"Greiman!" Dr. Elkmore said. "Get this man out of here."

As Porter Gravois's pallbearers guided his flower-decked casket up the church aisle, his accused killer was led away in handcuffs. Gravois's funeral was taped, and later, people would talk about that remarkable coincidence, as if Tritt's arrest were divinely inspired.

Tritt, cruelly handcuffed with his hands behind his back, was led away, a hostage in a Forest war he never understood.

CHAPTER 41

The hospital's driveway was blocked by half a dozen police cars and a TV truck. A handcuffed Tritt was roughly shoved into a police cruiser. Angela winced when he hit his head on the door frame. The pack of cop cars took off, sirens flashing, the TV truck roaring after them.

Angela went back to her gloomy room and listened as the emaciated young man in the next room moaned and wept for his mother.

That poor man, Angela thought. *He doesn't even have the comfort of imaginary visitors.*

She wondered if she should sit with him and hold his hand, but she knew she was still at risk of getting an infection.

Reggie's home-grown bouquet, the weedy warning delivered by her mentor, Emily, was dying. The rose heads drooped, the iris shriveled, and the phlox shed their purple petals. *I'm in death's waiting room,* she thought.

She curled up on the bed and hoped she'd sleep. Instead, Katie burst into the room.

"Tritt's been arrested," she said.

"Greiman did it in the worst possible way," Angela said, "with maximum publicity and drama. He even had a TV camera there— and I'm sure he tipped off the station. Tritt will be all over the news tonight. And he couldn't keep his big mouth shut. After he got a Miranda warning, he still kept attacking Porter Gravois. On the day of the man's funeral!"

"It's on TV as a breaking-news bulletin," Katie said. "I was getting some water in the cafeteria when it came on. The place stopped dead to watch it. First, the station showed Gravois's funeral at Our Lady of the Forest Church. All the bigwigs were there in black, along with enough flowers for a mob funeral. Next, the station interviewed his teary-eyed wife at the cemetery. She wore a Jackie Kennedy veil, like she was a presidential widow, and boo-hooed about the loss of her wonderful, loving husband, who was cut down in his prime. Half the people in the SOS cafeteria—staff and visitors—were crying along with her. Many of them didn't even know the bastard."

Angela groaned.

"Then the station switched to Tritt's arrest," Katie said.

"Did they show his handcuffs?" Angela said.

"They showed a lot more than that. Tritt was screaming, 'I never killed that asshole, but he deserved to die. Do you know how many people he killed? Legally? And got away with it?' The halfwit wouldn't shut up. I called Monty and asked him to recommend a criminal lawyer. I just hope it isn't too late."

"Why?" Angela said.

"The station has run that breaking news story three times already. The jury pool is as contaminated as an open sewer, Angela. Tritt has been electronically lynched. Who sent the dead flowers?" Katie asked.

"Emily delivered them with a message from old Reggie." Angela was so angry, she had trouble speaking.

"What message?" Katie said.

"Terry, the security guard, must have told Reggie that I was asking about Bobbi Heagy, the nurse who had an affair with Perfect Porter. You said you'd never heard any scandal about Gravois playing around."

"Right," Katie said.

"The Du Pres family must have known about his fling," Angela said. "I asked Terry if Bobbi was in the hospital the afternoon Porter Gravois died, and the next day Emily stops by and orders me to keep my nose out of the investigation if I want my job back."

"That old bat threatened you?" Katie said.

"It gets better—or worse. Emily reminded me that my parents bought the Du Pres guest cottage, but they didn't own the land, and Reggie could claim it anytime. All he has to do is write me a check for what my parents paid fifty years ago—twenty-five thousand dollars."

"You gotta be kidding. That's pocket change for Reggie," Katie said.

"So, if I keep looking for Gravois's real killer, I'm going to be homeless and jobless."

"You're not going to stop, are you?"

"Hell, no," Angela said. "There are death investigators all over the country. I can work anywhere."

"The Du Preses are a powerful family," Katie said. "I'm worried what they could do to you."

"They aren't going to kill me," Angela said. "The worst they can do is hurt me financially. Their reach doesn't extend past the Forest."

Katie was gone when Angela's bedside phone rang, and she found herself talking to Rick, the handyman. She swore that a wisp of pot smoke wafted out of the clunky receiver. "Some old dude came by and said I should give you a message," Rick said. "Thought I better call before I forgot it. Dude's name is Rodney Beck—he works for old Reggie Du Pres."

"I know him. He's about fifty, sunburned, pale-blue eyes, bit of a beer belly, right?" Angela said. "I'm not sure of his title, but he helps manage things for Reggie."

"That's him. He stopped by while I was working this afternoon and asked what I was doing. I said I was putting in a new bathroom after a pipe burst. He said something really strange: 'Tell Angela not to spend too much money. Mr. Du Pres may want his house back.' What's that mean?"

"Nothing," Angela said. "Nothing at all."

CHAPTER 42

A new nurse, Laurie, came in to take Angela's vitals. Angela felt like an empty box that had been dutifully checked on a form. The man next door moaned and cried for his mother. And the shadows in Angela's room seemed to shift and gather in the corners, waiting for her. Even her fury at the Du Pres family couldn't warm her unnaturally cold room.

I need something else to think about. Time to tackle those envelopes Katie brought me, Angela thought.

The envelopes were covered with a fine layer of slightly gritty dust. By the time Angela had plowed through half a stack, she was overwhelmed and bewildered, and her hands were gray.

Some envelopes held EOBs—explanations of benefits from her insurance company that didn't explain anything. One said: "Laboratory services 05/12/2016: Amount billed $55.16. Not covered $50.03 (1) The amount billed is greater than the amount allowed for this service. Based on our agreement with this provider, you will not be billed the difference."

The amount covered was $5.13. Did that mean some poor sap who didn't have insurance got walloped with an overpriced lab test for $55.16? And what exactly did the hospital test for? There was no explanation.

The bills were even more inexplicable. Angela waded through charges for X-rays, blood tests, MRIs without dye, physical therapy, drug therapy, medication monitoring solutions. A battalion of doctors had poked, prodded, cut, examined—and billed her. Angela found statements from anesthesiologists, radiologists, pathologists, immunologists, and emergency department physicians.

She had a vision of herself lying in her hospital bed, a feast for vultures and carrion crows.

When she found a $500 bill for an "emergency neurology consult" with Dr. Porter Gravois, she screamed and threw down the bill in disgust. She could feel her blood pressure skyrocket.

She had to pay for her own misdiagnosis? Outrageous. Porter Gravois's rotting corpse would have to rise out of his grave to collect that money.

Angela stood up, shaking with anger, and pushed her walker into the bathroom so she could wash her hands. Then she headed down the hall to get a cup of coffee in the family waiting room. She needed to calm down. She had to think. With shaking hands, she poured herself a cup of sludge from the pot on the burner, then took the thick bitter brew back to her room. She was ready to tackle more bills. The next one was an explanation of benefits from her insurance company for surgery. She wondered if Tritt really did get $3,000 for her brain surgery, like he said.

Except this wasn't a bill for a craniotomy. The explanation of benefits said Angela's insurance company had paid SOS $3,422.18 for a "total hysterectomy."

A what? She read the EOB again. Carefully. She couldn't believe it said that, but the words were right on the paper.

I never had a hysterectomy, Angela thought. *I can't tell how many blood tests and X-rays I've had, but a womb is a body part a woman keeps track of.*

When was this mythical operation? The EOB said 05/10/2016—May 10. *But I was taking physical therapy for my strokes then. Who performed this operation?* The EOB didn't explain.

But Angela knew the surgeon's bill had to be somewhere in the stack. She ripped through three more EOBs before she found it: her insurance company had paid $1,746 to Dr. Du Barry of Du Barry Surgery Associates.

Who is Dr. Du Barry? Angela wondered. *And where is Du Barry Surgery Associates?* She knew a lot of the medical professionals in the Forest because of her work, but she'd never heard of any doctor named Du Barry.

Angela fired up her laptop and Googled the names. She couldn't find a Dr. Du Barry in the Forest—or in Missouri, for that matter.

Just to make sure, she called SOS. "I'm sorry, ma'am," the hospital operator said. "We have no Dr. Du Barry on staff, and no physician by that name is affiliated with Sisters of Sorrow Hospital."

But the name was familiar, and not just because of Madame Du Barry. There was a Du Barry in the Forest. Then the answer hit her. Of course. Du Barry Circle. That's where Porter Gravois's mansion was located. She remembered the midnight rant when she'd told Dr. Tritt that Du Barry Circle was "the top of the tree in the Forest."

Only the Forest, which loved all things French, would name the grandest street after the official mistress of Louis XV—a woman of the streets.

Angela had thought because Porter Gravois lived in Du Barry Circle in a French castle, that was proof he was old money—and had plenty of it. After all, he'd donated $50 million for the pediatric oncology wing. But Tritt claimed Gravois's mother had donated that wing "anonymously" but wanted her son to get the credit. Gravois had named the wing after his mother.

Dr. Tritt had sworn that Porter Gravois had money trouble: "His father was a lush and lost most of the family fortune on bad investments," including the money his wife left. "Gravois was short of cash. He sold his private plane and joined some kind of rich people's club where they pool their money to buy and maintain a plane. There's a hefty discount if you pay your Chouteau County taxes early. Gravois didn't take it. In fact, he hasn't paid them yet . . . His wife stiffed the Forest Party Shoppe in Toonerville nine hundred bucks for her annual holiday party."

Now Angela had to face another painful memory: her disastrous visit to Monty Bryant's office, when she'd accused the lawyer of killing Gravois. Monty had told her the same story as Tritt: Gravois was in financial trouble. "I hired a gardener he'd let go, and his pool man," Monty had said. "Both told me they hadn't been paid in weeks. His widow has quietly put their estate up for sale."

Those three facts showed that Gravois was short of money when he died. Worse, his lack of cash was starting to be noticed in the Forest.

Cash. Cash was part of another puzzle, Angela thought.

Gina Swinny in the billing office wanted me to pay $100,000 because I didn't have a primary insurance. Then Gina offered me a bargain. She'd take only $10,000. Instead I called my lawyer, Tom Wymen, and he had said, "Tell her to pound sand. What's she gonna do, repossess your brain? Better yet, I'll call this Gina now and end this today." Gina had backed off.

Angela knew that wasn't standard billing procedure. That was extortion.

During his midnight rants, Dr. Tritt had insisted that Gravois was a crook. The brain surgeon swore that Gravois's lavish life "needed an endless flow, and someone was turning off the tap . . . You ask me, he was doing something sneaky with the billing office."

Angela had thought Tritt was blinded by hatred. She hadn't believed him. And Tritt had told her, "I'll give you a place to start your investigation. The hospital billing office. I used to see Gravois hanging around there all the time, talking to Gina Swinny."

Tritt had laughed at the idea that Gravois was having an affair with grandmotherly Gina and insisted their shenanigans were financial, not sexual.

Gina Swinny. The same woman who'd tried to hold Angela up for $100,000, then $10,000—until Angela's attorney had chased Gina away.

But Angela didn't start her investigation with Gina in the billing office. Instead, she'd dismissed Tritt's accusations. But he was right. The billing office was running a scam. And Angela was sure the late Porter Gravois had been part of it.

This time, I'm not crazy, she thought. *This bill for my imaginary hysterectomy is proof. In writing.*

CHAPTER 43

Why was Gina Swinny running a scam out of the hospital billing office? Did the office director need money? How did she live? Where did she live?

What did Angela know about the woman?

Not enough.

The Internet might have the answers. Angela Googled Gina Lorraine Swinny's name and discovered she lived in Toonerville. Google Earth showed a neat, 1970s two-bedroom brick rambler with white trim and a manicured yard.

Angela found a few news stories in the *Chouteau Forest Chronicle*, the local free paper.

On February 17, 2014, the hospital public relations department announced in the Promotions section, "Mrs. Gina Swinny, age sixty-two, has been promoted to billing office director at Sisters of Sorrow Hospital." Yep, that was Gina in the photo: a matronly woman with short, neat gray hair and eyes hard as agates.

In May of that year, the *Forest Chronicle* had this one line:

Mrs. Gina Swinny Elected President of the Ladies' Sodality at Our Lady of the Forest Catholic Church.

A position of influence and importance in the Forest, Angela thought.

She kept reading. Last September, the SOS website announced, "Mrs. Gina Swinny has been awarded a twenty-five-year service pin at the annual luncheon honoring our valued hospital employees." Twenty other employees and their titles were also listed. Their frozen smiles were captured in a stilted photo.

Angela wondered if the honorees' luncheon was catered by the hospital cafeteria. She hoped not, for their sakes.

So far, all Angela saw were the hallmarks of a modest, hardworking life. There was no hint that Gina was a crook. But why would a model citizen embezzle money in a billing scam?

Angela needed more information, and the Internet was her only way to search. Gina was a faithful Facebook user. Angela looked up her page.

Unlike some Facebook users, who limited their personal posts to family or friends, Gina was a trusting soul who shared all her information. Nothing was off-limits.

Gina came alive on her page. She was a widow who'd been married for forty-one years to Percival Swinny. She'd posted their wedding picture, a faded color snapshot of a slim, brunette Gina in an empire-waist gown, and her shy, sideburned groom in a black tux with a ruffled shirt and a butterfly bowtie. The two were the height of seventies fashion.

Angela already knew Gina was a grandmother, but on Facebook, Grandma Swinny was a tireless paparazzo, photographing her grandchildren at every holiday and life event. Angela saw that five-year-old Ian was a carrot in the Healthy Food Pyramid Pageant at his kindergarten. Baby Mason was an adorable bumblebee last Halloween.

Tow-haired Amy had a pink princess cake for her sixth birthday, baked by her mother, Maybelle.

Gina liked to quilt. Her colorful projects got dozens of Likes, and she donated them to the church auction.

Gina often dined with friends and family. In February, she had photographed her plate of chicken parmigiana at the Olive Garden, then took a selfie at the restaurant with a smiling, buxom redhead. "My favorite drug dealer," she wrote, "Marcie from the SOS pharmacy."

Gina was plagued by health problems, and she bared them all. She talked about her bunions in loving detail, as if they were naughty pets. "Little buggers are really aching in this rainy spring weather."

She was a martyr to sciatica. "Streaks of pain running down my legs. No relief. No sleep." A week later, she posted, "Hallelujah! My doctor prescribed Ambien. Now I'm sleeping a solid eight hours."

This March, she wrote, "At work, but not feeling well. Popping aspirin like crazy, but can't make the headache go away. Having trouble breathing. Corinne, my secretary, says since I work at a hospital, I should get this checked out ASAP."

Sixteen people Liked this post, though Angela wasn't sure why.

Two days later, Gina was back online. "Problem solved! I have high blood pressure. In the ER, it was one hundred sixty over one hundred! Doc put me on diuretics, and I'm peeing like a racehorse, but she promises I'll lose ten pounds fast. Almost worth it! So glad to be back working."

This post had twice as many Likes and thirteen get-well wishes.

But as Angela advanced through the Swinny chronicles, she noticed a change. At the beginning of this year, Gina had started posting fewer quilt and family pictures. She announced that she was resigning from the Sodality. "The new head, Mrs. Stephens, will do a splendid job. I need more me time." Sixty-three Facebook friends Liked that announcement.

Now Gina wrote more about her health and started showing off expensive purchases.

In January, she wrote, "Bought this green Kate Spade purse on sale! Only $400."

Only? Her Facebook friends liked that one. Gina's new purse got eighty-two Likes and comments like "Beautiful" and "Wow!"

In February, Gina was seated on the hood of a gleaming silver Lexus. "My new car after decades of Mom-mobiles," she wrote. "Sorry, grandbabies, but no stops at Mickey D's in this car. Grandma is not going to have french fries on her leather seats."

Her followers gave that post 206 Likes.

In early March she posted, "Happy birthday to me! I bought four Lladro Disney princesses: Snow White, Cinderella, Aurora, and Belle. Each princess will have her own shelf in my china cabinet!"

The Likes exploded, along with congratulations. "You deserve them all, Gina," said one. Another wistfully commented, "Wish I could afford Disney collectibles."

How much did those Lladro figurines cost? Angela did a quick check. The Lladro princesses were two hundred bucks each—$800 was a pricey passel of princesses.

But the capper came in mid-March, when Angela was lingering in her own coma-induced dream world.

Gina wrote, "A little real estate bird told me my dream house may be on the market soon. Please pray for me."

Torrents of prayers and good wishes followed that post, as well as four Page Likes.

By June 1, those prayers were answered. Gina posted the photo of a whopping, redbrick Greek Revival mansion with six massive, white pillars. The mansion was festooned with cornices, gables, and friezes, and overwhelmed by a *Gone with the Wind* portico.

"At last!" she wrote. "A house big enough for my whole family during the holidays. Twenty rooms, a dining room that seats thirty, three fireplaces, and twelve bathrooms. Five acres and a heated pool! I'm moving to the Forest and buying a house from a doctor!!!!!"

A doctor? Angela thought. Was that Tritt? Hadn't he sold his house during his divorce? He'd told Angela that his wife, Donatella, didn't like the place.

Angela remembered the brain surgeon's midnight rant: "I bought her a big house with twenty rooms, but she says it's too close to Toonerville. She's ashamed to have her friends there. I'll be happy to sell that fucking white elephant. It's a money pit with pillars."

Gina is touchingly proud of her new home, Angela thought. *The same house Tritt's wife hated because it was on the wrong side of the tracks.*

How could a glorified hospital clerk afford a mansion on her salary? How could she pay for the upkeep of the pillared money pit? Who would mow the five-acre lawn, look after the pool, and shovel the circular drive in the winter?

Gina was a widow. Had her husband left her money?

Angela looked up Percy Swinny's obituary. The beloved husband, father, and grandfather had worked as a mechanic at Chouteau Forest Motors for thirty-seven years before dying of a heart attack.

Percy could have provided Gina with a well-kept rambler, but his job wouldn't have paid for a twenty-room mansion. Where had Gina gotten the money for her dream house?

On May 2, Gina posted on her Facebook page, "I must have been born under a lucky star! After more than twenty-five years at SOS and a promotion to director of the billing office, I'm getting my own private office. Next week they'll start tearing out the walls. I'll have to put up with construction noise and dust all summer, but it's worth it! My staff will get new cubicles, too, with extra soundproofing. The plans look amazing. I thought my life was over when I had to drop out of nursing school in my last year because I was preggers (not that I don't love my darling daughter), but now I have a special place in this hospital. Thank you, SOS, for my dream office."

Two days later, on May 4, Gina's luck ran out. She posted this worried status update, studded with untypical typos: "Not feeling welk at all. I'm so weak I can hadly walk, and I achej like I have the flu—but no fever. Heart palpitapations are scarring me. Once again, Corinne insists I go to the a doctor here at SOS. I'll keep you posted."

But Gina didn't. Not a peep for four days. Then she wrote, "I'm back, after way too much excitement. Turned out I was low on potassium, and that caused those scary symptoms. An IV in the ER got me feeling better, but I had to stay in SOS for observation. Doc gave me potassium pills. My daughter drove me home yesterday. Slept in my own bed last night. Bliss!"

Angela reread Gina Swinny's posts three times and saw the pattern in that storm of information: Gina had developed a taste for luxury, buying herself a designer purse, then a luxury car, and finally a doctor's mansion.

As her need for luxury grew, Gina seemed to pull away from her family and her church projects. And Angela remembered Tritt saying he had noticed that Porter Gravois was hanging around the hospital billing office.

When I was admitted to the hospital in a coma, I had insurance, Angela thought. *Double insurance. But Gina threatened me with fraud charges and ordered me to pay her an outrageous amount—$100,000 cash— up front. Then she tried to negotiate it down to $10,000. She only backed off after I called my lawyer. But she's still running her billing scam. She billed my insurance company $3,422.18 for a total hysterectomy, then turned around and billed them for $1,746 for Dr. Du Barry of Du Barry Surgery Associates. There is no Dr. Du Barry in Missouri, though Dr. Gravois lived on Du Barry Circle. That's a total of $5,168.18 for a mythical doctor and a procedure that never took place.* Angela checked her bills again. Weird. Hospitals didn't bill for doctors' services. The doctors' practices did that. Another sign of a scam.

How many other false charges did Gina hide in the hospital's claims to insurance companies for patients with catastrophic illnesses? People overwhelmed by strokes, heart attacks, cancer, or car accidents might not take the time to go through each bill and EOB—or understand them if they did.

Porter Gravois's lavish life was a facade, according to Monty and Tritt. Angela might be able to discount what her neurosurgeon said. He was blinded by hatred. But Monty had a more clear-eyed view. Cracks were appearing in Gravois's faultless facade.

Tritt is right, Angela thought. *Gina Swinny was in cahoots with Porter Gravois, and the neurologist was seriously short of money. I bet Gravois wanted to cut Gina's share of the take—or worse, expose the scam. He'd go free. No one would question the beloved Gravois. But Gina was a lowly clerk with a taste for high living. She'd photographed and posted her greed on Facebook. If Gina got rid of Porter Gravois, she could keep all the money. And she had the tools to kill him. Gina took Ambien. She could get needles and syringes at the hospital or order them online. But where did she get the potassium?*

Angela stared at Gina's Facebook page and saw the answer in the Olive Garden selfie with the cheerful redhead: "My favorite drug dealer," she'd written, "Marcie from the SOS pharmacy."

Angela thought back to the Great Reconciliation in the cafeteria. She replayed the cafeteria scene in her mind again—the scene that so misled her she'd accused Monty of murder.

This time, she saw the three coffee mugs, for Tritt, Monty, and Chip Gravois, were on the same tray. Monty carried the tray to the reserved table in the cafeteria. As Monty carried the tray, a grandmotherly woman greeted him and walked next to him, trying to talk to him. Monty had snubbed her, which wasn't like him.

That woman was Gina Swinny. She could have easily dropped Ambien into the closest coffee mug. There were so many distractions, no one would have noticed.

Monty had carried Tritt's tray to the meeting spot and handed the first cup to Gravois, talking to him briefly and pointing to something in the newspaper. He left Tritt's cup. Then Monty sat down one table over on the same bench with his coffee and a newspaper. Dr. Elkmore and three more big shots took the table across from him. When Tritt sat down, the reserved section was filled.

Angela couldn't see everything, but she'd heard Tritt and Porter Gravois making awkward small talk for a few minutes. Then Gravois had yawned and didn't bother covering his mouth. The Ambien must have been taking effect.

"I'm tired," he'd said. "I want to read."

But he didn't get a chance to, even though he rudely stuck his nose in the newspaper. Gravois's supporters were lined up to see him. They patted him on the shoulder or simply smiled at him. They all shunned Tritt.

Angela remembered the same grandmotherly woman saying, "So good to see you, Dr. Gravois." She'd smiled and kept patting his hand while she talked to him.

That's when Stan Elkmore, the hospital's head enchilada, cut short the receiving line by saying, "Please respect Dr. Gravois's privacy, Gina. His time is limited."

And Gina left. But did she really pat Gravois's hand? Or did she inject it with a fatal dose of potassium?

By the time I discovered Porter Gravois's body, Gina was safely in her office, Angela thought. *Did she kill Porter Gravois?*

I was dead wrong about Monty Bryant killing Gravois.

I had good reasons to suspect that nurse Bobbi killed Gravois, her ex-lover, but I was right when I investigated those suspicions and found out she couldn't have murdered him.

I was wrong again when I concluded that the Angel of Death killed Gravois, and Detective Ray Greiman had covered up the evidence.

But I'm convinced that Gina Swinny killed Porter Gravois. And she's right here in the hospital.

Angela called the billing office on her room phone and got a recording: "The Sisters of Sorrow Patient Billing Services is open from eight a.m. to five p.m. and closes for lunch from noon to two o'clock. If you have a question about your bill, please leave a message, and we'll get back to you."

Angela checked her wall clock: 1:10.

I have a lot of questions, Gina, Angela thought. *And I want to hear your answers in person.*

CHAPTER 44

Katie breezed into Angela's grim hospice room with a huge, white carry-out bag and two coffees. Angela was glad her friend had left her white coat at the morgue. She didn't need another reminder of death.

Katie's lavender-gray suit and pale-pink shirt were practically tropical splashes of color compared to her usual grays, browns, and blacks.

"Hey, look what I brought," Katie said. Then she noticed Angela sitting on her bed in an avalanche of hospital bills. "Angela, what's wrong?"

"I've been going through my bills, and I found a scam," Angela said. "Gina Swinny billed my insurance company $3,422.18 for a total hysterectomy I didn't have, and $1,746 for a surgeon who doesn't exist. That's a total of $5,168.18."

"You're shittin' me," Katie said.

Katie handed Angela a turkey-bacon and avocado sandwich nearly four inches high, slathered with mayo and served on thick whole wheat bread. "Eat while you talk," she said. "You'll feel better. Gina is the billing office lady who looks like Grandma of the Year?"

"Yep. If you check her out on Facebook, this grandma has big eyes for Kate Spade purses, a taste for luxury cars with leather seats, and she just bought a twenty-room mansion—Dr. Tritt's old house, the one he sold when he got divorced." She took a big bite of her sandwich. "Yum."

"You are fucking kidding me," Katie said. "How much did she charge you?"

"Nothing," Angela said. "She only billed my insurance company." Angela licked mayo off her thumb.

"Clever," Katie said. "Hospitals deal with major insurance money every day. Insurance companies wouldn't notice a bill for five thousand dollars. That's like jabbing an elephant with a straight pin—the beast won't feel a thing. Gina could have flown under the radar forever if you hadn't checked your bills and EOBs. When you finish your sandwich, there's peach pie."

"I'm only halfway through that stack," Angela said. "My strokes— and Gravois's misdiagnosis—are going to cost me nearly sixty thousand dollars. I wonder how many other people who've had a major illness have these land mines hidden in their EOBs."

"The good sisters are gonna wear out their knees praying for a miracle," Katie said. "They'll need one to avoid this scandal. It's a medical Watergate. It's like Monica Lewinsky got caught blowin' Richard Nixon."

She handed Angela a generous slice of peach pie and said, "Once word gets out, the insurance companies will attack the hospital like rabid dogs, demanding SOS send them the records for every patient they've had during the time Gina Swinny was in charge. And when the patients find out, they'll want their bills reviewed. This is a giant monkey wrench in the SOS money machine. It's fuckin' financial chaos."

Angela saw the glee in her friend's face.

"This is the biggest scandal to hit SOS—" Katie began.

"Since the Angel of Death murders?" Angela interrupted. "The murder of Dr. Porter Gravois in the hospital cafeteria? Or the arrest of Jeb Travis Tritt? SOS has been triply blessed with scandal lately. The billing office reopens at two," she said and ate another bite of peach pie. "I'm going down there to ask Gina about that fraudulent bill."

"Why?" Katie was wary now.

Angela knew Katie would not care if she asked about a bill. But she wouldn't approve of Angela's hidden agenda: she planned to confront the head of the billing office about her role in Porter Gravois's death.

"I need to make sure Gina is responsible for this error," Angela said. "The problem could be with a staffer. Maybe it's a billing code error. I want to show Gina Swinny the EOBs and see what she says. Otherwise, I could be slandering—as you said—the Grandma of the Year."

Katie studied her. Angela hoped her best friend couldn't tell that she was lying like a used car dealer. She shifted her eyes to her dessert.

"All I want is half an hour in the billing office," Angela said.

"You should have backup," Katie said. "I'll go with you."

"Why?" Angela asked. "Gina has a secretary and a staffer. If you show up, she'll be on her guard. She sees me as a brain-damaged cripple."

And there's no evidence that Gina Swinny is violent, Angela thought. *Gravois was drugged with sleeping pills and poisoned with potassium. She won't attack me. This visit is worth the risk. The physical risk, anyway. If it got back to Reggie Du Pres that I'm investigating Porter Gravois's murder, I could lose my house and my job. But I can't let Tritt go to prison for a murder he didn't commit. I can find work in another city. I just hope Mom's peonies survive the move.*

Katie said, "Okay, on one condition. I come back to the billing office at two thirty and escort you back to your room. I know the difference between half-dead and really dead. If you don't look good, I'm calling Doc Bartlett."

"Deal," Angela said, feeling only slightly guilty at deceiving her friend. She had no doubt that greedy Gina was guilty of fraud.

After Katie left, Angela changed into the clothes she'd worn to the hospital. They were a bit wrinkled, but at least she wasn't risking the hospital gown's indecent exposure. As Angela buttoned her shirt, she realized it didn't hang on her quite so much. She was starting to gain back that lost weight. She was growing stronger. *Maybe I can graduate to a cane,* she thought.

She'd already had her morning infusion of Cubicin, so she wouldn't be dragging an IV pole to see Gina.

Angela discovered that her digital recorder was still in her shirt pocket from her disastrous visit to Monty's office. She erased the embarrassing conversation that she'd had with Monty and wished it could be so easily removed from her memory—and his.

Now she was ready to confront Gina Swinny.

In half an hour, either Tritt would be free—or Angela's life and livelihood would be destroyed.

CHAPTER 45

Gina Swinny looked like a perfect grandma. Her pillowy figure was meant to cuddle and comfort children. Her plump, pretty hands would pat their heads and bake them cookies.

It was only when Angela got to those calculating, dark eyes that the fairytale grandma disappeared. A wolf was hiding in Grandma's clothes, and Angela reminded herself not to underestimate Gina.

Angela sat across from the head of the billing office on a gritty plastic chair, her walker open beside her, the troublesome EOBs on her lap. Angela was uncomfortably aware that this office was isolated at the end of a long, windowless hall.

"How can I help you, Ms. Richman?" Gina asked, brushing gray dust off a stack of papers on her desk. Her short, gray hair was the same color as her lightweight gray pantsuit. Her pink blouse had a gray dirt smear.

I must be getting better, Angela thought. *I don't think she recognizes me.*

In the construction chaos, Gina's desk was rigidly organized. Her computer was directly in front of her. Papers were stacked neatly on each side, and the stapler, scissors, and paper clip holder were arranged with precision, as if Gina had lined them up with a ruler.

Angela noticed there were no family photos on the desk.

"My office is being gutted for remodeling," Gina said. "That powdery dust is everywhere. So bad for my sinuses. At least the wallboard is up in this section. When it's finished, this will be the new office for my secretary, Corinne. Sherry, my other staffer, will have a nice, quiet cubicle over there." Gina pointed to an alcove draped in heavy plastic.

"Right now both girls are working in the corner." Two half-size desks were shoved together in a space no bigger than a handicapped bathroom stall and mounded with papers.

"But my office will be there on the right," Gina said. She pointed to an area twice the size of the rest of the office.

Angela heard her pride.

"It's huge," she said.

Angela could see dusty concrete floors and bare brick being framed for drywall behind another flapping plastic shroud. Tools were laid out on rough wood benches. Angela thought she saw a power sander, an electric drill, and a yellow nail gun much like Rick the handyman's. Cans were stacked everywhere, and orange power cords snaked across the floor.

"Three square feet less than the hospital director's office," Gina said. "But who's counting?"

Gina smiled, and Angela knew the billing office head had measured every inch. "My new office will have a door, a window, and wall-to-wall carpeting," Gina said.

"All the perks of success," Angela said. "When will your office be finished? No one's working there now." Her heart was pounding. She didn't want to make small talk, but she had to if she was going to catch this killer. She'd turned on her digital recorder before she came into the office but realized she had forgotten to put in fresh batteries.

Angela didn't want her recorder to die before Gina admitted killing Dr. Gravois.

Gina sighed. "They've all left for lunch. I don't expect them back for at least an hour. The contractors take more coffee breaks than work breaks, but if I complain, they work even slower. They encourage my girls to play hooky. Sherry is sweet on the carpenter—though I don't think her mother would be happy if she knew. Sherry is in college and shouldn't be dating a blue-collar boy. And Corinne is such a flirt. Really, I don't know what gets into women during menopause. What man is going to look at her wrinkled face and turkey neck? But Corinne's been plain silly since the remodeling started. I can't even get her to answer the phone anymore."

Gina's phone rang as if to demonstrate her woes. "I just let it go to voice mail," she said, waving helplessly at the phone.

"My new office is supposed to be ready by September, but at this rate, it won't be done before Thanksgiving. Well, you don't need to hear my problems. You came in here with a walker, a young girl like you. You must have troubles of your own."

Big ones, Angela thought and launched into her speech before she lost her nerve.

"There's a problem with my insurance bills," Angela said, pulling out the two EOBs. "This one here says my insurance company was billed $3,422.18 for a total hysterectomy."

"Yes, I see that," Gina said.

"But I didn't have a hysterectomy," Angela said. "I was in for a craniotomy. Wrong end." She started to laugh but looked into Gina's cold eyes. The laugh was strangled at birth.

"It could be a billing code error," Gina said, turning to her computer. "Let me look up your file. Angela Richman, regular spelling, correct?"

"Yes," Angela said.

Gina tapped some keys, then asked, "What's your date of birth, dear?"

Angela told her, and Gina found her file.

"Oh my," she said, scrolling through Angela's records. "You have been through a lot, you poor thing. You're lucky to be alive, much less walking and talking. And worse, you had to deal with Dr. Tritt."

"He's a good doctor," Angela said, then wished she hadn't defended Dr. Tritt to the woman who'd framed him for murder.

"Oh, I have no doubt," Gina said. "He did save your life. But I've seen how he treats the pretty girls in this hospital—he thinks they're his personal harem. And he's a killer, besides."

Those hard eyes studied Angela, daring her to disagree. Angela forced herself to stare back until Gina returned to scrolling through Angela's records.

"Looks like you were one sick kitten when you came to the emergency room March tenth. And—oh my, you were in a coma, too. You are a lucky girl. A strong one, too. I see weeks and weeks of stroke rehab. You've worked hard for your good health. Rehab is very expensive. You were released quite recently, I see."

"Wednesday, June eighth," Angela said.

"And it says here you came back again June tenth. What happened? Did you go home too soon?"

"Yes. That's what Dr. Tritt said. I had a scalp infection," Angela said.

"And Dr. Tritt was arrested right in the lobby today. I wasn't there, but I saw the arrest on TV. He's such a clodhopper, isn't he?"

Angela didn't answer. Her hands were clenched and sweating with tension. How was she going to confront this killer? It was like punching a pillow.

"Ah, here's your insurance bill. But I don't see a problem, dear." Gina looked at Angela and smiled. The smile didn't reach those frosty eyes.

"Why not?" Angela asked.

"We didn't charge you a penny."

"No, but you did charge my insurance company," Angela said.

"But that's an insurance company," Gina repeated. "You don't have to pay anything."

"I don't like insurance companies," Angela said. "But they shouldn't be charged for a nonexistent operation."

"Oh, I agree, I agree," Gina said quickly. "Now that I look at your bill, I'm sure it's simply a wrong billing code. I haven't memorized all the codes, but I'll certainly check."

Here goes, Angela thought.

"Maybe," she said. "But there's also this insurance explanation of benefits, which says Dr. Du Barry of Du Barry Surgery Associates charged $1,746 for performing that operation I didn't have."

"I'm sure Dr. Du Barry isn't aware of that, either," Gina said. "But I'll correct it."

"How?" Angela said.

"I'm not sure what you mean." Gina turned those cold eyes on Angela, who felt like she was staring into an arctic cave. "I can explain how I'll do it step by step, but it's not very interesting, and you're not trained to understand it."

"How can you fix the bill for the surgeon when there is no Dr. Du Barry?" Angela asked.

"Of course there's a surgeon." Grandma Gina made little fluttery motions with her small, plump hands, like a mother bird trying to distract a predator away from her baby chick.

"There is no Dr. Du Barry," Angela repeated. "There is no Du Barry Surgical Associates in the Forest. In fact, there's no Dr. Du Barry and no office by that name in Missouri. And this hospital confirmed there's no doctor by that name on the staff or associated with Sisters of Sorrow Hospital. My insurance company was billed a total of $5,168.18 for a doctor who doesn't exist and a procedure that never took place. We all have to pay for that in higher premiums."

"I'm sure if there's a mistake," Gina said, "it must have been one of the girls. They've been so careless during this construction, not paying attention to their work at all. And they're still not back from lunch. Now, if you'll excuse me, I have work to do."

But Angela was not to be stopped. She gathered her courage and pressed on, determined to confront this killer. "And I'm quite sure your 'girls' have nothing to do with this billing scam."

"Scam!" Gina said. "You think I'm involved in a scam! There's a mistake, yes, but it's an innocent one. A slip of the fingers."

"Your fingers did the slipping," Angela said.

"Young woman, I am a widow and a grandmother. I'll have you know I'm the head of the church's Ladies' Sodality."

"You resigned," Angela said. "You need money, and you need it bad. You bought yourself an expensive purse."

"How do you know that?" Gina was indignant. "What I buy is none of your business."

"You made it everyone's business when you posted a photo of your four-hundred-dollar purse on Facebook. Then you showed us your new Lexus. And now you've bought a twenty-room mansion with a five-acre yard and a pool. How can you afford all that? You've developed a raging thirst for luxury."

"I've worked hard all my life," Gina said. "I'm entitled."

"Maybe so, but you aren't entitled to rip off insurance companies. You were working with Porter Gravois, weren't you? He was Dr. Du Barry. He lived on Du Barry Circle."

"Six families live there," Gina said.

"But only one was a doctor at SOS," Angela said. "Porter Gravois steered you to patients who had had catastrophic illnesses. You could bury the fraudulent charges in their colossal bills. Who would notice five thousand dollars when their insurance bills were two hundred thousand dollars or three hundred thousand dollars, or half a million? Better yet, you didn't charge the patients, just their insurance companies. So no one complained, did they?"

"I—"

But Angela was relentless now. "Porter Gravois gave you my name, didn't he? He thought I was gaga after six strokes, brain surgery, and a coma. He never noticed me after I was in the hospital, so he never knew I'd made an amazing recovery. You could hide that fake operation and the surgical charges in my bills. You even tried to get one hundred thousand dollars cash out of me. Then you offered me a deal of ten thousand dollars cash, but I called my lawyer, and you backed off. Did you need the cash for your mansion's down payment, Gina? Is that when Gravois started demanding a bigger cut? He was desperate for money, wasn't he? Behind on his taxes, selling his private plane. His wife quietly sold her diamonds. He threatened to turn you in and destroy your cushy little scheme, didn't he? Until you killed him."

"Until I *what?* I did nothing of the kind." Gina no longer looked like the World's Greatest Grandma. Her gray hair stuck out like a bristle brush, and her hands shook. She steadied them on her open desk drawer.

Angela pushed on. "Sure you did. If you killed Porter Gravois, you could have all the money. You were in the cafeteria the afternoon Dr. Gravois died. He was drugged with Ambien, which you took when you couldn't sleep with your sciatica. You dropped the tablets in his coffee cup when you stopped to talk to Monty in the cafeteria. Gravois was injected with potassium, which you got from your good buddy, Marcie, the SOS pharmacy 'drug dealer.' You were in the receiving line and talked to Gravois for a long time, patting him on the hand. That's when you injected him, isn't it?"

"You can't prove a thing," Gina said. She turned those dead eyes on Angela.

She admitted it! Angela thought. *I have it on tape.* She was so excited by this triumph that she didn't realize she was staring at the muzzle of a revolver.

"Stand up," Gina said, gesturing with the weapon. Angela recognized the gun as a .38, probably a six-shot. She'd seen enough of them at death investigation scenes. They were notoriously inaccurate, but Gina was at close range. She could blow a hole in Angela's chest.

Angela sat there, mesmerized by the gun. She would have put the World's Greatest Grandma at the bottom of a list of potential gun owners.

"You have a gun in your office?" she asked.

"It's isolated back here," Gina said. "I work late. My dear husband insisted I keep a gun for protection. Now go."

"Nope," Angela said. "I'm not moving. You can't shoot me. You'll get blood all over your floor."

"Up!" Gina said. "Or I'll shoot you here and say you attacked me. You had a head injury. You turned violent."

Angela saw those scary eyes. Gina would kill her. *If I can keep moving, I'll have time to think of a way to save myself.* Angela stood up on wobbly legs.

"The chute to the construction dumpster is in my new office," Gina said. "Where the window is. If I shoot you in front of it, I can shove your body down it, and no one will know. The dumpster is almost full. The construction trash gets hauled away tomorrow. Now move."

Angela needed the walker to move, her legs were shaking so badly. She scooted slowly across the floor, looking for a way to distract Gina or something to hit her with. There was nothing. The wastebasket was too light. Angela pushed through the construction plastic and felt it brush against her shoulders. She sneezed from the dust.

"Bless you," Gina said.

She's going to shoot me, and she remembers to bless me? Angela thought. She felt the hard muzzle of the .38 in her back.

"Move," Gina said.

The room was lit by a single bulb. The corners were filled with shadows. At the very end of the room, Angela could make out the tall, boarded window with a big chute near the floor. Angela shivered. That's where Gina wanted to send her body.

Angela looked around wildly for something to stop Gina. The power sander was too far away. The electric drill was unplugged. *There!* She spotted the big yellow nail gun. It was almost in reach.

"Faster!" Gina said, prodding Angela with the .38.

Angela felt like she might faint. Then her foot felt a fat extension cord. Salvation. She pretended to trip and catch herself, then fell backward against Gina. Her walker clanged against the concrete floor.

The well-upholstered Gina went down with an *oof!* Her gun fired. Angela saw the muzzle flash in the dimly lit room and was deafened by the noise. She reached for the nail gun, wrapped her hands around its awkward bulk, and fired.

Nothing happened. She thought Gina was laughing, but Angela couldn't hear her.

Gina brought the .38 up to shoot her again. This time she wouldn't miss. Time slowed, and Angela remembered what Rick had said during his nail gun demonstration: "My gun has a sliding safety tip. The safety tip has to be pushed down first. You can't just pull the trigger and shoot."

But Gina could. She was rising up to pull the trigger on her gun when Angela grabbed the nail gun with both hands and held the tip to Gina's forehead. She fired once.

Ka-chunk!

Gina's hand twitched. She fired the .38 again. And shot out the light.

CHAPTER 46

Katie was standing over Angela, saying something profane no doubt, but Angela couldn't hear her. She was still deaf from the two gunshots.

Angela pointed to Gina's gun and then to her ears and fired a finger pistol. Katie got the point. She knelt next to Gina and checked for a pulse, then ran to the phone.

Gina must be alive, Angela thought, *despite a nail in her forehead.* She was surprised there was so little blood. Angela felt better that Gina was alive, even though the woman had tried to kill her.

When Katie came back after making the call, she asked Angela, "Are you hurt?" with exaggerated mouth movements. Angela shook her head, then pulled out her digital recorder and turned it on. Katie cocked her head to listen to the chitchat and yawned.

But Angela motioned for Katie to keep listening, and she watched Katie's eyes grow wider. By the time the billing office was filled with medics and stretchers, Katie knew that Gina had killed Dr. Porter Gravois and tried to murder Angela. She shook her head, gave Angela a thumbs-up, and stowed the recorder in her pocket.

Gina was loaded onto a stretcher and hustled out of the room. Angela thought she saw the woman's chest rise and fall and hoped she would make it.

Angela thought Katie told everyone that the billing office was a crime scene. She definitely shooed everyone out of there. By that time, the construction workers had returned. They pointed to their tools, but Katie shook her head and pushed them out the door. She handed the weeping Sherry and Corinne their belongings and pushed them out, too. Then Katie had a security guard posted at the door.

Next, Katie made sure Angela was carefully helped onto a stretcher. She ignored Angela's protests and produced a clipboard. Katie wrote, "Doc Bartlett on the way to check you."

"What about you? You're a doctor," Angela said.

"For dead people," Katie wrote. "Don't want ur scrawny butt on my slab. Got enough work. Don't trust ER."

Angela gave up. She knew Katie was determined.

"Gina in surgery," Katie wrote, and Angela nodded. She thought she'd feel good about firing that nail gun into the woman who'd tried to take her money and her life, but she didn't.

She couldn't stop shivering. Doc Bartlett checked Angela's head and took her vitals, then ordered X-rays, for reasons no one explained. Katie and the tech looked at the X-rays, smiling and nodding. Katie's next clipboard note said, "U R OK. Cops on way. Will make a copy of recording for cops & keep original."

Angela nodded her approval. That was smart. Inconvenient information had a habit of disappearing in the Forest, and this recording was going to make a lot of people unhappy.

Angela was loaded on a gurney and parked in the hall like leftover laundry. Someone covered her with a warm blanket, and she fell asleep.

She was awakened by muffled voices in a dark room. People were talking right next to her, but her ears were stuffed with cotton.

"I told the detective she was in no fucking shape to talk to anyone tonight," a woman said. Katie? Yep, she recognized that *F*-word. It was Katie.

"But she's been asleep for six hours," she heard a man say. "She isn't drugged, is she?" Monty.

"No, she's in shock," Katie said. "She's tired, and the World's Greatest Grandma tried to shoot her."

Angela opened her eyes and said, "You saw that mug, too?"

She was lying in a hospital bed, but not in the horrible hospice section.

"Angela, you're alive," Monty said.

"Fucking suffering mahogany son of a bitch, don't you ever scare us like that again," Katie said. "I turn my back on you for half an hour, and you get in a shoot-out with a church lady. A nail-gun shoot-out!"

"She had a real gun," Angela said. "I had the nail gun. Rick the handyman's gun demo saved my life. I can't believe Gina is alive after I shot her in the forehead."

Angela heard another silence this time. A different, denser silence. She looked at their faces and said, "She died, didn't she?"

"On the operating table," Katie said. "She might have survived. You'd be surprised how many people survive nail-gun shots to the head. Some meth head on the West Coast tried to kill himself by shooting twelve nails into his skull, and he lived. Gina wasn't so lucky. The best brain surgeon in the Forest was in jail. The B team was on call, and Gina didn't make it. As far as I'm concerned, she's responsible for her own death. If Tritt wasn't locked up in jail, he might have saved her."

Angela started crying. She couldn't stop. She didn't like Gina. She wasn't even sure she was crying for her, but the tears kept flowing. Angela wept for her lost husband, for the pain she felt, for the job she missed, for the missing days, even for her lost hair.

"Hey, it's okay," Monty said, awkwardly patting her shoulder. "Gina wasn't some sweet little grandma. She was a greedy woman who cheated sick and dying people. She tried to extort money out of you when she thought you were dying. Hell, I wish *I* could have shot her."

"She's dead," Katie said. "You're not. She got what she deserved. If you're going to cry for anybody, save some tears for me. You just added to my fucking workload. I'll have to slice and dice her tomorrow."

Angela managed a smile. "I caught Gravois's killer. I proved I wasn't crazy."

"Jury's still out on that last verdict, but your head is definitely screwed on straight again," Katie said. "You took a crazy risk, but you were right, and you proved it. Congratulations. Consider yourself cured."

"Can I go home now?" Angela asked, sniffling back the last of the tears.

"Yes, you can go home. Doc Bartlett gave the okay," Katie said. "You still need about six more days of IV antibiotics, but your insurance will cover your home health care. You can go back to your house. In a few months, you can go back to your job. You can live happily ever after in the Forest, checking out dead bodies."

"That's all it takes to make me happy," Angela said.

EPILOGUE

Angela didn't live happily ever after, not after losing Donegan. She learned to live with his loss. Angela had lost the love of her life. But at least she'd had that love. And in that, she really was lucky.

She enjoyed her friends and found satisfaction in her work.

After Angela shot Gina Swinny with a nail gun, Katie called the Forest Police Department. Dr. Porter Gravois's murder was Detective Ray Greiman's investigation, and Angela expected him to give her a hard time. But Detective Greiman had left for the day and turned off his cell phone.

Instead, Detective Butch Chetkin caught the call. Angela considered him the best detective on the force. He listened to Angela's recording with Gina Swinny several times and got a search warrant for Mrs. Swinny's home.

"I could have searched her house without the warrant," he told Angela when he took her statement the next day, "but I'm a belt and suspenders kind of guy." That's why Angela loved working with Butch Chetkin.

Under the detective's guidance, the search backed up Angela's recorded conversation with Gina Swinny. Police found a prescription for Ambien. Checking the prescription date and the suggested dosage, the police determined that Gina had used six more pills than were prescribed for that period. They also found an empty potassium vial with the same lot number as those from SOS.

Marcie in the SOS pharmacy denied giving Gina the potassium. The police believed Gina pocketed the vial when her friend was distracted, but Marcie lost her job.

Gina had learned injections in nursing school, but she'd refreshed her skills with a video and a medical training hand used to teach students how to give injections and insert IV lines. She'd bought them on the Internet. The training hand had cost $126.

The police found the receipt for the training hand, the video, the syringes, and needles, all purchased on the Internet. They were in a folder marked "Taxes—Medical Expenses." Mrs. Swinny had planned to deduct her expenses for murdering Porter Gravois.

Dr. Jeb Travis Tritt was released from the Chouteau County jail within forty-eight hours. He sued the Forest Police Department for false arrest and violating his civil rights. Tritt's lawsuit detailed his humiliating, invasive body cavity search and was the cause of much giggling in the Forest.

A police officer had manually searched his rectum, saying he was "looking at the biggest asshole in the Forest." The officer probed the surgeon's mouth and other orifices. A flashlight was used to illuminate Tritt's nostrils, navel, ears, and penis, and the officer required the doctor to pull back his foreskin, then mocked him for "pulling his pud," according to the suit.

The court ruled that the strip search was an "unnecessary violation." Tritt settled out of court for an undisclosed amount, but Katie told Angela that Tritt got at least $1 million. Nobody in the Forest was laughing now.

Tritt left Sisters of Sorrow Hospital and started his own neurosurgery practice in Louisville, Kentucky.

If old Reggie Du Pres had had his way, Angela would have lost her house and her job for interfering in the Porter Gravois investigation, but the Forest patriarch was soon preoccupied with his own legal troubles. He ruled the Forest, but the Sisters of Sorrow Hospital billing scandal extended beyond his realm. The hospital insurance carriers, major contributors to both political parties, demanded a thorough investigation, wanting to know if any hospital board members were implicated in, or had profited from, the billing fraud. Reggie narrowly escaped indictment and retreated to his stronghold—after he made sure that Detective Ray Greiman was given a substantial raise.

When the investigation into Reggie's role in the billing scandal was over, his niece, Emily Du Pres, announced that she'd had enough of the capricious Missouri weather. "It's hot, it's cold. I'm freezing, or there's a damn tornado—all in the same day," she told him. "I'm going home to Palm Beach where the weather's good." Emily refused to train another death investigator and went home to play bridge. She was chagrined when the International Palm Beach Bridge Tournament was cancelled because of a hurricane.

Jillian Du Pres, the surviving JJ twin, left SOS in early September. She still walks with a cane and is facing more reconstructive surgery but is expected to recover. Vehicular manslaughter charges were dropped against Jillian in the death of her cousin, Jordan Hobart, and her license was suspended for six months. Since her suspension started while Jillian was in the hospital, she was able to drive after she was discharged. But Jillian, racked with guilt, imposed her own punishment: she lectures student and adult groups about the dangers of texting and driving while drunk and high. Jillian always mentions her cousin Jordan and shows before and after photos of her own face.

Sixteen-year-old Jillian shocked her parents by announcing that she was not coming out as a DV queen when she turned eighteen. She also refused to apply to the exclusive Vernet Academy in the Forest, the college preferred by the best families. Instead she plans to go to law school at the University of Chicago and hopes to practice environmental law. Her parents believe these choices were caused by a possible brain injury.

The charges against Lucy Chantilly, the senator's daughter, were pleaded down to community service and a drug rehab program. Lucy's court-directed community service was similar to Jillian's self-imposed one: Lucy spoke at high schools about the dangers of texting and driving while drunk and high. She had her father's knack for public speaking. Lucy's father, who had run on a family values ticket, was not reelected.

Sandiclere "Sandy" Warburton was charged with DWI, reckless driving, and vehicular manslaughter in the death of Jordan Hobart. His New York lawyer plea-bargained the charges down to a year of community service, and Sandy helped clean up the Missouri roadsides with a work crew. Sandy saw so much roadkill, he became a temporary vegetarian.

Sandy was also found liable for Jillian's injuries and Jordan's death. His license was suspended for one year, and his Ferrari with the weed in plain view was confiscated. The red Ferrari was sold at auction to fund the state school system. His father, defense contractor Otto Warburton, refused to buy his son another one.

Sandy was also sued in civil court by the Hobart and Du Pres families. Sandy was ordered to pay all of Jillian's medical bills, therapy, and future operations, and $2 million for her pain and suffering. Jordan's parents settled out of court for $2 million and donated the money to the no-kill animal shelter where she'd volunteered, as a memorial to their daughter.

Sandy's defense contractor father was so incensed that he was on the hook for several million dollars, he forced his son to get a job—a real job, not a cushy, unpaid internship. Sandy worked as a stock boy at a big-box store that summer and took two buses to work.

Nurse Daniel Cullen Anniston, the Angel of Death, was convicted of six counts of first-degree murder and is serving a life sentence. The families of all nine of his victims have filed suit against SOS. Results are pending.

Six major health insurance carriers filed suit against SOS and demanded billing records for more than five hundred patients. The records filled an entire semi. The suits are still wending their way through the courts. There are hundreds of health insurance carriers, and the hospital expects more suits.

Monty Bryant filed a class-action suit on behalf of the patients who received bills from SOS while the late Gina Lorraine Swinny was head of the billing office. SOS agreed to "forgive"—i.e., forget—the debts of the plaintiffs, including Angela. Her co-pays had totaled more than $60,000.

Monty filed a separate suit against the hospital on behalf of Mariah Fargo, mother of the late Patrick Fargo. Thanks to that suit, Mariah is no longer in debt to SOS. She quit her job in the hospital laundry and her second job cleaning houses. Monty made sure the money she'd already paid SOS was returned in a lump sum and invested it for her. Mariah currently works only one job and volunteers for the Kidney Foundation.

Katie continues to date Monty Bryant. She still refuses to discuss her romance, but she did buy herself a fine pair of Vogel riding boots, a sign she is serious. Monty gave her an insanely expensive, custom-made Hermès Senlis saddle. Angela was disappointed that its sleek lines didn't have any leather tooling or silver trim, but Katie explained those were for Western saddles, and this was an English saddle. "A Senlis is recommended for outdoor riding, and it's designed and padded so I can spend hours in the saddle," she said. "Make one joke about being in the saddle," she added, "and you're a dead woman."

"The thought never crossed my mind," Angela said, struggling to keep a straight face.

Angela's hair grew back as thick as ever, and Mario keeps it stylish. Chic bangs cover the front of the cobblestone-shaped scar in her head. Thanks to Mrs. Raines's good care and cooking, Angela gained back all but five pounds of the weight she lost during her illness and told Katie, "I wanted to lose five pounds, anyway."

"That's a hell of a diet," Katie said.

In early September, almost six months after the strokes and the brain surgery, Angela graduated from a walker to a cane. She refused to carry a medical cane or to consider herself even temporarily disabled. Instead, she used a stylish, high-tech REI Austrian walking stick.

The day she was cleared to drive, Angela tossed the cane in the back of her black Dodge Charger and drove with Mrs. Raines through the Forest at a stately pace. Once Angela had a feel for the road, she dropped her caregiver off at the house, took her muscle car out on the highway, and let 'er rip.

In December, Angela went back to work as a death investigator, and Mrs. Raines went to care for a new patient. Angela met Katie and Monty at their favorite Mexican restaurant, Gringo Daze, to celebrate.

"To your health," the couple toasted Angela. "And your amazing recovery."

Angela raised her own glass and toasted them. "Recovery is a group project," she said. "I couldn't have done it without you."

ACKNOWLEDGMENTS

In 2007, my husband, Don Crinklaw, took me to a top-ranked hospital because I had blinding headaches and neurological problems similar to death investigator Angela Richman's. The respected neurologist on call told me I was "too young and fit to have a stroke" and scheduled a PET scan for the following Wednesday.

Wednesday never happened. Two days later, I had six strokes, including a hemorrhagic stroke, then brain surgery, and was in a medically induced coma. I lost a third of my right frontal lobe. It took four years to recover.

No one recovers from a catastrophic illness on her own. I have a good husband and good friends, and I had good medical care, except for the neurologist who misdiagnosed me. The hospital medical billing scam was real. Please check your bills and Explanations of Benefits.

The mystery writing community saved my career. I'd been about to leave on tour for *Murder with Reservations* when the strokes hit. Mystery writers from coast to coast pitched in and sold my novels—at the expense of their own books. Readers sent more than four hundred cards. I've kept them all.

I hope I've remembered all the people who've helped me with *Brain Storm*.

Thanks to retired agent and longtime friend David Hendin, who told me, "It's time to write this story." To my current agent, Jill Marr of the Sandra Dijkstra Agency. My Thomas & Mercer team, including acquisitions editor JoVon Sotak, development editor Bryon Quertermous, author relations manager Sarah Shaw, and Dennelle Catlett in Amazon Publishing PR. Thanks, too, to copy editor Hilary Handelsman.

Thank you, Kristy ("P.J. Parrish") Montee, coauthor of *She's Not There*, and Christine Kling, author of *Knight's Cross*, for introducing me to Thomas & Mercer. I'm grateful to *Alfred Hitchcock's Mystery Magazine* editor Linda Landrigan for introducing Angela in the short story "Gotta Go." Thank you, Ian Kern, manager of the Mysterious Bookshop. Your good advice helped me return to the dark side.

This mystery contains lots of forensic and medical information. I've checked it with many experts, but all mistakes are mine.

Thank you to the teachers, staff, and other students at the Medicolegal Death Investigators Training Course for being so welcoming. Special thanks to Mary Fran Ernst, St. Louis County Medicolegal Death Investigator, who helped devise the death investigator course and coauthored *Medicolegal Death Investigator: A Systematic Training Program for the Professional Death Investigator*.

Thanks also to death investigator Krysten Addison, who advises me on DI procedure.

The Harold R. Messler Award is an imaginary award named for a real forensic pathologist. Harold Messler was director of the St. Louis Police Department Crime Laboratory for thirty-seven years and teaches at the Medicolegal Death Investigators Training Course.

Nora E. Saunders, Saunders & Taylor Insurance, Inc., Fort Lauderdale, explained the mysteries of Angela's insurance. Thank you to my friend Joanna Campbell Slan, bestselling mystery author and Daphne du Maurier Award winner. Special thanks to Gregg Brickman, nurse and writer, for a tutorial on the mysteries of potassium. Gregg has a fine mind for murder.

Thank you, Detective R. C. White, Fort Lauderdale Police Department (retired) and licensed private eye. Thanks to Houston private eye and mystery writer William Simon and poison expert Luci Zahray, who fortunately uses her powers for good.

Thank you, Donna Mergenhagen, Dr. Robin Waldron, Molly Weston, Dick Richmond, Valerie Cannata, and Mystery Lovers Bookshop founders Mary Alice Gorman and Richard Goldman and their review site, www.revuzeit.com.

Thank you, Femmes Fatales Charlaine Harris, Dana Cameron, Marcia Talley, Toni L. P. Kelner, Kris Neri, Mary Saums, Hank Phillippi Ryan, Donna Andrews, Catriona McPherson, and Frere Dean James/ Miranda James, for your encouragement and advice. Read our blog at www.femmesfatales.typepad.com.

Thanks also to my fellow bloggers at The Kill Zone for your entertaining writing advice. Read us at killzoneauthors.blogspot.com.

But most of all, thank you to my husband, Don Crinklaw, who saved my life and then stayed with me on the long journey to recovery.

You can reach me at eviets@aol.com.

ABOUT THE AUTHOR

Award-winning author Elaine Viets has written twenty-nine mysteries in three series, including the bestselling Dead-End Job series, featuring south Florida private detectives Helen Hawthorne and her husband, Phil Sagemont; the Josie Marcus, Mystery Shopper mystery series; and the dark Francesca Vierling mysteries. She is a director-at-large of the Mystery Writers of America and a frequent contributor to *Alfred Hitchcock Mystery Magazine* as well as anthologies edited by Charlaine Harris and Lawrence Block. Viets has won the Anthony, Agatha, and Lefty Awards.

The Angela Richman, Death Investigator series returns the prolific author to her hard-boiled roots and draws on her personal experiences as a stroke survivor, as well as her studies in the Medicolegal Death Investigators Training Course at St. Louis University's School of Medicine.